THE
ONE HUNDRED YEAR OLD MAN WHO CLIMBED OUT THE WINDOW
AND DISAPPEARED

JONAS JONASSON

ALLEN&UNWIN
SYDNEY • MELBOURNE • AUCKLAND • LONDON

This edition published in 2013
First published in Australia and New Zealand by Allen & Unwin in 2012
First published in the United States in 2012 by Hyperion,
an imprint of Hachette Book Group Inc.
First published in the Swedish language by Piratförlaget, Sweden

Allen & Unwin
83 Alexander Street
Crows Nest NSW 2065
Australia
Phone: (61 2) 8425 0100
Email: info@allenandunwin.com
Web: www.allenandunwin.com

Cataloguing-in-Publication details are available
from the National Library of Australia
www.trove.nla.gov.au

ISBN 978 1 74331 793 8

Printed in Australia by McPherson's Printing Group

25 24 23 22 21 20

The paper in this book is FSC® certified.
FSC® promotes environmentally responsible,
socially beneficial and economically viable
management of the world's forests.

*No one was better at captivating an audience than Grandpa,
when he sat on his favorite bench telling stories, leaning on his
walking stick and chewing tobacco.*

*"But Grandpa . . . Is that really true?" we grandchildren
would ask, wide-eyed.*

*"Those who only says what is the truth, they're not worth
listening to," Grandpa replied.*

This book is dedicated to him.

JONAS JONASSON

THE
ONE HUNDRED YEAR OLD MAN WHO CLIMBED OUT THE WINDOW
AND DISAPPEARED

ONE

Y*ou might think he could have made up his mind earlier, and* been man enough to inform his surroundings of his decision. But Allan Karlsson had never been given to pondering things too long.

So the idea had barely taken hold in the old man's head before he opened the window of his room on the ground floor of the Old Folks' Home in the town of Malmköping, and stepped out—into the flower bed.

This maneuver required a bit of effort, since Allan was 100 years old, on this very day in fact. There was less than an hour to go before his birthday party would begin in the lounge of the Old

Folks' Home. The mayor would be there. And the local paper. And all the other old people. And the entire staff, led by bad-tempered Director Alice.

It was only the Birthday Boy himself who didn't intend to turn up.

TWO

Monday, May 2, 2005

Allan Karlsson hesitated as he stood there in the flower bed that ran along one side of the Old Folks' Home. He was wearing a brown jacket with brown trousers and on his feet he had a pair of brown indoor slippers. He was not a fashion plate; people rarely are at that age. He was on the run from his own birthday party, another unusual thing for a 100-year-old, not least because even being 100 is pretty rare.

Allan thought about whether he should make the effort to crawl back in through the window to get his hat and shoes, but when he felt his wallet in his inside pocket, he decided that it would suffice. Besides, Director Alice had repeatedly shown that she had a sixth sense (wherever he hid his vodka, she found it), and she might be nosing around in there even now, suspicious that something fishy was going on.

Better to be on his way while he could, Allan thought, as he stepped out of the flower bed on creaking knees. In his wallet, as far as he could remember, he had a few notes saved—a good thing since it probably wouldn't be free to go into hiding.

He turned to take one last look at the Old Folks' Home that—until a few moments ago—he had thought would be his last residence on Earth, and then he told himself that he could die some other time, in some other place.

The 100-year-old man set off in his pee-slippers (so called because men of an advanced age rarely pee farther than their shoes), first through a park and then alongside an open field where a market was occasionally held in the otherwise quiet provincial town. After a few hundred yards, Allan went around the back of the district's medieval church and sat down on a bench next to some gravestones to rest his aching knees. The piety in the area was not such that Allan worried about being disturbed. He noted an ironic coincidence. He was born the same year as a Henning Algotsson who lay beneath the stone just across from the bench. But there was an important difference—Henning had given up the ghost sixty-one years earlier. If Allan had been more curious he might have wondered what Henning died of, at the age of thirty-nine. But Allan did not get into other people's business—if he could avoid it, which he usually could.

Instead, he thought that he had probably been mistaken when he'd sat in the Old Folks' Home, feeling as if he might as well be dead. However many aches and pains he suffered, it had to be much more interesting and instructive to be on the run from Director Alice than to be lying rigid six feet under.

Upon which thought the Birthday Boy, despite his complaining knees, got up and said good-bye to Henning Algotsson and continued on his badly planned flight.

Allan cut across the churchyard to the south, until a stone wall appeared in his path. It wasn't more than three feet high, but Allan was a centenarian, not a high jumper. On the other side was Malmköping's bus station and the old man suddenly realized that his rickety legs were taking him toward a building that could be very useful. Once, many years earlier, Allan had crossed the Himalayas. That was no picnic. Allan thought about that experience now, as he stood before the last hurdle between himself and the station. He considered the matter so intently that the stone wall in front of his eyes seemed to shrink. And when it was at its very lowest, Allan crept over it, age and knees be damned.

Malmköping is not what you'd call a bustling town, and this sunny weekday morning was no exception. Allan hadn't met a living soul since he had suddenly decided not to show up at his own hundredth birthday party. The station waiting room was almost empty when Allan shuffled in. Almost. On the right were two ticket windows, one closed. Behind the other sat a little man with small, round glasses, thin hair combed to one side, and a uniform vest. The man gave him an irritated look as he raised his eyes from his computer screen. Perhaps the current crowd was too much for him, because over in the corner stood a young man of slight build, with long, greasy blond hair, a scraggly beard, and a jean jacket with the words *Never Again* on the back.

Perhaps the young man was illiterate since he was pulling at the door to the handicapped restroom, as if the sign Out of Order in black lettering against an orange-colored background had no meaning.

After a moment, he did move to the door to the restroom next to it, but there he faced a different problem. Evidently he didn't want to be parted from his big, gray suitcase on wheels, but the restroom was simply too small for the two of them. It seemed to Allan that the young man would either have to leave the suitcase outside while he relieved himself, or allow the suitcase to occupy the restroom, while he himself remained outside.

But Allan had more pressing concerns. Making an effort to lift his legs in the right sequence, he shuffled with small steps up to the little man in the open ticket window and inquired as to the possibility of public transport in some direction, any at all would do, within the next few minutes, and if there was, what would it cost?

The little man looked tired. He had probably lost track of things halfway through Allan's inquiry, because after a few seconds, he said:

"And where is it you want to go?"

Allan took a deep breath, and reminded the little man that he had already stated that the actual destination, and for that matter the means of transport, were of less importance than a) the time of departure, and b) the cost.

The little man silently inspected his timetables and let Allan's words sink in.

"Bus number 202 departs for Strängnäs in three minutes. Would that work?"

Yes, Allan thought it would. The little man told him that the bus departed from outside the terminal door and that it would be most convenient to buy a ticket directly from the driver.

Allan wondered what the little man did behind the window if he didn't sell tickets, but he didn't say anything. The little man possibly wondered the same thing. Allan thanked him for his help and tried to tip the hat he had in his haste not brought along.

The 100-year-old man sat down on one of the two empty benches, alone with his thoughts. The wretched birthday party at the home would start at three o'clock, and that was in twelve minutes. At any moment they would be banging on the door to Allan's room, and then all hell would break loose. He smiled at the thought.

Then, out of the corner of his eye, Allan saw that somebody was approaching. It was the slightly built young man heading straight for Allan with his big suitcase trailing behind him on four small wheels. Allan realized that he might not be able to avoid engaging the long-haired youth in conversation. Perhaps that wasn't so bad. He might gain insight into what today's young people thought about this and that.

A conversation did take place, but without the depth of social analysis Allan had anticipated. The young man came to a halt a few yards away, seemed to study the old man for a moment, and then said:

"Hey."

Allan replied in a friendly tone, saying that he wished him a good afternoon, and then asked him if there was some way he could be of service. It turned out that there was. The young man wanted Allan to keep an eye on the suitcase while the owner relieved himself. Or as he expressed it:

—I need to take a dump.

Allan replied that, although he was old and decrepit, his eyesight was still in good repair and it did not sound like too arduous a task to keep an eye on the young man's suitcase. He did recommend that the young man relieve himself with some urgency—without, of course, using the young man's own terminology—as Allan had a bus to catch.

The young man did not hear the last bit. His urgent need drove him toward the toilet before Allan had finished speaking.

The 100-year-old man had never let himself be irritated by people, even when there was a good reason to be, and he was not annoyed by the uncouth manner of this youth. But he couldn't warm to him either, and that probably played some part in what happened next.

Bus number 202 rolled up outside the entrance to the terminal, just a few seconds after the young man had closed the toilet door behind him. Allan looked at the bus and then at the suitcase, then again at the bus and then again at the suitcase.

It has wheels, he said to himself. And there's a strap to pull it by too.

And then Allan surprised himself by making what—you have to admit—was a decision that said "yes" to life.

The bus driver was conscientious and polite. He stepped down and helped the very old man with the big suitcase to get on the bus.

Allan thanked him and pulled out his wallet from the inside pocket of his jacket. The bus driver wondered if the gentleman was possibly going all the way to Strängnäs. But Allan thought it best to be frugal and so he held out a fifty-crown note and asked:

—How far will this get me?

The driver said jovially that he was used to people who knew where they wanted to go but not what it would cost, but this was quite the opposite. Then he looked in his schedule and replied that for forty-eight crowns you could travel on the bus to Byringe Station.

Allan thought that sounded fine. The driver put the newly stolen suitcase in the baggage area behind his seat, while Allan sat down in the first row on the right-hand side. From there he could see through the window of the station's waiting room. The restroom door was still closed when the bus rolled off. Allan hoped for the young man's sake that he was having a pleasant time in there, bearing in mind the disappointment that was awaiting him.

The bus to Strängnäs was not exactly crowded that afternoon. In the back row there was a middle-aged woman, in the middle a young mother who had struggled on board with her two children, one of them in a baby carriage, and at the very front an extremely old man.

This passenger was wondering why he had stolen a big gray suitcase on four wheels. Was it because he could and because the owner was a lout or because the suitcase might contain a pair of shoes and even a hat? Or was it because the old man didn't have anything to lose? Allan really couldn't say why he did it. When life has gone into overtime it's easy to take liberties, he thought, and he made himself comfortable in the seat.

So far, Allan was satisfied with the way the day had developed. Then he closed his eyes for his afternoon nap.

At that same moment, Director Alice knocked on the door to room 1 at the Old Folks' Home. She knocked again and again.

—Stop fooling around, Allan. The mayor and everyone else have already arrived. Do you hear me? You haven't been at the bottle again, have you? Come out this minute, Allan! Allan?

At about the same time, the door opened to what was, for the time being, the only functioning toilet in Malmköping Station. Out stepped a young man who was doubly relieved. He took a few steps toward the middle of the waiting room, tightening his belt with one hand and combing his hair with the fingers of the other hand. Then he stopped, stared at the two empty benches, and looked left and right. Upon which he exclaimed:

—What the damned hell . . . !

Then words failed him, before he found his voice again:

—You're a dead man, you old bastard. Once I've found you.

THREE

Monday, May 2, 2005

Just after three o'clock in the afternoon on May 2 the calm of Malmköping was shattered for what would be several days. At first
Director Alice at the Old Folks' Home was worried rather
than angry, and pulled out her master key. Since Allan had not concealed his escape route, it was immediately obvious that the Birthday Boy had climbed out of the window. Judging by the tracks, he
had then stood among the pansies in the flower bed, before disappearing.

By virtue of his position, the mayor felt he should take command. He ordered the staff to search in pairs. Allan couldn't be far
away; the searchers should concentrate on the immediate vicinity.
One pair was dispatched to the park, one to the state-run liquor
store (a place that Allan had occasionally frequented, Director

Alice knew), one to the other shops on Main Street, and one to the Community Center up on the hill. The mayor himself would stay at the Old Folks' Home to keep an eye on the residents who hadn't vanished into thin air and to ponder the next move. He told the searchers that they should be discreet; there was no need to generate unnecessary publicity about this affair. In the general confusion, the mayor forgot that one of the pairs of searchers he had just sent out consisted of a reporter from the local paper and her photographer.

The bus station was not included in the mayor's primary search area. In that location, however, a very angry, slightly built young man with long, greasy blond hair, a scraggly beard, and a jean jacket with the words *Never Again* on the back had already searched every corner of the building. Since there was no trace of either a very old man or a suitcase, the young man took some decisive steps toward the little man behind the only open ticket window, for the purpose of obtaining information as to the old man's possible travel plans.

Although the little man was generally bored with his work, he still had his professional pride. So he explained to the loudmouthed young man that the passengers' privacy was not something that could be compromised, adding firmly that under no circumstances whatsoever would he give him any information of the type that he wished to obtain.

The young man stood in silence for a moment. He then moved five yards to the left, to the not very solid door to the ticket office. He didn't bother to check whether it was locked. Instead he took a step back and kicked the door in with the boot on his right foot so that splinters flew in every direction. The little man did not even have time to lift the telephone receiver to phone for help, before he was dangling in the air in front of the young man, who grasped him firmly by the ears.

—I might not know anything about privacy, but I'm good at

getting people to talk, said the young man to the little ticket seller before he let him drop down with a bump onto his revolving office chair.

At which point the young man explained what he intended to do with the little man's genitals, with the help of a hammer and nails, if the little man did not comply with his wishes. The description was so realistic that the little man immediately decided to say what he thought, namely that the old man in question had presumably taken a bus in the direction of Strängnäs. Whether the man had taken a suitcase with him, he couldn't say, as he was not the sort of person who spied on his customers.

The ticket seller then stopped talking to ascertain how satisfied the young man was with what he had said, and immediately determined that it would be best for him to provide further information. So he said that on the journey between Malmköping and Strängnäs there were twelve stops and that the old man could of course get out at any one of those. The person who would know was the bus driver, and according to the timetable he would be back in Malmköping at ten after seven that same evening, when the bus made its return journey to Flen.

The young man sat down beside the terrified little man with throbbing ears.

—Just need to think, he said.

So he thought. He thought that he should certainly be able to shake the bus driver's mobile phone number out of the little man, and then call the driver and say that the old man's suitcase was actually stolen property. But then of course there was a risk that the bus driver would involve the police and that was not something the young man wanted. Besides, it was probably not so urgent really, because the old man seemed dreadfully old and now that he had a suitcase to drag around, he would need to travel by train, bus, or taxi if he wanted to continue his journey from the station in Strängnäs. He would thus leave new tracks behind him, and there would always be somebody who could be dangled by the ears to say where the old man was heading. The young man had confidence in his ability to persuade people to tell him what they knew.

When the youth had finished thinking, he decided to wait for the bus in question to return so he could interview the driver without undue politeness.

When he had decided, the young man got up again, and explained to the ticket seller what would happen to him, his wife, his children, and his home if he told the police or anybody else what had just occurred.

The little man had neither wife nor children, but he was eager to keep his ears and genitals more or less intact. So he gave his word as an employee of the national railways that he wouldn't say a peep.

That was a promise he kept until the next day.

The two-man search groups came back to the Old Folks' Home and reported on what they had seen. Or rather hadn't seen. The mayor instinctively did not want to involve the police and he was desperately trying to think of alternatives, when the local newspaper reporter dared to ask:

—And what are you going to do now, Mr. Mayor?

The mayor was silent for a few moments; then he said:

—Call the police, of course.

God, how he hated the free press!

*A*llan woke when the driver kindly nudged him and announced that they had now reached Byringe Station. Shortly afterward, the driver maneuvered the suitcase out the front door of the bus, with Allan close behind.

The driver asked if he could now manage on his own, and Allan said that the driver had no need to worry in that respect. Then Allan thanked him for his help and waved good-bye as the bus rolled out onto the highway again.

Tall fir trees blocked the afternoon sun and Allan was starting to feel a bit chilly in his thin jacket and indoor slippers. He could see no sign of Byringe, let alone its station. There was just forest, forest, and forest in all directions—and a little gravel road leading to the right.

Allan thought that perhaps there were warm clothes in the suitcase he had on impulse brought along with him. Unfortunately the suitcase was locked and without a screwdriver or some other tool it was surely hopeless to try to open it. There was no other option but to start moving, otherwise he would freeze to death. And given past experiences, he was pretty sure he wouldn't succeed in doing that even if he tried.

The suitcase had a strap at the top and if you pulled it, the suitcase rolled along nicely on its small wheels. Allan followed the gravel road into the forest with short, shuffling steps. The suitcase followed just behind him, skidding on the gravel.

After a few hundred yards, Allan came to what must be Byringe Station—a closed-down building next to a most definitely and absolutely former railway line.

Allan was in excellent shape as far as centenarians went, but it was all getting to be a bit too much. He sat down on the suitcase to gather his thoughts and strength.

To Allan's left stood the shabby, yellow two-story station. All the windows on the bottom floor were covered with planks. To his right you could follow the no longer used railway line into the distance, straight as an arrow even deeper into the forest. Nature had not yet succeeded in entirely eating up the tracks, but it was only a matter of time.

The wooden platform was evidently no longer safe to walk on. On the outermost planking you could still read a painted sign: Do Not Walk on the Track. The track was certainly not dangerous to walk on, thought Allan. But who in his right mind would voluntarily walk on the platform?

That question was answered immediately, because at that very moment the shabby door of the station building was opened and a man in his seventies wearing a cap stepped out of the house. Given his big boots, he clearly trusted the planks not to give way and he was entirely focused on the old man in front of him. His initial attitude was hostile, but then he seemed to change his mind, possibly as a result of seeing what a decrepit specimen of humanity had invaded his territory.

Allan sat on the newly stolen suitcase, not knowing what to say and in any case lacking the energy to say it. But he looked steadily at the man, letting him make the first move.

—Who are you, and what are you doing in my station? asked the man with the cap.

Allan didn't answer. He couldn't decide whether he was dealing with friend or foe. But then he decided that it would be wise not to argue with the only person around, someone who might even let Allan inside before the evening chill set in. He decided to tell it like it was.

Allan told the man that his name was Allan, that he was exactly one hundred years old and spry for his age, so spry in fact that he was on the run from the old age home. He had also had time to steal a suitcase from a young man who by now would certainly not be particularly happy about it; his knees were not for the moment at their best and he would very much like to give them a break.

Allan then fell silent, awaiting the court's verdict.

—Is that so, said the man in the cap; then he smiled. A thief!

He jumped nimbly down from the platform and went over to the centenarian to have a closer look.

—Are you really one hundred years old? he asked. In that case, you must be hungry.

Allan couldn't follow the logic, but of course he was hungry. So he asked what was on the menu and if a nip of the hard stuff might be included.

The man with the cap stretched out his hand, introduced himself as Julius Jonsson, and pulled the old man to his feet. He then announced that he would personally carry Allan's suitcase, and that roast elk was on the bill if that suited, and that there would absolutely be a nip of the hard stuff to go with it, or rather enough to take care of the knees and the rest of him too.

Julius Jonsson had not had anybody to talk to for several years, so he was pleased to meet the old man with the suitcase. A drop of the hard stuff first for one knee and then for the other, followed by a drop more for the back and neck, and then some to whet the appetite, all in all made for a convivial atmosphere. Allan asked what Julius did for a living, and got his whole story.

Julius was born in the north of Sweden, the only child of Anders and Elvina Jonsson. Julius worked as a laborer on the family farm and was beaten every day by his father who was of the opinion that Julius was good for nothing. When Julius was twenty-five, his mother died of cancer—which Julius grieved over—and shortly afterward his father was swallowed by the bog when he tried to rescue a heifer. Julius grieved over that too—because he was fond of the heifer.

Young Julius had no talent for the farming life (in this his father had essentially been right) nor did he have any desire for it. So he sold everything except a few acres of forest that he thought might come in handy in his old age. He went off to Stockholm and within two years had squandered all his money. He then returned to the forest.

With great enthusiasm, Julius put in a bid to supply five thousand electricity poles to the Hudiksvall District Electricity Company. And since Julius didn't concern himself with such details as payroll taxes, he won the bid, and with the help of a dozen Hungarian refugees he even managed to deliver the poles on time, and was paid more money than he knew existed.

So far, all was well. The problem was that Julius had been obliged to cheat a little. The trees were not yet fully grown, so the poles were a yard shorter than what had been ordered. This would probably have gone unnoticed if it hadn't been for the fact that virtually every farmer in the area had just acquired a combine harvester.

The Hudiksvall District Electricity Company stuck up the poles crisscrossing fields and meadows in the area, and when it was harvest time, on one single morning the cables were pulled down in twenty-six locations by twenty-two different newly bought combine harvesters. The entire region had no electricity for weeks; harvests were lost and milking machines stopped working. It was not long before the farmers' fury—at first directed against the Hudiksvall District Electricity Company—was turned against young Julius.

—The town slogan "Happy Hudiksvall" was not on many people's lips at that time, I can tell you. I had to hide at the Town Hotel in Sundsvall for seven months and then I ran out of money. Shall we have another swig of the hard stuff?

Allan thought that they should. The elk had been washed down with beer too, and now Allan felt so comprehensively satisfied that he began to be almost afraid of dying.

Julius continued his story. After being nearly run down by a tractor in the center of Sundsvall (driven by a farmer with a murderous look in his eyes), he realized that the locals weren't going to forget his little mistake for the next hundred years. So he moved a long way south and ended up in Mariefred where he did a bit of small-time thieving for a while until he tired of town life and managed to acquire the former station building in Byringe for 25,000 crowns he happened to find one night in a safe at the Gripsholm Inn.

Here at the station, he now lived essentially through handouts from the state, poaching in his neighbor's forest, small-scale production and sale of alcoholic spirits from his home-distilling apparatus, and resale of what goods he could get hold of from his neighbors. He wasn't particularly popular in the neighborhood,

Julius went on, and between mouthfuls Allan answered that he could imagine as much.

When Julius suggested having one final snifter "for dessert," Allan answered that he had always had a weakness for desserts of that kind, but that first of all he must seek out a toilet if there possibly happened to be one in the building. Julius got up, turned on the ceiling lamp since it was starting to get dark, and then pointed to the stairs saying that there was a functional water closet on the right. He promised to have two newly poured drams ready and waiting when Allan returned.

Allan found the toilet where Julius had said it would be. He stood in position to pee, and as usual the last drops didn't quite make it to the bowl. Some of them landed softly on his pee slippers instead.

Halfway through the process, Allan heard a noise on the stairs. His first thought was that it was Julius, going off with his newly stolen suitcase. The noise got louder. Somebody was climbing the stairs.

Allan realized that there was a chance that the steps he heard outside the door belonged to a slightly built young man with long, greasy blond hair, a scraggly beard, and a jean jacket with the words *Never Again* on the back. And that, if it was him, then it probably wasn't going to be a pleasant encounter.

The bus *returning from Strängnäs arrived at Malmköping Station* three minutes early. The bus carried no passengers and the driver had accelerated a little bit extra after the last bus stop to have time to catch his breath before continuing the journey to Flen.

But the driver had barely lit his cigarette before a slightly built youth with long, greasy blond hair, a scraggly beard, and a jean jacket with the words *Never Again* on the back arrived. Of course, the driver couldn't see the words on the back of the jacket, but they were there nevertheless.

—Are you going to Flen? The driver asked a little hesitantly, because there was something about the young man that didn't feel right.

—I'm not going to Flen. And neither are you, answered the young man.

Hanging around waiting for four hours for the bus to come back had been a bit too much for what little patience the youth could muster. Besides, after half that time he had realized that if instead he had immediately stolen a car, he could have caught up with the bus long before Strängnäs.

On top of it all, police cars had started to cruise around in the little town. At any time the police could stumble into the station, and start interrogating the little man behind the window in the ticket office as to why he looked terrified and why the door to his office was hanging at an angle on one hinge.

The young man had no idea what the cops were doing there. His boss in Never Again had chosen Malmköping as the transaction venue for three reasons: first, it was close to Stockholm; second, it had relatively good transportation options; and third—and most important—because the long arm of the law wasn't long enough to reach there. There were simply no cops in Malmköping.

Or, to be more precise: there shouldn't be, and yet the place was crawling with them. The young man had seen two cruisers and a total of four policemen; from his perspective that was a crowd.

At first, the young man thought that the police were after him. But that would assume that the little man had squawked, and the young man could categorically discount that possibility. While waiting for the bus to come, the young man hadn't had much to do other than keep an eye on the little man, smash his office phone to bits, and patch up the office door as best he could.

When the bus eventually did come and the young man noted that it had no passengers, he had immediately decided to kidnap both the driver and the bus.

It took all of twenty seconds to persuade the bus driver to turn the bus around and drive northward again. Close to a personal record, the young man reflected as he sat down in the exact seat where the geriatric he was now chasing had been sitting earlier the same day.

The bus driver quivered with fear, but got through the worst of it with a calming cigarette. Smoking was, of course, forbidden on board the bus, but the only law the driver was subject to at that moment was sitting just diagonally behind him in the bus and was slightly built, had long, greasy blond hair, a scraggly beard, and a jean jacket with the words *Never Again* on the back.

On the way, the young man asked where the elderly suitcase thief had gone. The driver said that the old man had gotten off at Byringe Station and that was probably entirely random, explaining the backward way the old man had gone about things, offering a 50-crown note and asking how far he could get with that.

The driver didn't know much about Byringe Station, except that it was rare for anyone to get on or off there. Supposedly there was a closed-down railway station some way in the forest, and Byringe village was somewhere in the vicinity. The geriatric couldn't have gotten much farther than that, the driver guessed. The man was very old and the suitcase was heavy, even though it had wheels.

The young man immediately calmed down. He had refrained from calling the boss in Stockholm, because the boss was one of the few people who could scare people more effectively than the young man himself. The young man shivered at the thought of what the boss would say about the suitcase going astray. Better to solve the problem first and tell him later. And seeing as how the old man hadn't gone all the way to Strängnäs or even beyond, the suitcase should be back in the hands of the young man quicker than he had feared.

—Here's the Byringe Station bus stop . . .

The driver slowly rolled to the side of the road, prepared to die.

But it turned out that his time had not come, although his mobile phone wasn't so lucky. It met a rapid death under one of the young man's boots. And a whole stream of death threats directed at the driver's relatives spewed out of the young man's mouth, designed to avert any possible thought of the driver contacting the police instead of turning the bus around and continuing the journey to Flen.

Then the young man got off and let the driver and the bus escape. The poor driver was so terrified that he didn't dare turn the bus around; he continued all the way to Strängnäs, parked in the middle of Trädgårds Street, and walked in shock into the Delia Hotel where he rapidly downed four glasses of whiskey. Then to the bartender's horror, he started to cry. After a further two glasses of whiskey, the bartender offered him a telephone in case he wanted to phone somebody. The bus driver started to cry again—and called his girlfriend.

The young man thought he could make out tracks in the gravel on the road, tracks of a suitcase on wheels. This would be over in no time, which was a good thing, because it was getting dark.

Off and on, the young man wished that he had done a bit more planning. It struck him that he was standing in a rapidly darkening forest, and it would soon be pitch black. What would he do then?

These troubled thoughts ended abruptly when he first caught sight of a shabby, partly boarded-up yellow building near the bottom of the hill. And when somebody turned on a light on the upper floor, the young man mumbled:

—Now I've got you, old geezer.

Allan quickly stopped peeing. Then he carefully opened the toilet door and tried to hear what was happening in the kitchen. Soon enough he had his worst fear confirmed. Allan recognized the young man's voice, bellowing at Julius Jonsson to reveal where "the other old bastard" was.

Allan snuck over to the kitchen door, silently because he was wearing bedroom slippers. The young man had grasped Julius by both ears, the same hold he had earlier practiced on the little man at the station in Malmköping. While he shook poor Julius, he continued his interrogation. Allan thought the young man should have been satisfied with finding the suitcase, which was standing right in the middle of the room. Julius grimaced but made no move to answer. Allan reflected that the old timber merchant was quite a tough guy, and looked around for a suitable weapon. Amid the junk he saw a small number of candidates: a crowbar, a plank, a container of insect spray, and a packet of rat poison. Allan first settled on the rat poison but couldn't just then figure out a way to get a spoonful or two into the young man. The crowbar, on the other hand, was a bit too heavy for the centenarian to lift, and the insect spray. . . . No, it would have to be the plank.

So Allan took a firm hold of his weapon and with four sensationally fast steps—for his age—he was right behind his intended victim.

The young man must have sensed that Allan was there, because just as the old man took aim the youth loosened his hold on Julius Jonsson and spun around.

He received the plank slap bang in the middle of his forehead, stood where he was and stared for a second before he fell backward and hit his head on the edge of the kitchen table.

No blood, no groaning, nothing. He just lay there, with his eyes closed.

—Good one, said Julius.

—Thanks, said Allan, now where's that dessert you promised?

Allan and Julius sat down at the kitchen table, with the long-haired youth sleeping at their feet. Julius poured the brandy, gave one glass to Allan, and raised his own in a toast. Allan raised his glass too.

—So, said Julius when they'd emptied their glasses. I'm betting that's the owner of the suitcase?

Allan realized that it was time for him to explain a thing or two in more detail.

Not that there was so much to explain. Most of what had happened during the day was hard for Allan himself to understand. But he described the events—his defection from the home, his spontaneous seizure of the suitcase at the station in Malmköping, and the fear at the back of his mind that the young man who now lay unconscious on the floor would probably quickly catch up with him. And he sincerely apologized for the fact that Julius now sat there with red and throbbing ears. But Julius said that Allan most certainly shouldn't be apologizing for the fact that there was finally a bit of action in Julius Jonsson's life.

Julius was back in good form. He thought it was high time that they both had a look at what was in the suitcase. When Allan pointed out that it was locked, Julius told him not to be silly.

—Since when has a lock stopped Julius Jonsson? asked Julius Jonsson.

But there is a time for everything, he went on. First there was the matter of the problem on the floor. It wouldn't do if the young man were to wake up and then carry on from where he left off when he passed out.

Allan suggested that they tie him to a tree outside the station building, but Julius objected that if the young man shouted loudly enough when he woke up he would be heard down in the village. There was only a handful of families still living there, but all had—with more or less good reason—a bit of a grudge against Julius and they would probably be on the young man's side if they got the chance.

Julius had a better idea. Off the kitchen was an insulated freezer room where he stored his poached and butchered elks. For the time being the room contained no elks, and the fan was turned off. Julius didn't want to use the freezer unnecessarily because it used a hell of a lot of electricity. Julius had of course hot-wired it, and it was Gösta at Forest Cottage farm who unknowingly paid, but it was important to steal electricity in moderation if you wanted to keep taking advantage of the perk for a long time.

Allan inspected the turned-off freezer and found it to be an excellent cell, without any unnecessary amenities. The six-by-nine feet were perhaps more space than the youth deserved, but there was no need to make things unnecessarily hard.

The old men jointly dragged the young man into the freezer. He groaned when they put him on an upturned wooden chest in one corner and propped his body against the wall. He seemed about to wake up. Best to hurry out and lock the door properly!

No sooner said than done. Upon which Julius lifted the suitcase onto the kitchen table, looked at the lock, licked clean the fork he had just used for the evening's roast elk with potatoes, and picked the lock in a few seconds. Then he motioned Allan over for the actual opening, on the grounds that it was Allan's booty after all.

—Everything of mine is yours too, said Allan. We share and share alike, but if there is a pair of shoes in my size then I call first dibs.

Upon which Allan opened the lock.

—What the hell, said Allan.

—What the hell, said Julius.

"Let me out!" could be heard from the freezer room.

FOUR

1905–1929

Allan Emmanuel Karlsson was born on May 2, 1905. The day before, his mother had marched in the May Day procession in Flen and demonstrated on behalf of women's suffrage, an eight-hour working day, and other utopian demands. The demonstrating had at least one positive result: her contractions started and just after midnight her first and only son was born. She gave birth at home with the help of the neighbor's wife, who was not especially talented at midwifery but who had some status in the community because as a nine-year-old she had had the honor of curtsying before King Karl XIV Johan, who in turn was a friend (sort of) of Napoléon Bonaparte. And to be fair to the neighbor's wife, the child she delivered did indeed reach adulthood, and by a very good margin.

Allan Karlsson's father was of both a considerate and an angry nature. He was considerate with his family; he was angry with society in general and with everybody who could be thought of as representing that society. Finer folks disapproved of him, dating back to the time he had stood on the square in Flen and advocated for the use of contraceptives. For this offense he was fined ten crowns, and relieved of the need to worry about the topic any further since Allan's mother out of pure shame decided to ban any further entry to her person. Allan was then six and old enough to ask his mother for a more detailed explanation of why his father's bed had suddenly been moved into the woodshed. He was told that he shouldn't ask so many questions unless he wanted his ears boxed. Since Allan, like all children at all times, did not want his ears boxed, he dropped the subject.

From that day on, Allan's father appeared less and less frequently in his own home. In the daytime he more or less coped with his job on the railways, in the evening he discussed socialism at meetings far and wide, and where he spent his nights was never really clear to Allan.

His father did however take his financial responsibilities seriously. He handed over the greater part of his wage to his wife each week, until one day he was fired after he had turned violent with a passenger who happened to announce that he was on his way to Stockholm with thousands of others to visit the King in the royal palace and assure him of their will to defend their fatherland.

—You can start by defending yourself against this, Allan's father had said and punched the man with a hard right so that he fell to the ground.

The immediate dismissal meant that Allan's father could no longer support his family. The reputation he had acquired as a man of violence and an advocate of contraception meant that it was a waste of time for him to look for another job. All that was left was to wait for the revolution, or best of all to speed up its arrival, because every little thing nowadays went so damned slowly. Allan's father was a man who wanted to see results. Swedish socialism needed an international model. That would light a fire under everything and make things hellishly hot for Mr. Wholesale Merchant Gustavsson and his ilk.

So Allan's father packed his bag and went off to Russia to depose the Czar. Allan's mother missed his salary of course, but she was otherwise satisfied that her husband had left not only the district but also the country. After the family breadwinner had emigrated, it was up to Allan's mother and the just-ten-year-old Allan himself to keep the family afloat financially. His mother had the fourteen fully grown birch trees they owned felled and then she cut them up and split them herself to sell as firewood, while Allan managed to get a miserably paid job as an errand boy at Nitroglycerin Ltd.'s production branch.

In the regular letters she received from St. Petersburg (which soon after was renamed Petrograd), Allan's mother noted to her increasing surprise that Allan's father had started to waver in his belief in the blessings of socialism.

In his letters, Allan's father often referred to friends and acquaintances from Petrograd's political establishment. The person who was most often quoted was a man called Carl. Not an especially Russian name, Allan thought, and it didn't get any more Russian when Allan's father began to call him Uncle Carl or just Uncle.

According to Allan's father, Uncle's thesis was that people in general didn't know what was best for them, and that they needed somebody whose hand they could hold. That was why autocracy was superior to democracy, as long as the educated and responsible segment of society made sure the autocrat concerned did a good job. Seven out of ten Bolsheviks can't read, Uncle had snorted. We can't hand over power to a load of illiterates, can we?

Allan's father had nevertheless defended the Bolsheviks on

that particular point, because, as he wrote in one letter, "You can't imagine what the Russian alphabet looks like. It's no wonder people are illiterate."

What was worse was how the Bolsheviks behaved. They were filthy, and they drank vodka like the riffraff back home: the ones who laid the rails crisscrossing central Sweden. Allan's father had always wondered how the rails could be so straight considering the extent of the workers' consumption of spirits, and he had felt a twinge of guilt every time Swedish rails swung to the right or left.

Be that as it may, the Bolsheviks were at least as bad as the Swedes. Uncle maintained that socialism would end with everybody trying to kill everybody else until there was only one person left to make all the decisions. So it would be better to rely from the start on the Czar, a good and educated man with a vision for the world.

In a way, Uncle knew what he was talking about. He had actually met the Czar, indeed more than once. Uncle claimed that Nicholas II had a genuinely good heart. The Czar had had a lot of bad luck, but surely that couldn't go on. Failed harvests and Bolshevik revolution had made a mess of things. And then the Germans started to growl just because the Czar was mobilizing his forces. But he did that in order to keep the peace. After all, it wasn't the Czar who had killed the Archduke and his wife in Sarajevo, was it?

That was evidently how Uncle (whoever he was) saw it all, and somehow he got Allan's father to see it the same way. Besides, Allan's father felt an affinity with the Czar because of all the bad luck he suffered.

Sooner or later such bad luck must change, for Russian Czars as well as for ordinary honest folk from the vicinity of Flen.

His father never sent any money from Russia, but once, after a couple of years, a package came with an enamel Easter egg that his father said he had won in a game of cards from a Russian comrade, who besides drinking, arguing, and playing cards with Allan's father didn't do much more than make these kinds of eggs.

His father sent the Easter egg to his "dear wife" who just got angry and said that the damned layabout could at least have sent a real egg so that the family could eat. She was about to throw the present out the window, when she reconsidered. Perhaps Mr. Wholesale Merchant Gustavsson might be interested in it. He always tried to be special and special was exactly what Allan's mother thought the egg was.

Imagine Allan's mother's surprise when Mr. Wholesale Merchant Gustavsson after two days' consideration offered her eighteen crowns for Uncle's egg. Not real money of course, just canceling a debt, but even so.

After that, his mother hoped to receive more eggs, but instead in the next letter she found out that the Czar's generals had abandoned their autocrat who then had to leave his throne. In his letter, Allan's father cursed his egg-producing friend, who had now fled. Allan's father himself planned to stay on and do battle with the upstart clown who had taken over, a man they called Lenin.

For Allan's father, the whole thing had acquired a personal dimension since Lenin had forbidden all private ownership of land the very day after Allan's father had purchased 130 square feet on which to grow Swedish strawberries. "The land didn't cost more than four rubles, but they won't get away with nationalizing my strawberry patch," wrote Allan's father in his very last letter home, concluding: "Now it's war!"

And war it certainly was—all the time. In just about every part of the world, and it had been going on for several years. It had broken out about a year before little Allan had got his errand-boy job at Nitroglycerin Ltd. While Allan loaded his boxes with dynamite, he listened to the workers' comments on events. He wondered how they could know so much, but above all he marveled at how much misery grown men could cause. Austria declared war on

Serbia. Germany declared war on Russia. Then, Germany conquered Luxembourg a day before declaring war on France and invading Belgium. Great Britain then declared war on Germany, Austria declared war on Russia, and Serbia declared war on Germany.

And on it went. The Japanese joined in, as did the Americans. In the months after the Czar abdicated, the British took Baghdad for some reason, and then Jerusalem. The Greeks and Bulgarians started to fight each other while the Arabs continued their revolt against the Ottomans. . . .

So "Now it's war!" was right. Soon afterward, one of Lenin's henchmen had the Czar executed together with all his family. Allan noted that the Czar's bad luck had persisted.

A few months later, the Swedish consulate in Petrograd sent a telegram to Yxhult to inform them that Allan's father was dead. Although it wasn't really the job of the civil servant in the consulate to go into detail, he did.

Apparently Allan's father had nailed some plank around a little bit of earth, and proclaimed the area to be an independent republic. He called his little state The Real Russia but then two government soldiers came to pull down the fence. Allan's father had put up his fists in his eagerness to defend his country's borders, and it had been impossible for the two soldiers to reason with him. In the end, they could think of no better solution than to put a bullet between his eyes, so they could go about their task in peace.

—Couldn't you have chosen to die in a less idiotic manner? said Allan's mother to the telegram from the consulate.

She hadn't really expected her husband to come home again, but recently she had nevertheless started to hope, because she had troublesome lungs, and it wasn't easy to keep up her old pace when splitting logs. Allan's mother made a croaky sigh and that was the extent of her mourning. She told Allan philosophically that it was what it was, and that in the future whatever would be would be. Then she ruffled her son's hair kindly before going out to split more logs.

Allan didn't really understand what his mother meant. But he understood that his father was dead, that his mother coughed, and that the war was over. He himself, at the age of thirteen, was particularly accomplished when it came to making explosions by mixing nitroglycerin, cellulose nitrate, ammonium nitrate, natrium nitrate, wood flour, dinitrotoluen, and a few other ingredients. That ought to come in handy someday, thought Allan, and he went out to help his mother with the wood.

Two years later, Allan's mother finished coughing, and she entered that possible heaven where his father was already established. Then, on the threshold of the little house, Allan found an angry Mr. Wholesale Merchant, who thought that Allan's mother should have paid her debt of nine crowns before she—without telling anyone—went and died. But Allan had no plans to give Gustavsson anything.

—That's something you'll have to talk to her about yourself, Mr. Wholesale Merchant. Do you want to borrow a spade?

As wholesalers often are, the man was lightly built, compared with the fifteen-year-old Allan. The boy was on his way to becoming a man. If he was half as crazy as his father, then he was capable of anything was how Mr. Wholesale Merchant Gustavsson saw it, and since he wanted to be around quite a bit longer to count his money, the subject of the debt was never raised again.

Young Allan couldn't understand how his mother had managed to scrape together several hundred crowns in savings. But the money was there anyway, and it was enough to bury her and to start the Karlsson Dynamite Company. Maybe the boy was only fifteen years old when his mother died, but Allan had learned all he needed at Nitroglycerin Ltd.

He experimented freely in the gravel pit behind the house; once so freely that two miles away the closest neighbor's cow had a miscarriage. But Allan never heard about that, because just like

Mr. Wholesale Merchant Gustavsson, the neighbor was a little bit afraid of crazy Karlsson's possibly equally crazy boy.

Since his time as an errand boy, Allan had retained his interest in current affairs. At least once a week, he rode his bicycle to the public library in Flen to get updated on the latest news. When he was there he often met young men who were keen to debate and who all had one thing in common: they wanted to tempt Allan into some political movement or other. But Allan's great interest in world events did not include any interest in trying to change them.

In a political sense, Allan's childhood had been bewildering. On the one hand, he was from the working class. You could hardly use any other description of a boy who ends his schooling when he is ten to get a job in industry. On the other hand, he respected the memory of his father, and his father during far too short a life had managed to hold views right across the spectrum. He started on the Left, went on to praise Czar Nicholas II, and rounded off his existence through a land dispute with Vladimir Illich Lenin.

His mother, in between her coughing fits, had cursed everyone from the King to the Bolsheviks, and, in passing, even the leader of the Social Democrats, Mr. Wholesale Merchant Gustavsson, and—not least—Allan's father.

Allan himself was certainly no fool. True, he spent only three years in school, but that was plenty for him to have learned to read, write, and count. His politically conscious fellow workers at Nitroglycerin Ltd. had also made him curious about the world.

But what finally formed young Allan's philosophy of life were his mother's words when they received the news of his father's death. It took a while before the message seeped into his soul, but once there, it was there forever:

Things are what they are, and whatever will be will be.

That meant, among other things, that you didn't make a fuss, especially when there was good reason to do so: for example, when they heard the news about his father's death. In accordance with family tradition, Allan reacted by chopping wood, although for an unusually long time and without saying a word. Or when his mother followed his father's example, and as a result was carried out to the waiting hearse. Allan stayed in the kitchen and followed the spectacle through the window. And then he said so quietly that only he could hear:

—Well, good-bye, Mom.

And that was the end of that chapter of his life.

*A*llan worked hard in his dynamite company and during the first years of the 1920s built up a considerable circle of customers in the county. On Saturday evenings, when his contemporaries were attending barn dances, Allan sat at home and developed new formulas to improve the quality of his dynamite. And when Sunday came, he went to the gravel pit and tested the new explosives. Not between eleven and one, though—he promised the local pastor in exchange for not complaining too much about Allan's absence from church.

Allan liked his own company and that was good, because he lived an isolated life. Since he didn't join the ranks of the labor movement he was despised by socialists, while he was far too working class (not to mention related to his father) to be allowed a place in any bourgeois gathering. Gustavsson, for one, would rather die than end up in the company of that Karlsson brat. Just think what would happen if the boy discovered what Gustavsson had been paid for the enamel egg, the one that he had once bought from Allan's mother for next to nothing and now sold to a diplomat in Stockholm. Thanks to that bit of business, Gustavsson had become the district's third proud owner of an automobile.

That time he had been lucky. But one Sunday in August 1925, after the church service, Gustavsson's luck ran out. He went out for a drive, mainly to show off his expensive car. Unluckily for him, he happened to choose the road that passed Allan Karlsson's house. At the turn, Gustavsson had gotten nervous (or perhaps God or fate had a hand in the events), and the gears got stuck and one thing led to another and Gustavsson and his automobile went straight into the gravel pit behind the house, instead of following the gentle curve of the road to the right. It would have been bad enough for Gustavsson to set foot on Allan's land and have to explain himself, but things turned out much worse than that, because just as Gustavsson managed to bring his runaway automobile to a halt, Allan set off the first of that Sunday's trial explosions.

Allan, himself, was curled up for protection behind the outhouse and could neither see nor hear anything. Not until he returned to the gravel pit, did he realize that something had gone wrong. Bits of Gustavsson's automobile were spread out over half the pit, and here and there lay bits of Gustavsson himself.

Gustavsson's head had landed softly on a patch of grass. It stared vacantly out over the destruction.

—What business did you have in my gravel pit? Allan asked.

Gustavsson did not reply.

During the next four years, Allan had plenty of time to read and improve his knowledge of how society worked. He was immediately locked up, though it was hard to say exactly what for. After a while, his father was brought up. This occurred after a young and enthusiastic disciple of Professor Bernhard Lundborg, an expert on Racial Biology at Uppsala University, decided to build his career on Allan's case. When Allan was delivered into the clutches of Professor Lundborg, he was immediately sterilized for "eugenic and social reasons" on the basis that Allan was probably a bit slow and there was probably too much of his father in him for the state to allow further reproduction of the Karlsson genes.

The sterilization did not bother Allan. On the contrary, he felt he was well treated at Professor Lundborg's clinic. Now and then, he had to answer all sorts of questions such as why he needed to blow people and things into bits and whether he had any knowledge of having Negro blood. Allan answered that he saw a certain difference between things and people when it came to the pleasure of lighting the fuse of a load of dynamite. Splitting a rock down the middle—that could make you feel good. But if instead of a rock, it was a person, well, Allan couldn't see why a person wouldn't move out of the way under the circumstances. Didn't Professor Lundborg feel the same way?

But Bernhard Lundborg was not the sort of man to involve himself in philosophical discussions with his patients; he repeated the question about Negro blood. Allan answered that you never really know, but both his parents had had skin that was as pale as his; perhaps the professor could settle for that as an answer? And then Allan added that he was dying to see a black man for real if the professor had one on hand.

Professor Lundborg and his assistants did not answer Allan's questions, but they made notes and hummed and then left him in peace, sometimes for days at a stretch. Allan devoted those days to all kinds of reading: the daily newspapers of course, but also books from the hospital's extensive library. Add to that three square meals a day, an indoor toilet, and a room of his own, and you can see why Allan found it very comfortable to be locked up in an asylum. The atmosphere had been a little unpleasant only once, and that was when Allan asked Professor Lundborg what was so dangerous about being a Negro or a Jew. For once, the professor didn't respond with silence, but bellowed that Karlsson should mind his own business and not interfere in other people's affairs. Allan was reminded of that time many years ago when his mother had threatened to box his ears.

The years passed and the interviews with Allan became few and far between. Then parliament appointed a committee to investigate the sterilization of "biologically inferior individuals" and when the report was issued, Professor Lundborg suddenly had so much to do that Allan's bed was needed for somebody else. In the spring of 1929, Allan was pronounced rehabilitated and fit once again to enter society, and was sent out onto the streets with just enough cash to get him a train ticket to Flen. He had to walk the last few miles to Yxhult, but Allan didn't mind. After four years behind bars, he needed to stretch his legs.

FIVE

Monday, May 2, 2005

T he local newspaper lost no time in posting the news about the old man who had disappeared into thin air on his hundredth birthday. As the newspaper's reporter was starved for real news from the district, she managed to imply that you could not exclude the possibility of kidnapping. According to witnesses, the centenarian was all right in the head and probably wasn't roaming around confused.

There is something special about disappearing on your hundredth birthday. The local radio station soon followed the local newspaper, and then came national radio, the Web sites of the national newspapers, and the afternoon and evening TV news.

The police in Flen had to hand the case over to the county crime squad, which sent two police cars with uniformed police officers and a Detective Chief Inspector Aronsson who was not in uniform.

They were soon joined by assorted reporters who wanted to help search every corner of the area. The presence of the mass media in turn gave the county police chief reason to lead the investigation himself and perhaps to appear on camera in the process.

Initially the police work involved the police cars driving back and forth across the municipality, while Aronsson interrogated people at the Old Folks' Home. The mayor, however, had gone home, and turned off his phone. In his opinion, only harm would come from being involved in the disappearance of an ungrateful geriatric.

A scattering of tips did come in: everything from Allan being seen on a bike, to standing in line and behaving badly at the pharmacy. But these, as well as similar observations, could soon be dismissed for various reasons. For example, he could not have been biking at the same time as he was definitely observed eating lunch in his room at the Old Folks' Home.

The head of the county police organized search parties with the help of about a hundred volunteers from the area, and he was genuinely surprised when this gave no results. Up to now he had been pretty certain that it was an ordinary case of a demented person disappearing, despite the statements of witnesses as to the good quantity of marbles possessed by the hundred-year-old man.

So the investigation didn't at this stage go anywhere, not until the police dog borrowed from Eskilstuna arrived at about half past seven in the evening. The dog sniffed a few moments at Allan's armchair and the footprints among the pansies outside the window before it set off toward the park and out the other side, across the street, into the grounds of the medieval church, over the stone wall, coming to a halt outside the bus station waiting room.

The waiting room door was locked. An official told the police that the station locked its doors at 7:30 in the evening on weekdays, when the official's colleague finished work for the day. But, the official added, if the police absolutely couldn't wait until the following day, they could visit his colleague at home. His name was Ronny Hulth and he was sure to be listed in the telephone directory.

While the head of the county police stood in front of the cameras outside the Old Folks' Home and announced that the police needed the public's help to continue with search parties during the evening and through the night since the centenarian was lightly dressed and possibly in a state of confusion, Detective Chief Inspector Göran Aronsson rang Ronny Hulth's doorbell. The dog had clearly indicated that the geriatric had gone into the waiting room, and Mr. Hulth, who had been in the ticket office, ought to be able to say whether the old man had left Malmköping by bus.

But Ronny Hulth did not open the door. He sat in his bedroom with the blinds drawn, hugging his cat.

—Go away! Ronny Hulth whispered toward the front door. Go away!

And in the end that is precisely what the chief inspector did. Partly he agreed with his boss's belief that the geriatric was wandering about locally, or that if the old guy had gotten on a bus, he was presumably capable of looking after himself.

Ronny Hulth was probably visiting his girlfriend. The first task tomorrow morning would be to seek him out on the job. If the geriatric hadn't turned up by then, that is.

At 9:02 p.m., the county police received a call:
—My name is Bertil Karlgren and I'm calling . . . I'm calling on behalf of my wife you could say. Well, yes, anyway, my wife, Gerda Karlgren, has been in Flen for a few days visiting our daughter and her husband. They're going to have a baby. . . . So there's always a lot to do. But today it was time to go home and she took—I mean Gerda—Gerda took the early afternoon bus, and the bus goes via Malmköping, we live here in Strängnäs. . . . Well, this might not be anything—the wife doesn't think so—but we heard on the radio about a hundred-year-old man who'd disappeared.

Perhaps you've already found him? You haven't? Anyway, the wife says that there was an incredibly old man who got on the bus in Malmköping and he had a large suitcase as if he was going for a long journey. The wife sat at the back and the old man sat right at the front so she couldn't see so well and she didn't hear what the old man and the driver talked about. What did you say, Gerda? Well, Gerda says that she isn't one of those people who listen to other people's conversations. . . . The old man got out only half-way to Strängnäs. Gerda doesn't know what the bus stop is called. It was sort of in the middle of the forest. . . .

The conversation was recorded, transcribed, and sent by fax to the detective chief inspector's hotel in Malmköping.

SIX

Monday, May 2–Tuesday, May 3, 2005

The suitcase was stuffed with bundles of 500-crown notes. Julius did some quick math in his head: ten rows across, five rows high, fifteen bundles in every pile . . .

—Thirty-seven-and-a-half million if I counted correctly, said Julius.

—That's a decent amount of money, said Allan.

—Let me out, you bastards, the young man shouted from inside the freezer.

The young man was acting crazy in there; he yelled and kicked and yelled some more. Allan and Julius needed to collect their thoughts about the surprising turn of events, but they couldn't do it with all that noise. In the end, Allan thought it was time to cool the young man's temper a little, so he turned on the freezer fan.

It didn't take many seconds for the young man to notice that his situation had worsened. He quieted down to try to think clearly, not something he usually had much aptitude for, let alone with a pounding headache when trapped in a rapidly cooling freezer.

After a few minutes deliberation, he decided that threatening or trying to kick his way out of the situation was unlikely to be effective. All that was left was to call for help from outside. All that was left was to call the boss. It was a dreadful thought. But the alternative seemed even worse.

The young man hesitated for a minute or two, while it got colder and colder. Finally, he pulled out his mobile phone.

No signal.

The evening turned into night, and the night became morning. Allan opened his eyes but couldn't figure out where he was. Had he gone and died in his sleep, after all?

A chipper male voice wished him a good morning and informed him that there were two pieces of news to be conveyed, one good and one bad. Which did Allan want to hear first?

First of all, Allan wanted to know where he was and why. His knees were aching, so he was alive despite everything. But hadn't he . . . and didn't he then take. . . . Was the man called Julius?

The pieces were falling into place; Allan was awake. He lay on a mattress on the floor in Julius's bedroom. Julius stood in the doorway and repeated his question.

—Do you want the good or the bad news first?

—The good news, said Allan. You can skip the bad news.

—Okay.

Julius told him that the good news was that breakfast was on the table. There was coffee, sandwiches with cold roast elk, and eggs from the neighbors.

To think that Allan was going to enjoy one more breakfast

THE ONE HUNDRED YEAR OLD MAN   43

without porridge in his life! That was good news indeed. When he sat down at the kitchen table, he felt that he was now ready to hear the bad news after all.

—The bad news, said Julius, lowering his voice a little, the bad news is that when we were well and truly pissed last night, we forgot to turn off the fan in the freezer room.

—And? said Allan.

—And . . . the guy inside must be dead cold—or cold dead—by now.

With a worried look, Allan scratched his neck while he decided whether to let news of this carelessness spoil the day.

—Oh dear, he said. But I must say that you've got these eggs just right, not too hard and not too runny.

Detective Chief Inspector Aronsson woke at about eight a.m. in a bad mood. A geriatric who goes astray, on purpose or otherwise, should not be a case for somebody with the chief inspector's qualifications.

Aronsson showered, got dressed, and went down to breakfast on the ground floor of the Plevna Hotel. On his way he met the receptionist who gave him a fax that had come in just after reception had closed the previous evening.

An hour later, the chief inspector saw the case in a different light. The importance of the fax from the county police was unclear until Aronsson met a pale Ronny Hulth at the station's ticket office. It didn't take long before Hulth broke down and told Aronsson what had happened.

Shortly afterward, there was a call from Eskilstuna reporting that the county bus company in Flen had just discovered that a bus had been missing since the previous evening. Could Aronsson call a Jessica Björkman, the live-in girlfriend of a bus driver who had evidently been kidnapped but released?

Chief Inspector Aronsson went back to the Plevna Hotel for a cup of coffee and to put all this newly gained information together. He wrote down his observations:

An elderly man, Allan Karlsson, goes AWOL from his room at the Old Folks' Home just before his hundredth birthday is to be celebrated in the lounge. Karlsson is or was in sensationally good condition for his age. The simple physical fact that he managed to get himself out through a window attests to this—unless the geriatric got help from outside of course, but later observations would suggest that he was acting on his own. Furthermore, Director Alice Englund has testified that "Allan may be old, but he is also one hell of a rascal and he damned well does exactly what he feels like."

According to the tracking dog, Karlsson, after trampling down a bed of pansies, walked through parts of Malmköping and eventually into the waiting room at the bus station where, according to witness Ronny Hulth, he had gone straight up to Hulth's ticket window—or rather shuffled up, since Hulth noticed Karlsson's short steps and that Karlsson was wearing slippers, not shoes.

Hulth's further comments indicate that Karlsson wanted to get away from Malmköping as quickly as possible, with the direction and the means of transport seeming to be of lesser importance.

That is incidentally confirmed by Jessica Björkman, the live-in girlfriend of bus driver Lennart Ramnér. The bus driver has not been interrogated as yet, on account of his having taken too many sleeping pills. But Björkman's statement seemed sound. Karlsson bought a ticket from Ramnér for a predetermined amount of money. The destination happened to be Byringe Station. Happened to be. There was thus no reason to believe that anybody or anything was waiting for Karlsson.

There was another interesting detail. The ticket seller had not noticed whether Karlsson had a suitcase before he climbed on board the bus to Byringe, but this fact had very soon become apparent to him on account of the violent behavior of a supposed member of the criminal organization Never Again.

There wasn't a suitcase in the story Jessica Björkman had managed to get out of her boyfriend, but the fax from the police confirms that Karlsson had presumably—albeit incredibly—stolen the suitcase from the Never Again member.

The rest of Björkman's story, together with the fax from Eskilstuna, tells us that Karlsson, at 3:20 in the afternoon, give or take a few minutes, and then the Never Again member, about four hours later, got off at Byringe Station before walking toward an unknown destination. The former is one hundred years old, dragging a suitcase with him; the latter is about seventy-five years younger. Chief Inspector Aronsson closed his notebook and drank the last of the coffee. It was 10:25 a.m.

Next stop, Byringe Station.

*A*t breakfast, Julius told Allan everything that he had accomplished and plotted during the early morning hours while Allan still slept.

First, the unfortunate accident in the freezer room: when Julius realized that the temperature had been below freezing for at least ten hours during the evening and night, he had armed himself with the crowbar and opened the door. If the young man was still alive, he wouldn't be even close to as awake and alert as he would need to be to stand up to Julius and his crowbar.

But the crowbar safety measure was unnecessary. The young man sat hunched up on his empty box, his threatening and kicking days over. He had ice crystals on his body and his eyes stared coldly out at nothing—dead as a butchered elk, in short.

Julius thought it was too bad, but also very convenient. They wouldn't have been able to let that wild man out just like that. Julius turned the fan off and left the door open. The young man was dead, but he didn't have to be frozen solid.

Julius lit the stove in the kitchen to keep the place warm, and checked on the money. It wasn't the thirty-seven million that he had hurriedly estimated the evening before. It was exactly fifty million.

Allan listened to Julius's account with interest, while he ate his breakfast with a better appetite than he'd had for as long as he could remember. He didn't say anything until Julius reached the money part.

—Fifty million is easier to split into two than thirty-seven. Nice and equal. Would you be so kind as to pass me the salt?

Julius did as Allan requested, saying that he would probably have been able to divide thirty-seven into two as well if it had been necessary, but he agreed that it was easier with fifty. Then Julius became serious. He sat down at the kitchen table opposite Allan, and said that it was high time they left the disused station for good. The young man in the freezer could do no more harm, but who knows what he might have stirred up behind him on the way here? At any moment there could be ten new young men standing there shouting in the kitchen, each one just as ornery as the one who was done shouting.

Allan agreed, but reminded Julius of his advanced age and pointed out that he wasn't as mobile as he once had been. Julius promised to see to it that there would be as little walking as possible involved. But get away they must. And it would be best if they took the young man in the freezer with them. It would do the two old men no good if people found a corpse in their wake.

Breakfast was done with; now it was time to get going. Julius and Allan lifted the dead young man out of the freezer and into the kitchen, where they put him in a chair while they gathered their strength.

Allan inspected him from top to toe, and then said:

—He has unusually small feet for someone so big. He has no use for his shoes anymore, does he?

Julius answered that although it was clearly cold outside at this time of the morning, the risk was greater that Allan would get frostbitten toes than would the young man. If Allan thought the shoes would fit, then he should go ahead and take them. If the young man didn't object, that meant he agreed.

The shoes were a bit too large for Allan, but solid and much better suited to being on the run than a pair of well-worn indoor slippers.

The next step was to shove the young man out into the hall and tip him down the steps. When all three found themselves out on the platform, two standing and one lying down, Allan wondered what Julius had in mind now.

—Don't go anywhere, Julius said to Allan. Not you, either, he said to the young man, and jumped down from the platform and headed for a shed at the end of the station's only siding.

Shortly afterward, Julius rolled out of the shed on an inspection trolley.

—Vintage 1954, he said. Welcome aboard.

Julius did the heavy pedaling at the front. Just behind him, Allan let his feet follow the movement of the pedals, and the corpse sat on the seat to the right with his head propped up on a broom handle and dark sunglasses covering his staring eyes.

It was five to eleven when the party set off. Three minutes later, a dark blue Volvo arrived at Byringe's former railway station. Chief Inspector Göran Aronsson stepped out of the car.

The building did undeniably seem to be abandoned, but he should probably take a closer look before he moved on to Byringe village to knock on doors.

Aronsson stepped cautiously up onto the platform, since it didn't look entirely stable. He opened the door and called out:

—Is anybody home?

Not receiving an answer, he went up the stairs to the first

floor. In fact, the building did seem to be inhabited. Downstairs, there were glowing embers in the kitchen stove and an almost-finished breakfast for two on the table.

On the floor sat a pair of well-worn slippers.

Never Again described itself officially as a motorcycle club, but in fact it was a small group of young men with criminal records, led by a middle-aged man with an even longer criminal record, all of them with ongoing criminal intentions.

The leader of the group was called Per-Gunnar Gerdin, but nobody dared call him anything but the "Boss," because that's what the Boss had decided and he was almost six-and-a-half feet tall, weighed about 500 pounds, and was apt to wave a knife around if anybody or anything crossed him.

The Boss had started his criminal career in a rather low-key way. Together with a partner, he imported fruit and vegetables into Sweden and faked the country of origin in order to deprive the state of taxes and get a higher price from consumers.

The only problem with the Boss's partner was that his conscience wasn't sufficiently flexible. The Boss wanted to diversify into more radical schemes such as soaking food in formaldehyde. He had heard that was how they did things in some parts of Asia and the Boss had the idea of importing Swedish meatballs from the Philippines, cheap and by sea. With the right amount of formaldehyde the meatballs would stay fresh for three months if necessary, even at 100 degrees.

They would be so cheap that the partners wouldn't even have to label them as "Swedish" to sell them at a profit. "Danish" would suffice, thought the Boss, but his partner said no. In his opinion, formaldehyde was fine for embalming corpses, but not for giving eternal life to meatballs.

So they went their separate ways and nothing more came of the formaldehyde meatballs. Instead, the Boss discovered that he

could pull a ski mask over his face and rob his most serious com-
petitor, Stockholm Fruit Import AB, of their day's takings.

With the help of a machete and an angry shout of "Gimme the
cash or else!" in an instant and to his own surprise, he had become
forty-one thousand crowns richer. Why slave away with imports
when you could earn such nice money for almost no work at all?

And thus the course was set. Usually it went well. In almost
twenty years as an entrepreneur in the robbery business, he had
only had a couple of short involuntary vacations.

But after two decades, the Boss felt it was time to think bigger.
He found a couple of younger henchmen. The first thing he did was
to give each of them a suitably idiotic nickname (one was called Bolt
and the other, Bucket), and with their help he then carried out two
successful armored car robberies.

A third armored car robbery, however, ended with four-and-
a-half years in a maximum-security prison for all three of them. It
was there that the Boss got the idea for Never Again. During stage
one, the club would consist of about fifty members, divided into
three operative branches: "robbery," "narcotics," and "extortion."
The name Never Again came from the Boss's vision of creating such
a professional and watertight structure for crime that they would
never again find themselves in a maximum-security prison. Never
Again would be the Real Madrid of organized crime (the Boss was
crazy about soccer).

In the beginning, the recruitment process in prison went well.
But then a letter to the Boss from his mom happened to go astray
in the prison. His mom wrote, among other things, that her little
Per-Gunnar should take care not to mix with bad company in the
prison, that he should be careful with his delicate tonsils, and that
she was looking forward to playing the Treasure Island Game with
him again when he got out.

After that, it didn't help that the Boss sliced up a couple of
Yugoslavs in the lunch line and generally acted like a violent psy-
chotic. His authority was damaged. Of the thirty recruits so far,

twenty-seven dropped out. Besides Bolt and Bucket, only a Vene-zuelan named José Mariá Rodriguez stayed on, the latter because he was secretly in love with the Boss, which he never dared admit to anybody, even himself.

The Venezuelan was given the name Caracas, after the capital city of his home country. However much the Boss threatened and swore, no one else joined his club. And one day, he and his three henchmen were released from prison.

At first, the Boss thought of abandoning the whole idea of Never Again, but Caracas happened to have a Colombian comrade with a flexible conscience and dubious friends, and after one thing and another, Sweden (through Never Again) became the gateway country to eastern Europe for the Colombian narcotics trade. The deals got bigger and bigger, and there was neither need nor staff to activate the "robbery" and "extortion" branches.

The Boss convened a war council in Stockholm with Bucket and Ca-racas. Something had happened to Bolt, the clumsy idiot who had been trusted to carry out the club's largest transaction so far. The Boss had been in contact with the Russians in the morning and they swore that they had gotten the merchandise—and handed over the payment. If Never Again's courier had run off with the suitcase then that wasn't the Russians' problem.

The Boss assumed for the time being that the Russians were telling the truth. Would Bolt voluntarily have skipped town with the money? No, he dismissed the idea; Bolt was too stupid for that. Or too wise, however you wanted to look at it.

Somebody must have known about the transaction, have waited for the right moment in Malmköping or on Bolt's journey back to Stockholm, knocked out Bolt, and grabbed the suitcase.

But who? The Boss presented the question to the war council and didn't get an answer. The Boss wasn't surprised; he had long ago decided that his henchmen were idiots, all three of them.

Anyhow, he ordered Bucket out into the field, because the Boss
thought that the idiot Bucket was still not quite as big an idiot as
the idiot Caracas. The idiot Bucket would thus have a greater
chance of finding idiot Bolt, and perhaps even the suitcase with the
money.

—Go down to Malmköping and poke around a bit, Bucket.
But don't wear your jacket; police are all over the town. A hundred-
year-old guy has disappeared.

J ulius, Allan, and the corpse rolled along through the forest. At Vidkärr they had the misfortune to meet a farmer. The farmer was
there inspecting his crops when the trio came racing by on the
inspection trolley.

—Good morning, said Julius.

—Nice day, said Allan.

The corpse and the farmer didn't say anything. But the farmer
stared at the trio for a long time as they went off into the distance.

The closer the trolley got to the local steel works, the more worried Julius got. He had thought they might pass a lake on the way
and that they'd be able to dump the corpse in it. But they didn't. And
before Julius had time to worry any further, the trolley rolled into
the foundry yard. Julius applied the brakes just in time. The corpse
fell forward and hit its forehead on an iron handle.

—That would have been really painful if the circumstances
had been a little different, said Allan.

—There are undoubtedly advantages to being dead, said Julius.

Julius climbed down from the trolley and positioned himself
behind a birch tree to survey the area. The enormous doors into
the factory halls were open, but the yard seemed deserted. Julius
looked at his watch. It was ten past twelve. Lunchtime, he realized. He spotted a large container and announced that he intended
to go off and do a bit of reconnaissance. Allan wished Julius the
best of luck and asked him not to get lost.

There wasn't much risk of that, because Julius was only going to walk the thirty yards to the container. He climbed in and was out of Allan's sight for just over a minute. Once back at the trolley, Julius announced that he now knew what to do with the corpse.

The container had been packed half full of steel cylinders of some sort, each one of them in a protective wooden box with a lid. Allan was totally exhausted once the heavy corpse was finally in place inside one of the innermost cylinders. But when he closed the wooden lid and saw the address label, he livened right up.

Addis Ababa.

—He's going to see the world if he keeps his peepers open, said Allan.

—Hurry up, Julius said. We can't stay here.

The operation went well, and the two men were back under the birch trees well before the lunch break was over. They sat down on the trolley to rest, and soon things started to liven up in the factory yard. A truck driver filled the container with a few more cylinders. Then he closed and locked it, brought over a new container, and continued the loading.

Allan wondered what they actually manufactured there. Julius knew it was a works with a history; as far back as the seventeenth century they had cast and supplied cannons to everybody in the Thirty Years' War who wanted to do their killing more efficiently.

Allan thought it sounded unnecessary for the people in the seventeenth century to kill each other. If they had only been a little patient they would all have died in the end anyway. Julius said that you could say the same of all epochs. Then he announced that the break was now over and that it was time to make themselves scarce. Julius's simple plan was that the two friends would walk the short distance into the more central parts of Åker and once there decide on their next move.

Chief Inspector Aronsson *went through the old station building in* Byringe without finding anything of interest except a pair of slippers that might have belonged to the centenarian. He would take them with him to show the staff at the Old Folks' Home.

There *were* pools of water here and there on the kitchen floor, leading to an open walk-in freezer, which was switched off. But that was unlikely to be of any significance.

Aronsson continued into Byringe village to knock on doors. There were people at home in three of the houses, and from all three families he learned that a Julius Jonsson lived on the first floor of the station building, that Julius Jonsson was a thief and a con man whom nobody wanted to have anything to do with, and that nobody had heard or seen anything strange since the previous evening. But they all took it for granted that Julius Jonsson was up to no good.

—Put him behind bars, one of the angriest neighbors demanded.

—For what reason? the chief inspector wondered in a tired voice.

—Because he steals my eggs from the henhouse at night, because he stole my newly purchased sled last winter and painted it and called it his own, because he orders books in my name, goes through my mailbox when they arrive and lets me pay the bill, because he tries to sell privately distilled vodka to my fourteen-year-old son, because he—

—Okay, Okay, fine. I'll put him behind bars, said the chief inspector. I just have to find him first.

Aronsson turned back toward Malmköping and was about halfway there when his mobile rang. A farmer had just phoned in with an interesting tip. An hour or so earlier, a known petty criminal from the district had passed his fields on an inspection trolley on the disused railway line between Byringe and Åker Foundry. On the trolley he saw an old man, a big suitcase, and a young man with sunglasses. The young man seemed to be in charge, according to the farmer. Even though he wasn't wearing any shoes . . .

—I don't get it, said Chief Inspector Aronsson and turned his car around at such a speed that the slippers on the passenger seat fell onto the floor.

A fter a couple of hundred yards, Allan's already glacial walking pace slowed. He didn't complain, but Julius could see that the old man's knees were causing problems. In the distance stood a hot dog stand. Julius promised Allan that if he made it to the hot dog stand, then Julius would treat him—he could afford it—and then he would find a solution to the transportation problem. Allan replied that never in his life had he complained over a bit of discomfort and that he wasn't going to start now, but that a hot dog would hit the spot.

Julius increased his pace; Allan stumbled after him. When he arrived, Julius had already eaten half of his hot dog. A fancy grilled one. And that wasn't all.

—Allan, he said, come and say hello to Benny. He's our new private chauffeur.

Benny, the owner of the hot dog stand, was about fifty, and still in possession of all his hair, including a ponytail. In about two minutes, Julius had managed to buy a hot dog, an orange soda, and Benny's silver 1988 Mercedes, including Benny himself, all for one hundred thousand crowns.

Allan looked at the owner of the hot dog stand.

—Have we bought you too, or just hired you? he asked finally.

—The car has been bought, the chauffeur has been hired, Benny answered. For ten days to start with, then it seems we are going to have a new discussion. A hot dog is included in the price. Can I tempt you with a Viennese wurst?

No, he couldn't. Allan just wanted an ordinary boiled sausage if that was all right. And besides, said Allan, one hundred thousand for such an old car was an extremely high price even if it included a driver, so now it was only fair that he throw in a bottle of chocolate milk too.

Benny agreed instantly. He would be leaving his kiosk behind and a chocolate milk more or less made no difference. His business was losing money anyway; running a hot dog stand in a small village had turned out to be just as bad an idea as it had seemed at the beginning.

In fact, Benny informed them, even before the two gentlemen had so conveniently turned up, he had been toying with plans to do something different with his life. But a private chauffeur, well, he hadn't pictured that.

In light of what the hot-dog-stand manager had just told them, Allan suggested that Benny load an entire carton of chocolate milk into the trunk of the car. And Julius, for his part, promised that Benny would get his own private chauffeur's cap at the first opportunity, if only he would take off his hot-dog-stand chef's hat and exit the stand because it was time for them to be on their way.

Benny didn't think it was part of his job to argue with his employers, so he did as he was told. His chef's hat ended up in the garbage, and the chocolate milk went into the trunk. But Julius wanted to keep the suitcase on the backseat with him. Allan had to sit in the front where he could stretch out his legs properly.

So the only hot-dog-stand manager in Åker went and sat in the driver's seat of what a few minutes earlier had been his own Mercedes, now honorably sold to the two gentlemen in Benny's company.

—And where do you two gentlemen want to go? asked Benny.

—What about north? said Julius.

—Yes, that would be fine, said Allan. Or south.

—Then we'll say south, said Julius.

—South it is, said Benny.

Ten minutes later, Chief Inspector Aronsson arrived at Åker. By following the railway tracks, he discovered an old inspection trolley behind the factory.

But the trolley provided no obvious clues. The workers in the yard were busy loading cylinders of some type into containers. None of them had seen the trolley arrive. But just after lunch they had seen two elderly men walking along the road, one of them dragging a large suitcase. They were headed in the direction of the gas station and the hot dog stand.

Aronsson asked if there were really only two men, not three. But the workers hadn't seen a third person.

Driving to the gas station and the hot dog stand, Aronsson considered this new information. But it was harder than ever to make sense of it all.

First, he stopped at the hot dog stand. He was getting hungry, so it was perfect timing. But it was closed. It had to be tough to run a hot dog stand out in this wilderness, Aronsson thought, and continued on to the gas station. There, they had seen nothing and heard nothing. But at least they could sell Aronsson a hot dog, even though it tasted of gas.

After his quick lunch, Aronsson went to the supermarket, the flower shop, and the Realtor. And he stopped and spoke to any natives who had ventured out with dogs, baby carriages, or a husband or wife. But nobody had seen two or three men with a suitcase. The trail simply came to an end somewhere between the foundry and the gas station. Chief Inspector Aronsson decided to return to Malmköping. At least he had a pair of slippers that required identification.

Aronsson phoned the county police chief from his car and updated him. The county police chief was grateful because he was giving a press conference at the Plevna Hotel at two o'clock and so far he had had nothing to say.

The police chief had something of a theatrical bent; he was not inclined to understatement. And now Chief Inspector Aronsson had given him just what he needed for today's show.

So the police chief pulled out all the stops during the press conference, before Aronsson had time to get back to Malmköping to stop him (which he wouldn't have succeeded in doing anyway). The police chief announced that the police had to assume that Allan Karlsson's disappearance had developed into a kidnapping, just as the local newspaper's Web site had suggested the previous day. The police now had information that Karlsson was alive but in the hands of people from the underworld.

There were of course a lot of questions, but the police chief skillfully avoided them. What he *could* tell the press was that Karlsson and his presumed kidnappers had been seen in the little village of Åker as recently as around lunchtime that very day. And he urged the police authority's best friend—the General Public—to keep their eyes open.

To the disappointment of the police chief, the TV team hadn't stayed around for his dramatic announcement. They would surely have been hooked if that sluggard Aronsson had managed to dig up the kidnapping story a little earlier. But at least the national tabloid was there, as were the local paper and a reporter from the local radio. And at the back of the hotel dining room stood another man whom the police chief didn't recognize. Was he from the national news agency?

Bucket wasn't from a news agency. But he was becoming convinced that Bolt *had* skipped town with all the dough—in which case he was now as good as dead.

When Chief Inspector Aronsson arrived at the Plevna Hotel, th press had dispersed. On his way, Aronsson had stoppe at the Old Folks' Home and they had confirmed that the did indeed belong to Allan Karlsson. (Director Alice sniffed at them and nodded with a disgusted look on her face.)

Aronsson had the misfortune to stumble upon the county police chief in the hotel lobby. The chief told him about the press conference and ordered him to solve the crime, preferably in such a way that it didn't conflict with what the police chief had said to the press.

Then the police chief went on his way. He had a lot of work to do. It was, for example, high time to bring a prosecutor on board.

Aronsson sat down with a cup of coffee to reflect on the latest developments. He decided to focus on the relationship between the three trolley passengers. If the farmer had been wrong about Karlsson and Jonsson's relationship to the trolley's third passenger, then it might be a hostage drama. The police chief had just said as much at his press conference, but since he was rarely right, that might be a strike against the kidnapping theory. Besides, witnesses had seen Karlsson and Jonsson walking around in Åker—with a suitcase. So the question was, had the two old men, Karlsson and Jonsson, somehow managed to overpower the young and strong Never Again member and throw him into a ditch?

An incredible but not impossible idea. Aronsson decided to call in the Eskilstuna police dog again. The dog and her handler would need to take a long walk all the way from the farmer's fields to the foundry in Åker. Somewhere in between, the Never Again member had disappeared.

Karlsson and Jonsson themselves managed to disappear into thin air somewhere between the back of the foundry and the gas station—a distance of 200 yards. They disappeared from the face of the earth without anyone noticing. The only thing along the route was a closed hot dog stand.

Aronsson's mobile rang. The police had received a new tip. This time the centenarian had been seen in Mjölby, probably kidnapped by the middle-aged man with the ponytail who sat behind the wheel of a silver Mercedes.

—Should we check it out? his colleague asked.

—No, said Aronsson, sighing.

Years of experience had taught Aronsson to distinguish between good and bad tips. That was a consolation when most things were clouded in mist.

B enny stopped in Mjölby to get gas. Julius carefully opened the suitcase and pulled out a 500-crown note to pay with.

Then Julius said he wanted to stretch his legs a little, and asked Allan to stay in the car and guard the suitcase. Allan was tired after the day's hardships, and promised not to move an inch.

Benny came back first, and got behind the wheel. Shortly after, Julius returned. The Mercedes continued its journey south.

After a while, Julius started to rustle something in the backseat. He held out an opened bag of candy to Allan and Benny.

—Just look what I found in my pocket, he said.

Allan raised his eyebrows:

—You stole a bag of candy, when we've got fifty million in the suitcase?

—You've got fifty million in the suitcase? asked Benny.

—Oops, said Allan.

—Not quite, said Julius. We gave you one hundred thousand.

—Plus five hundred for the gas, said Allan.

Benny was silent for a few seconds.

—So you've got forty-nine million, eight hundred and ninety-nine thousand, five hundred crowns in the suitcase?

—You have a head for numbers, said Allan.

Silence reigned until Julius said that it might be better to explain everything to the private chauffeur. If Benny wanted to break their contract, then that would be quite all right.

The part of the story Benny found hardest to stomach was that a person had been put to death and subsequently packed for ⸗ port. But on the other hand, it had clearly been an accident though vodka was involved. For his part, Benny never touched the hard stuff.

The newly employed chauffeur thought it through and decided that the fifty million had most certainly been in the wrong hands from the very beginning, and now the money might be of more use to humanity. Besides, it seemed wrong to resign on the very first day of a new job.

So Benny promised to stay on and wondered what the two old men were planning next. Until then, he hadn't wanted to ask; in Benny's opinion, curiosity was not a desirable quality in private chauffeurs, but now he had become a bit of a conspirator.

Allan and Julius admitted that they didn't actually have any plan at all. Maybe they could follow the road until it started to get dark, and then spend the night somewhere where they could discuss the matter in more detail.

—Fifty million, said Benny and smiled, while he put the Mercedes into first gear.

—Forty-nine million, eight hundred and ninety-nine thousand, five hundred crowns, Allan corrected him.

Then Julius had to promise to stop stealing things for the sake of stealing. He said it wouldn't be easy; he had it in his blood and wasn't suited to anything else. But he did promise, and one thing Julius knew about himself was that he rarely failed to keep his promises.

The journey continued in silence. Allan soon fell asleep. Julius ate another candy. And Benny hummed a song whose name he didn't remember.

A *tabloid journalist who sensed a story is not easy to stop. It didn't take long for the reporters to form a much clearer picture of* the true course of events than the one the county police chief had presented at the afternoon's press conference. This time around, the *Express* was the first to get hold of ticket seller Ronny Hulth,

visit him at his home, and—upon promising to find a live-in partner for Ronny Hulth's lonely cat—manage to persuade him to follow the reporter to a hotel in Eskilstuna for the night—out of reach
of the rival paper. At first, Hulth had been afraid to talk; he remembered only too well what the young man had threatened him with.
But the reporter promised that Hulth could remain anonymous
and assured him that nothing would happen to him since the police were now involved in the case.

But the *Express* did not stop at Hulth. The bus driver too had
been caught in the net, as had the villagers in Byringe, the farmer
in Vidkärr, and various people in the Åker village. All in all, this
offered fodder for several dramatic articles the next day. They
were of course full of incorrect assumptions, but considering the
circumstances the reporter had done well.

The silver Mercedes drove on. Eventually, Julius too fell asleep. Allan
was snoring in the front seat, Julius in the back with the suitcase as an uncomfortable pillow. All of this while Benny charted
their course as best he could. Eventually Benny decided to leave the
highway, continuing south, deep into the Småland forests. Here he
was hoping to find suitable lodging for the night.

Allan woke up and wondered whether it wouldn't soon be time
to go to bed. That conversation woke up Julius, who looked around,
seeing forest everywhere, and asked where they were.

Benny told them that they were now about fifteen miles north
of Växjö and that he had been thinking while the gentlemen slept.
What he had concluded was that for reasons of security it would be
best to find a discreet place to stay the night. They didn't know who
was chasing them, but if you stole a suitcase with fifty million, you
should not expect to be left in peace. So Benny had turned off the
road that led to Växjö, and headed toward a much humbler place
called Rottne. Perhaps there might be a small hotel there where
they could spend the night.

—Smart, said Julius appreciatively. But perhaps not smart enough.

Julius explained what he meant. In Rottne there might be, at best, a little shabby hotel that nobody ever found their way to. If three gentlemen without a reservation suddenly turned up one evening it would attract considerable attention from the villagers. Better, in that case, to find a farm or a house somewhere in the forest and bribe their way into a room for the night and something to eat.

Benny found Julius's reasoning wise, and thus turned on to the first insignificant gravel road he saw.

It had just started to get dark when after almost two winding miles the three men saw a mailbox at the side of the road. On the mailbox it said: Lake Farm, and next to it was an even narrower track, which they presumed would lead to the farm. And that turned out to be correct. A hundred yards farther on they came across a house. It was a proper red two-story farmhouse with white window frames and a barn. Farther along beside a lake there was something that had once been a tool shed.

The place seemed to be inhabited and Benny brought the Mercedes to a halt just in front of the entrance to the farmhouse. Then, out through the front door came a woman in her early forties, with frizzy red hair, wearing an even redder track suit, and with an Alsatian at her heel.

The three men got out of the Mercedes. Julius glanced at the dog, but it didn't look as if it would attack them. In fact, it gave the guests a curious, almost friendly look.

So Julius dared to take his eyes off it. He said a polite "Good evening" and explained their quest for a place to sleep and perhaps a bite to eat.

The woman looked at the motley crew in front of her: an old man, a less-old man, and a . . . rather stylish guy, she had to admit. And the right age too. And with a ponytail! She smiled to herself and Julius thought they were set, but then she said:

—This is not a damn hotel.

Allan sighed. He really was longing for something to eat and a bed. Life was exhausting now that he had decided to live a little longer. Say what you like about the Old Folks' Home; at least it didn't give him aches and pains all over his body.

Julius looked disappointed too and said that he and his friends were lost and tired, and that they were naturally prepared to pay their way if only they could stay there the night. If absolutely necessary they could skip the food bit.

—We'll pay one thousand crowns per person if you give us somewhere to sleep, Julius offered.

—One thousand crowns? said the woman. Are you on the run?

Julius brushed her rather perceptive question aside and explained again that they had come a long way, and although *he* could probably keep going, Allan here was advanced in years.

—Yesterday was my hundredth birthday, said Allan in a pathetic voice.

—One hundred? said the woman, almost frightened. Well, I'll be damned!

And then she was silent for a moment.

—What the hell, she finally said. I suppose you can stay. But forget the thousand crowns. Like I said, this is not a damn hotel I'm running here.

Benny gave her an admiring look. He had never heard a woman swear so much in such a short time. He thought it sounded delightful.

—My Beauty, he said. May I pet your dog?

—Beauty? said the woman. Are you blind? But sure, pet away. Buster is friendly. You can each have a room upstairs; there's plenty of room here. The sheets are clean, but watch out for the rat poison on the floor. Dinner will be on the table in an hour.

The woman headed past the three guests toward the barn, with Buster faithfully at her side. Benny inquired in passing what her name might be. Without turning she said it was Gunilla but that

she thought "Beauty sounded fine, so just stick the fuck to that."
Benny promised.

—I think I'm in love, said Benny.

—I know I'm tired, said Allan.

At that very moment, they heard a bellowing from the barn that
made even the exhausted Allan stand up straight. It must have come
from a very large and possibly pained animal.

—Cool it, Sonya, said the Beauty. I'm on my damn way.

SEVEN

1929–1939

The little house in Yxhult was a mess. During the years Allan had been in Professor Lundborg's care, the tiles had blown off the roof and lay scattered on the ground, the outhouse had fallen over, and one of the kitchen windows was flapping in the wind.

Allan peed in the open air, since there was no longer an outhouse in working order. Then he went in and sat in his dusty kitchen. He left the window open. He was hungry but resisted the urge to check the larder; it wouldn't improve his mood, he was sure.

He had grown up here, but home had never felt as distant as it did at that moment. Was it time to cut his ties with the past and move on? Most definitely.

Allan got out several sticks of dynamite and set about a familiar task before packing his bike trailer with the few valuables he owned. At dusk on the third of June 1929, he took off. The dynamite exploded as it was meant to exactly thirty minutes later. The little house was blown to bits and the neighbor's cow had another miscarriage.

An hour later, Allan was behind bars at the police station in Flen, eating dinner while being yelled at by Superintendent Krook. The Flen police had just acquired a police car and it hadn't taken long to catch the man who had blown his own house to bits and pieces.

This time, the offense was more obvious.

—Negligent destruction, said Superintendent Krook authoritatively.

—Could you pass me the bread? Allan asked.

No, Superintendent Krook could not. He could, however, dress down his poor assistant who had weakly complied with the wishes of the delinquent when he had requested an evening meal. In the meantime, Allan finished his dinner and then let himself be taken to the same cell as last time.

—You don't happen to have today's paper? Allan asked. Something to read before bed, that is.

Superintendent Krook replied by turning off the ceiling light and slamming the door. The next morning, the first thing he did was phone "that loony bin" in Uppsala to tell them to come and get Allan Karlsson.

But Bernhard Lundborg's colleagues turned a deaf ear. Karlsson's treatment was complete, and now they had others to castrate and analyze. If only the police superintendent knew how many people the nation must be saved from: Jews and Gypsies and Negroes and imbeciles and others. The fact that Mr. Karlsson had blown his own house to bits did not qualify him for a new journey to Uppsala. Aren't you allowed to do what you want with your own house? We live in a free country, don't we?

Police Superintendent Krook hung up. He could make no headway with these big-city types. He regretted that he had not let Karlsson bike away the previous evening.

And that is why Allan Karlsson, after a morning of negotiations, was back on his bicycle with the trailer in tow. This time he had food for three days in neat packets and double blankets to keep him warm if the weather turned cool. He waved good-bye to Superintendent Krook, who didn't wave back, and then turned north, because that direction seemed to Allan to be as good as any.

By afternoon, the road had taken him to Hälleforsnäs, and that was far enough for one day. Allan stopped beside a grassy slope, spread out a blanket, and opened one of his food packets. While he chewed away at a slice of syrupy bread with salami, he studied the industrial premises that he'd happened to choose for his picnic site. Outside the factory was a heap of cannon pipes from the foundry. Perhaps the people who made cannons could use someone to make sure that they went off when they were meant to go off. There was no point in biking as far away from Yxhult as possible. Hälleforsnäs would do as well as anywhere else. If there was work to be had, that is.

Allan's assumption that the presence of cannon pipes might mean work for him was perhaps a little naive. Nevertheless it turned out to be exactly right. After a short talk with the director, during which Allan omitted details of certain recent life events, he secured employment as an ignition specialist.

He was going to like it here, thought Allan.

The manufacture of cannons was at a low point at the foundry in Hälleforsnäs, and the orders continued to decline. The minister of defense, in the aftermath of the First World War, had reduced the funds available to the military, while King Gustav V sat in the palace gnashing his teeth. The defense minister, a man with an analytic bent, realized in hindsight that Sweden should have been better armed when the war broke out, but that didn't mean that there was any point in arming now, ten years later.

The consequences for the Hälleforsnäs foundry were that production was switched to more peaceful products, and the workers lost their jobs.

But not Allan—ignition specialists being hard to come by. The factory owner had hardly believed his ears and eyes when Allan appeared one day and turned out to be an expert on explosives of every type. Up until then, he had been forced to rely entirely upon the ignition specialist he had, and that was not a good thing, because the man was a foreigner, could hardly speak Swedish, and had black hair all over his body. He also doubted whether the man was reliable. But the owner had not had much choice.

Allan, on the other hand, did not think of people in terms of their color. He had always found Professor Lundborg's ideas strange. But he was curious to meet his first black man. It was with longing that he read the advertisements in the paper announcing that Josephine Baker was to appear in Stockholm, but he had to settle for Estebán, his white but dark-skinned Spanish ignition specialist colleague.

Allan and Estebán got along well, and shared a room in the workers' barracks next to the foundry. Estebán told Allan his dramatic story. He had met a girl at a party in Madrid and secretly embarked upon a fairly innocent relationship with her, without realizing that she was the daughter of the prime minister, Miguel Primo de Rivera. The prime minister was not a man you argued with; he governed the country as he wished, with the King trailing helplessly along behind him. "Prime minister" was a polite word for "dictator," in Estebán's opinion. But Primo de Rivera's daughter was a knockout.

Estebán's proletarian background had not in any way appealed to his potential father-in-law. So in his first, and only, meeting with Primo de Rivera, Estebán was informed that he had two alternatives. One was to disappear as far away from Spanish terri-

THE ONE HUNDRED YEAR OLD MAN 69

tory as possible, the other was to receive a bullet through his neck on the spot.

While Primo de Rivera cocked his rifle, Estebán said that he had at that moment decided in favor of the first alternative, and backed rapidly out of the room without so much as a glance in the direction of the sobbing girl.

As far away as possible, thought Estebán, and he went north, and then even farther north and finally so far north that the lakes froze to ice in the winter. He had been in Sweden ever since. He had gotten the job at the foundry three years earlier with some interpreting help from a Catholic priest and, may God forgive him, a made-up story about having worked with explosives back home in Spain, when in actual fact he had mainly picked tomatoes.

Gradually, Estebán had managed to learn workable Swedish and had become a fairly competent ignition specialist. And now, with Allan at his side, he became a real professional.

Allan felt at home in the workers' barracks. After a year, he could make himself understood in the Spanish that Estebán taught him. After two years, his Spanish was virtually fluent. But it took three years before Estebán gave up his attempts to impose his Spanish variety of international socialism on Allan. He tried everything, but Allan was not susceptible. Estebán could not understand that particular facet of his best friend's personality. It wasn't that Allan took an opposite view of the ways of the world and argued accordingly. No, he simply had no opinion whatsoever.

Allan had the same problem. Estebán was a good friend. It wasn't his fault that he had been poisoned by those damned politics. He certainly wasn't the only one.

The seasons came and went for some time before Allan's life took a new turn. It started when Estebán finally received the news that Primo de Rivera had resigned and fled the country. Now proper democracy was just round the corner, perhaps even socialism, and Estebán didn't want to miss that.

So he planned to go home as soon as possible. The foundry

was getting fewer and fewer orders because Señor Defense Minister had decided that there wouldn't be any more wars. Estebán was sure that both ignition specialists would be fired any day. What did his friend Allan have in mind for the future? Did he want to come along to Spain?

Allan thought about it. On the one hand, he wasn't interested in any revolution, Spanish or otherwise. It would probably only lead to a new revolution, in the opposite direction. On the other hand, Spain was actually abroad, just like every other country except Sweden, and after having read about countries abroad all his life perhaps it wouldn't be such a bad idea to experience them for real. On the way, they might even meet up with a black man or two.

When Estebán promised that they would meet at least one black man on the way to Spain, Allan had to say yes. The two friends then discussed more practical matters. In doing so they came to the conclusion that the owner of the foundry was a "stupid bastard" (that was exactly how they put it) and did not deserve their consideration. They decided to await that week's wages and then discreetly disappear.

So it was that Allan and Estebán got up at five in the morning the following Sunday to depart by bicycle with trailer attached, headed in a southerly direction, leading—eventually—to Spain. On the way, Estebán planned to stop outside the foundry owner's residence to drop off a complete sample of the result of his morning visit to the outhouse, delivered in a milk-filled jug that looked just like the one that arrived early every morning at the factory owner's gate. Estebán had been forced to put up for a long time with being called "the ape" by the factory owner and his two teenage sons.

—Revenge is not a good thing, Allan warned him. Revenge is like politics: one thing always leads to another until bad has become worse, and worse has become worst.

But Estebán insisted.

—Just because you had slightly hairy arms and didn't speak the foundry owner's language that didn't make you an ape, did it?

Allan had to agree, so the two friends arrived at a reasonable compromise. Estebán would limit himself to pissing into the milk.

That same morning witnesses had tattled to the foundry owner that Allan and Estebán had been seen on bikes with trailers on the way toward Katrineholm, or perhaps even farther south, so the foundry owner was prepared for the coming week's immediate decrease in staff. He sat brooding on the veranda of his lavish foundry owner's villa while he sipped the glass of milk that Sigrid had kindly served him, together with an almond biscuit. The foundry owner's mood darkened because there seemed to be something wrong with the biscuits. They had a distinct taste of ammonia.

The foundry owner decided to wait until after church to tell Sigrid off. For the time being, he would drink another glass of milk, hoping to remove the unpleasant taste in his mouth.

So it was that Allan found himself in Spain. It took them three months to make their way down through Europe, and on the way he got to meet more black men than he ever dreamed of. But after the first one, he lost interest. It turned out that there was no difference other than the color of their skin, except of course that they spoke weird languages, but the whites did that too, from southern Sweden onward. Professor Lundborg must have been frightened by a black man when he was a child, thought Allan.

Allan and his friend Estebán came to a land in chaos. The King had fled to Rome and been replaced by a republic. The Left called for *revolución*, while the Right was terrified by what had gone on in Stalin's Russia. Would the same thing happen here?

For a moment Estebán forgot that his friend was incorrigibly apolitical and tried to drag Allan in the direction of revolution. But Allan stuck to his habit of not getting involved. It seemed all too familiar, and Allan was still unable to understand why everything always had to become the exact opposite of what it was.

An unsuccessful military coup from the Right was followed by a general strike from the Left. Then there was a general election.

The Left won, and the Right got grumpy, or was it the other way around? Allan wasn't really sure. In the end, there was war.

Allan was in a foreign country and had no better idea than to follow half a step behind his friend Estebán, who joined the army and was immediately promoted to sergeant when his platoon leader realized that Estebán knew how to blow things up.

Allan's friend wore his uniform with pride and looked forward to his first contribution to the war. The platoon was ordered to blow up a couple of bridges in a valley in Aragon, and Estebán's group was told to deal with the first bridge. Estebán was so exalted by the trust placed in him that he got up onto a rock, grabbed his rifle in his left hand, raised it in the air, and shouted:

—Death to fascism, death to all . . .

He didn't manage to finish the sentence before half of his head and one shoulder were shot away by what might possibly have been one of the first enemy mortars fired in the war. Allan was about twenty yards away when it happened, and thus avoided being dirtied by the parts of his comrade that were spread around the rock that Estebán had been stupid enough to stand on. One of the soldiers in Estebán's group started to cry. For his part, Allan looked around at what was left of his friend and decided that it wasn't worth picking up the bits.

—You should have stayed in Hälleforsnäs, said Allan and suddenly felt a sincere longing to be chopping wood outside his little house in Yxhult.

The mortar that killed Estebán may well have been the first in the war, but it certainly wasn't the last. Allan considered going home, but suddenly the war was all around him. Besides, it was one hell of a long walk back to Sweden, and nobody was waiting for him.

So Allan sought out Estebán's company commander, introduced himself as Europe's leading pyrotechnical expert, and said that he would be prepared to blow up bridges and other infrastructural constructions for the company commander, in exchange for three square meals a day and enough wine to get drunk on when circumstances allowed.

The company commander was about to have Allan shot because he stubbornly refused to sing the praises of socialism and the republic and, almost worse, he insisted on serving in civilian clothes. As Allan expressed it:

—One more thing . . . if I am going to blow up bridges for you, then I'm going to do it wearing my own jacket; otherwise you can blow up the bridges yourself.

No company commander has ever been born who would let himself be browbeaten by a civilian in that way. The problem for this particular company commander was that the most skilled explosives expert in his company was spread in pieces across a rock on a nearby hill.

While the company commander sat in his foldable military field chair and ruminated upon whether Allan's immediate future was employment or execution, one of the platoon leaders whispered in his ear that the young sergeant who so unfortunately had just been shot to bits had previously affirmed this strange Swede's abilities as a master in the field of explosives.

That decided the matter. Señor Karlsson could a) stay alive, b) be fed three square meals a day, c) have the right to wear his jacket, and d) have exactly the same right as all the others to sample the wine now and then, in reasonable quantities. In return, he would blow up exactly what the commanders around him requested. Two foot soldiers were asked to keep a special eye on the Swede, because there was no way of knowing for certain that he wasn't a spy.

The months turned to years. Allan blew up what he was told to blow up, and he did so with considerable skill.

The job was not without its risks. You often had to crawl along the ground in order to sneak up on the object that was to be blown up, place an explosive charge there with a time fuse, and then zigzag your way back to safe ground. After three months, one of Allan's two soldier guards lost his life (by mistake he crawled right into an enemy camp). Six months later, the other one met the same fate (he got up to stretch his back and immediately that same body part was shot in two). The company commander didn't bother to replace them, since Señor Karlsson had done such a good job with the explosives.

Allan couldn't see the point of killing lots of people unnecessarily, so he tried to make sure the bridge in question was empty when the charge went off. That was true as well for the very last bridge he was ordered to blow just before the war ended. But this time, just as he had finished his preparations and had crawled back to some bushes beyond one of the bridge foundations, an enemy patrol came walking toward him with a medal-wearing little man in the middle. They approached from the other side and seemed to be totally unaware that the republicans were close by, and that they were just about to join Esteban and tens of thousands of other Spaniards in eternity.

But Allan had had enough. So he got up out of the bushes and started to wave his arms.

—Go away! he hollered at the little man with the medals and his entourage. Be off, before you get blown up!

The little man with the medals gave a start. Then his entourage dragged him over the bridge and didn't stop until they had reached Allan's bush. Eight rifles were suddenly pointed at the Swede and at least one of them would have been fired if it hadn't been for the bridge suddenly blowing up behind them all. The pressure wave knocked the little man with the medals into Allan's bush. In the tumult, none of the little man's entourage dared send a bullet in Allan's direction, since it might hit the wrong person. Besides, he appeared to be a civilian. And when the smoke settled there was no longer any question of killing Allan. The little man with the medals shook his hand and explained that a real general knows how to show his appreciation and that the best thing now was for the group to withdraw to the other side again, with or without a bridge. If his savior wanted to come along, he was more than welcome. Once there the general would invite him to dinner.

—Paella Andaluz, said the general. My cook is from the south. ¿Comprende?

Yes, indeed, Allan understood. He understood that he had saved the life of the generalissimo himself; he understood that it was probably to his advantage to be standing there in his dirty jacket instead of in an enemy uniform; he understood that his friends on the hill a few hundred yards away would be watching the whole thing through binoculars and he understood that for the sake of his health it would be best to change sides in the war—the purpose of which he hadn't in any case understood.

Besides, he was hungry.

—Sí, por favor, mi general, said Allan. Paella would hit the spot. Perhaps with a glass or two of red wine?

When, ten years earlier, Allan had applied for a job as an ignition specialist at the foundry in Hälleforsnäs, he had chosen to exclude from his résumé the fact that he had been in an asylum for four years, after which he had blown up his own house. Perhaps that was precisely why the job interview went so well.

Allan thought back to that while he chatted with General Franco. On the one hand, you shouldn't lie. On the other, it would be best not to reveal to the general that it was Allan who had set the charge under the bridge and that he had, for the last three years, been a civilian employee of the republican army. Allan wasn't shy, but in this particular case there was a dinner and good booze on offer. The truth could temporarily be set aside, Allan thought.

So, Allan told the generalissimo that he had found himself in the bush while fleeing from the republicans. Luckily he had personally observed how the charge had been set, so he was able to warn the general. Furthermore, the reason he had ended up in Spain and the war at all was that he had been tempted there by a friend, a man who had a close relationship with the deceased Miguel Primo de Rivera. But since that friend had been killed by an enemy mortar shell, Allan had been forced to struggle on his own to stay alive. He had been in the clutches of the republicans, but eventually managed to break out.

And then Allan quickly changed the subject, telling instead of how his father had been in the inner circle of the court of the Russian Czar Nicholas and that his father had died a martyr's death in a hopeless battle with the leader of the Bolsheviks, Lenin.

Dinner was served in the general staff's tent. The more red wine Allan downed, the more colorful the descriptions of his father's heroic deeds. General Franco could not fail to be impressed. First his life is saved, then it turns out that his savior is practically related to Czar Nicholas II.

The food was excellent; the Andulasian cook did not dare let it be anything else. And the wine flowed in an endless series of toasts in honor of Allan, of Allan's father, of Czar Nicholas II, and of the Czar's family. And finally the general fell asleep just as he was giving Allan a big hug to seal the fact that they had just progressed to the familiar *tú*.

When the two now-firm friends woke up again, the war was over. General Franco took charge of the government of the new Spain and offered Allan the position as head of his internal bodyguard. Allan thanked him for the offer, but said that it was high time for him to be heading home, if Francisco would allow it. And Francisco would, even writing a letter giving the generalissimo's unconditional protection ("just show this if you need any help") and then providing Allan with a princely escort all the way to Lisbon from where the general thought boats would leave for the north.

From Lisbon, boats left in every direction imaginable, it turned out. Allan stood on the quay and thought about it for a while. Then he waved the letter from the general in front of the captain of a ship sailing under the Spanish flag, and he soon had a free passage. There was no question of his having to pay his way.

The ship wasn't actually going to Sweden, but on the quay Allan had asked himself what he would do there anyway, and he hadn't really come up with a good answer.

EIGHT

After the afternoon's press conference, Bucket sat down with a beer to think things over. But however much he thought he couldn't make heads or tails of it. Would Bolt have started kidnapping centenarians? Or did one thing have nothing to do with the other? All this thinking gave Bucket a headache, so he stopped and phoned the Boss instead, reporting to him that nothing at all had happened that was worth reporting. He was told to stay in Malmköping and await further orders.

The conversation over, Bucket was alone again with his beer. The situation was becoming too taxing. He didn't like having no idea what was going on, and now his headache came back again. So in his mind he fled to the past, remembering his youth back home.

Bucket had started his criminal career in Braås, not far from where Allan and his new friends now found themselves. There, he had gotten together with some like-minded peers and started the motorcycle club called The Violence. Bucket was the leader; he decided which newsstand was to be robbed of cigarettes next. He was the one who had chosen the name—The Violence, in English, not Swedish. And he was the one who unfortunately asked his girlfriend Isabella to sew the name of the motorcycle club onto ten newly stolen leather jackets. Isabella had never really learned to spell properly at school, not in Swedish, and certainly not in English.

The result was that Isabella sewed *The Violins* on the jackets instead. As the rest of the club members had had similar academic success, nobody in the group noticed the mistake.

So everyone was very surprised when one day a letter arrived for The Violins in Braås from the people in charge of the concert hall in Växjö. The letter suggested that, since the club obviously concerned itself with classical music, they might like to put in an appearance at a concert with the city's prestigious chamber orchestra, Musica Vitae.

Bucket felt provoked; somebody was clearly making fun of him. One night he skipped the newsstand, and instead went into Växjö to throw a brick through the glass door of the concert hall. This was intended to teach the people responsible a lesson in respect.

It all went off well, except that Bucket's leather glove happened to follow the stone into the lobby. Since the alarm went off immediately, Bucket felt it would be unwise to try to retrieve the personal item in question.

Losing a glove was not good. Bucket had traveled to Växjö by motorbike and one hand was extremely cold all the way home to Braås that night. Even worse was the fact that Bucket's luckless girlfriend had written Bucket's name and address inside the glove, in case he lost it. So by the following morning the police had worked out who the primary suspect was, and picked up Bucket for questioning.

In the interrogation, Bucket explained that there were extenuating circumstances and described how he had been provoked by the management of the concert hall. The story of how The Violence became The Violins ended up in the local newspaper, and Bucket became the laughingstock of all Braås. In a rage, he decided that the next newsstand they were robbing should be burned down instead of just having its door smashed in. This in turn led to the Turkish-Bulgarian owner—who had gone to bed in his storeroom to guard against thieves—narrowly escaping with his life. Having decided that one glove was better than none on a cold evening, Bucket wore his remaining glove to the scene of the crime (with the address noted just as neatly as in the first glove), lost it, and not long after found himself on his way to prison for the first time. There he met the Boss, and when he had served his sentence Bucket decided it was best to leave Braås and his girlfriend behind. Both seemed only to bring him bad luck.

But The Violence lived on, and the members retained the misspelled jackets. Lately, however, the club had changed its focus. Now it concentrated on stealing cars and on fixing the odometers. Or as the new leader of the group, Bucket's little brother, used to say: "Nothing makes a car prettier than when you suddenly discover it has driven only half the mileage."

Bucket was occasionally in touch with his brother and the old life, but had no wish to be back there.

—What a fuckup, was how Bucket concisely summed up his own history.

It was tough to think in new ways and equally tough to remember the old. Better to have a third beer and then, in accordance with the Boss's orders, check in to the hotel.

It was almost dark when Chief Inspector Aronsson accompanied by the police dog handler and Kicki, the dog, arrived at Åker village, after the long walk along the railway track from Vidkärr.

The dog hadn't reacted to anything along the way. Aronsson wondered if she actually realized that they were working, not just out on an evening stroll. But when the trio came to the abandoned inspection trolley, the dog stood to attention, or whatever it was called. And then she raised one paw and started to bark. Aronsson's hopes were raised.

—Does that mean something? he asked.

—Yes, it certainly does, answered the dog handler.

And then he explained that Kicki had different signs, depending on what she wanted to convey.

—Well then, what is she trying to tell us?! asked the increasingly impatient Aronsson and pointed at the dog, still standing on three legs and barking.

—That, said the dog handler, means there has been a dead body on the trolley.

—A dead body? A corpse?

—A corpse.

Chief Inspector Aronsson saw in his mind's eye how the Never Again member killed the unfortunate centenarian Allan Karlsson. But then this new information merged with what he already knew.

—It must be the exact opposite, he mumbled and felt strangely relieved.

The Beauty served beef and potatoes with lingonberries and beer, followed by a glass of bitters. The guests were hungry, but first they needed to know what sort of animal they had heard from the barn.

—That was Sonya, said The Beauty. My elephant.

—Elephant? said Julius.

—Elephant? said Allan.

—I thought I recognized that sound, said Benny.

The former hot-dog-stand owner had been struck by love at first sight. And now, at second sight, he felt no different. This constantly swearing red-haired woman with the full figure seemed to have popped straight out of a novel!

The Beauty had discovered the elephant early one August morning in her garden stealing apples. If she had been able to talk she would have said that the previous evening she had absconded from a circus in Växjö to look for something to drink, because the elephant keeper had gone to do the same in town instead of doing his job.

When darkness fell the elephant had reached the shores of Helga Lake and decided to do more than simply quench her thirst. A cooling bath would be very nice, the elephant thought, and waded out in the shallow water.

But suddenly it wasn't so shallow anymore, and the elephant had to rely on her innate ability to swim. Elephants in general are not as logical in their thinking as are people. This elephant was a prime example; she decided to swim one-and-a-half miles to the other side of the cove to reach firm ground again, instead of just turning around to swim four yards back to the shore.

The elephantine logic had two consequences. One was that the elephant was quickly declared dead by the circus people and the police, who rather belatedly thought to follow her tracks all the way to Helga Lake and onto the shore of its fifty-foot-deep water. The other was that the still-very-much-alive elephant, under cover of darkness, managed to spirit herself all the way to The Beauty's apple orchard, without a single soul observing it.

The Beauty didn't know that, of course, but afterward she worked out most of what happened when she read in the local paper about an elephant that had disappeared and was now declared dead. How many elephants could be running around the area and at that particular time? The dead elephant and the still-very-much-alive elephant were presumably the same.

The Beauty began by giving the elephant a name. It became Sonya, after her idol Sonya Hedenbratt. This was followed by several days' negotiations between Sonya and the Alsatian, Buster, before the two agreed to get along.

Winter arrived, meaning an endless search for food for poor Sonya who ate like the elephant she was. Conveniently, The Beauty's father had just conked out and left an inheritance of one million crowns to his only daughter. (When he became a pensioner twenty years earlier, he had sold his successful brush-making factory and subsequently looked after his money well.) So The Beauty resigned from her job at the local clinic in Rottne, to be a stay-at-home mom for a dog and an elephant.

Then spring arrived and Sonya could once more sustain herself with grass and leaves, and then that Mercedes drove into the yard—the first visitors since Daddy, bless his dear departed soul, had come to see his daughter one last time two years before. The Beauty said that she wasn't one to argue with fate, so it never occurred to her to try to keep Sonya a secret from the strangers.

Allan and Julius sat quietly and let The Beauty's story sink in, while Benny said:

—But what was that bellowing from Sonya? I feel she must be in pain.

The Beauty stared at him wide-eyed:

—How the hell could you hear that?

Benny took a bite to give himself time to think. Then he said:

—I'm almost a vet. Do you want the long or the short story?

They all agreed that they would prefer the long version, but The Beauty insisted that first she and Benny should go to the barn so the almost-vet could have a look at Sonya's painful left front foot.

Allan and Julius remained at the dinner table, both wondering how a vet with a ponytail could end up as a failure of a hot-dog-stand proprietor in one of the most out-of-the-way places in the county of Södermanland. A vet with a ponytail, what sort of sense did that make? These really were strange times.

Benny examined poor old Sonya with confidence; he had done this sort of thing before, during the practical part of his studies. A broken-off twig had become jammed under her second toenail, and made part of her foot swell up. The Beauty had tried to get the twig out but she had not been strong or dexterous enough. It didn't take Benny more than a couple of minutes to manage it, with the help of calm talk with Sonya and a pair of tongs. But the elephant's foot was badly swollen.

—We need antibiotics, said Benny. A couple of pounds.

—If you know what we need, I know how to get it, said The Beauty.

But "getting it" would require a visit to Rottne in the middle of the night, and to pass the evening Benny and The Beauty returned to the dinner table.

They all ate with a good appetite and washed the food down with beer and bitters, all except Benny who drank juice. After the last bite, they moved into the living room and the armchairs beside the fire, where Benny was asked to explain how he came to be an almost-vet.

It all began when Benny and his one-year-older brother, Bo, who grew up just south of Stockholm, spent several summers with their uncle Frank in Dalarna. Uncle Frank, who was never called anything other than Frasse, was a successful entrepreneur who owned and ran a number of different local businesses. Uncle Frank sold everything from campers to gravel and most things in between. Besides eating and sleeping, work was his great passion. He had some failed romances behind him, since all the ladies soon got tired of Uncle Frasse just working and working, eating and sleeping (and showering on Sundays).

Anyway, during a number of summers in the 1960s, Benny and Bo had been sent to Dalarna by their father, Uncle Frasse's older brother, on the grounds that the children needed some fresh air. It is doubtful whether they got much of that, because Benny and Bo were quickly trained to look after the big stone-crushing machine at Uncle Frasse's gravel pit. The boys liked working there, even though it was hard, and for two months they had to breathe in stone dust rather than fresh air. In the evenings, Uncle Frasse delivered moral sermons, regularly exhorting:

—You boys make sure you get a proper education; otherwise you'll end up like me.

Now, neither Benny nor Bo thought it would be such a bad thing to end up like Uncle Frasse—at least until he fell into the stone crusher and came to a gravelly end—but Uncle Frasse had always been bothered by his own limited schooling. He could hardly write, he was no good at math, he didn't understand a word of English; it was only with difficulty he could remember that Norway's capital was called Oslo if anybody happened to ask. The only thing Uncle Frasse knew was how to do business. And he ended up rolling in money.

Exactly just how much money Uncle Frasse had at the time of his departure was hard to say. It happened when Bo was nineteen and Benny almost eighteen. One day, a lawyer contacted Bo and Benny, and informed them that they were both mentioned in Uncle Frasse's will but that the matter was somewhat complicated and that a meeting was required.

Benny and Bo met the lawyer at his office and discovered that a considerable amount—unspecified—of money awaited the brothers the day they both completed their education.

And as if that wasn't enough, the lawyer would supply the brothers with a generous monthly allowance (to be regularly increased according to the rate of inflation) while they were studying. But the monthly allowance would stop if they abandoned their studies, just as it would when they had passed a final examination and thus should be able to support themselves. There was more to the will, some more- or less-complicated details, but on the whole what it meant was that the brothers would only be rich once they had both finished their studies.

Bo and Benny immediately started on a seven-week course in

welding skills and the lawyer confirmed that according to the will that would suffice, "although I suspect that your uncle Frank might have had something more advanced in mind."

Two things happened halfway through the course. One, Benny finally had enough of his brother's bossiness. That's the way he had always been but it was time to make it clear to big brother that they were both grown and he needed to find someone else to order around. Two, Benny realized that he didn't want to become a welder and that in any case he had no talent for it. The two brothers argued about this for a while, until Benny managed to talk his way into a course on botany at Stockholm University. According to the lawyer, the will allowed for a change of subject, as long as there was no interruption.

Bo finished his welder's training, but didn't get a penny of Uncle Frasse's money because his brother Benny was still studying. In addition, the lawyer immediately ended Bo's monthly allowance, in accordance with the will.

This, of course, meant that the brothers became enemies. And when Bo, in a bout of drunken confusion, smashed up Benny's newly purchased motorcycle (bought with money from his generous study allowance), that was the end of all brotherly love, the end of any relationship whatsoever.

Bo started to do business deals in the spirit of Uncle Frasse, yet perhaps without his uncle's talent. After a while he moved to Västergötland, partly in search of new business opportunities, partly to avoid the risk of bumping into his damned brother. Benny, on the other hand, stayed in the academic world, year after year. The monthly allowance was, as explained earlier, generous and by changing his subject just before taking final exams and starting on something new, Benny could live well, while his bullying jerk of a brother had to wait for his money.

And Benny continued like this for thirty years, until the extremely aged lawyer one day contacted him and announced that the money in the will was now used up, that there wouldn't be any more monthly allowances, and of course there was no other money available for anything else. The brothers could forget the inheritance, said the lawyer who was now more than ninety years old and who appeared to have stayed alive for the sake of the will, because just a couple of weeks later he died in his television armchair.

All this had happened just a few weeks ago. Benny had suddenly found himself forced to get a job. But despite being one of the best-educated people in Sweden, he discovered that the labor market was not interested in the number of years he had studied, but rather in his final-exam grades. Benny had almost finished at least ten academic degrees, but still found himself investing in a hot dog stand in order to have something to do. Benny and Bo were compelled to be in each other's presence in connection with the lawyer's announcement that the inheritance had now been used up but on that occasion Bo expressed himself in such a way that Benny did not make any immediate plans to go and visit him.

Having gotten this far in Benny's story, Julius was beginning to worry that it might lead to all too personal questions from The Beauty, such as how Benny had ended up with Julius and Allan. But The Beauty didn't bother with the details, thanks to the beer and the bitters. Instead, she had to admit that she was feeling a bit infatuated, old as she was.

—So what else have you almost become over the years, besides a vet? she asked with sparkling eyes.

Benny understood just as well as Julius that the developments of the last few days shouldn't be described in too much detail, so he was grateful for the direction of The Beauty's question. He couldn't remember everything, he said, but you can cover a lot if you sit at a school desk for three decades, and do your homework once in a while. Benny was an almost-vet, almost-doctor, almost-architect, almost-engineer, almost-botanist, almost-language teacher, almost-sports teacher, almost-historian, and almost quite a few other things. And for a bit of variety he had taken some shorter courses of varying quality and importance. Sometimes he had even taken two courses at the same time.

Then Benny remembered something else that he almost was. He leapt to his feet, facing The Beauty, and declaimed a love poem in very poetic Swedish.

Complete silence followed; then The Beauty mumbled an inaudible expletive while she blushed.

—Erik Axel Karlfeldt, Benny explained. With those words I would like to thank you for the food and the hospitality. I don't think I said that I am an almost-literary expert too?

Benny might have gone too far when he asked The Beauty if she would like to dance in front of the fire, because she quickly said no, adding that there must be some damned limit to these stupidities. But Julius noticed that she was flattered. She zipped up her tracksuit jacket and smoothed it down to look her best for Benny.

After which Allan retired for the night while the other three moved on to coffee, cognac optional. Julius happily said yes to the entire offer, while Benny settled for half.

Julius showered The Beauty with questions about the farm and her own story, partly because he was curious, partly because he wanted to avoid the subject of who they were, where they were going, and why. But he didn't have to worry. The Beauty had now gotten up steam and was talking about her childhood; about the man she married when she was eighteen and kicked out ten years later (that part of the story contained even more expletives); about never having children; about Lake Farm, which had been her parents' summer house before her mother died seven years ago and that her father had let The Beauty take over; about the inheritance that was starting to run out; and about it soon being time to move on.

—I'm already forty-three, said The Beauty. That is damn well halfway to the grave.

—I wouldn't be so sure about that, said Julius.

The dog handler gave Kicki new instructions and she moved away from the trolley, sniffing constantly. Chief Inspector Aronsson hoped that the corpse in question would turn up somewhere in the vicinity, but only thirty yards inside the grounds, Kicki started walking in circles, and seemed to be searching at random, before looking up pleadingly at her handler.

—Kicki says she's sorry, but she can't figure out where the corpse has gone, the dog handler translated.

The dog handler did not convey this message as precisely as he perhaps should have. Chief Inspector Aronsson interpreted the answer as meaning that Kicki had lost track of the corpse as soon as she walked away from the trolley. But if Kicki had been able to talk, she would have told him that the body had definitely been moved a few yards into the grounds before disappearing. And then Chief Inspector Aronsson might have investigated whether any shipments had left the foundry in the last few hours. The answer would have been just one: a tractor trailer with a container bound for Gothenburg harbor. Then, the police could have been notified and the tractor trailer intercepted on the highway. But now the corpse had disappeared beyond the borders of Sweden.

Almost three weeks later, a young Egyptian watchman sat on a barge that had just emerged from the southern end of the Suez Canal. He noticed a terrible stench from the cargo.

Finally he couldn't stand it any longer. He wet a rag and tied it around his nose and mouth. In one of the wooden boxes he found the explanation: a half-rotten corpse.

The Egyptian seaman deliberated. He had no desire to leave the corpse there to ruin the rest of the journey. Besides, he would almost certainly be subjected to long police interrogations in Djibouti, and everybody knew what the police were like in Djibouti.

Moving the body himself wasn't a pleasant thought either, but in the end he made up his mind. First he emptied the corpse's pockets of everything of value—he deserved something for his trouble—and then he shoved it overboard.

And that is how what had once been a young man of slight build, with long blond and greasy hair, a scraggly beard, and a jean jacket with the words *Never Again* on the back, was turned with a splash into fish food in the Red Sea.

The group at Lake Farm split up just before midnight. Julius went upstairs to sleep, while Benny and The Beauty got into the Mercedes to visit the health clinic in Rottne after hours. Halfway there they discovered Allan under a blanket on the backseat. He woke up and explained that he had gone out for a breath of fresh air and once outside he had realized that the car would be a good place to sleep because the stairs up to the bedrooms were a bit too much for his shaking knees, after such a long day.

—I'm no longer ninety, he said.

The duo had become a trio for the nocturnal exercise, but it didn't matter. The Beauty described her plan in more detail. They would get into the clinic with the help of the key The Beauty had forgotten to return when she resigned. Once inside, they would log in to Doctor Erlandsson's computer and in Erlandsson's name send a prescription for antibiotics, made out in The Beauty's name. For that you needed Erlandsson's password, but that was no problem said The Beauty, because Doctor Erlandsson was not just pompous, he was also a fool. When the new computer system was installed a couple of years earlier, it was The Beauty who had to teach the doctor how to file electronic prescriptions, and she was the one who chose his user name and password.

The Mercedes arrived at the intended crime scene. Benny, Allan, and The Beauty got out and inspected the surroundings before committing the actual crime. Of course, a car passed by slowly at that moment. The driver was as surprised by the trio as they were by him. A single living being awake at that time of night in Rottne was a sensation. On this particular night there were four.

But the car drove on and darkness and silence settled on Rottne once more. The Beauty led Benny and Allan in through the staff entrance in the back, and then to Doctor Erlandsson's room. There she turned on his computer and logged in.

Everything went according to plan and The Beauty giggled happily until, suddenly, she let loose a long stream of curses. She had just realized that you couldn't simply send a prescription for "a couple of pounds of antibiotics."

—Write erythromycin, rifampin, and gentamicin, three hundred grams each, said Benny. Then we can attack the inflammation from several different angles.

The Beauty looked admiringly at Benny. Then she invited him to sit down and spell it all out. Benny did and added various other medicines, useful to have on hand in case of future bad luck.

Breaking out of the clinic was just as easy as breaking in. And their journey home was without incident. Benny and The Beauty helped Allan upstairs and when it was almost half past two in the morning, the last light was turned off at Lake Farm.

*A*fter ten at night there weren't many people awake in that sleepy area. But in Braås, not far from Lake Farm, a young man lay in bed turning restlessly, desperate for a cigarette. It was Bucket's little brother, the new leader of The Violence. Three hours earlier, he had finished his last cigarette and soon felt an unstoppable need to have another. He cursed himself for having forgotten to buy smokes before everything shut for the evening.

At first he had intended to hold out until the following morning, but by midnight he couldn't stand it any longer. That was when he got the idea of reliving old times, of simply gaining entry to a newsstand with the help of a crowbar. But it couldn't be in Braås, where he had a reputation to uphold. Besides, he would be suspected of the crime almost before it was discovered.

It would be best to go a bit farther afield, but he needed a smoke so badly that he had to compromise. And the compromise was Rottne, about fifteen minutes away. Dressed inconspicuously he rolled slowly into the little town in his old Volvo 240, a little after midnight. When he drove past the health clinic he was surprised to see three people on the sidewalk: a woman with red hair, a man with a ponytail, and just behind them a terribly old man.

Bucket's little brother didn't analyze the event deeply. (He rarely analyzed anything deeply or even superficially.) Instead, he drove on, stopped under a tree quite close to the newsstand he'd been seeking, failed to break in because the owner had secured the door against crowbars, and then drove home again, just as desperate for a smoke as before.

W hen Allan woke up just after eleven o'clock the next morning he felt reinvigorated. He looked out of the window where the forest spread out around a lake. The landscape reminded him of Södermanland. It looked like it was going to be a nice day.

He got dressed, putting on the only clothes he had, and thinking that he could perhaps afford to renew his wardrobe a little. Neither he nor Julius nor Benny had even managed to bring a toothbrush with them.

When Allan came downstairs, Julius and Benny were eating breakfast. Julius had been out for a walk while Benny had slept deeply and for a long time. The Beauty had put out plates and glasses and left written instructions about self-service in the kitchen. She herself had gone to Rottne. The note ended with an order that the gentlemen should make sure to leave a reasonable amount of breakfast on the plates, so Buster could have some too.

Allan said good morning and received the same greeting in return. After which Julius added that he had had the idea of staying another night at Lake Farm because the surroundings were so enchanting. Allan asked if perhaps the private chauffeur had had some influence over that decision, considering the passion that had been in the air the previous evening. Julius answered that Benny had indeed given a wealth of reasons for staying on at Lake Farm for the rest of the summer, but that the conclusion was his own. Where would they go anyway? Didn't they need an extra day to think? All they needed in order to stay was a plausible story explaining who they were and where they were going—and The Beauty's permission, of course.

Benny followed Allan and Julius's conversation with interest, clearly hoping that it would end with another night at the same place. His feelings for The Beauty had not diminished since the previous day. On the contrary he was disappointed she wasn't around when he came down for breakfast. But she had written "thanks for last night" in the letter. Could she have been referring to the poem that Benny had recited? If only she would come back soon!

But it was almost an hour before The Beauty turned into the yard. When she climbed out of her car, Benny saw that she was even more beautiful than the last time he saw her. She had exchanged her red tracksuit for a dress and she might even have been to the hairdresser. He took some eager steps toward her, and exclaimed:

—My Beauty! Welcome home!

Behind him stood Allan and Julius, enjoying the tender scene. But their smiles disappeared as soon as they saw her demeanor. First she walked straight past Benny and then past the other two, before stopping on the steps of Lake Farm, where she turned round and said:

—You bastards! I know everything! And now I want to know the rest. Assemble in the living room. NOW!

Upon which The Beauty disappeared into the house.

—If she already knows everything, what more does she want to know? asked Benny.

—Just be quiet, Benny, said Julius.

—My words exactly, said Allan.

And then they went inside to meet their fate.

The Beauty had started the day by feeding Sonya some newly cut grass and then decided to smarten up a little. Reluctantly, she had admitted to herself that she wanted to be beautiful for that Benny guy. So she had swapped the red tracksuit for a light yellow dress and her frizzy hair had now been tidied into two pigtails. She had also added a little makeup and a touch of smell-good before she got into her red VW Passat to drive to Rottne for supplies.

Buster sat as he always did in the passenger seat and licked his chops when the car headed for the supermarket. Afterward, The Beauty wondered whether in fact Buster had seen the newspaper headlines—the one for the *Express* was lit up outside the shop and had two photos, one at the bottom of old man Julius, and one at the top of very old man Allan. The headline read:

CENTENARIAN KIDNAPPED BY CRIMINAL GANG.
HUNT ON TODAY FOR NOTORIOUS MASTER THIEF—POLICE

The Beauty turned bright red in the face, her thoughts flying in all directions. She was furious and immediately abandoned plans to buy supplies, because those three sly devils would be out of her house before lunch! But first The Beauty went into the pharmacy to pick up the medicine that Benny had ordered the night before, and then she bought a copy of the *Express* to find out in more detail what on earth was going on.

The more The Beauty read, the angrier she became. But at the same time she couldn't really piece it all together. Was it Benny who was Never Again? Was Julius a master thief? And who had kidnapped whom? They all seemed to get along so well.

In the end, her anger won over her curiosity. Whatever had happened, she had been conned. And you didn't con Gunilla Björklund and get away with it! *My Beauty!* Hah!

She sat in her car and read the article once more: "On his hundredth birthday on Monday, Allan Karlsson disappeared from the Old Folks' Home in Malmköping. The police now suspect that he has been kidnapped by the criminal organization Never Again. According to information received by the *Express*, the master thief Julius Jonsson is involved."

This was followed by a mishmash of information and witness statements. "Allan Karlsson had been seen at the bus station in Malmköping, then he had climbed on the bus to Strängnäs, and this had made a member of Never Again furious. . . ." But hang on . . . "Blond man in his thirties . . ." That did not describe Benny. The Beauty felt . . . relieved?

The confusion continued when she read that Allan Karlsson had been seen the day before on a rail inspection trolley in the middle of the Södermanland forest, together with master thief Jonsson and the Never Again member who had been so angry with him. The *Express* could not give an exact description of the relationship between the three men, but the current theory was that Allan Karlsson was in the clutches of the others. That at least was the opinion of the farmer Tengroth in Vidkärr.

Finally, the *Express* had yet another scoop. According to the assistant at the nearby gas station, the proprietor of a local hot dog stand, by the name of Benny Ljungberg, had disappeared without a trace the day before, close to the last known location of the centenarian and the master thief.

The Beauty folded the paper and placed it in Buster's mouth. Then she headed back to her farmhouse in the forest, where she now knew her visitors consisted of a centenarian, a master thief, and the proprietor of a hot dog stand. This last one was handsome as well as charming and clearly had some medical knowledge, but there was no room for romance here. For a moment, The Beauty was more sad than angry, but she worked up to a fury again just as she drove into her yard.

The Beauty pulled the *Express* out of Buster's mouth, unfolded the first page with the pictures of Allan and Julius, and started swearing and shouting before reading aloud from the article. Then she demanded an explanation and promised that all three of them would be on their way in five minutes, come what may. Then she folded the paper again and put it back in Buster's mouth, crossed her arms, and ended with a frigid:

—Well?

Benny looked at Allan who looked at Julius, who strangely enough broke into a smile.

—Master thief, he said. I'm a master thief. Not bad!

But The Beauty was not impressed. She was already red in the face and became even redder when she informed Julius that he would soon be a very beaten-up master thief if The Beauty didn't immediately find out what was going on. And then she told the assembled guests what she had already told herself, namely that nobody conned Gunilla Björklund at Lake Farm and got away with it. To put force behind her words, she pulled an old shotgun down from the wall. It didn't work, of course, The Beauty admitted, but it would serve well to smash the skulls of master thieves, hot-dog-stand proprietors, and old geezers, if necessary, and it seemed it would be necessary.

Julius Jonsson's smile quickly faded. Benny stood there, nailed to the floor, with his arms hanging limply by his side. As far as he could see, his chance of romance was rapidly evaporating. Then Allan stepped in, and asked The Beauty for time to think. With The Beauty's permission, he would like to have a private conversation with Julius in the adjacent room. The Beauty agreed with a bit of muttering, but warned Allan not to try any tricks. Allan promised to behave and then he took Julius by the arm and led him into the kitchen, closing the door behind them.

Allan asked Julius if he had any ideas which, unlike previous attempts, would not just make The Beauty even angrier. Julius answered that the only way they could save the situation was by inviting The Beauty to partake in some sort of part ownership of the suitcase. Allan agreed, although he pointed out that no good would come of telling a new person each day that they had stolen someone's suitcase, killed that person when he wanted to get it back, and sent the corpse to Africa packed neatly in a steel cylinder.

Julius thought Allan was exaggerating. So far only one person had paid with his life and surely he got what he deserved. If they could just stay hidden until things calmed down, then nobody else need meet the same fate.

Upon which Allan said that he himself had had a new idea. He thought that it was just as well to divide the contents of the suitcase in four: Allan, Julius, Benny, and The Beauty. Then there would be no risk of the last two talking too much to the wrong people. And as a bonus they would all be able to stay at Lake Farm for the summer, by which time the motorcycle gang would certainly have stopped looking for them, if they were looking for them at all, which one must assume they were.

—Twenty-five million for a few months' room and board and a chauffeur, Julius sighed. But he accepted Allan's suggestion.

The meeting in the kitchen was finished. Julius and Allan went back into the living room. Allan asked The Beauty and Benny for another thirty seconds' patience, while Julius went up to his room and returned with the suitcase trailing behind him. He put it on the long table in the middle of the living room and opened it.

—Allan and I have decided that the four of us will share this equally.

—Jesus bloody Christ! said The Beauty.

—Have a seat, and I'll explain, said Julius.

The Beauty found it just as hard as Benny had to digest the part about the corpse, but she was impressed with Allan for climbing out of a window and just disappearing from his earlier life.

—I should have done the same after fourteen days with that asshole I married.

Calm returned to Lake Farm. The Beauty and Buster went off again to pick up supplies. She bought food, drink, clothes, toiletries, and lots of other stuff. She paid for everything with a wad of 500-crown bills.

Chief Inspector Aronsson questioned the witness from the gas station in Mjölby, a woman in her fifties. Her profession and the way she described what she had seen made her a credible witness. She could also identify Allan in pictures from an eightieth birthday party at the Old Folks' Home a week or two earlier, pictures that Director Alice had been kind enough to provide not only to the police but also to the press.

Chief Inspector Aronsson was forced to admit to himself that he had wrongly dismissed this tip the day before. But there was no point in looking back. Instead, Aronsson concentrated on his analysis. From a flight perspective, there were two possibilities: Either the old men and the hot-dog-stand proprietor knew where they were going, or they were simply traveling south at random. Aronsson preferred the first alternative, given that it was easier to follow someone who knows where he's going. But with these people it was hard to know. There seemed to be no obvious link between Allan Karlsson and Julius Jonsson on the one hand, and Benny Ljungberg on the other. Jonsson and Ljungberg might be acquaintances; after all, they lived fairly close together. But it was possible that Ljungberg had been kidnapped and forced to drive the car. The centenarian too could have been forced to follow along, although that interpretation had two strikes against it: 1) the fact that Allan Karlsson had gotten off the bus at Byringe Station and, it would seem, of his own volition sought out Julius Jonsson; and 2) witness statements that Julius Jonsson and Allan Karlsson seemed to be on good terms: a) on the inspection trolley through the forest and b) on their walk outside the foundry.

Whatever the circumstances, the gas station attendant had noticed that the silver Mercedes had left the highway and continued toward Tranås. Although twenty-four hours had passed, that fact remained of interest. Somebody heading south along the highway who turns off at Mjölby has immediately limited the number of likely final destinations. They might be going to Oskarshamn and then on to the island of Gotland but there was no sign of them on the ferry passenger lists. All that remained was northern Småland, in which case the Mercedes had hardly chosen the fastest route. But if the old men and the hot-dog-stand proprietor felt they were being chased, then it would be sensible to choose smaller roads.

What spoke in favor of their still being in the area that Chief Inspector Aronsson had just zeroed in on was first, the car contained two people without valid passports. They would hardly be going abroad. Second, Chief Inspector Aronsson's colleagues had phoned every imaginable gas station in a southern, southeastern, and southwestern direction between 200 and 300 miles from Mjölby. No one had seen a silver Mercedes with three conspicuous travelers. Of course, they could have gotten gas at an unmanned station, but people usually went to full-service gas stations because after having driven a certain distance they invariably required a bag of chips, a bottle of soda, or a hot dog. And what additionally spoke in favor of the full-service gas stations was that they had chosen one before, in Mjölby that time.

—Tranås, Eksjö, Nässjö, Vetlanda, Åseda . . . and thereabouts, said Chief Inspector Aronsson to himself in a congratulatory tone, before frowning.

—And then where?

When the leader of The Violence in Braås woke after a terrible night, he immediately made his way to the gas station to do something about his desperate need for a smoke. On the wall outside the entrance the newspaper headlines screamed down at him. The big picture in the *Express* showed . . . the same old guy he had seen in Rottne the previous night.

In his haste he forgot to ask for cigarettes. But he did buy the *Express*, was astounded by what he read, and then phoned his big brother, Bucket.

The mystery of the vanished and presumably kidnapped centenarian caught the attention of the nation. More than one-and-a-half-million viewers, including the centenarian himself and his new comrades at Lake Farm, watched a report that didn't actually reveal anything more than the *Express*.

—If I hadn't known it was me, I would have felt sorry for that old guy, said Allan.

The Beauty was less easygoing; she thought that Allan, Julius, and Benny had better keep well out of sight for a long time. And from now on the Mercedes would remain parked behind the barn. And the next morning she would go off and buy the large bus she had had her eye on for a while. Since many of the seats had been cleared away and it had been fitted with an unusually wide side door, it was perfect for moving especially large cargo. They might have to make a quick getaway very soon, and in that case the whole family was going, including Sonya.

NINE

1939–1945

O n September 1, 1939, Allan's ship, sailing under the Spanish
flag, arrived in New York. Allan had contemplated taking
a quick look at the big country to the west of Europe, and
then sailing back again, but on the same day one of the generalissimo's dear friends marched into Poland and once again war was
raging in Europe. The Spanish-registered ship was impounded,
confiscated, and then did service in the U.S. Navy until the war
ended in 1945.

Everyone on board was sent over to the immigration office on
Ellis Island. There, every passenger was asked the same four questions: 1) Name? 2) Nationality? 3) Profession? 4) Purpose of visit to
the United States of America?

All of Allan's comrades from the ship said, through a Spanish
interpreter, that they were simple Spanish seamen who now had

nowhere to go because their ship had been impounded. After which they were quickly admitted to the United States, where they had to manage as best they could.

But Allan was different. He had a name that the Spanish interpreter couldn't pronounce; he said he came from Suecia; and, most important, he revealed that he was an explosives expert, with all sorts of experience ranging from running his own explosives business, to the manufacture of cannons, and most recently to participating in the war between Spaniards and Spaniards.

After which Allan pulled out his letter from General Franco. Terrified, the Spanish interpreter translated it for the immigration officer who immediately summoned his superior who immediately summoned his superior.

At first the inferior and the two superiors agreed that the fascist Swede should immediately be sent back where he had come from.

—As long as you can find a ship for me, I'll be happy to go, said Allan.

This was not a practicable suggestion, and so the interrogations continued. And the more the immigration officer got out of Allan, the less fascistic the Swede seemed to be. He wasn't a communist either. Or a national socialist. He was nothing at all, it would seem, other than an expert on explosives. As for the story of how he came to be on first-name terms with General Franco, it was so ridiculous that it had to be true—he could hardly have made it up.

Since he had no better ideas, the senior immigration officer arranged for Allan to be locked up for a couple of months. Unfortunately, the months turned into years, and the immigration boss mostly forgot about Allan, until one day he found himself discussing the case with his brother when they met at the family farm in Connecticut for Thanksgiving. His brother was working on some kind of explosive device for the military. The brother was not thrilled at the idea of having a potential Franco supporter on his hands, but they were desperately in need of all the expertise they could muster down at Los Alamos, and they could probably find some suitably unqualified and not-too-secret work for this odd Swede, if it would help out his brother.

The immigration director answered that it most definitely would be a favor, and then the brothers tucked into the turkey.

Some time later in the winter of 1943 Allan flew for the first time ever—destination: the U.S. national laboratory in Los Alamos, where it was soon discovered that he didn't speak a word of English. A Spanish-speaking lieutenant was given the task of finding out the extent of the Swede's professional skills, and Allan was required to write down his most explosive chemical formulas for the lieutenant. The latter looked through these, finding evidence of a considerable innovative ability, but pointing out that the force of Allan's explosive charges would barely blow up a car.

—Oh, but it would, answered Allan. A car with a man in it. I've tried it.

Allan was allowed to stay on, at first in the most remote corner of the compound, but as the months and years went by and he started to speak English, he was allowed to move about more and more freely. As an extremely meticulous observer, during the days Allan learned how to make explosive charges of a substantially different nature from those he'd been in the habit of setting off on Sundays back home in the gravel pit. And in the evening, when most of the young men at the Los Alamos lab went out to town to chase women, Allan sat in the restricted-access library and learned about new realms in the world of explosives.

The war in Europe was escalating, but these events largely passed Allan by as he acquired knowledge, which, as a lowly assistant, he couldn't really use. It was no longer about familiar chemicals like nitroglycerin and sodium nitrate—that was for amateurs—but about exotic relationships between atoms like hydrogen and uranium, which turned out to be far more complicated elements than he could ever have imagined.

From 1943 on, extremely strict security restrictions came into force at Los Alamos. The scientists had been given a secret mission by President Roosevelt to create a big bomb: a bomb that, Allan guessed, could destroy ten or even twenty Spanish bridges with a single explosion. Someone needed to help out on even the most secret activities, and the hugely popular Allan was given the highest security clearance.

He had to admit that they knew their stuff, these Americans. Instead of working with the conventional materials Allan had been brought up on, these scientists had found ways of unlocking the power that held the nuclei of atoms together, trying to create more enormous explosions than anything the world had seen before.

By April 1945, they were almost there. The researchers—and for that matter Allan—knew how to achieve a nuclear reaction, but they didn't know how to control it. The problem fascinated Allan, and when he sat in the library in the evenings he worried away at the problem that nobody had asked him to worry about—and he solved it.

Every week that spring, the most important military people met for hours with the leading physicists, led by chief scientist J. Robert Oppenheimer, while Allan filled their coffee cups—and listened.

The scientists pulled at their hair and asked Allan for more coffee. The military people scratched their heads and asked Allan for more coffee. The military people and the scientists all despaired of finding a solution and asked Allan for more coffee. And so it went on, week after week. Allan had been sitting on the solution to the group's problem for some time but he didn't think it was the waiter's task to tell the chef how to prepare dinner, so he kept what he knew to himself.

Until on one occasion, to his own surprise, he heard himself say:

—Excuse me, but why don't you divide the uranium into two equal parts?

It just sort of slipped out, while he was pouring coffee into Robert Oppenheimer's cup.

—*What* did you say? said Oppenheimer who was so shocked that the waiter had opened his mouth that he hadn't even listened to what Allan said.

Allan had no choice but to go on.

—Well, if you divide the uranium into two equal parts and slap them together only when it is time, then they'll explode when you want them to.

—*Equal* parts? said Oppenheimer. There was a lot more going on in his head at that moment, but "equal parts" was what he managed to say.

—Well, perhaps you have a point there, Professor. The parts don't have to be equal in size. The important thing is that they are big enough when they come together.

Lieutenant Lewis, who had vouched for Allan's suitability as an assistant, looked as if he wanted to murder the Swede, but one of the scientists around the table reacted with considerable interest:

—But how do we slap them together? And when? In the air?

—Exactly, Professor. You see, it's not hard to make it all explode. The problem is that you can't control the moment of explosion. But a critical mass divided into two gives you two *uncritical* masses, doesn't it? And the opposite applies too, because from two uncritical masses you can get one critical mass.

—And how do you propose we slap them together Mr. . . . excuse me, but who are you? said Oppenheimer.

—I'm Allan, said Allan.

—And, Mr. Allan, how do we slap them together?

—With a good old, everyday explosive charge, said Allan. That's the sort of thing I'm good at, but I am sure you can manage it yourselves.

Professors of physics in general and top military scientists in particular are not stupid. In a few seconds, Oppenheimer had worked his way through thickets of equations and come to the conclusion that it was extremely likely that the waiter was right. Just imagine that something so complicated could have such a simple solution! A good old everyday explosive charge at the back of the bomb could be activated from a distance and would send an uncritical mass of uranium-235 forward to a meeting with another uncritical mass. It would immediately become critical. The neutrons would start to move, the uranium atoms would start to split. The chain reaction would be in process and. . . .

—Bang! said Oppenheimer to himself.

—Exactly, said Allan. I see that you have already worked it out, Professor. Would anyone like some more coffee?

At that very moment the door to the secret room was opened and in walked Vice President Truman on one of his rare and always unannounced visits.

—Sit down, said the vice president to the men who were all standing to attention.

To be on the safe side, even Allan sat down. If a vice president told you to sit down then it was probably best to sit down; that was how it worked in America, he thought.

The vice president asked for a status report from Oppenheimer, who quickly stood up again. Somewhat flustered, the only thing he could think to say was that Mr. Allan over there in the corner had just solved the remaining problem of how the detonation could be controlled. Mr. Allan's solution was not yet tested, but Oppenheimer was speaking for all those present when he said that the problem had just become history and that within three months they could have a trial explosion.

The vice president looked round the table and got nods of agreement. Lieutenant Lewis had gradually started to breathe again. In the end, the vice president's eyes fell on Allan.

—I do believe, Mr. Allan, that you are the hero of the day. As for me, I need to have a bite before I return to Washington. Would you like to join me?

Following on less than a decade after the generalissimo's dinner invitation, Allan surmised that it must be a common characteristic of world leaders to invite you to eat as soon as you did something they liked, but he didn't say so. Instead he thanked the vice president for the invitation and the two men walked out of the room together. Oppenheimer was left at the conference table looking both relieved and unhappy.

V*ice President Truman had ordered his favorite Mexican restaurant* in the center of Los Alamos to be sealed off, so Allan and Truman had the place to themselves, except for a dozen or so bodyguards spread out in various corners.

The head of the security unit had pointed out that Mr. Allan was not an American and not even cleared to be alone with the vice president, but Truman dismissed the security official's objections with the comment that today Mr. Allan had done the most patriotic thing anyone could imagine.

The vice president was in excellent spirits. Straight after dinner, instead of going to Washington, he had decided to fly to Georgia, where President Roosevelt was staying at a polio clinic. The president would want to hear this news directly, Harry Truman was sure of that.

—I'll order the food, so you can choose the drinks, said Harry Truman jovially and handed the wine list to Allan.

Truman turned to the head waiter who bowed as he received a large order for tacos, enchiladas, corn tortillas, and salsa.

—And to drink, sir?

—Two bottles of tequila, Allan answered.

Harry Truman laughed and asked if Allan wanted to drink him under the table. Allan answered that the last year had taught him that the Mexicans could make spirits with as much oomph as akvavit, but that the vice president could of course drink milk if he considered that more suitable.

—No, I've given my word, said Vice President Truman, and he made sure the order included lime and salt.

Three hours later the two men were calling each other Harry and Allan, which goes to show what a couple of bottles of tequila can do for international relations. Allan told Truman how the local bigwig had been blown to bits and how he saved the life of General Franco. The vice president, for his part, amused Allan by imitating President Roosevelt's attempts to get up out of his wheelchair.

When the two men were on the most jovial of terms, the head of the security staff discreetly approached the vice president.

—Could I have a word please, sir?

—Go ahead, said the vice president in a slurred voice.

—Preferably in private, sir.

—I'll be damned if you don't look just like Humphrey Bogart! Have you seen him, Allan?

—Sir . . . , said the increasingly troubled security man.

—Yes, what the hell do you want? the vice president hissed.

—Sir, it is about President Roosevelt.

—What about that old goat? The vice president guffawed.

—He's dead, sir.

TEN

B ucket sat outside the supermarket in Rottne for four days, hoping to see his colleague Bolt, first of all, and then a hundred-year-old man, a red-haired woman of a slightly younger model, a guy with a ponytail (otherwise of unknown appearance), and a Mercedes. It wasn't his idea to sit there; it was the Boss's. Bucket had immediately reported his fortuitous conversation with his little brother and leader of The Violence in Braås about the centenarian who had most definitely been outside a health clinic in Småland in the middle of the night. That was when the Boss had ordered a watch on the town's most popular supermarket. He assumed that a person who was out walking in Rottne in the middle of the night must be holed up somewhere thereabouts, and everyone needs to go food shopping sooner or later. The logic was indisputable. It was not for nothing the Boss was the boss. But of course that was five days ago. Now, Bucket had started to despair.

His concentration was no longer top-notch either. So he didn't notice the red-haired woman when she drove into the parking lot in a red VW Passat instead of the expected silver Mercedes. But as she had the good taste to walk right past Bucket's nose on her way into the store, he didn't miss her. He couldn't be certain that it was the right woman, but she was about the right age, and she did have exactly the right hair color.

Bucket phoned the Boss in Stockholm. He wasn't nearly as enthusiastic. It was primarily Bolt they were hoping to find, or at least that damned geriatric.

Still Bucket was told to make a note of the license plate and then discreetly follow the redhead to see where she went. Then he was to report back again.

Chief Inspector Aronsson had spent the last four days at the hotel in Åseda. The idea had been that he would be close to the center of events when new witnesses turned up.

But none did, and Aronsson was just about to set off for home when his colleagues in Eskilstuna phoned. They had got some results from the bug they had planted on the Never Again troublemaker Per-Gunnar Gerdin.

Gerdin, or the Boss, as he was known, had been something of a celebrity several years earlier in connection with the establishment of a criminal organization in the maximum-security prison where he resided. The media had taken note, even printing Gerdin's name and picture. The enterprise had fizzled out as a result of a letter Per-Gunnar Gerdin's mother had sent him, but that part of the story never reached the media.

A couple of days earlier, Chief Inspector Aronsson had ordered Gerdin's phone bugged, and now they had a bite. The conversations were taped, transcribed, and then sent by fax to Åseda:

—Hello?

—Yes, it's me.

—Anything new?

—Maybe. I'm sitting outside the supermarket and I just saw a red-haired dame go in to do some shopping.

—Just the dame? Not Bolt? Not a hundred-year-old?

—No, just the dame. I don't know if. . . .

—Was she driving a Mercedes?

—Err, I didn't have time to see . . . but there wasn't a Mercedes in the parking lot, so she must have been driving something else.

[Silence for five seconds]

—Hello?

—Yeah, I'm still here, I'm thinking, damn it. Somebody has to.

—Yeah, but I only. . . .

—There must be more than one red-haired dame in Småland. . . .

—Yeah, but she's the right age, according to. . . .

—Follow her in your car, write down the license plate, don't do anything stupid, but find out where she's going. And make damned sure no one sees you. Then report back to me again.

[Silence for five seconds]

—Did you get that?

—Well, err, yeah. I'll be in touch as soon as I know more. . . .

—And next time call my pay-as-you-go mobile. Haven't I told you to use it for all business calls?

—Yeah, sure, but isn't that only when we do business with the Russians? I didn't think you'd have it turned on now that. . . .

—Idiot. [Followed by grunting and then the conversation ends.]

Chief Inspector Aronsson read the transcript and then put the new bits of the puzzle into place.

The "Bolt" that was mentioned must be Bengt Bylund, one of the known members of Never Again, now presumably dead. And the one who phoned Gerdin was presumably Henrik "Bucket" Hultén, hunting down Bolt somewhere in Småland.

Aronsson now had proof that he was on the right track:

Somewhere in Småland, as he had previously surmised, was Allan Karlsson, together with Julius Jonsson, Benny Ljungberg and his Mercedes, together with a red-haired lady of unknown age. Still she could hardly be particularly young because she had just been called a dame. On the other hand, for somebody like Bucket you wouldn't have to be very old to become a dame.

At Never Again in Stockholm they thought that Bolt was also with the group. Did that mean he was on the run from his own lot? Otherwise why hadn't he been in touch? Because he was dead, of course! But the Boss hadn't fathomed that, so the Boss thought that Bolt was hiding in Småland together with . . . but where did the redhead come into the picture?

So Aronsson ordered a family background check on Allan, Benny, and Julius. Was there possibly a sister or a cousin or some other relative who lived in Småland and who happened to have the right color of hair?

"But she's the right age, according to . . ." Bolt had said. According to what? What somebody had said to them? Someone who had seen the group in Småland and phoned to tip them off? What a pity the bug hadn't been activated earlier.

And by now, of course, Bucket would have followed the redhead from the supermarket and then either dropped the case if she turned out to be the wrong redhead, or . . . Bucket now knew where Allan Karlsson and his friends were holed up. In that case, the Boss would soon be on his way down to Småland too, to make Allan and his companions spill the beans as to what had happened to Bolt and his suitcase.

Aronsson phoned Conny Ranelid, the prosecutor in charge in Eskilstuna. At first Ranelid had not been particularly interested, but his engagement increased with every new complication that Aronsson reported in to him.

—Now, don't let Gerdin and his henchman slip away, said Prosecutor Ranelid.

The Beauty put two shopping bags from the supermarket in the trunk of her VW Passat and set off for home.

Bucket followed at a safe distance. As soon as they reached the highway, he phoned the Boss (on his pay-as-you-go phone, of course; Bucket did have some survival instinct) to inform him of the make of the car the redhead was driving and its license plate, and he promised to call again when they reached their destination.

The two cars drove out of Rottne but the redhead soon turned off down a gravel road. Bucket recognized it. He had once come in last at a car rally here. His then-girlfriend had been the map-reader; halfway through the rally she had realized she was holding the map upside down.

The gravel road was dry, and the redhead's car left a cloud of dust behind it. Bucket could safely follow her without even keeping her in sight. But then after a few miles the cloud of dust suddenly disappeared. Damn it!

First, he started to panic, but then he calmed down. The dame must have turned off somewhere along the road. Less than a mile back on the road, Bucket thought he had solved the puzzle. A little track went off to the right next to a mailbox. She must have gone down there.

Bearing in mind how things soon developed, you could say that Bucket was a little too enthusiastic. He sent the car and himself at a decent speed down the little track, wherever it might lead. The idea of being discreet and cautious was discarded early on.

Bucket was driving too fast, and before he realized it the track had come to an end and was replaced by a little yard. And if he had been driving just a little faster, he wouldn't even have had time to stop but would have driven straight into the old man who was standing there feeding an . . . an . . . elephant?

Allan had quickly found a new friend in Sonya. They had quite a lot in common. One had climbed out through a window one day and thus given his life a totally new direction, while the other had waded out into a lake with the same result. And both of them had—before that—been out and about and seen some of the world. Furthermore, Sonya had deep furrows on her face, more or less like a wise centenarian, Allan thought.

Sonya was not about to do circus tricks for just anybody, but she happened to like this old man. He gave her fruit, scratched her trunk, and chatted with her in a friendly way. She didn't understand much of what he said, but that didn't matter. It was pleasant. So when the old man asked Sonya to sit down, she sat down, if he asked her to turn around, she was happy to do just that. She even showed him how she could stand up on her back legs, although the old man didn't know the command for that. The fact that she got an apple or two for her trouble and an extra bit of scratching on her trunk was a pure bonus. Sonya could not be bought.

While this was going on, The Beauty liked to sit on the veranda steps with Benny and Buster, with a cup of coffee and some doggy treats for the dog. They looked on while Allan and Sonya bonded in the yard, and Julius fished for perch down at the lake.

The spring heat wave continued. The sun had been shining a whole week and the weather forecasters were predicting that the high pressure would continue.

Benny, who apart from all his other skills was an almost-architect, had sketched out how the bus that The Beauty had just purchased could be fitted out to suit Sonya. When The Beauty discovered that Julius was not just a thief but also a former timber merchant and he knew how to handle a hammer and nails, she said to Buster that these friends were not bad. It was a good thing that she hadn't slammed the door on them. It didn't take Julius more than an afternoon to nail together the new bus interior according to Benny's instructions. After which Sonya walked in and out of the bus together with Allan to test it, and Sonya seemed to like it. It was a bit of a squeeze for her, but there were two kinds of dinner to chew on, one to the left and one straight ahead, and water to drink to the right. The floor was raised and slightly sloped, and Sonya's droppings had their own pit running along the back. The pit was filled to the brim with hay, which was intended to absorb most of what might come out during the journey.

In addition there was a substantial ventilation system in the form of holes drilled along both sides of the bus, and a sliding glass panel behind the driver's cabin so that Sonya could see her benefactor and feeder while they were on the road. The bus had, to put it simply, been transformed into a luxury elephant transporter.

The more prepared they got, the less eager the group was to set off. Life at Lake Farm had developed quite pleasantly. Not least for Benny and The Beauty who by the third night had decided that it was a pity to wear out sheets in different rooms when they could just as well share. The evenings had been passed in front of the log fire, with good food, good drink, and episodes from Allan Karlsson's remarkable life.

But on Monday morning the fridge and the pantry were almost empty, and it was high time for The Beauty to go off to Rottne to stock up. For reasons of security, the journey was undertaken in her old VW Passat. The Mercedes remained hidden behind the barn.

She filled one shopping bag with this and that for her and the old men, and another one with fresh, Argentinean apples for Sonya. When The Beauty got home, she gave the bag of apples to Allan and put the rest of the groceries away before joining Benny and Buster on the veranda with a basket of Belgian strawberries. Julius was there too, taking a rare break from fishing.

That was when a Ford Mustang roared into the yard and almost ran down both Allan and Sonya.

Sonya was the calmest of them all. She was so focused on receiving the next apple from Allan that she neither saw nor heard what happened around her. Or perhaps she did, despite everything, because she stopped in the middle of a twirl and froze with her bottom toward Allan and the new visitor.

The second calmest was Allan. He had been close to death so many times in his life that a bolting Ford Mustang hardly made any difference. If it stopped in time, so be it.

The third calmest was probably Buster. He was strictly brought up not to run off and bark when strangers came to visit. But his ears stuck up and he was all eyes, ready to follow developments.

But The Beauty, Benny, and Julius all jumped up from the veranda and stood there in a row waiting to see what would happen next.

Bucket, somewhat disconcerted for a moment, got unsteadily out of his Mustang and felt about for a revolver in a bag on the floor of the backseat. He pointed it first at the elephant's behind, then had a better idea and aimed it at Allan and the three friends standing in a row on the veranda, and then he said (perhaps rather unimaginatively):

—Hands up!

—Hands up??

That was the most stupid thing Allan had heard in a long time. What did this man think would happen? That he himself, one hundred years old, would throw apples at him? Or that the delicate lady over there would bombard him with Belgian strawberries? Or that . . .

—Okay, Okay, do what the hell you want with your hands, but don't try any tricks.

—Tricks?

—You keep your mouth shut, you old bastard! Tell me where that damned suitcase is—and the guy who took it.

Well there we are, thought The Beauty. That was the end of their luck in life. Reality had caught up with them all. Nobody answered. They all racked their brains so you could hear the creaking, all except the elephant that was facing away from all the drama and thought it was time to relieve herself. And an elephant relieving itself is not something you can miss if you happen to be in the vicinity.

—Oh, shit, said Bucket and took a few rapid steps away from the mess that poured out of the elephant. . . . Why the hell do you have an elephant?

Still no answer. But now Buster couldn't restrain himself any longer. He obviously felt that things weren't quite right. And he really wanted to have a good bark at the stranger. And even though he knew the rules, he let out a deep growl. Discovering the Alsatian on the veranda, Bucket instinctively took two steps backward, raised his revolver, and looked as if he was ready to shoot.

At that point Allan's hundred-year-old brain gave birth to an idea. It was a wild idea, and there was an evident risk that he would get shot in the process, unless of course he really was immortal after all. He took a deep breath and with a naive smile on his lips, he walked straight toward the troublemaker. And he said in his most doddery voice:

—That really is one hell of a nice pistol you've got there. Is it real? Can I hold it?

Benny, Julius, and The Beauty all thought that the geriatric had lost his marbles.

—Stop, Allan! Benny shouted out.

—Yeah, stop, you old bastard, or I'll shoot you, said Bucket.

But Allan kept shuffling toward him. Bucket took a step backward, stretched out his hand with the revolver even more threateningly toward Allan, and then . . . he did it.

If you've ever stepped in a heap of sticky, very fresh elephant shit then you'll know it's virtually impossible to keep your balance. Bucket didn't know, but he quickly learned. His back foot slipped, and Bucket tried to counter this with his hands but fell helplessly, landing softly on his back.

—Sit, Sonya, sit! said Allan as the final part of his daring plan.

—No damn it, Sonya, don't sit, shouted The Beauty who suddenly realized what was about to happen.

—Fucking hell, said Bucket where he lay on his back in the elephant's excrement.

Sonya, who stood with her back to them all, had clearly and distinctly heard Allan's command. And the old man was nice to her, and she liked to do as he wanted. Besides, his benefactor and feeder had confirmed the order. The function of the word "Don't" to countermand an order was not something Sonya had ever grasped.

So Sonya sat down. Her bottom landed on something soft and warm, with a dull crushing sound and something that sounded like a squeak before complete silence reigned. Sonya was ready for another apple.

—There went number two, said Julius.

—Jesus, bloody, fucking Christ, said The Beauty.

—Yuck, said Benny.

—Here's an apple, Sonya, said Allan.

Henrik "Bucket" Hultén didn't say anything at all.

The Boss waited for three hours for Bucket to get in touch again. Then he decided that something had happened to that good-for-nothing. The Boss found it desperately hard to understand why people didn't just do as he said and nothing more.

Time to deal with it all himself; that much was obvious. The Boss began by checking the registration number that Bucket had given him. It didn't take many minutes to ascertain via the national vehicle registry that it referred to a red VW Passat, owned by a Gunilla Björklund, of Lake Farm, Rottne, Småland.

ELEVEN

1945–1947

I *f it is possible to become stone-cold sober instantly after having just* downed a whole bottle of tequila, then that was what Vice President Harry S. Truman did.

The news of President Roosevelt's sudden demise meant that the vice president had to conclude the pleasant dinner with Allan and fly immediately to Washington. Allan was left behind in the restaurant to argue with the headwaiter about the bill. In the end, the headwaiter accepted Allan's argument that the future president of the United States was probably reasonably creditworthy and that, in any case, the headwaiter now knew his address.

Allan took a refreshing walk back to the lab and resumed his duties as coffeemaker and assistant to America's foremost physicists, mathematicians, and chemists, even though they now felt somewhat embarrassed in Allan's company. The atmosphere was uncomfortable and after a few weeks Allan was considering whether to move on. A telephone call from Washington settled the matter:

—Hi, Allan, it's Harry.

—Which Harry?

—Truman, Allan. Harry S. Truman, the president, damn it!

—How nice! That was a good meal we had, Mr. President, thank you. I hope you weren't required to fly the plane home?

No, the president had not. Despite the gravity of the situation, he had passed out on a sofa and had not woken up again until it was time to land five hours later.

But now, Harry Truman had some things to deal with that he had inherited from his predecessor, and for one of these the president might need Allan's help, if Allan thought that possible?

Allan certainly did, and the next morning he checked out from the Los Alamos National Laboratory for good.

The Oval Office was just about as oval as Allan had imagined. And there he was, sitting across from his Los Alamos drinking partner.

It turned out that the president was having some trouble with a woman whom he—for political reasons—couldn't ignore. Her name was Soong Mei-ling. Perhaps Allan had heard of her? No?

Well, she was the wife of the anticommunist Kuomintang leader Chiang Kai-shek in China. She was also extremely beautiful, educated here in America, and a best friend of Mrs. Roosevelt. She drew an audience of thousands wherever she turned up, and had even given a speech to Congress. And now she was hounding President Truman almost to death to ensure that he would make good on all the promises that she claimed President Roosevelt had made with regard to the struggle against communism.

—I should have guessed that this was about politics, said Allan.

—It's pretty hard to avoid that if you are president, said Harry Truman.

Just for the moment there was a brief period of calm in the struggle between the Kuomintang and the communists, for they were more or less fighting for a common cause in Manchuria. But soon the Japanese would surrender, and then the Chinese would certainly start to fight among themselves again.

—How do you know that the Japanese are going to surrender? asked Allan.

—You, of all people, ought to be able to work that out, answered Truman and immediately changed the subject.

The president proceeded with what for Allan was a boring overview of developments in China. Intelligence reports said that the communists had the advantage in the civil war, and at the Office of Strategic Services there were questions about Chiang Kai-shek's military strategy. He was concentrating on the towns, leaving the rural areas open for communist propaganda. The leader of the communists, Mao Tse-tung, would of course soon be eliminated by the Americans, but there was an obvious risk that his ideas might gain a foothold among the population. Even the irritating Soong Mei-ling acknowledged that something had to be done. So she simply followed her own military course.

The president continued to describe military strategy, but Allan had stopped listening. He looked absentmindedly around the Oval Office, wondering whether the windowpanes were bulletproof and where the door to the left might lead. He thought it must be difficult to drag the gigantic carpet out for cleaning. . . . In the end, he felt he had to interrupt the president in case he started asking questions to make sure that Allan had understood.

—Excuse me, Harry, but what do you want me to do?

—Well, as I said, it's about stopping the communists' freedom of movement in the rural areas. . . .

—What do you *actually* want me to do?

—Soong Mei-ling is pushing for increased American weapons' support, and now she wants even more equipment than what they've already been offered.

—And what *specifically* do you want me to do?

When Allan had asked the question for the third time, the president fell silent. Then he said:

—I want you to go to China and blow up bridges.

—Why didn't you say that right away? said Allan, his face brightening.

—As many bridges as possible, so that you cut off as many of the communist roads as you can. . . .

—It'll be nice to see a new country, said Allan.

—I want you to train Soong Mei-ling's men in the art of blowing up bridges and that. . . .

—When do I leave?

Although Allan was an explosives expert, and had rapidly and drunkenly become good friends with the future American president, he was still Swedish. If Allan had been the slightest bit interested in politics, he might have asked the president why he was the one to have been chosen for this mission. Had the president been asked he would have answered truthfully that the United States couldn't be seen to support two parallel and potentially contradictory military projects in China. Officially they supported Chiang Kai-shek and his Kuomintang party. Now they were adding to that support on the sly with a whole shipload of equipment for blowing up bridges on a major scale, ordered and pushed through by the beautiful, serpentlike (in the president's view), and half-Americanized Soong Mei-ling. Worst of all, Truman couldn't rule out that everything *had* actually been settled over a cup of tea between Soong Mei-ling and Mrs. Eleanor Roosevelt. What a mess! But now all that remained was for the president to introduce Allan Karlsson and Soong Mei-ling to each other. Then as far as the president was concerned the matter was over and done with.

The next item on his agenda was more of a formality, because he had already made his decision. There was no need for him physically to push the button, so to speak. On an island east of the Philippines the crew of a B-52 bomber was waiting for the go-ahead from the president. All the tests had been carried out. Nothing could go wrong.

The next day was the sixth of August 1945.

Allan Karlsson's delight that something new was going to happen in his life soon faded when he met Soong Mei-ling for the first time. Allan had instructions to call on her at a hotel suite in Washington. After managing to negotiate his way through a couple of rows of bodyguards, he stood in front of the lady herself and holding out his hand said:

—How do you do, Madame, I'm Allan Karlsson.

Soong Mei-ling did not shake his hand. Instead, she pointed to an armchair close by.

—Sit! she said.

Over the years, Allan had been accused of being everything from crazy to fascist, but never a dog. He considered pointing out the unsuitability of the lady's tone, but refrained from doing so, since he was curious to see what would come next. Besides, the armchair looked comfortable.

When Allan sat down, Soong Mei-ling embarked upon something that Allan felt a particular aversion to, namely a political explanation. Oddly, she referred to President Roosevelt as the man behind the entire plan, and Allan found that strange. Surely you couldn't lead military operations from beyond the grave?

Soong Mei-ling described the importance of putting a stop to the communists, of preventing that clown Mao Tse-tung from spreading his political poison from province to province, and—rather strangely, thought Allan—of her husband, Chiang Kai-shek, not understanding anything about this business.

—How are things really between you two on the romantic side? said Allan.

Soong Mei-ling informed Allan that such a matter was of no concern to an insignificant person like him. Karlsson was appointed by President Roosevelt to be directly under her command in this operation, and from now on he should only answer when spoken to, and otherwise be silent.

Allan didn't get angry—the word didn't seem to be in his vocabulary—but he took advantage of the fact that he had been spoken to, to answer.

—The last thing I heard about Roosevelt was that he was dead, and if anything has changed about that it would have been in the papers. I am doing this because President *Truman* asked me to. But if your madameship is going to keep on being angry then I don't think I'll bother. I can always visit China another time, and I've already blown up more than enough bridges.

No one had confronted Soong Mei-ling like this since her mother had tried to stop her daughter's marriage to a Buddhist, and that was many years ago. Besides, her mother had later had to apologize because the marriage had led her daughter all the way to the top.

Now Soong Mei-ling had to stop and think. She had evidently misjudged the situation. Up to now, all Americans had started to tremble when she described President Roosevelt and the First Lady as personal friends. How should she deal with this person who didn't react in the same way as everybody else? Who on earth had that incompetent Truman sent her?

Soong Mei-ling was not a person who would fraternize with just anybody, but her goal was more important than her principles. So she changed tactics:

—I think we forgot to introduce ourselves properly, she said, and held out her hand in the western manner. But better late than never.

Allan was not one to harbor a grudge. He took her hand and smiled indulgently. But he didn't agree in general with better late than never. His father, for example, became a faithful supporter of Czar Nicholas the day before the Russian Revolution.

Two days later Allan was on his way to Los Angeles, with Soong Mei-ling and twenty men from her personal bodyguard. There awaited the ship that would take them and their cargo of dynamite to Shanghai.

Allan knew that it would be impossible for him to keep out of the way of Soong Mei-ling for the whole of the long voyage across the Pacific Ocean—the vessel simply didn't have enough hiding places. So he made up his mind not even to try, and he accepted a permanent seat at the captain's table during dinner every evening. The advantage was the good food. The disadvantage was that Allan and the captain were not alone; they had the company of Soong Mei-ling, who seemed to be incapable of talking about anything but politics.

And to be honest, there was yet another disadvantage; instead of vodka, they were served a green, banana liquor. Allan accepted what he was served, but he reflected that it was the first time he had drunk something that was essentially undrinkable. Drinks with an alcoholic content ought to go down your throat and into your belly as quickly as possible, not stick to your palate.

But Soong Mei-ling liked the taste of the liquor and the more glasses she put away during an evening, the more personal was the tone of her everlasting political ramblings.

What Allan quite effortlessly learned during the dinners on the Pacific Ocean was, for example, that the clown Mao Tse-tung and his communists could very well win the civil war and that such an outcome would essentially have been caused by Chiang Kai-shek. Soong Mei-ling's husband was incompetent as commander in chief. At this very moment he was partaking in peace negotiations with Mao Tse-tung in the south Chinese city of Chongqing. Had Mr. Karlsson and the captain heard anything so stupid? Negotiating with a communist? Where would that lead, other than nowhere!

Soong Mei-ling was certain that the negotiations would break down. Her intelligence reports also revealed that a considerable part of the communist army was waiting for its leader Mao in the desolate mountains in Sichuan province not far from Chongqing. Soong Mei-ling's handpicked agents, like Soong Mei-ling herself, believed that the clown and his forces would next move to the northeast, toward Shaanxi and Henan, in their disgusting propaganda procession through the nation.

Allan made sure to keep quiet so that the evening's political lecture would be no longer than necessary, but the hopelessly polite captain asked question after question while he repeatedly filled her glass with the sweet green banana goo.

The captain wondered, for instance, in what way Mao Tse-tung actually posed any sort of threat. The Kuomintang did, after all, have the USA behind it and was, as the captain understood it, militarily completely superior.

That question extended the evening's misery by almost an hour. Soong Mei-ling explained that her pathetic husband was just about as intelligent and charismatic as a cow and possessed the same leadership qualities. Chang Kai-shek had completely embraced the erroneous belief that it was all about who controlled the cities.

It was not Soong Mei-ling's intention to confront Mao in battle. How could she do that with the little project she had cooked up with Allan and a handful of her bodyguards? Twenty poorly armed men, twenty-one with Mr. Karlsson, against a whole army of very able opponents in the mountains of Sichuan. . . . That would be ugly.

Instead, the first stage in the plan was to limit the clown's mobility, to make it more difficult for the communist army to move around. The next stage was to get her miserable husband to realize that he must now seize the opportunity to lead his forces out into the rural areas and show the Chinese people that the Kuomintang would protect them from communism, and not vice versa. Soong Mei-ling had understood, just like the clown, what Chiang Kai-shek so far had not—namely, that it was easier to be the leader of a nation if you had the nation behind you.

Sometimes, of course, even a blind hen will find a grain of corn on the ground, and it was good that Chiang Kai-shek had invited his opponents to the peace negotiations in Chongqing. Because with a little luck, the clown and his soldiers would still be there south of the Yangtze, after the negotiations had broken down, when her troop of bodyguards and Karlsson arrived on the scene. Then Karlsson could blow up bridges with maximum effect! And for a long time to come, the clown would be confined to the mountains halfway to Tibet.

—But if he should happen to be on the wrong side of the river, then we simply regroup. There are five thousand rivers in China, so wherever the parasite goes there will be a river in his path.

A clown and a parasite, Allan thought, doing battle with a cowardly, incompetent figure who to cap it all had the intelligence of a cow, and between them, a serpent drunk on green, banana liquor.

—It'll definitely be interesting to see how it all turns out, Allan said sincerely. Incidentally and apropos of nothing at all, Captain, do you by any chance have a few drops of vodka somewhere, to wash down this green liquor?

No, unfortunately the captain didn't. But there were a lot of other flavors if Mr. Karlsson wanted some variety for his palate: lemon liquor, cream liquor, mint liquor. . . .

—Apropos of nothing at all again, said Allan, when do you think we will reach Shanghai?

Allan Karlsson and a force of twenty men from Soong Mei-ling's bodyguard traveled on the Yangtze by riverboat in the direction of Sichuan, as part of their plan to make life more difficult for the communist upstart Mao Tse-tung. They departed on October 12, 1945, two days after the peace negotiations had, as predicted, broken down.

They proceeded at a leisurely pace since the bodyguards wanted to have fun in every harbor. And there were lots of harbors. First Nanjing, then Wuhu, Anqing, Jiujiang, Wuhan, Yueyang, Yidu, Fengjie, Wanxian, Chongqing, and Luzhou. And every stop featured drunkenness, prostitution, and a general lack of morals.

Since such a lifestyle tends to use up funds very quickly, the twenty bodyguards devised a new tax. The peasants who wanted to unload their products onto the ship in the harbor could not do so unless they paid a fee of five yuan. And anyone who complained was shot.

This new tax revenue was immediately spent in the darkest quarters of the city in question, and those quarters were nearly always close to the harbor. Allan thought that if Soong Mei-ling believed it was important to have the people on her side, she might have conveyed that message to her subordinates. But that, thank God, was her problem, not Allan's.

It took two months for Allan and the twenty soldiers to reach Sichuan province, and by then Mao Tse-tung's forces had long since left for the north. And they didn't sneak off through the mountains, but went down into the valley and did battle with the Kuomintang regiment that had been left to defend the city of Yibin.

Yibin was soon on the verge of falling into communist hands. Three thousand five hundred Kuomintang soldiers were killed in the battle, at least two thousand five hundred of them because they were too drunk to fight. In comparison, three hundred communists died, presumably sober.

The battle for Yibin had nevertheless been a success for the Kuomintang, because among the fifty captured communists there was one jewel. Forty-nine of the prisoners could simply be shot and pushed into a hole in the ground, but the fiftieth! Mmmm! The fiftieth was none other than the beautiful Jiang Qing, the actress who became a Marxist-Leninist and—far more important—Mao Tse-tung's third wife.

A palaver immediately started up between, on the one side, Kuomintang's company command in Yibin and, on the other, Soong Mei-ling's bodyguards. The argument was about who would have the responsibility for the star prisoner, Jiang Qing. So far, the company commander had just kept her locked up, waiting for the boat with Soong Mei-ling's men to arrive. He hadn't dared to do otherwise because Soong Mei-ling could be on board. And you didn't argue with her.

But it turned out that Soong Mei-ling was in Taipei, which simplified things considerably as far as the Kuomintang company commander was concerned. Jiang Qing would first be raped in the most brutal manner and then, if she was still alive, she would be shot.

Soong Mei-ling's bodyguards did not object to the rape bit. They could even see themselves joining in, but Jiang Qing must definitely not be allowed to die. Instead she should be taken to Soong Mei-ling or Chiang Kai-shek for them to decide her fate. This was big-time politics, the internationally experienced soldiers explained in a superior tone to the provincially schooled company commander in Yibin.

The company commander grudgingly promised that he would hand over his jewel the same afternoon. The meeting broke up and the soldiers decided to celebrate their victory with a drinking spree. They were going to have a lot of fun with the jewel on the trip home!

The final negotiations had been carried out on the deck of the riverboat that had brought Allan and the soldiers all the way from the sea. Allan was astounded by the fact that he understood most of what was said. While the soldiers had been amusing themselves in various cities, Allan had been sitting on the stern deck together with the good-natured mess boy, Ah Ming, who turned out to have considerable pedagogical talent. In two months, Ah Ming had helped Allan make himself understood pretty well in Chinese (with a special proficiency in expletives and profanity).

A s a child, Allan had been taught to be suspicious of people who didn't have a drink when the opportunity arose. He was no more than six years old when his father laid a hand on his little shoulder and said:

—You should beware of priests, my son. And people who don't drink vodka. Worst of all are priests who don't drink vodka.

Acting on his own counsel, Allan's father had certainly not been completely sober when one day he punched an innocent traveler in the face, upon which he was immediately fired from the national railways. This in turn had caused Allan's mother to give some words of wisdom of her own to her son:

—Beware of drunks, Allan. That's what I should have done.

The little boy grew up and added his own opinions to those he had acquired from his parents. Priests and politicians were equally bad, Allan thought, and it didn't make the slightest difference if they were communists, fascists, capitalists, or any other political persuasion. But he did agree with his father that reliable people didn't drink fruit juice. And he agreed with his mother that you had to make sure you behaved, even if you had drunk a bit more than was wise.

In practical terms, that meant that during the course of the river journey Allan had lost interest in helping Soong Mei-ling and her twenty drunken soldiers (in fact there were only nineteen left, since one had fallen overboard and drowned). Nor did he want to be around when the soldiers raped the prisoner who was now locked up belowdecks, regardless of whether she was a communist or not, and of who her husband was.

So Allan decided to abandon ship and take the prisoner with him. He told his friend, the mess boy, of his decision and humbly asked that Ah Ming provide the future escapees with some food for their journey. Ah Ming promised to do that, but on one condition— that he could come along.

Eighteen of the nineteen soldiers from Soong Mei-ling's bodyguard, together with the boat's cook and the captain, were out enjoying themselves in the pleasure district in Yibin. The nineteenth soldier, the one who had drawn the shortest straw, sat grumpily outside the door to the stairs that led down to Jiang Qing's prison cell.

Allan sat down with the guard and suggested that they should have a drink together. The guard said that he had been entrusted with responsibility for possibly the most important prisoner in the nation so it would not be right to indulge in rice vodka.

—I entirely agree, said Allan. But one glass can't hurt, can it?

—No, said the guard, upon reflection. One glass certainly can't hurt.

Two hours later, Allan and the guard had each emptied a bottle, while the mess boy Ah Ming had scuttled back and forth and served goodies from the pantry. Allan had become a bit tipsy while on the job, but the guard had fallen asleep right on the open deck.

Allan looked down at the unconscious Chinese soldier at his feet.

—Never try to outdrink a Swede, unless you happen to be a Finn or at least a Russian.

The bomb expert, Allan Karlsson; the mess boy, Ah Ming; and the eternally grateful communist leader's wife, Jiang Qing, slipped away from the riverboat under cover of darkness and were soon in the mountains where Jiang Qing had already spent much time to-gether with her husband's troops. The Tibetan nomads in the area knew her and the fugitives had no problem in eating their fill even after the supplies carried by Ah Ming had run out. The Tibetans had good reason, or so they thought, for being on friendly terms with the People's Liberation Army. It was generally assumed that if the communists won the struggle for China, Tibet would im-mediately gain its independence.

Jiang Qing suggested that she, Allan, and Ah Ming should hurry northward, in a wide circle round Kuomintang-controlled territory. After months of walking in the mountains, they would eventually reach Xi'an in the province of Shaanxi—and Jiang Qing knew that her husband would be there, as long as they didn't take too long.

The mess boy, Ah Ming, was delighted by Jiang Qing's promise that he would be able to serve Mao himself. The boy had secretly become a communist when he saw how the soldiers behaved, so he was fine with changing sides and advancing his career at the same time.

Allan, however, said that he was certain the communist strug-gle would manage just fine without *him*. So he assumed it would be okay if he went home. Did Jiang Qing agree?

Yes, she did. But "home" was surely Sweden and that was ter-ribly far away. How was Mr. Karlsson going to manage?

Allan replied that boat or airplane would have been the most practical method but poor placement of the world's oceans had ruled out catching a boat from the middle of China, and he hadn't seen any airports up there in the mountains. And anyway he didn't have any money to speak of.

—So I'll have to walk, said Allan.

The head of the village who had so generously received the three fugitives had a brother who had traveled more than anybody else. The brother had been as far afield as Ulan Bator in the north and Kabul in the west. Besides which, he had dipped his toes into the Bay of Bengal on a journey to the East Indies, but now he was home in the village again and the headman sent for him and asked him to draw a map of the world for Mr. Karlsson so that he could find his way back to Sweden. The brother promised to do that and he had completed the task by the next day.

Even if you're well bundled up, it is bold to cross the Himalayas with only the help of a homemade map of the world and a compass. In fact, Allan could have walked north of the mountain chain and the Aral and Caspian seas, but reality and the homemade map didn't exactly match up. So Allan said good-bye to Jiang Qing and Ah Ming and started upon his perambulation, which was to go through Tibet, over the Himalayas, through British India, Afghanistan, into Iran, on to Turkey, and then up through Europe.

After two months on foot, Allan discovered that he must have chosen the wrong side of a mountain range and the best way to deal with that was to turn back and start over. Another four months later (on the right side of the mountain range) Allan realized he was making rather slow progress. At a market in a mountain village he haggled as best he could about the price of a camel, with the help of sign language and the Chinese he knew. Allan and the camel-seller finally came to an agreement, but not until the seller had been forced to accept that Allan was not going to take his daughter as part of the purchase.

Allan did consider the part about the daughter. Not for purely physical reasons, because he no longer had any such urges. They had been left behind in Professor Lundborg's operating theater. It was rather her companionship that attracted him. Life on the Tibetan highland plateau could sometimes be lonely.

But since the daughter spoke nothing other than a monotonous-sounding Tibeto-Burmese dialect that Allan didn't understand, he thought that where intellectual stimulation was concerned he could just as well talk to the camel. Besides, one couldn't rule out that the daughter might have certain sexual expectations as to the arrangement. Something in the way she looked at him led Allan to believe that to be the case.

So another two months of loneliness ensued, with Allan wobbling across the roof of the world on the back of a camel, before he came across three strangers, also on camels. Allan greeted them in the languages he knew: Chinese, Spanish, English, and Swedish. Luckily, English worked.

Allan told his new acquaintances that he was on his way home to Sweden. The men looked at him wide-eyed. Was he going to ride a camel all the way to northern Europe?

—With a little break for the ship across Öresund, said Allan.

The three men didn't know what Öresund was so Allan told them that it was where the Baltic Sea met the Atlantic Ocean. After they had ascertained that Allan was not loyal to the British-American lackey, the Shah of Iran, they invited him to accompany them.

The men told him that they had met at the university in Tehran where they had studied English. After their studies, they had spent two years in China, breathing the same air as their communist hero, Mao Tse-tung, and they were now on their way back home to Iran.

—We are Marxists, one of the men said. We are pursuing our struggle in the name of the international worker; in his name we will carry out a revolution in Iran and the whole world; we will build a society based upon the economic and social equality of all people: from each according to his ability, to each according to his need.

—I see, comrade, said Allan. Do you happen to have any spare vodka?

The men did. The bottle went from camelback to camelback and Allan began to feel that the journey was working out nicely.

Eleven months later, the four men had managed to save each others' lives at least three times. They had survived avalanches, bandits, extreme cold, and repeated periods of hunger. Two of the camels had died, a third had had to be slaughtered and eaten, and the fourth had been given to an Afghan customs officer so that they would be allowed to enter the country instead of being arrested.

Allan had never imagined it would be easy to cross the Himalayas. But later he had realized just how lucky he had been to bump into those kind Iranian communists. It would not have been pleasant to wrestle alone with the valley sandstorms and the flooding rivers or the minus forty degrees Fahrenheit in the mountains—even if he could have managed the bitter cold on his own, with his long experience of the Swedish winters. The group had set up camp at an altitude of just under 7,000 feet to wait for the 1946–47 winter to end.

The three communists tried to get Allan to join their struggle, especially after they discovered his talent for working with dynamite. Allan wished them the best of luck, but said that he had to go home to Sweden to look after his house in Yxhult. (Allan momentarily forgot that he had blown the house to bits eighteen years earlier.)

In the end, the men gave up their attempts to persuade Allan of the rightness of their cause, and settled for his being a good comrade, and someone who didn't complain about a bit of snow. Allan's standing improved further when, while the group was waiting for better weather, he figured out how to make alcohol from goats' milk. The communists couldn't fathom how he managed, but the end result was definitely potent and made everything a bit warmer and less boring.

In the spring of 1947 they finally made it over to the southern side of the world's highest mountain chain. The closer they came to the Iranian border, the more eager the communists were to talk about the future of Iran. Now was the time to chase the foreigners out of the country once and for all. The Brits had supported the corrupt Shah for years and years, and that was bad enough. But when the Shah finally tired of being their lapdog and started to protest, then the Brits simply lifted him off his throne and put his son there instead. Allan was reminded of Soong Mei-ling's relationship to Chiang Kai-shek; he reflected that family relations could be weird out in the big wide world.

The son was evidently easier to bribe than the father, and now the Brits and Americans controlled the Iranian oil. Inspired by Mao Tse-tung, these Iranian communists were determined to put a stop to that. The problem was that some other Iranian communists leaned more toward the brand of communism practiced in Stalin's Soviet Union, and there were other irritating revolutionary elements that mixed religion into it all.

—Interesting, said Allan, and meant the opposite.

They replied with a long Marxist declaration on the theme that the situation was more than interesting. The trio would, in short, be victorious or die!

The very next day, the latter turned out to be the case, because as soon as the four friends set foot on Iranian soil they were arrested by a border patrol. The three communists unfortunately each had a copy of the *Communist Manifesto* (in Persian!), and that got them shot on the spot. Allan survived because he had no literature with him. Besides, he looked foreign and required further investigation.

With the barrel of a rifle against his back, Allan took his cap off and thanked the three dead communists for their company across the Himalayas. He couldn't really get used to the way people he befriended went and died right in front of his eyes.

Allan didn't have time for a longer period of mourning. His hands were tied behind his back and he was thrown into the back of a truck. With his nose buried in a blanket he asked in English to be taken to the Swedish Embassy in Tehran, or to the American one if Sweden didn't have any representation in the city.

—*Khafe sho!* was the answer, in a threatening tone.

Allan didn't understand the words, but he understood the sentiment. It probably wouldn't hurt to keep his mouth shut for a while.

On the other side of the globe, in Washington D.C., President Harry Truman had problems of his own. Election time was coming up, and it was important for him to make his policies clear. And that meant deciding what they were. The biggest strategic question was how much he would be prepared to support the Negroes in the South. You had to maintain a fine balance between seeming modern and not seeming too soft. That was how you maintained your support in the opinion polls.

And in the world arena, he had Stalin to deal with. There, however, he was not prepared to compromise. Stalin had managed to charm quite a few people, but not Harry S. Truman.

In light of everything else, China was now history. Stalin pumped in help to Mao Tse-tung, and Truman couldn't refrain from doing the same to that amateur Chiang Kai-shek. Soong Mei-ling had so far gotten what she wanted, but now that would have to end too. He wondered what had happened to Allan Karlsson. A very nice guy.

Chiang Kai-shek suffered more and more military defeats. And Soong Mei-ling's project failed because the explosives expert assigned to it disappeared, taking the clown's wife with him.

Soong Mei-ling asked time and time again for a meeting with President Truman, hoping to be able to strangle him with her bare hands for having sent her Allan Karlsson, but Truman never had time to receive her. Instead, the United States turned its back on the Kuomintang; in China, the corruption, hyperinflation, and famine all played into the hands of Mao Tse-tung. In the end, Chiang Kai-shek, Soong Mei-ling, and their subordinates had to flee to Taiwan. Mainland China became communist China.

TWELVE

Monday, May 9, 2005

The friends at Lake Farm realized that it was high time to get in their bus and leave for good. But first they had some things to take care of.

The Beauty put on a raincoat with a hood and rubber gloves and rolled out the hose to rinse off the remains of the thug that Sonya had just sat on to death. But first, she eased the revolver out of the dead man's right hand and carefully laid it on the veranda (where she later forgot it), with the barrel pointing at the thick trunk of a fir tree four yards away. You never knew when those things could go off.

When Bucket was cleansed of Sonya's excrement, he was put under the backseat of his own Ford Mustang. Normally there wouldn't have been room for him, but now he was neatly flat.

Then Julius got behind the wheel of the thug's car and drove

THE ONE HUNDRED YEAR OLD MAN   139

off, with Benny right behind him in The Beauty's Passat. The idea
was to seek out a deserted place a safe distance from Lake Farm
and then pour gasoline over the thug's car and set fire to it, just as
real gangsters would have done.

But that required a can and gas. So Julius and Benny stopped at
a gas station in Braås, Benny went in to do what was necessary and
Julius to buy something yummy to chew on.

A new Ford Mustang with a V8 of more than 300 horsepower
outside a gas station is as sensational in Braås as a Boeing 747 would
be on a street in downtown Stockholm. It didn't take more than a
second for Bucket's little brother and one of his colleagues in The
Violence to seize the opportunity. The little brother jumped into
the Mustang while his colleague kept an eye on the man he presumed was the owner who was looking at the candy in the gas station shop. What a find! And what an idiot! He'd even left the keys
in the ignition.

When Benny and Julius came out again—one with a newly
purchased gas can, the other with a newspaper under his arm and
his mouth full of candy—the Mustang was gone.

—Didn't I park the Mustang here? asked Julius.

—Yes, you did, said Benny.

—Do we have a problem now? asked Julius.

—Yes, we do, said Benny.

And then they took the unstolen Passat back to Lake Farm.

The Mustang was black with two bright yellow stripes running the
length of the roof. A really deluxe specimen that Bucket's little
brother and his buddies would get good money for. The theft had
been just as accidental as it had been easy. Less than five minutes
after the unplanned seizure, the car was safely tucked away in The
Violence's garage.

The next day, they changed the registration plates before the
little brother let one of his henchmen take the car to their business

companions in Riga. Using false registration plates and documents, the Latvians would arrange for a car to be sold as a private import back to somebody in The Violence, and magically a stolen car had now become a legal car.

But this time things didn't go as planned, because the car from the Swedes started to stink while it stood in the garage in Ziepniek-kalns in Riga's southern suburbs. The garage boss looked for the cause and discovered a corpse under the backseat. He turned the air purple with his swearing, and ripped off all the registration plates and anything else that could provide a clue as to where the car had come from. Then he started to dent and scratch the body-work of the once-fantastic specimen of a Mustang and didn't stop until the car looked like a write-off. Next he went out and found a drunk and in exchange for four bottles of wine persuaded him to drive the wreck to the scrapyard for destruction—corpse and all.

The friends at Lake Farm were ready to depart. They were of course somewhat worried about the theft of the Mustang with the corpse, but then Allan pointed out that it was what it was, and that thereafter whatever will be will be. Besides, in Allan's opinion, there was good reason to hope that the car thieves would never contact the police. Car thieves generally tended to keep a certain distance from the police.

It was now six o'clock in the evening, and they needed to be on their way before it got dark, because the bus was large and the roads for the first part of the journey were small and winding.

Sonya was standing in her stall on wheels. All tracks of the ele-phant had been carefully swept away from the farmyard and barn. The Passat and Benny's old Mercedes were left behind; they hadn't been involved in anything illegal and besides, what else could they do with them?

The bus started on its way. The Beauty had at first intended to drive herself; after all, she knew perfectly well how to drive a large bus. But then it transpired that Benny was an almost-truck driver and had every possible category included in his driving license, so it was best that he got behind the wheel. There was no reason to act more illegally than they had already.

When he reached the mailbox, Benny turned left. According to The Beauty, snaking along gravel roads they would eventually reach Åby and then get to the highway. It would take just over half an hour to get there, so meanwhile they could discuss the not unimportant question of where they were actually going.

Four hours earlier, the Boss had been sitting impatiently and waiting for the only one of his henchmen who hadn't yet disappeared. As soon as Caracas returned from his errand, whatever it was, he and the Boss would set off south—but not on their bikes and not in uniform. Now it was time to be careful.

The Boss had already started to doubt his previous strategy with the Never Again symbol on the club jackets. From the beginning, the point had been to create a feeling of identity and fellowship in the group, and to make outsiders respect them. But first, the group was much smaller than the Boss had once imagined. Keeping a quartet together consisting of Bolt, Bucket, Caracas, and himself, he could manage without jackets. And the tinge of illegality in their activities meant that the club jacket as a signal became counterproductive. Bolt's orders for the transaction in Malmköping had been somewhat contradictory in this respect: on the one hand he was to travel there discreetly by public transportation and on the other hand he was to wear the club jacket with the Never Again symbol on the back to show the Russian who he was dealing with.

And now Bolt was on the run . . . or whatever it was that had happened. And on his back he had a sign that more or less said: "Any questions, phone the Boss."

Damn it! thought the Boss. When this mess was over, he would burn all the jackets. But where the hell was Caracas? Their planned departure time was now!

Caracas turned up eight minutes later and explained the delay by the fact that he had been at the 7-Eleven and bought a watermelon.

—Thirst quenching and tasty, Caracas explained.

—Thirst quenching and tasty? Half the organization has disappeared together with fifty million crowns, and you go off to buy fruit?

—Not fruit, a vegetable, said Caracas. In the same family as cucumbers, in fact.

That did it for the Boss, who picked up the watermelon and split it open on Caracas's head. Upon which Caracas started to cry and said that he didn't want to be in the club anymore. He had had nothing but shit from the Boss since first Bolt and then Bucket vanished, just as if it had been him, Caracas, who lay behind it. No, the Boss would have to manage as best he could; Caracas was going to phone for a taxi, drive to the airport, and fly all the way home to his family in . . . Caracas. Then at least he could get his real name back.

—¡Vete a la mierda! Caracas howled, and rushed out of the door.

The Boss sighed. Everything was getting messier and messier. First Bolt disappeared, and in retrospect the Boss had to admit that he should not have taken out his frustration on Bucket and Caracas. And then Bucket disappeared and the Boss in retrospect had to admit that he should not have taken out his frustration on Caracas. And then Caracas disappeared—to buy a watermelon. And the Boss now in retrospect had to admit that he . . . should never have whacked him over the head with the melon.

And now, he was all alone in his hunt for. . . . Well, he didn't even know what he was hunting. Would he find Bolt? But then had Bolt pinched the suitcase? Could he be so stupid? And what had happened to Bucket?

The Boss drove a car that reflected his standing in society, the latest BMW X5. And most of the time he drove it extremely fast. The police in the unmarked car shadowing him passed the time counting the number of traffic violations he committed during the journey from Stockholm down to Småland, and after 200 miles they agreed that the man behind the wheel in the BMW in front of them ought to be deprived of his driving license for the next four hundred years if everything he had done so far on the journey went to court, which of course it never would.

Be that as it may, the journey took them past Åseda where Chief Inspector Aronsson intercepted his Stockholm colleagues, thanked them for their help, and informed them that he would take over the surveillance himself.

With the help of the GPS in the BMW, the Boss had no trouble getting all the way to Lake Farm. But the closer he came, the more impatient his driving. His already-illegal speeds increased so much Chief Inspector Aronsson had trouble keeping up. He had to keep a certain distance so that Per-Gunnar "Boss" Gerdin wouldn't notice that he was being shadowed, but now Aronsson was beginning to lose sight of his quarry. It was only on the really long straight stretches that he could occasionally glimpse the BMW until . . . he couldn't see it anymore!

Where had Gerdin gone? He must surely have turned off somewhere, or . . . ? Aronsson slowed down. He could feel the sweat breaking out on his forehead. This was definitely not what was supposed to happen.

There was a road off to the left. Perhaps the BMW had gone that way. Or had it continued straight ahead and then gone to. . . . Rottne, wasn't that the name of the place? Unless Gerdin had turned off earlier?

That must be what happened. Aronsson turned around and then turned down the side road where he thought Gerdin must have gone.

The Boss stood on the brakes to slow down from 180 to 20 and quickly steered his way onto the gravel road indicated by the GPS. Now there was only a mile or so left to his destination.

Two hundred yards from the mailbox at Lake Farm the road made a final turn, and round the bend the Boss saw the rear end of a bus that had just maneuvered its way out from the exit that the Boss was being directed toward. What should he do now? Who was in the bus? And was anyone still left at Lake Farm?

The Boss decided to let the bus go on its way. He turned down a winding track, which led him to a farmhouse, a barn, and a lakeside shed that had seen better days.

But no Bucket. No Bolt. No oldie. No dame with red hair. And absolutely no gray suitcase with wheels.

The Boss took another minute to inspect the place. It was obviously empty of people, but behind the barn two cars had been hidden: a red VW Passat and a silver Mercedes.

—The right place, that's for sure, said the Boss. But a few minutes too late.

And so he decided to catch up with the bus. That shouldn't be too hard; it had a start of only three or four minutes on the winding gravel road.

The Boss pressed his foot down on the accelerator and disappeared in a cloud of dust. The fact that a blue Volvo was approaching from the direction in which he had originally come did not concern him one bit.

At first, Chief Inspector Aronsson was pleased to have regained visual contact with Gerdin, but considering Gerdin's speed, the chief's enthusiasm for the chase diminished. There was no way he would be able to keep up. Might it be better to go and have a look at the place? Gunilla Björklund was the name on the mailbox.

—It wouldn't surprise me if you're a redhead, Gunilla, said Chief Inspector Aronsson.

So that is how Aronsson's Volvo arrived in the same farmyard as Henrik "Bucket" Hultén's Ford Mustang had nine hours earlier, and that Per-Gunnar "Boss" Gerdin's BMW had some minutes earlier.

Chief Inspector Aronsson could see, just as the Boss had, that Lake Farm was abandoned. But he did devote a bit more time than the Boss had to searching for various pieces of the puzzle. He found one in the form of that day's newspapers in the kitchen, and some fresh greens in the fridge. So they hadn't broken camp until earlier that very same day. Another bit of the puzzle was of course the Mercedes and the Passat behind the barn. One of those told Aronsson a great deal, and he guessed that the other one belonged to Gunilla Björklund.

Two more clues were waiting to be discovered by Chief Inspector Aronsson. First, he found a revolver lying on the edge of the wooden floor of the farmhouse veranda. What was it doing there? And whose fingerprints were on it? Aronsson guessed Bucket Hultén, and he carefully slipped the revolver into a plastic bag.

The other discovery was in the mailbox when Aronsson was leaving. Among the day's post there was an official letter from the Vehicle Licensing Authority which confirmed that a 1992 yellow Scania K113 had changed owners.

So you are driving around in a bus, the chief inspector said to himself.

The bus wound its way slowly through the forest. It didn't take long for the BMW to catch up. But on the narrow road the Boss couldn't do much more that just stay behind and fantasize about who was in the bus and whether they were transporting a gray suitcase with wheels.

Blissfully unaware of the danger only five yards behind them, the friends in the bus discussed the situation as it had developed and quickly concluded that things would certainly calm down if they could find somewhere to hide for a few weeks. That had been their intention at Lake Farm, of course, but that good idea had suddenly become terribly bad after they received the unexpected visitor and Sonya sat down on him.

The problem now was that Allan, Julius, Benny, and The Beauty had one thing in common: an almost total absence of relatives and friends. How were they going to find someone who would shelter a yellow bus with four people, a dog, and an elephant?

Allan explained his lack of relatives and friends by the fact that he was one hundred years old, and they had died from one cause or another and that anyway they would have been dead by now for reasons of age. Few people were lucky enough to survive everything, year after year.

Julius said that his specialty was *enemies*, not friends. He would like to deepen his friendship with Allan, Benny, and The Beauty, but now wasn't really the time or place.

The Beauty admitted that she had been extremely antisocial during the years following her divorce, so for her too there was nobody to contact and ask for help.

That left Benny. He had a brother, didn't he? The angriest brother in the world.

Julius wondered whether they could bribe the brother, and then Benny's face lit up. They did have millions in the suitcase! They might not be able to bribe him, because Bosse was more proud than greedy. But now they were getting into semantics. And Benny had the solution. He would tell his brother that he wanted to do the right thing after all these years.

Having worked that out, Benny phoned his brother and didn't manage to do more than say who he was before he was informed that Bosse had a loaded shotgun and that his little brother was welcome to visit if he wanted a load of pellets up his butt.

Benny said that such a fate was not something he desired, but that he—together with some friends—planned to visit anyway, because he wished to settle their financial dealings. There was, you might say, a certain disagreement between the two brothers over Uncle Frasse's money.

Bosse replied that his brother should stop expressing himself in such a bloody complicated way. And then he got straight to the point:

—How much have you got with you?

—What about three million? asked Benny.

Bosse said nothing for a few moments. He was thinking the situation over. He knew his brother well enough to feel certain that Benny would never call and joke about something like that. My little brother is filthy rich! Three million! Absolutely fantastic! But . . . perhaps he even had more?

—What about four million? Bosse tried.

But Benny had decided once and for all that he would never allow his big brother to steamroll him again, so he said:

—We can of course stay at a hotel instead, if you think we are too much trouble.

Bosse said that his little brother had never been any trouble. Benny and his friends were heartily welcome and if Benny wanted to settle the old differences with three million—or even three and a half if he felt like it—then that was just a plus.

Bosse gave Benny directions to his house; he thought it would take them a couple of hours to get there.

Everything seemed to be working out for the best. And now the road was going to be both wide and straight.

That was just what the Boss needed too, a wider and straighter road. For ten minutes, he had been stuck behind the bus while the BMW had been telling him that he hadn't filled up with gas since Stockholm, but when had he had time?

The nightmare he feared was running out of gas there in the middle of the forest and not being able to do anything except just look on as the yellow bus disappeared in the distance, perhaps with Bolt and Bucket and the suitcase or whoever and whatever it happened to contain.

So the Boss acted with the energy and drive that he thought became a boss of a criminal club in Stockholm. He put his foot down on the accelerator, and in a second had passed the bus, continuing for another 150 yards before he put the BMW in a controlled skid and stopped, so his car now blocked the road. Then he pulled out his revolver and prepared to meet the vehicle he had just overtaken.

The Boss was of a more analytical bent than his now-dead or emigrated assistants. The idea of using his car to block the road and force the bus to stop originated of course from the fact that he was about to run out of gas. But the Boss had also made the completely correct assumption that the bus driver would choose to stop. His conclusion was based on his belief that in general people do not deliberately ram other people on the roads, risking the lives and health of both.

And indeed, Benny stood on the brakes as soon as he saw the BMW. The Boss had been right—about that, anyway.

But in his calculations, he had failed to take into account the risk that the bus's load might include an elephant weighing in at several tons. Had he done so, he would then have considered the effect this might have on the bus's braking distance, not least bearing in mind that they were still on a gravel road.

Benny really did do his very best to avoid a collision, but his speed was still almost thirty miles per hour when the fifteen-ton bus, elephant and all, torpedoed the car in its path, upon which the car was thrown up into the air and flung twenty yards, landing hard against an eighty-year-old fir tree.

—That was probably number three, Julius guessed.

All the two-legged passengers in the bus jumped out (easier for some than for others) to inspect the demolished BMW.

Hanging over the steering wheel, looking suspiciously dead, was a man the friends did not know, and he was still holding a revolver of exactly the same make as thug number two had threatened them with earlier that day.

—They must have thought that three is the charm, said Julius. They can think again.

Benny lamely objected to Julius's light tone. Surely it was

enough to kill one thug a day, but today they had already reached two and it wasn't yet six in the evening. There was time for more if they were unlucky.

Allan proposed that they hide corpse number three some-where because no good at all could come of being too closely as-sociated with people you have done away with, unless you wanted to admit to people that you've done away with them and Allan didn't think that the friends had any reason to do that.

Upon which, The Beauty started shouting angrily at the corpse slumped over the steering wheel, her theme being how the hell he could have been so stupid as to position his car across the road like that.

The corpse responded by gurgling weakly and moving one of his legs. . . .

The only plan that made sense to Chief Inspector Aronsson was to continue his journey in the same direction Boss Gerdin had taken just over half an hour earlier. There was of course no hope of catching up with the Never Again leader, but something inter-esting might turn up on the road. Besides, Växjö wasn't so very far away, and the chief inspector needed to find a hotel so he could think through the situation and get a few hours' sleep.

After some time, Aronsson spotted the wreck of a new BMW X5 wrapped round a fir tree. At first, Aronsson wasn't surprised that Gerdin had crashed, considering the speed with which he had left Lake Farm. But a closer look suggested a different story.

First, the car was empty. It was full of blood on the driver's seat, but there was no driver anywhere to be seen.

Second, the right-hand side of the car seemed to be unnatu-rally dented, and here and there were signs of yellow paint. Some-thing big and yellow had rammed the car at full speed.

—For example, a yellow 1992 Scania K113, Chief Inspector Aronsson murmured to himself.

This was hardly a difficult inference to make, and it became easier when it turned out that the registration plate of the yellow Scania was firmly impressed into the right back door of the BMW. Aronsson only had to compare the numbers and letters with what the Vehicle Licensing Authority said about the change of ownership to have his suspicions confirmed.

Chief Inspector Aronsson still couldn't fathom what was actually going on. But one thing seemed more and more clear, however incredible: centenarian Allan Karlsson and his entourage seemed to be pretty accomplished at killing people and then spiriting away their corpses.

THIRTEEN

1947–1948

Allan had most certainly experienced more comfortable nights than those he spent lying on his stomach in the back of a truck on the road to Tehran. It was cold, and there was no specially treated goats' milk to warm him up. And that would have been difficult anyway because his hands were tied behind his back.

No wonder Allan felt pleased when the journey was over. It was late afternoon when the truck stopped outside the main entrance of a large brown building in the middle of the capital.

Two soldiers helped the stranger to his feet and brushed off the worst of the dirt. Then they loosened the ropes that had tied Allan's hands and picked up their rifles to guard him.

If Allan had mastered Persian, he would have been able to read where he had ended up on a little yellow sign by the entrance. But he couldn't. And he couldn't care less. More important to him was whether anyone was going to serve breakfast. Or lunch. Or preferably both.

But, of course, the soldiers knew exactly where they had brought the suspected communist. And when they pushed Allan through the doors, one of the soldiers said good-bye to Allan with a grin and a "good luck" in English.

Allan thanked him for the good wishes even though he realized they were meant ironically, and then he thought that he probably needed to pay attention to his surroundings now.

The officer in the group that had arrested Allan formally handed his prisoner over to somebody of equivalent rank. When Allan was properly registered, he was moved to a holding cell down a nearby corridor.

The holding cell was pure Shangri-La compared with what Allan had been used to recently. Four beds in a row, double blankets on each bed, an electric light in the ceiling, a washbasin with running water in one corner, and in the other an adult-size bucket with a lid. Allan also received a decent-size bowl of porridge and a whole quart of water to satisfy his hunger and quench his thirst.

Three of the beds were unoccupied, but in the fourth lay a man on his back, with his hands clasped and his eyes closed. When Allan arrived, the man woke from his slumber and got up. He was tall and thin and had a white clerical collar, a contrast to his otherwise black clothing. Allan held out his hand to introduce himself and said that unfortunately he didn't know the local language. Did the clergyman perhaps speak a word or two of English?

The man in black explained that he did, since he was born and bred in Oxford, and educated there too. He introduced himself as Kevin Ferguson, an Anglican pastor who had been in Iran for twelve years searching for lost souls to recruit to the true faith. And where did Mr. Karlsson stand?

Allan answered that in a purely physical sense he was lost, since he had no control of where he stood, but that didn't mean he was spiritually lost. Allan had always reasoned about religion that if you couldn't know for sure then there was no point in going around guessing.

Allan saw that Father Ferguson was about to embark on a longer sermon, so he quickly added that the pastor should be so kind as to respect Allan's sincere wish to avoid becoming an Anglican, or for that matter anything else.

Father Ferguson wasn't a man who took a no for a no. Nevertheless, he hesitated just this once. Perhaps he shouldn't be too eager to convert against his will the only person—besides God—who might be able to save him from his dire situation.

Father Ferguson settled for a compromise. He made a half-hearted attempt to suggest that it wouldn't hurt Mr. Karlsson if the pastor could at least shed some light upon the Trinity. That happened to be the first of the thirty-nine articles in the Anglican creed.

Allan answered that the pastor couldn't begin to appreciate just how uninterested Allan was in that Trinity.

—Of all the groupings here on Earth, I would think that the Trinity is the one I am least interested in, said Allan.

Father Ferguson thought that was so stupid that he promised he would leave Karlsson in peace as far as religion was concerned, "even though God must have had some purpose in placing us in the same cell."

Instead, he turned to the matter of his and Allan's plight.

—It doesn't look good, said Father Ferguson. We might both of us be on our way to meeting the Creator, and if I hadn't just promised not to, I would add that it might be high time for you to embrace the true faith.

Allan looked sternly at the cleric, but said nothing. The pastor explained that they were now both in the holding cell of the department for domestic intelligence and security: in other words, the secret police. Perhaps Mr. Karlsson thought that sounded safe and good, but the truth was that the secret police cared only about the Shah's security, and their purpose was actually to keep the Iranian populace suitably terrified and respectful, and whenever possible to hunt down and destroy socialists, communists, Islamists, and other disturbing elements.

—Such as Anglican pastors?

Pastor Ferguson answered that Anglican pastors didn't have anything to fear, because they had freedom of religion in Iran. But that this particular Anglican pastor had probably gone too far.

—The prognosis is not good for somebody who ends up in the clutches of the secret police, and for my part I am afraid that this is the last stop, said Father Ferguson and suddenly looked very sad.

Allan immediately found himself feeling sorry for his cell mate, even though he was a cleric. He said consolingly that they would probably find a way to get out, but that there was a time for everything. First of all he wanted to know what the pastor had done to find himself in this pickle.

Father Kevin Ferguson sniffed and pulled himself together. It wasn't that he was afraid to die, he explained, he just thought that he had so much more to do here on our Earth. The pastor had always put his life in the hands of God, but if Mr. Karlsson, while they were waiting for God to decide, could find a way out of this, then the pastor was certain that God would not be offended.

Then the pastor told his story. The Lord had spoken to him in a dream when the pastor had just finished his studies. "Go out into the world to do missionary work," the Lord had said, but then he hadn't said any more so the pastor himself had to decide where to go.

An English friend and bishop had tipped him off about Iran—a country where the existing freedom of religion was grossly abused. For example, you could count the Anglicans in Iran on the fingers of only a few hands, but the place was seething with Shiites,

Sunnis, Jews, and folk who adhered to pure mumbo-jumbo religions. To the extent that there were any Christians at all, they were Armenians or Assyrians.

Allan said that he hadn't known that, but now he did, and he thanked the pastor for the information.

The pastor went on. Iran and Great Britain were on good terms and with the help of the Church's highly placed contacts the pastor had managed to get a lift to Tehran on an official British airplane.

This was more than ten years earlier, around 1935. Since then, he had worked his way through religion after religion, in a growing ring around the capital. At first he concentrated on the various religious ceremonies. He sneaked into mosques, synagogues, and temples of every kind and waited for a suitable moment before he quite simply interrupted the ceremony and with the help of an interpreter preached the true faith.

Allan praised the pastor for his courage but said he had some doubts about his mental abilities. Surely these visits had rarely ended well?

Father Ferguson conceded that in fact they had not ended successfully on a single occasion. He had never been able to have his full say. He and the interpreter had been thrown out and usually both of them had been knocked about too. But none of this had prevented the pastor from continuing his struggle. He knew that he was planting tiny Anglican seeds in the souls of all the people he met.

In the end, however, the reputation of the pastor had spread so far and wide that it became difficult to find interpreters who would work with him.

So the pastor took a break and put more effort into studying Persian. While doing so, he worked out how to refine his tactics and one day he felt so comfortable in the language that he launched his new plan.

Instead of going to temples and services, he visited markets where he knew that the teachings he considered false had a lot of followers among the shoppers, and he would stand on a wooden box and preach.

This method had not resulted in as many beatings as during his first years, but the number of souls saved was still not at all what Father Ferguson had hoped for.

Allan asked by how many converts Father Ferguson had fallen short of his target, and was told that it depended on how you looked at it. On the one hand, Father Ferguson had exactly one convert from every religion he had worked on, which amounted to eight in all. On the other hand, he had realized a few months ago that all eight could actually be spies from the secret police, sent out to keep track of the missionary pastor.

—Between zero and eight genuine converts, then, said Allan.

—Probably closer to zero than eight, answered Father Ferguson.

—In twelve years, said Allan.

The pastor admitted that he had become discouraged when he realized that his already meager results were actually even more meager. And he also realized that he would never succeed in this country, because however much the Iranians might like to convert, they wouldn't dare. The secret police were everywhere and if someone changed his religion a dossier would definitely be created with his name in their archives. And from a dossier in the archives to disappearing without trace was rarely a long step.

Allan said that, in addition, it might be the case that an Iranian or two—whatever Father Ferguson might think—went around generally satisfied with their current religion, couldn't he see that?

The pastor answered that he had rarely heard such ignorant talk, but that he was prevented from providing a proper answer because he had promised Mr. Karlsson he would eschew all Anglican preaching. Could Mr. Karlsson listen to the rest of the pastor's story without interrupting more than necessary?

Father Ferguson went on to describe how, with his newly acquired insights as to the manner in which the secret police had infiltrated his missionary work, he had started to think in new ways. He had started to think big.

So the pastor shook off his eight possible spying disciples, and contacted the underground communist movement. He told them he was a British representative for the True Faith and he wanted to meet them to discuss the future.

It took time to get a meeting arranged, but he eventually found himself sitting with five gentlemen from leading communist circles in the province of Razavi Khorasan. He would have preferred to meet the Tehran communists because Father Ferguson thought that they probably made the important decisions, but this meeting would do for starters.

Or not.

Pastor Ferguson presented his big idea to the communists. In brief, that Anglicanism would become the state religion in Iran the day the communists took over. If the communists went along with this, Father Ferguson promised to accept the job of government minister of religion and ensure that right from the beginning there would be enough Bibles for everyone. The churches could be built afterward, but to start with, the synagogues and mosques—which would have been closed by decree—could be used. There was just one thing Father Ferguson wanted to know: how long did the gentlemen think it would be before the communist revolution?

The communists had not reacted with the enthusiasm, or even curiosity, that Father Ferguson had expected. Instead, he was told in no uncertain terms that there wouldn't be any Anglicanism or for that matter any other sort of -ism besides communism when the day came. In addition, he got a loud telling-off for having requested this meeting under false pretenses. The communists had never experienced such a dreadful waste of time.

With a vote of 3–2 in favor, it was then decided that Father

Ferguson would be given a good beating before being put on the
train back to Tehran, and with a unanimous vote it was decided
that it would be best for the pastor's health if he didn't come
back.

Allan smiled and said that—with permission—he in no way
could eliminate the possibility that the pastor was completely mad.
To bring about a religious agreement with the communists was,
of course, quite hopeless. Didn't the pastor understand that?

The pastor answered that heathens like Mr. Karlsson would do
well not to judge what was wise or unwise. But of course he *had*
understood that there was little chance of success.

—But just think, Mr. Karlsson, if it had actually worked. Just
think of being able to send a telegram to the Archbishop of Can-
terbury and report fifty million new Anglicans all at once.

Allan admitted that the difference between madness and ge-
nius was subtle, and that he couldn't with certainty say which it
was in this case, but that he had his suspicions.

Be that as it may, it turned out that the Shah's cursed secret
police were bugging the Razavi Khorasan communists, and Father Ferguson was picked up as soon as he got off the train in the
capital, and taken in for questioning.

—And I admitted everything and a bit more besides, said
Father Ferguson, because my thin body is not created to withstand
torture. A good beating is one thing, but torture is something
else.

With that immediate and exaggerated confession, Father Ferguson had been transported to this holding cell, and he had been
left in peace for two weeks because the head of the secret police,
the vice prime minister, was on a business trip to London.

—The vice prime minister? Allan wondered.

—Yes, or the boss of the murderers, said Father Ferguson.

It was said of the secret police that no organization was more
controlled from the top. Putting fear in the hearts of the popula-

tion on a more routine basis, or killing communists, socialists, or Islamists—these of course didn't require the blessing of the boss. But as soon as something happened that was the slightest bit out of the ordinary, then it was he who decided. The Shah had given him the title vice prime minister, but in effect he was a murderer, in Father Ferguson's opinion.

—And according to the prison guards, you'd better forget the "vice" bit of his title when you address him, if things go so badly that you need to meet him, which they seem to be doing in both your case and mine.

Perhaps the pastor had spent more time with underground communists than he cared to admit, thought Allan, because he went on:

—Ever since the end of the Second World War, the American CIA has been here and has built up the Shah's secret police.

—CIA? said Allan.

—Yes, that's what they are called now. They were the OSS before, but it's the same dirty business. They're the ones who have taught the Iranian police all the tricks and tortures. What can he be like, the man who allows the CIA to destroy the world in this way?

—You mean the American president?

—Harry S. Truman will burn in hell, believe you me, said Father Ferguson.

—You think so? said Allan.

The days passed. Allan had told his own life story to Father Ferguson, without leaving anything out at all. And after this, the pastor stopped talking to Allan because he realized what sort of relationship his cell mate had to the American president and—even worse—to the bombs over Japan.

Instead, the pastor turned to God and prayed for advice. Was it the Lord who had sent Mr. Karlsson to help him, or was it the Devil who lay behind it?

But God answered with silence. He did that sometimes, and Father Ferguson always interpreted it to mean that he should think for himself. Admittedly, it didn't always work out well when the pastor thought for himself, but you couldn't just give up.

After two days and two nights of deliberation, Pastor Ferguson came to the conclusion that for the time being he should make his peace with the heathen in the next bed. And he informed Allan that he now intended to speak to him again.

Allan said that although it had been nice and quiet while the pastor kept silent, it was probably preferable in the long run that when one man spoke, the other answered.

—Besides, we're going to try to get out of here, and it would perhaps be best if we can do so before the murder boss gets back from London. So we can't just sit, grumpily, in our corners, can we?

Father Ferguson agreed. When the murder boss came back, they would probably face a short interrogation and then simply disappear. That was what Father Ferguson had heard happened.

The holding cell was not in a real prison, with all the security and locks that went with that. On the contrary, the guards sometimes didn't even bother to lock the door properly. But there were never fewer than four guards at the building's entrance and exit, and they were unlikely to just stand and stare if Allan and the pastor tried to slip out.

Would it be possible to create some sort of tumult or distraction? Allan wondered. And then sneak out in the midst of the general disarray?

Allan wanted peace to work, and he therefore assigned the pastor the task of finding out from the guards how long they had. That is, exactly when would the murder boss be back?

The pastor promised to ask as soon as he got an opportunity.

Perhaps even right away, because there was a rattling sound at the door. The youngest and kindest of the guards stuck his head in and with a sympathetic look said:

—The *prime minister* is back from England and it's time for questioning. Which of you wants to go first?

The head of the department of domestic intelligence and security was in a dreadful mood.

He had just been to London where he had been told off by the Brits. He, the prime minister (well, as good as), head of a government department, one of the most important elements of the Iranian society, had been told off by the Brits!

The Shah did nothing but make sure that the arrogant Englishmen were kept happy. The oil was in the hands of the Brits, and he himself made sure they weeded out everybody and anybody who tried to bring about change in the country. And that was no easy matter, because who was really satisfied with the Shah? Not the Islamists, not the communists, and definitely not the local oil workers who literally worked themselves to death for the equivalent of one British pound a week.

And for this he had now been told off, instead of being praised!

The secret police chief knew he had made a mistake when a while ago he had been a little heavy-handed with a provocateur of unknown origin. The provocateur had demanded to be set free because the only thing he was guilty of was insisting that the line in the butcher's shop should be for everyone, not just employees in the state's secret police.

When the provocateur had put forward his case, he folded his arms and refused to answer any more questions. The police chief didn't like the look of the provocateur (it was indeed provocative), so he made use of a couple of the CIA torture methods (the police chief admired the inventiveness of the Americans). It was only at that point that it transpired that the provocateur was an assistant secretary in the British Embassy and that, of course, was most unfortunate.

The solution was first to tidy up the assistant as best they could, then let him go, but only so that he could immediately be run over by a truck, which then disappeared from the scene. That is how you avoid diplomatic crises, the police chief reasoned, pleased with himself.

But the Brits picked up what was left of the assistant secretary, and sent all the pieces to London where they went through them with a magnifying glass. After which the police chief was summoned by the Brits and asked to explain how the assistant secretary suddenly turned up on a street outside the head office of the secret police and was immediately so drastically run over that marks of the torture he had previously been subjected to were barely visible.

The police chief had of course firmly denied all knowledge of the affair; this was how the diplomatic game worked, but the assistant secretary happened to be the son of some lord or other who in turn was a good friend of the recent prime minister, Winston Churchill, and now the Brits were going to take a firm stand.

As a result of all this, the department for domestic intelligence and security had now been relieved of responsibility for the visit that same Winston Churchill was to make to Tehran in just a couple of weeks. Instead, the amateurs in the Shah's own bodyguard would take care of the visit, which was of course far beyond their competence. This was a major loss of prestige for the police chief. And it estranged him from the Shah in a way that did not feel good.

To dispel his bitter thoughts, the police chief had summoned the first of the two enemies of the state that were said to be waiting in the holding cell. He anticipated a short interrogation, a quick and discreet execution, and a traditional cremation of the corpse. Then lunch and in the afternoon he would probably have time for the other enemy of the state too.

A*llan Karlsson had volunteered to be first. The police chief met him* at the door of his office, shook hands, asked Mr. Karlsson to have a seat, and offered him a cup of coffee and a cigarette.

Though he had never met a murder boss before, Allan had assumed that they would be more unpleasant of manner than this murder boss seemed to be. And then he thanked him for the coffee and asked if it would be OK with Mr. Prime Minister if he declined the cigarette.

The police chief always chose to start his interrogations in a civilized manner. Just because you were soon going to kill someone, you didn't have to behave like a bumpkin. Besides, it amused the police chief to see how a flutter of hope rose in the eyes of his victims. People in general were so naive.

This particular victim didn't look so terrified, not yet. And he had addressed the police chief in the manner in which he liked to be addressed—an interesting and positive beginning.

During the interrogation, Allan—lacking a well-thought-out survival strategy—provided selected episodes from the later part of his life story: namely that he was an expert on explosives who had been sent by President Harry S. Truman on an impossible mission to China to combat the communists, and he had subsequently started his long walk home to Sweden and that he now regretted that Iran had lain in the way of that walk, and that he had been obliged to enter the country without the requisite visa, but that he now promised to leave the country immediately if Mr. Prime Minister would just let him do so.

The police chief asked him a lot of supplementary questions, not least why Allan Karlsson was in the company of Iranian communists when he was arrested. Allan answered truthfully that he and the communists had met by chance and agreed to help each other across the Himalayas. Allan added that if Mr. Prime Minister planned a similar walk, then he shouldn't be too fussy about whose help he accepted because those mountains were dreadfully high when they were in the mood for it.

The police chief didn't have any plans to cross the Himalayas on foot, nor did he intend to set Allan free. But perhaps he could make some use of this explosives expert with his international experience before letting him disappear for good? With a voice that perhaps sounded a little too keen, the police chief asked Mr. Karlsson what experience he had with secretly killing people who were famous and well guarded.

Allan had never done that sort of thing, to sit and consciously plan to kill a person as if you were blowing up a bridge. And he had no wish to do so either. But now he had to think ahead. Could this chain-smoking murder boss have something special in mind?

Allan searched his memory and in his haste found nothing better than:

—Glenn Miller.

—Glenn Miller? the police chief repeated.

Allan could remember from his time at Los Alamos a couple of years earlier how shocked everyone had been on hearing the news that the young jazz musician Glenn Miller was missing after his U.S. Army Air Forces plane had disappeared off the coast of England.

—Exactly, Allan confirmed with a hush-hush tone. It was supposed to look like an accident and I succeeded in that. I made sure both engines burned up, and he crashed somewhere in the middle of the English Channel. Nobody has seen him since. A fitting fate for a defector to the Nazis, if you ask me, Mr. Minister.

—Was Glenn Miller a Nazi? asked the astonished police chief.

Allan nodded in confirmation (and silently apologized to all of Glenn Miller's surviving family). The police chief, for his part, tried to accustom himself to the news that his great jazz hero had been running errands for Hitler.

Now Allan thought it was perhaps best to take charge of the

conversation before the murder boss asked a lot of other question about what happened to Glenn Miller.

—If Mr. Prime Minister so wishes, I am prepared to get rid of anybody, with maximum discretion of course, in exchange for us then parting as friends.

The chief of police was still shook up after the sad unmasking of the man behind "Moonlight Serenade," but that didn't mean that he was anyone's fool. He certainly wasn't planning to negotiate about Allan Karlsson's future.

—If I want you to get rid of somebody, you will do as you are told. And it is just *possible* that I will *consider* letting you live, said the police chief as he leaned across the table to stub out his cigarette in Allan's half-full coffee cup.

—Yes, that is what I meant, of course, said Allan, although I expressed myself a little vaguely.

This particular morning's interrogation had turned out differently from what the police chief was used to. Instead of getting rid of an enemy of the state, he had adjourned the meeting to accustom himself to the new situation in peace and quiet. After lunch, the police chief and Allan Karlsson met again and plans were laid.

The intention was to kill Winston Churchill while he was being protected by the Shah's own bodyguard. But it must happen in such a way that nobody could find any possible link to the department for domestic intelligence and security, let alone to its boss. Since it could safely be assumed that the Brits would investigate the event with extreme attention to detail, there must be no slip-ups. If the project succeeded, the consequences in every possible way would be to the police chief's advantage.

First and foremost it would shut those arrogant Brits up, the Brits who had taken away the police chief's responsibility for the security arrangements during the visit. And furthermore, the police chief would most certainly be entrusted with sorting out the bodyguard, after its failure. And when the smoke had cleared, the police chief's standing would be greatly strengthened, instead of what it was now—weakened.

The police chief and Allan worked out a plan as if they were best friends, although the police chief did stub out his cigarette in Allan's coffee every time he felt the atmosphere became too intimate.

The police chief told Allan that Iran's only bulletproof motor car was in the department's garage in the cellar below them. It was a specially built DeSoto Suburban. It was wine-red and very stylish, the police chief said. There was the greatest likelihood that the Shah's bodyguard would soon request the car, to transport Churchill from the airport to the Shah's palace.

Allan said that a well-proportioned explosive charge on the car's chassis might be the solution to the problem. But bearing in mind Mr. Prime Minister's need not to leave any clues that could lead back to him, Allan proposed two special measures.

One was that the explosive charge should consist of exactly the same ingredients that Mao Tse-tung's communists used in China. This was something Allan knew a lot about, and he was certain that he could make it all look like a communist attack.

The other measure was that the charge in question should be hidden in the front part of the DeSoto's chassis, but that it should not detonate immediately but be designed to drop from the car and explode a few tenths of a second later when it hit the ground.

During that time the car would have traveled a short distance so that the position where Winston Churchill would be sitting and smoking his cigar would now be directly above the explosion, which would rip a hole in the floor of the car and send Churchill to eternity. It would also leave a large crater in the ground.

—In this way we'll get people to think the explosive charge was buried in the street instead of somebody having hidden it in the car. The little deception would surely suit Mr. Prime Minister perfectly?

The police chief giggled with joy and anticipation, and flicked a lighted cigarette into Allan's newly poured coffee. Allan said that Mr. Prime Minister could do as he wished with his cigarettes and with Allan's coffee, but that if he really wasn't satisfied with the ashtray he had in front of him, and if Mr. Minister would consider giving Allan a short period of leave, then he would go out and buy a nice new ashtray for the Prime Minister.

The police chief ignored Allan's talk about ashtrays, but immediately approved Allan's explosive plan and asked for a complete list of what he needed to prepare the car in the shortest possible time.

Allan listed the names of the nine ingredients that he needed to make up the formula. In addition, he included a tenth—nitroglycerin—which he thought might be useful, and an eleventh—a bottle of ink.

Furthermore, Allan asked to borrow one of Mr. Prime Minister's most trusted colleagues as an assistant and a purchasing manager, and to have his cell mate, Father Ferguson, as his interpreter.

The police chief muttered that what he would like most of all was to do away with the pastor straightaway, because he didn't like clerics, but now there wouldn't be time. Yet again he stubbed out his cigarette in Allan's coffee, to indicate that the meeting was at an end and to remind Allan who was boss.

The days passed, and everything went according to plan. The boss of the bodyguard did indeed get in touch and announce that he would pick up the DeSoto the following Wednesday. The police chief boiled with anger. It had been an announcement rather than a request. But in fact, it fit perfectly with Allan's plan. What if the bodyguard hadn't contacted the department about the car? And in any case, the boss of the bodyguard would soon get his comeuppance.

Allan now knew how much time he had to prepare the charge. Unfortunately, Father Ferguson had also eventually fathomed what was going on. Not only was he going to be an accomplice in the murder of former prime minister Churchill, but he also had good reason to believe that his own life would end shortly afterward. To stand before the Lord as a murderer was not something Father Ferguson looked forward to.

But Allan calmed the pastor, promising that he had a plan to solve both those problems. First, there was a good chance that Allan and the pastor would be able to escape, and second, it need not necessarily happen at the cost of Mr. Churchill's life.

But the whole scheme required the pastor to do what Allan said when the right moment arrived, and the pastor promised to do so. Allan was his only hope of survival, since God still wasn't answering his prayers. And it had been like that for almost a month now. Could God possibly be angry with the pastor for his attempt to ally himself with the communists?

Wednesday arrived. The DeSoto was rigged and ready. The explosive charge on the car's chassis happened to be rather larger than the task demanded, and yet it was still completely hidden, if anyone were to look to see if there was anything strange there.

Allan showed the police chief how the remote control worked, and explained in detail what the final result would be when it went off. The police chief smiled and looked happy. And stubbed out that day's eighteenth cigarette in Allan's coffee.

Allan then pulled out a new cup, one that he had kept hidden behind the toolbox, and placed that strategically beside the table next to the stairs leading to the corridor, the holding cell, and the entrance. Without making a fuss of it, Allan then took the pastor by the arm and left the garage, while the police chief walked round and round the DeSoto, puffing on the day's nineteenth cigarette, delighting in the thought of what would soon happen.

The pastor understood from Allan's firm grasp that this was for real. Time to obey Mr. Karlsson to the letter.

They walked past the holding cell and continued toward reception. Once there, Allan didn't bother to stop by the armed guards, but continued right past them, still keeping a firm hold on the pastor.

The guards had become accustomed to Karlsson and the pastor and they had not thought there was any risk of an escape attempt, so it was with some surprise that the officer in charge called out:

—Halt! Where do you think you are going?

Allan stopped with the pastor on the very threshold to freedom and looked very surprised.

—We are free to go. Hasn't Mr. Prime Minister informed you?

Father Ferguson was terrified, but forced a little oxygen into his nostrils so as not to faint.

—Stay exactly where you are, said the officer in charge, in an authoritative tone. You are not going anywhere until I have Mr. Prime Minister's confirmation.

The three guards were ordered to keep a careful eye on the pastor and Mr. Karlsson, while the officer in charge went down the corridor to the garage to ask for confirmation. Allan smiled encouragingly at the pastor and said that soon everything would be sorted out—unless the opposite happened and it all blew up.

Since first the police chief had not given Allan and the pastor permission to leave, and, second, did not have any plans to do so, he reacted forcefully to the officer's query.

—What? They're standing by the entrance and brazenly lying? They are bloody well going to pay for that. . . .

The police chief rarely swore. He had always been careful to keep a certain dignity about him. But now he was furious. And as was his custom, he stubbed his cigarette into that damned Karlsson's coffee cup, before heading for the stairs.

Or rather, that was his intention, but he didn't get any farther than the coffee cup. Because this time it didn't contain coffee, but pure nitroglycerin mixed with black ink. There was a huge explosion and the vice prime minister and the officer in charge of the guards were ripped to bits. A white cloud billowed out of the garage and made its way along the corridor at the other end of which Allan, the pastor, and the three guards stood.

—Time to go, Allan said to the pastor. And off they went.

All three guards were sufficiently alert to think that they really ought to stop Karlsson and the pastor from leaving, but only a few tenths of a second later—and as a logical consequence of the garage now being a sea of fire—the charge under the DeSoto, the one intended for Winston Churchill, also detonated. And in so doing, it proved to Allan that it would have amply served its intended purpose. The entire building immediately leaned over, and the ground floor was in flames when Allan changed his order to the pastor:

—Let's run out of here, instead.

Two of the three guards had been blown into a wall by the pressure wave and had caught on fire. The third found it impossible to gather his thoughts sufficiently to attend to his prisoners. For a few seconds, he wondered what had happened, but then he ran away to avoid ending up like his comrades. Allan and the pastor had gone off in one direction. The only remaining guard now ran off in the other.

After Allan in his own special way had arranged for himself and the pastor to be somewhere other than the headquarters of the secret police, it was now the pastor's turn to be useful. He knew where most of the diplomatic missions were located and he guided Allan all the way to the Swedish Embassy. Once there, Allan gave him a warm hug to thank him for everything.

Allan asked what the pastor himself was going to do. Where was the British Embassy?

It wasn't far away, said the pastor, but why would he need to go there? They were all Anglicans already. No, the pastor had thought up a new strategy. If there was something the last hour or so had taught him, it was that everything seemed to start and finish at the department for domestic intelligence and security. So it was a matter of changing that organization from the inside. Once all the people working for the secret police, and all those who helped them, were Anglicans—well, the rest would be easy as pie!

Allan said that he knew of a good asylum in Sweden if in the future the pastor should happen to come to some sort of self-understanding. The pastor answered that he didn't want to appear ungrateful, not in any way. But he had once and for all found his calling, and now it was time for him to say good-bye. The pastor was going to start with the surviving guard, the one who ran off in the other direction. He was basically a nice, easygoing boy, and he could probably be led down the path of the true faith.

—Farewell! said the pastor solemnly and walked off.

—Bye for now, said Allan.

He watched the pastor vanish into the distance, and thought that the world was crazy enough that the pastor might survive the course he was now taking.

But Allan was wrong. The pastor found the guard wandering around in a daze in the Park-e Shahr in the middle of Tehran, with burns on his arms and an automatic with the safety catch off in his hands.

—Well, there you are, my son, said the pastor and walked up to embrace him.

—You! shouted the guard. It's you!

And then he shot the pastor twenty-two times in the chest. It would have been more but he ran out of bullets.

Allan was allowed into the Swedish Embassy because of his regional Swedish accent. But then things got complicated, because he didn't have any documentation that proved who he was. So the embassy could not give him a passport, nor could they help him back to Sweden. Besides, said Third Secretary Bergqvist, Sweden had just introduced special personal identity numbers and if it was the case that Karlsson had been out of the country for many years, then there would be no Mr. Allan Karlsson in the Swedish system back home.

To that, Allan answered that regardless of whether all Swedes' names had now become numbers instead, he was and would remain Allan Karlsson from the village of Yxhult outside Flen and now he wanted Mr. Third Secretary to be so kind as to arrange papers for him.

Third Secretary Bergqvist was for the time being the most senior official at the embassy. He was the only one who hadn't been able to attend the diplomatic conference in Stockholm. It was just his luck that everything suddenly happened at once. It wasn't enough that some parts of the center of Tehran had been on fire for the last hour: now on top of that an unknown person turns up claiming to be Swedish. There were of course hints that the man was telling the truth, but this was a situation where it was important to follow the rules so as not to jeopardize his future career. So Third Secretary Bergqvist repeated his statement that no passport would be forthcoming unless Mr. Karlsson could be properly identified.

Allan said that he found Third Secretary Bergqvist to be exceptionally stubborn, but that they could perhaps solve everything if only the third secretary had a telephone available.

The third secretary did. But it was expensive to make long-distance phone calls. Whom did Mr. Karlsson intend to phone?

Allan was beginning to tire of the difficult third secretary so he didn't answer, but instead asked:

—Is Per Albin still the Swedish prime minister?

—No, said the astounded third secretary. Tage Erlander is prime minister. Prime Minister Hansson died last autumn. But why. . . .

—Could you please be quiet for a moment so we can clear this up?

Allan phoned the White House in Washington, and was put through to the president's senior secretary. She remembered Mr. Karlsson very well and she had also heard so many good things about him from the president and if Mr. Karlsson really considered it important then she would see if they could wake the president. It was only eight in the morning in Washington, you see, Mr. Karlsson, and President Truman was not an early riser.

A short while later the newly awoken President Truman came to the phone and he and Allan had a hearty chat for several minutes, catching up with each other's news before Allan finally mentioned his errand. Could Harry possibly do him a favor and phone the new Swedish Prime Minister Erlander and vouch for who Allan was, so that Erlander in turn could phone Third Secretary Bergqvist at the Swedish Embassy in Tehran and inform him that Allan should immediately be issued a passport.

Harry Truman would of course do this for him, but first please spell the third secretary's name so that he got it right.

—President Truman wants to know how you spell your name, Allan said to Third Secretary Bergqvist. It would be easier if you told him directly.

After Third Secretary Bergqvist, almost in a trance, spelled out his name letter by letter for the president of the United States, he replaced the receiver and didn't say anything for eight minutes. Which was exactly how long it took before Prime Minister Erlander phoned the embassy and ordered Third Secretary Bergqvist to 1) immediately issue a passport with diplomatic status to Allan Karlsson, and 2) without delay arrange to get Mr. Karlsson back to Sweden.

—But he hasn't got a personal identity number, Third Secretary Bergqvist attempted.

—I suggest that you, Third Secretary, solve that problem, said Prime Minister Erlander. Unless you wish to become the fourth or fifth secretary instead. . . .

—There is no such thing as a fourth or fifth secretary, the third secretary attempted.

—And what conclusions do you draw from that?

War hero Winston Churchill had somewhat unexpectedly lost the British elections in 1945, the British people's gratitude having run out.

But Churchill planned his revenge and marked time by traveling the world. The former prime minister suspected that the Labour incompetent who now governed Great Britain would introduce a planned economy at the same time as handing over the Empire to people who couldn't administer it.

Take British India for example, which was now on its way to falling to bits. Hindus and Muslims could not get along, and in the middle sat that damned Mahatma Gandhi with his legs crossed, having stopped eating because he was dissatisfied with something. What sort of war strategy was that? How far would they have gotten with such a strategy against the Nazi bombing raids over England?

It was not quite as bad in British East Africa, not yet, but it was only a matter of time before the Africans also wanted to become their own masters.

Churchill understood that not everything could remain as it was, but nevertheless the Brits needed a commander who could announce what was needed, and do so with authority. They did not need a sneaky socialist like Clement Atlee.

As regards India, the battle was lost, Churchill knew that. It had been developing that way for many years, and during the war it had been necessary to send signals about future independence to the Indians so that in the midst of the struggle for survival the British would not also have to deal with a civil war.

But in many other places there was still plenty of time to stop the process. Churchill's plan for the autumn was to travel to Kenya and evaluate the situation. But first he would drop in on Tehran and drink tea with the Shah.

He had the misfortune to land amid chaos. The day before, something had exploded at the department for domestic intelligence and security. The entire building had collapsed and burned up. The idiot of a police chief had evidently died in the explosion too, the same man who had previously been clumsy enough to use his harsh methods on innocent British Embassy staff.

The police chief was no great loss, but apparently the Shah's only bulletproof car had been consumed by the flames too, and this led to a much shorter meeting between the Shah and Churchill than had first been envisaged, and for reasons of security it took place at the airport.

Nevertheless, it was a good thing that the visit came off. According to the Shah the situation was under control. The explosion at the headquarters of the secret police was something of a bother, and so far they couldn't say anything about the cause. The fact that the police chief had died in the explosion the Shah could live with. The man had begun to lose his touch.

So they had a stable political situation. They were about to appoint a new chief of the secret police. And they were seeing record results for the Anglo-Iranian Oil Company. Oil provided fantastic wealth to both England and Iran. Mainly England, if the truth be told, but that was only fair because Iran's sole contribution to the project was cheap labor—and of course the oil itself.

—Mainly peace and prosperity in Iran then, Winston Churchill said to the Swedish military attaché who had been assigned a place in the plane on the way back to London.

—Glad to hear that you are satisfied, Mr. Churchill, Allan answered, adding that he thought Churchill was looking well.

A llan finally landed at Stockholm's Bromma airport, after a stopover in London, and stood on Swedish soil for the first time in eleven years. It was late December 1948, and the weather was the usual for that time of year.

In the arrivals hall, a young man was waiting for Allan. He said he was Prime Minister Erlander's assistant and that the PM wished to meet Allan as soon as possible, if that could be arranged.

Allan thought it could, and he willingly followed the assistant who proudly invited Allan to sit in the brand-new government car, a black, shiny Volvo PV444.

—Have you ever seen anything as swank, Mr. Karlsson? asked the assistant who was interested in cars. Forty-four horsepower!

—I saw a really nice wine-red DeSoto last week, Allan answered. But your car is in better condition.

The drive took Allan to the center of Stockholm and he looked around him with interest. To his shame, he had never been in the capital before. It was a beautiful city indeed, with water and bridges everywhere, and none of them had been blown up.

The prime minister welcomed Allan with a "Mr. Karlsson! I have heard so much about you!," upon which he pushed the assistant out of the room and closed the door.

Allan didn't say so, but he realized that he himself had heard nothing whatsoever about Tage Erlander. Allan didn't even know if the prime minister was Left or Right. He must certainly be one of them, because if there was one thing life had taught Allan, it was that people insisted on being either one or the other.

Anyway, the prime minister could be whichever he liked. Now it was a question of hearing what he had to say.

The prime minister had, it transpired, called President Truman back and had a longer conversation about Allan. So now he knew all about . . .

But then the prime minister stopped talking. He had been in

THE ONE HUNDRED YEAR OLD MAN   177

the job less than a year and there was a lot left to learn. He did, however, already know one thing: in certain situations it was best not to know or at least best not to leave any way of proving that you knew what you knew.

So the prime minister never finished his sentence. What President Truman had told him about Allan Karlsson would be forever a secret between them. Instead the prime minister came straight to the point:

—I understand that you don't have anything to come back to here in Sweden, so I have arranged a cash payment for services rendered to the nation . . . in a manner of speaking. . . . Here are ten thousand crowns for you.

And the prime minister handed over a thick envelope full of banknotes and asked Allan to sign a receipt. Everything had to be by the book.

—Thank you very much, Mr. Prime Minister. It occurs to me that with this fine and generous contribution I will be able to afford new clothes and clean sheets at a hotel tonight. Perhaps I'll even be able to brush my teeth for the first time since August 1945. . . .

The prime minister interrupted Allan just as he was about to describe the condition of his underpants, and informed him that the money was of course without any conditions, but that since some activities connected to nuclear fission were being carried out in Sweden at this time, the prime minister would like Mr. Karlsson to have a look.

The truth was that Prime Minister Erlander had inherited a number of important issues when his predecessor's heart had stopped the previous autumn, and he had no idea what to do about them. For example: what stance should Sweden take with regard to something called an atom bomb. The commander in chief had been telling him about how the country must defend itself against communism, since they only had little Finland between Sweden and Stalin.

There were two sides to the question. On the one hand, the

commander in chief happened to marry into a rich upper-class family and it was generally known that he sometimes drank a bit of the hard stuff with the old Swedish King. But Social Democrat Erlander couldn't stand the idea that Gustav V might even imagine that he could influence Swedish defense policy.

On the other hand, Erlander could not exclude the possibility that the C-in-C might be right. You couldn't trust Stalin and the communists, and if they should get it into their heads to widen their sphere of interest westward, then Sweden was unpleasantly close.

Sweden's military research department had just moved its few nuclear energy specialists to the newly created AB Atomic Energy. Now the experts who sat there were trying to figure out exactly what had happened at Hiroshima and Nagasaki. In addition, their mission in more general terms was to "analyze the nuclear future from a Swedish perspective." It was never spelled out, but Prime Minister Erlander had understood that the vaguely formulated task—had it been put in plain language—would have read:

How the hell do we build our own atom bomb, if necessary?

And now the answer was sitting right across from the prime minister. Tage Erlander knew that, but above all he knew that he didn't want anybody else to know he knew. Politics was about watching where you put your feet.

So the previous day, Prime Minister Erlander had contacted the head of research at AB Atomic Energy, Dr. Sigvard Eklund, and asked him to invite Allan Karlsson for a job interview during which he could thoroughly question him as to whether he could be of use in AB Atomic Energy's activities—assuming that Mr. Karlsson was interested.

Dr. Eklund was not at all pleased with the prime minister involving himself in the atom project. He even suspected that Allan Karlsson might be a Social Democrat spy. But he promised to interview Karlsson, even though, oddly, the prime minister would not say anything about the man's qualifications. Erlander had just emphasized the word "thoroughly" when he said that Dr. Eklund ought to *thoroughly* question Mr. Karlsson about his background.

Allan, for his part, said that he had nothing against meeting Dr. Eklund or any other doctor, if that would please the prime minister.

Ten thousand crowns was an almost excessive amount of money, Allan thought, and checked in at the most expensive hotel he could find.

The receptionist at the Grand Hôtel had his doubts about the dirty and badly dressed man until Allan showed proof of his identity with a Swedish diplomatic passport.

—Of course we have a room for you, Mr. Military Attaché, sir, the receptionist announced. Would you like to pay cash or should we send the bill to the Foreign Ministry?

—Cash would be fine, said Allan. Did he want payment in advance?

—Oh, no, Mr. Attaché, sir. Of course not! The receptionist bowed.

If the receptionist had been able to look into the future, he would most certainly have answered differently.

The next day, Dr. Eklund welcomed a newly showered and more-or- less well-dressed Allan Karlsson to his Stockholm office. The doctor offered him coffee and a cigarette, just as the murder boss in Tehran used to do. (Eklund, however, stubbed his cigarettes out in his own ashtray.)

Doktor Eklund was unhappy with the way the prime minister had interfered with Eklund's recruiting process. And Allan, for his part, felt the negative vibe in the room and for a moment was reminded of the first time he met Soong Mei-ling. People could do what they wanted, but Allan considered that in general it was quite unnecessary to be grumpy if you had the chance not to.

The meeting between the two men was short:

—The prime minister has asked me to question you thoroughly, Mr. Karlsson, to ascertain whether you would be suited to work in our organization. And that is what I shall do, with your permission, of course!

Yes, that's fine. Allan thought it was quite in order for the Mr. Doctor to want to know more about Allan and thoroughness was a virtue, so the Mr. Doctor should simply ask away.

—Well, then, said Dr. Eklund. If we can begin with your studies . . . ?

—Not much to boast of, said Allan. Only three years.

—Three years!? exclaimed Doktor Eklund. With only three years of academic studies, Mr. Karlsson, you can hardly be a physicist, mathematician, or a chemist?

—No, three years altogether. I left school after my tenth birthday.

Doktor Eklund made an effort to retain his composure. So the man didn't have any education! Could he even read and write?

—Do you, Mr. Karlsson, have any professional experience that might be seen as relevant for the work that you might assume we carry out here at AB Atomic Energy?

Well, yes, in a manner of speaking, Allan did. He had worked for a while in the USA, at Los Alamos in New Mexico.

Now Dr. Eklund's face lit up. Erlander might have had his reasons after all. What had been achieved at Los Alamos was general knowledge. What had Mr. Karlsson worked on there?

—I served coffee, Allan answered.

—Coffee? Dr. Eklund's face darkened again.

—Yes, and on occasion tea too. I was a general assistant and waiter.

—Were you ever involved in any decisions at all that were connected to nuclear fusion?

—No, Allan answered; the closest I came was probably that

time I happened to say something at a meeting when I was really meant to be serving coffee.

—So Mr. Karlsson happened to say something at a meeting where he in fact was a waiter . . . and then what happened?

—Well, we were interrupted . . . and then I was asked to leave the room.

Dr. Eklund was utterly dumbfounded. Did the prime minister think that a waiter who had dropped out of school before he was ten years old could be put to use to build atom bombs for Sweden?

Dr. Eklund thought that it would be a sensation if this beginner of a prime minister would even last the year out, then he said to Allan that if Mr. Karlsson had nothing to add then their meeting could end now. Dr. Eklund did not think that at present there was any opening for Mr. Karlsson. It was true that the assistant who made the coffee for the academics at AB Atomic Energy had never been to Los Alamos, but Dr. Eklund thought that she nevertheless managed to do a good job. Besides, Greta even found time to clean the offices and that must be seen as a plus.

Allan sat there in silence for a moment, and wondered whether he ought to point out to the doctor that, unlike all of Dr. Eklund's academics, and probably Greta too, he actually knew how to build an atom bomb.

But then Allan decided that Dr. Eklund didn't deserve his assistance if he hadn't the sense to ask the question. Besides, Greta's coffee tasted like dishwater.

*A*llan didn't get a job at AB Atomic Energy, his qualifications being seen as woefully inadequate. But he felt a quiet satisfaction as he sat on a park bench outside the Grand Hôtel, with a nice view of the Royal Palace across the water. And how could he feel otherwise? He still had most of the money that the prime minister had been so kind as to give him. He had been staying in a fancy hotel for a while now. He ate in a restaurant every evening, and on this particular early January day he sat with the sun in his face and felt how it warmed his body and soul.

Of course, it was a bit cold for his bottom, and so it was a little surprising when a man sat down right next to Allan.

Allan greeted him with a polite "Good afternoon" in Swedish.

—Good afternoon, Mr. Karlsson, the man answered in English.

FOURTEEN

Monday, May 9, 2005

W hen *Chief Inspector Aronsson reported his findings to Prosecutor* Conny Ranelid in Eskilstuna, the prosecutor immediately decided to issue a warrant for the arrest of Allan Karlsson, Julius Jonsson, Benny Ljungberg, and Gunilla Björklund.

Aronsson and the prosecutor in charge of the case had been in close touch ever since the centenarian climbed out of the window and disappeared, and the prosecutor's interest had continued to grow. Now he was reflecting upon the spectacular possibility of getting Allan Karlsson convicted for murder, or at least manslaughter, even though they hadn't found any victims. There were one or two cases in Swedish legal history that showed it could be done. But you needed exceptionally good evidence and an extremely skillful prosecutor. The latter was no problem for Prosecutor

Conny Ranelid, and as for the former he intended to construct a chain of circumstantial evidence, where the first link would be the strongest and no link would be really weak.

Chief Inspector Aronsson felt a little disappointed at the way things had developed. It would have been much more fun to save a geriatric from the clutches of a gang of criminals, rather than—as now—failing to save the criminals from the geriatric.

—Can we really prove that Allan Karlsson and the others were involved in Bylund's, Hultén's, and Gerdin's deaths when we still don't have any corpses? asked Aronsson, hoping that the answer would be "no."

—Don't sound so downcast, Göran, said Prosecutor Conny Ranelid. You'll see; that old fool will spill the beans as soon as you catch him for me. And if he is too senile, I'm sure the others will contradict one another and that'll give us all we need.

And then the prosecutor went through the case again with his chief inspector. First he explained the strategy. He didn't think they would be able to lock up all of them for murder, but there were still other charges—manslaughter, or assistance to commit this and that felony, or causing a death, or protecting a criminal. Even offenses against the law concerning corpses could come into play, but the prosecutor would need a bit of time to think that through.

Since some of the suspects got involved in the events later than others, and would be more difficult to convict, the prosecutor intended to focus on the man who had been in the thick of it all the whole time, the centenarian Allan Karlsson.

—In his case, I think we will be able to manage a life sentence in the true meaning of the word, Prosecutor Ranelid joked.

To start with, the old man had a motive for killing Bylund, Hultén, and Gerdin. The motive was that otherwise he risked the opposite—that Bylund, Hultén, and Gerdin would do away with him. The prosecutor had evidence that the three men from the Never Again organization had a tendency to resort to violence.

But that didn't mean that the old man could claim he acted in self-defense, because between Karlsson on the one side and the three victims on the other there was a suitcase with contents unknown to the prosecutor. From the very beginning the suitcase was clearly at the center of events, so the old man had actually had an alternative to killing the others—he could have refrained from stealing the suitcase, or at least given it back.

Furthermore, the prosecutor could point to several geographical connections between Mr. Karlsson and the victims. The first victim had, just like Mr. Karlsson, gotten off the bus at Byringe Station, even though it hadn't been at the same time. And, unlike Mr. Karlsson and his companion, victim number one had not been seen after the inspection trolley journey. However, "someone" had become a corpse and left a trail behind him. It seemed obvious who this was. Both the old man and the petty thief Jonsson had demonstrably been alive later that same day.

The geographical connection between Karlsson and victim number two was not quite as strong. They had not been observed together. But a silver Mercedes on the one hand, and a forgotten revolver on the other told Prosecutor Ranelid—and would soon tell the court—that Mr. Karlsson and victim Hultén, the one who was called Bucket, had both been at Lake Farm in Småland. Hultén's fingerprints on the revolver were not yet confirmed, but the prosecutor felt that was purely a matter of time.

The sudden appearance of the revolver was a gift from above. Besides the fact that it would prove that Bucket Hultén had been at Lake Farm, it strengthened the motive for killing victim number two.

As far as Karlsson was concerned, they now had the fantastic discovery of DNA to make use of. The old man would of course have spread it around everywhere. So now the prosecutor had the formula: Bucket + Karlsson = Lake Farm!

DNA would also be used to ascertain that the blood in the crashed BMW belonged to victim number three, Per-Gunnar

Gerdin, also known as the Boss. They would soon be able to carry out a more thorough examination of the demolished car, and that would certainly reveal that Karlsson and his companions had been there too and put their fingers on everything. How otherwise would they have got the corpse out of the car?

So the prosecutor could show a motive and a connection in time and space between Allan Karlsson on the one hand and all three dead thugs on the other.

The chief inspector risked asking whether the prosecutor could be certain that all three victims really were victims, that is, were actually dead? Prosecutor Ranelid sniffed and said that as far as number one and number three were concerned, they hardly needed any further explanation. As for number two, Ranelid would have to put his faith in the court—because when they accepted that number one and number three had indeed passed on, then number two would end up as a link in the famous chain of circumstantial evidence.

—Or are you suggesting, Chief Inspector, that number two quite voluntarily handed over his revolver to the people who had just killed his friend, before tenderly saying good-bye and leaving without waiting for the arrival of his boss a few hours later? asked Prosecutor Ranelid in an acid tone.

—No, I guess not, said the chief inspector, defensively.

The prosecutor admitted to Chief Inspector Aronsson that the case might be a little thin, but what really held it together was the chain of events. The prosecutor didn't have a murder weapon (except for the yellow bus). But the plan was to get Karlsson convicted for victim number one to begin with.

—At the very least, I'll get the old man locked up for man-slaughter or for being an accessory. And once I've got him convicted, then the others will fall with him—to varying degrees, but they will fall!

The prosecutor could not really arrest people on the grounds that during interrogation they would contradict each other so much that he would be able to hold them in custody. Nevertheless, that was plan B, because they were amateurs, the lot of them. A centenarian, a petty thief, a hot-dog-stand proprietor, and a woman: how the hell would they be able to withstand the pressure in an interrogation room?

—Make your way to Växjö, Aronsson, and check in at a decent hotel. I'll leak the news this evening that the centenarian is a veritable murder machine and early tomorrow morning you'll get so many tips about where he is that you'll be able to pick him up before lunch, I promise.

FIFTEEN

Monday, May 9, 2005

—*Here are your three million, dear brother. I would also like to take this* opportunity to apologize for how I behaved in connection with the money from Uncle Frasse.

Benny got straight to the point when he met Bosse for the first time in thirty years. He handed over a bag with the money before they even had time to shake hands. And he went on, in a serious voice, while his brother was still catching his breath:

—And now I'll tell you two things. The first is that we need your help, because we have created a real mess. And the second is that the money I have given you is yours, and you deserve it. If you have to send us packing then you can do so, the money is yours regardless.

The brothers stood in the light of the one still-functioning

headlight on the yellow bus, outside the entrance to Bosse's substantial residence, Bellringer Farm, on the Västgöta plain just a
few miles southwest of the little town of Falköping. Bosse gathered his wits as best he could, and then said he had some questions, if that was okay? And on the basis of the answers he promised
that he would then decide about any possible hospitality. Benny
nodded.

—Okay, said Bosse. This money you've just given me, is it hon-
estly gotten by?

—Definitely not, said Benny.

—Are the police after you?

—Presumably thieves and policemen, said Benny. But mainly
thieves.

—What happened to the bus? The front is all smashed in.

—We rammed a thief at full speed.

—Did he die?

—No, unfortunately. He's lying in the bus with a concussion,
broken ribs, a broken arm, and a big open wound on his right
thigh. His condition is serious but stable, as they say.

—You've brought him with you?

—Yes, it's as bad as that.

—Is there anything else I need to know?

—Well, perhaps that we killed a couple of other thieves on the
way, buddies of the half-dead one in the bus. They insisted on trying to get back the fifty million that happened to come into our
hands.

—Fifty million?

—Fifty million. Minus various expenses—for this bus, among
other things.

—Why are you driving around in a bus?

—We've got an elephant in the back.

—An elephant?

—She's called Sonya.

—An elephant?

—Asiatic.

—An elephant?

—An elephant.

Bosse was silent for a few moments. Then he said:

—Is the elephant stolen too?

—No, you couldn't really say that.

Bosse was silent again. Then he said:

—Grilled chicken with roast potatoes for supper. Would that be good?

—I am sure it would, said Benny.

—Does that include something to drink? said an elderly voice from inside the bus.

When it transpired that the corpse was still alive in the middle of his wrecked car, Benny immediately ordered Julius to go and fetch the first aid kit from behind the driver's seat in the bus. Benny said that he knew that he was causing them trouble but that with his being an almost-doctor he also had to think of his almost-doctor's ethics. It was thus unthinkable to leave the corpse sitting there to bleed to death.

Ten minutes later, they were on their way. The half-corpse had been eased out of the car wreck, Benny had examined him, made a diagnosis, and with the help of the first aid kit administered relevant medical care; above all, he had made sure that the heavy bleeding from the half-corpse's thigh was stopped.

Upon which Allan and Julius had to move into the back of the bus and join Sonya, to allow room for the half-corpse to lie across the backseat in the driver's cabin, with The Beauty as nurse on duty. Benny had already checked that the victim's pulse and blood pressure were in reasonable order. With an appropriate dose of morphine, Benny had also ensured that he could sleep despite all his injuries.

As soon as it became clear that the friends really were welcome to stay with Bosse, Benny examined his patient afresh. The half-corpse was still sleeping deeply, and Benny decided that they should wait to move him.

Then Benny joined the group in Bosse's spacious kitchen. While their host busied himself with a meal, the friends—one after the other—described the dramatic course of the last few days. Allan first, then Julius, after that Benny with a bit of help from The Beauty, and then Benny again when they came to the ramming of thug number three's BMW.

Although Bosse had just heard in detail how two people had lost their lives, and how the course of events had been concealed in a way that contravened Swedish law, there was just one thing he wanted them to confirm:

—Now, if I've understood you correctly . . . you've got an elephant in the bus.

—Yes, but tomorrow morning she needs to be let out, said The Beauty.

Otherwise, Bosse didn't find much to comment upon. The law often says one thing, while morality leads to a different conclusion, in his opinion, and he didn't think he needed to look further than his own small-scale activities to find examples of how the law can be set to one side as long as you hold your head high.

—A bit like how you dealt with our inheritance, except the other way round, Bosse happened to say to Benny.

—Oh yeah, who smashed up my new motorbike? Benny countered.

—But that was because you dropped out of the welding course, said Bosse.

—And I did that because you lorded it over me all the time, said Benny.

Bosse looked as if he had the answer to Benny's answer to

Bosse's answer, but Allan interrupted the two brothers by saying that he had been out and about in the world and if there was one thing he had learned it was that the very biggest and apparently most impossible conflicts on earth were based on the dialogue: "You are stupid, no, it's you who are stupid, no, it's you who are stupid." The solution, said Allan, was often to down a bottle of vodka together and then look ahead. But now there was an unfortunate problem in that Benny was a teetotaler. Allan could, of course, look after Benny's share of the vodka, but he didn't think it would be quite the same thing.

—So a bottle of vodka would solve the Israel-Palestine conflict? asked Bosse. That stretches all the way back to the Bible.

—For the particular conflict you mention, it is not impossible that you would need more than one bottle, Allan answered. But the principle is the same.

—Would it work if I drink something else? asked Benny, feeling—with his total abstinence—as if he was destroying the world.

Allan was pleased with the development. The argument between the brothers had lost its poison. He remarked on this, and added that the vodka in question, for that very reason, could be used for other things than solving conflicts.

The liquor would have to wait, Bosse said, since the food was ready. Chicken straight from the grill and roast potatoes with beer for the grown-ups and a soft drink for his little brother.

While they were starting their dinner in the kitchen, Per-Gunnar "Boss" Gerdin woke up. He had a headache, it hurt when he breathed, one arm was probably broken because it was in a sling, and when he struggled down from the bus's cabin, a wound in his right thigh began to bleed. Amazingly he found his own revolver in the glove compartment. It would seem that all the people in the whole world were idiots apart from him.

The morphine was still effective, so he could cope with the pain, but it also made it hard for him to sort out his thoughts. He limped about in the yard and peered in through various windows, until he was certain that all the people in the house were gathered together in the kitchen, including an Alsatian dog. And, it turned out, the kitchen door to the garden was unlocked. The Boss limped in through the door, and with considerable determination and the revolver in his left hand, said:

—Lock the dog in the pantry, otherwise I'll shoot it. After that I've got five bullets left, one for each of you.

The Boss was surprised how well he was keeping his anger under control. The Beauty looked unhappy rather than afraid when she led Buster into the pantry and closed the door. Buster was surprised and a bit worried, but above all satisfied. He discovered he had just been shut inside a pantry, and there are worse things to do to a dog.

The five friends were now lined up. The Boss informed them that the suitcase in the corner belonged to him, and that he was going to take it with him when he left. It was possible that he would leave one or two of the five alive, depending on their answers to his questions, and on how much of the contents of the suitcase had disappeared.

Allan was the first to speak. He said that a few million were indeed missing from the suitcase, but that Mr. Revolver Man could perhaps be satisfied with less, since for various reasons two of the revolver man's colleagues had died and that meant there were fewer people to share with.

—Are Bolt and Bucket dead? asked the Boss.

—Pike?! Bosse suddenly exclaimed. It is you, Pike. It's been a long time!

—Bosse Baddy! exclaimed Per-Gunnar "Pike" Gerdin in return.

And Bosse Baddy and Pike Gerdin met with a hug in the middle of the kitchen floor.

—I do believe I'll survive this too, said Allan.

Buster was let out of the pantry, Benny dressed "Pike" Gerdin's bleeding injury, and Bosse Baddy set another place at the table.

—Just a fork will do, said Pike; I can't use my right arm anyway.

—You used to be a dab hand with a knife in the old days, said Bosse Baddy.

Pike and Bosse Baddy had been close friends, and also colleagues in the food trade. Pike had always been the impatient one, the one who wanted to go that bit further. In the end they had gone their separate ways when Pike insisted that the friends should import Swedish meatballs from the Philippines, treated with formalin to increase their best-before date from three days to three months (or three years depending on how generously you applied the formalin). Bosse had said "stop" at that point. He didn't want to be involved with preparing food with stuff that could kill people. Pike thought Bosse was exaggerating. People didn't die from a few chemicals in their food, and with formalin it would surely be the opposite.

The friends separated amicably. Bosse moved to Västergötland, while Pike tried his hand at robbing a firm of importers and was so successful that he set aside his meatball plans and decided to become a full-time robber.

At first, Bosse and Pike had been in touch once or twice a year, but over the years they had gradually drifted apart—until that evening when Pike was suddenly standing unsteadily in Bosse's kitchen, just as threatening as Bosse remembered he could be when he was in the mood.

But Pike's anger subsided the moment he found the companion and comrade of his youth. He sat down at the table together with Bosse Baddy and his friends. It couldn't be helped that they had killed Bolt and Bucket. They could sort out the business with the suitcase and everything else the next day. For the moment they were going to enjoy their dinner.

—Cheers! said Per-Gunnar "Pike" Gerdin and fainted, his face landing right in his food.

They wiped the food off Pike's face, moved him to the guest room, and put him to bed. Benny checked his medical state and then gave the patient a new dose of morphine so he would sleep until the next day.

Upon which it was at last time for Benny and the others to enjoy the chicken and roast potatoes. And enjoy it they did!

—This chicken really is delicious! Julius praised the food, and they all agreed that they had never eaten anything tastier. What was the secret?

Bosse told them that he imported fresh chickens from Poland ("no junk, top-quality stuff"), and then he injected every chicken manually with up to one quart of his own special spicy water mixture. Then he repackaged them, and with all that he had added locally he thought he could just as well call them "Swedish."

—Twice as good on account of the spicy mixture, twice as heavy on account of the water, and twice as popular on account of the Swedish origin, was how Bosse summed it up.

Suddenly it had become a big business, despite the fact that he had started off on a really small scale. And everybody loved his chickens. But for reasons of security, he didn't sell to any of the wholesalers in the district, because one of them might come by and discover that there wasn't a single chicken out pecking in Bosse's farmyard.

That was what he meant by the difference between law and morality, Bosse said. The Poles were surely no worse at feeding hens and then killing them than the Swedes? Quality had nothing to do with national boundaries, did it?

—People are just stupid, Bosse maintained. In France, French meat is best. In Germany, German meat. The same thing in Sweden. So for everybody's benefit, I keep some information to myself.

—That is thoughtful of you, said Allan, without irony.

Bosse said that he had done something similar with the watermelons he also imported, although not from Poland. They came from Spain or Morocco. He preferred to call them Spanish because nobody would believe that they came from Skövde in the middle of Sweden. But before he sold them, he injected half a quart of sugar solution into each melon.

—That makes them twice as heavy—good for me!—and three times as tasty—good for the consumer!

—That is also thoughtful of you, said Allan. Still without irony.

The Beauty thought that there must be one or two consumers who for medical reasons should not gobble down a half quart of sugar solution, but she didn't say anything. Besides, the watermelon tasted almost as heavenly as the chicken.

*C*hief Inspector Göran Aronsson sat in the restaurant at the Hotel Royal Corner in Växjö and ate chicken cordon bleu. The chicken, which didn't come from Västergötland, was dry and tasteless. But Aronsson washed it down with a bottle of good wine.

By now, the prosecutor would surely have whispered in some reporter's ear, and the next day the pack of journalists would be out in force again. Prosecutor Ranelid was probably right in assuming that there would be lots of tipoffs about the whereabouts of the yellow bus with the smashed front. While he was waiting for them, Aronsson might as well stay where he was. He had nothing else to do: no family, no close friends, not even a sensible hobby. When this strange chase was over, he was definitely going to have his life overhauled.

Chief Inspector Aronsson ended the evening with a gin and tonic, and while he drank, he sat there feeling sorry for himself and fantasized about pulling out his service pistol and shooting the pianist in the bar. If he had managed to stay sober and carefully thought through what he already knew, the story would most certainly have developed differently.

That same evening in the editorial offices of the Express they had a short linguistic discussion before deciding on the billboards for the next day. In the end, the head of the news desk decided that one dead person could be murder, two dead people could be double murder, but three dead people could not be called mass murder as some of his colleagues wanted to. But he managed a nice headline in the end:

MISSING
CENTENARIAN
SUSPECTED OF
TRIPLE MURDER

They had a late evening at Bellringer Farm with one and all in very good spirits. Amusing stories were trotted out one after the other. Bosse was a hit when he pulled out the Bible and said that now he would tell them the story of how he, quite involuntarily, came to read the whole book from beginning to end. Allan wondered what devilish method of torture Bosse had suffered, but that wasn't what lay behind it. No outsider had forced Bosse to do anything, No, Bosse's own curiosity was responsible.

—I'm sure I'll never be that curious, said Allan.

Julius asked whether Allan could stop interrupting Bosse for once so that they could hear the story, and Allan said that he could. Bosse went on:

One day some months earlier he had received a phone call

from an acquaintance at the recycling center outside Skövde. The two of them had gotten to know each other at the racetrack. This acquaintance had learned that Bosse's conscience was flexible and that Bosse was always interested in opportunities that might provide new sources of income.

The recycling center had just received a pallet with half a ton of books that were to be pulped, because they had been classified as waste and not as literature, presumably because of some defect. Bosse's acquaintance had become curious as to what sort of literature it was, and he had opened the packaging only to find a Bible (his acquaintance had been hoping for something of a totally different kind).

—But this wasn't just your standard Bible, said Bosse, and passed a specimen around so they could see for themselves. We are talking ultrathin in genuine leather with golden lettering and stuff. . . . And just look at this: a list of characters, maps in color, an index. . . .

His acquaintance had been just as impressed as his friends now were, and instead of pulping the goodies, had phoned Bosse and offered to smuggle the books out of the recycling center in exchange for . . . say one thousand crowns.

Bosse jumped at the chance, and that very same afternoon he found himself with a half a ton of fancy Bibles in his barn. But try as he might, he couldn't find anything wrong with the books. It was driving him crazy. So one evening he sat down in front of the fire in the living room and started to read, from "In the beginning . . ." onward. To be on the safe side, he had his old confirmation Bible for reference. There must be a misprint somewhere, otherwise why would they throw out something so beautiful and . . . holy?

Bosse read and read, evening after evening, the Old Testament followed by the New Testament, and still he read on, comparing it with his old confirmation Bible—without finding anything wrong.

Then one evening he reached the last chapter, and then the last page, the last verse.

And there it was! That unforgivable and unfathomable misprint that had caused the owner of the books to order them to be pulped.

Now Bosse handed a copy to each of them sitting round the table, and they thumbed through to the very last verse, and one by one burst out laughing.

Bosse was happy to know that the misprint was where it actually was. He had no interest in finding out how it got there. He had satisfied his curiosity, and in the process had read his first book since his school days, and even gotten a bit religious while he was at it. Not that Bosse allowed God to have any opinion about Bell-ringer Farm's business enterprise, nor did he allow the Lord to be present when he filed his tax return, but—in other respects—Bosse now placed his life in the hands of the Father, the Son, and the Holy Spirit. And surely none of them would worry about the fact that he set up his stall at markets on Saturdays and sold Bibles with a tiny misprint in them? ("Only ninety-nine crowns each! Jesus! What a bargain!")

But if Bosse had cared, and if, against all odds, he had managed to get to the bottom of it, then after what he had told his friends, he could have gone on:

A typographer in a Rotterdam suburb had been through a personal crisis. Several years earlier, he had been recruited by the Jehovah's Witnesses but they had thrown him out when he discovered and rather too loudly questioned the fact that the congregation had predicted the return of Jesus on no less than fourteen occasions between 1799 and 1980—and sensationally managed to get it wrong all fourteen times.

Upon which, the typographer had joined the Pentecostal Church; he liked their teachings about the Last Judgment, he could embrace the idea of God's final victory over evil, the return of Jesus (without their actually naming a date), and how most of the people from the typographer's childhood including his own father, would burn in hell.

But this new congregation sent him packing too. A whole month's collections had gone astray while in the care of the typographer. He had sworn by all that was holy that the disappearance had nothing to do with him. Besides, shouldn't Christians forgive? And what choice did he have when his car broke down and he needed a new one to keep his job?

As bitter as bile, the typographer started the layout for that day's jobs, which ironically happened to consist of printing two thousand Bibles! And besides, it was an order from Sweden where, as far as the typographer knew, his father still lived after having abandoned his family when the typographer was six years old.

With tears in his eyes, the typographer arranged chapter upon chapter in the special software they used at the printing works. When he came to the very last chapter—the Book of Revelation—he just lost it. How could Jesus ever want to come back to Earth? Here where Evil had once and for all conquered Good, so what was the point of anything? And the Bible . . . It was just a joke!

So it came about that the typographer with the shattered nerves made a little addition to the very last verse in the very last chapter in the Swedish Bible that was just about to be printed. The typographer didn't remember much of his father's tongue, but he could at least recall a fairy tale that was well suited in the context. Thus the Bible's last two verses plus the typographer's extra verse were printed as:

20. He who testifies to these things says, Surely I am coming quickly. Amen. Even so, come, Lord Jesus!
21. The grace of our Lord Jesus Christ be with you all. Amen.
22. And they all lived happily ever after.

The late evening became night at Bellringer Farm. Vodka as well as brotherly love had flowed freely and would probably have continued to do so if it wasn't for the fact that teetotaler Benny realized how late it was. He informed those present that it was high time that everyone went to bed. There were a lot of things that needed to be sorted out the following day, and it would be best for one and all to be rested.

—If I was of a more curious disposition, I'd be eager to see what sort of mood the man with his face in his food is going to be in when he wakes up, said Allan.

SIXTEEN

1948–1953

T he man on the park bench had just said good afternoon, Mr.
Karlsson, in English, and from that Allan drew two conclusions. First, that the man was not Swedish, otherwise
he would probably have tried speaking his own language. Second,
that he knew who Allan was, because he had just called him by his
name.

The man was smartly dressed, in a gray hat with a black rim, a
gray overcoat and black shoes. He could very well be a business-
man. He looked friendly and definitely had something in mind. So
Allan said, in English:

—Is my life, by any chance, about to take a new turn?

The man answered that such a change could not be ruled out,
but added in a friendly tone that it depended on Mr. Karlsson him-

self. The fact was, the man's employer wanted to meet Mr. Karlsson to offer him a job.

Allan answered that at the moment he was doing quite well, but, of course, he could not remain sitting on a park bench for the rest of his life. Was it too much to ask for the name of his employer? Allan found it easier to say yes or no to something if he knew what he was saying yes or no to. Didn't the man agree?

The man agreed completely, but his employer was a bit special and would probably prefer to introduce himself in person.

—But I am prepared to accompany you to the employer in question without the slightest delay, if that would suit you?

Why not, Allan said, it might suit him. The man added that it was some distance away. If Mr. Karlsson would like to collect his belongings from the hotel room, the man promised to wait in the lobby. In fact, the man could give Mr. Karlsson a lift back to the hotel, because the man's car with a chauffeur was right beside them.

A stylish car it was too, a red Ford sedan of the latest model. And a private chauffeur! He was a quiet type. Didn't seem nearly as friendly as the friendly man.

—I think we can skip the hotel room, Allan said. I am used to traveling light.

—No problem, said the friendly man and tapped his chauffeur on the back in a way that meant "drive off."

The journey took them out to Dalarö, just over an hour south of the capital on winding roads. Allan and the friendly man conversed about this and that. The friendly man explained the endless magnificence of opera, while Allan told him how you cross the Himalayas without freezing to death.

The sun had given up for the day when the red sedan rolled into the little village on the coast that was so popular with archipelago tourists in the summers, but as dark and silent as can be in the winters.

—So this is where he lives, your employer, said Allan.

—No, not exactly, said the friendly man.

The friendly man's chauffeur said nothing. He just dropped Allan and the friendly man off by the harbor and left. Before that, the friendly man had managed to get a fur coat out from the trunk of the Ford, and he put it around Allan's shoulders in a friendly gesture while apologizing for the fact that they would now have to walk a short way in the winter cold.

Allan was not one to pin his hopes (or, for that matter, his fears) on what might happen in the immediate future. What happened happened. There was no point second-guessing it.

Nevertheless, Allan was surprised when the friendly man led him away from the center of Dalarö and instead set off across the ice into the jet-black archipelago evening.

The friendly man and Allan walked on and on. Sometimes the friendly man turned his flashlight on and flashed it a bit in the winter darkness before using it to get the right bearing on his compass. He didn't talk to Allan during the entire walk, but instead just counted his steps aloud—in a language that Allan hadn't heard before.

After a fifteen-minute walk at quite a good pace out into the void, the friendly man said that they had now arrived. It was dark around them, except for a flickering light on an island far away. The ground (or rather, the ice) under the two men's feet suddenly broke up.

The friendly man had possibly counted incorrectly. Or the captain of the submarine hadn't been exactly in the place he should have been. Whatever the cause, the three-hundred-foot-long vessel now broke through the ice far too close to Allan and the friendly man. They both fell backward and almost ended up in the icy water. But soon Allan was helped to climb down into the warmth.

—Well, now you can see how sensible it is not to start your day by guessing what might happen, said Allan. After all, how long would I have had to go on guessing before I guessed this?

At this point, the friendly man thought that he didn't have to be so secretive any longer. He told Allan that his name was Yury Borisovich Popov and that he worked for the Union of Soviet Socialist Republics; that he was a physicist, not a politician or a military man; and that he had been sent to Stockholm to persuade Mr. Karlsson to follow him to Moscow. Yury Borisovich was chosen for this mission because of Mr. Karlsson's possible reluctance, which could perhaps be overcome by Yury Borisovich's background as a physicist, meaning that Mr. Karlsson and Yury Borisovich both spoke the same language, so to speak.

—But I am not a physicist, Allan said.

—That may be the case, but my sources tell me that you know something that I would like to know.

—I do? Whatever could that be?

—The Bomb, Mr. Karlsson. The Bomb.

Yury Borisovich and Allan Emmanuel immediately took a liking to each other. To agree to follow him without knowing where he was going or why—that impressed Yury Borisovich and indicated that there was something devil-may-care about Allan that Yury himself lacked. And as for Allan, well, he appreciated the fact that for once he could talk with somebody who didn't try to fill him with politics or religion.

Besides, it soon transpired that both Yury Borisovich and Allan Emmanuel shared a boundless enthusiasm for vodka. The previous evening Yury Borisovich had had the opportunity to taste the Swedish variety while he had been keeping an eye on Allan Emmanuel in the dining room at the Grand Hôtel. At first, Yury

Borisovich thought that it was too dry, without the Russian sweetness, but after a couple of glasses he got used to it. And another two glasses later, he let a "not bad at all!" pass through his lips.

—But this is of course better, said Yury Borisovich and held up a whole bottle of Stolichnaya. He and Allan Emmanuel sat and had the officers' mess to themselves. And now we shall each take a glass!

—Sounds good, said Allan. The sea air tires you out.

After the very first glass, Allan insisted on a change in the way the two men addressed each other. To say Yury Borisovich to Yury Borisovich every time he needed to attract Yury Borisovich's attention just wasn't practical in the long term. And he didn't want to be called Allan Emmanuelson, because he hadn't used his middle name since he was baptized by the priest in Yxhult.

—So from now on, you are Yury and I am Allan, said Allan. Otherwise I'm getting off this boat now.

—Don't do that, dear Allan, we are at a depth of seven hundred feet, said Yury. Fill your glass again instead.

Yury Borisovich Popov was a passionate socialist and wanted nothing more than to keep working in the name of Soviet socialism. Comrade Stalin was a stern man but Yury knew that if you served the system loyally and well then you had nothing to fear. Allan said that he didn't have any plans to serve any system, but that of course he could give Yury one or two tips if they had gotten stuck in working out the atom bomb problem. But first of all Allan wanted to taste another glass of the vodka whose name was unpronounceable even when you were sober. And another thing: Yury would have to promise that he would continue not to talk politics.

Yury thanked Allan heartily for his promise to help, and said straight off that Marshal Beria, Yury's boss, intended to give the Swedish expert a one-off payment of 100,000 American dollars, on condition that Allan's help led to the production of a bomb.

—We'll figure it out, said Allan.

The contents of the bottle shrank steadily while Allan and Yury talked about everything on heaven and earth (except politics and religion). They also touched upon the atom bomb problems and although the topic really belonged to the days to come, Allan decided to give him a couple of simple tips and then a couple more.

—Hmmm, said senior physicist Yury Borisovich Popov. I think I understand. . . .

—Well, I don't, said Allan. Explain the thing with opera again. Isn't it just a lot of shouting?

Yury smiled, took a large gulp of vodka, stood up—and started to sing. In his drunkenness he didn't just choose any old folk song, but instead the aria "Nessun Dorma" from Puccini's *Turandot*.

—That was quite something, said Allan when Yury had finished.

—"*Nessun dorma!*" said Yury solemnly. Nobody is allowed to sleep!

R*egardless of whether anybody was allowed to sleep or not, they did* both soon drop off in their berths beside the officers' mess. When they woke up, the submarine was already docked in Leningrad harbor. There, a limousine was waiting to take them to the Kremlin for a meeting with Marshal Beria.

—Saint Petersburg, Petrograd, Leningrad. . . . Couldn't you make up your mind? said Allan.

—And a good morning to you too, said Yury.

Y*ury and Allan got into the backseat of a Humber Pullman limousine* for a day-long journey from Leningrad to Moscow. A sliding window separated the driver's seat from the salon where Allan and his newfound friend were sitting. The salon also boasted a refrigerator with water, soft drinks, and all the alcohol that these two passengers were not in need of at the moment. There was also a bowl of red gummy candies and a whole tray of fancy chocolates. The car and its fittings would have been a brilliant example of Soviet socialist engineering if it hadn't all been imported from England.

Yury told Allan about his background. He had studied under Nobel Prize laureate Ernest Rutherford, the legendary nuclear physicist from New Zealand, which was why Yury Borisovich spoke such good English. Allan, in turn, described (to an increasingly astounded Yury Borisovich) his adventures in Spain, America, China, the Himalayas, and Iran.

—And what happened to the Anglican pastor? Yury wondered.

—I don't know, said Allan. He has either Anglicized all of Persia, or he's dead. The least likely is probably something in between those two.

—That sounds a bit like challenging Stalin in the Soviet Union, said Yury candidly. Setting aside the fact that it would be a crime against the revolution, the chance of survival is poor.

On this particular day and in this particular company, Yury's candidness seemed to know no bounds. He opened his heart about what he thought of Marshal Beria, the boss of the secret service who suddenly had become the head of the project to make an atom bomb. Beria had no sense of shame at all. He abused women and children sexually and as for undesirable people, well, he sent them to prison camps—if he hadn't had them killed first.

—Undesirable elements must of course be weeded out as soon as possible, but they must be undesirable on the correct, revolutionary grounds. Those who don't further the aims of socialism must be gotten rid of! But not those who don't further the aims of Marshal Beria. No! Allan, that is dreadful. Marshal Beria is no true representative of the revolution. But you can't blame comrade Stalin for that. I have never had the privilege of meeting him, but he has the responsibility for an entire country, almost an entire continent. And if amid all that work, and in a hasty moment, he gave Marshal Beria more responsibility than he is capable of shouldering . . . well, comrade Stalin has every right to do that! And now, my dear Allan, I shall tell you something really fantastic. You and I, this very afternoon, are going to be honored with an audience not only with Marshal Beria, but also with comrade Stalin in person! He has invited us to dinner!

—I look forward to that, said Allan. But how are we going to manage until then? Are we supposed to survive on red gummy candies?

Yury saw to it that the limousine stopped in a little town on the way, to pick up a couple of sandwiches for Allan. Then their journey continued.

Between bites of his sandwich, Allan thought about this Marshal Beria character who, from Yury's description, seemed to resemble the recently deceased boss of the secret service in Tehran.

Yury, for his part, sat there trying to figure out his Swedish colleague. The Swede would soon be eating dinner with Stalin, and he had said that he was looking forward to it. But Yury had to ask whether it was the dinner he meant, or the leader.

–You have to eat to live, Allan said diplomatically and praised the quality of the Russian sandwiches. But, dear Yury, would you allow me to ask a question or two?

—But of course, dear Allan. Ask away, I'll do my best to answer.

Allan said that to be honest he hadn't really been listening while Yury had been spouting on about politics just now, because politics was not what interested Allan most in this world. Besides, he did distinctly recall from the previous evening that Yury had promised not to sail off in that direction.

But Allan had made a note of Yury's description of Marshal Beria's human failings. Allan believed that in his earlier life he had come across people of the same type. On the one hand, if Allan had understood correctly, Marshal Beria was ruthless. On the other hand, he had now seen to it that Allan was extraordinarily well cared for, with a limousine and everything.

—But it does occur to me to wonder why he didn't simply have me kidnapped and then make sure that you wring out of me what he wants to know, said Allan. Then he wouldn't have had to waste the red gummy candies, the fancy chocolates, the hundred thousand dollars, and a lot of other stuff.

Yury said that what was tragic about Allan's observation was that it did have some relevance. Marshal Beria had more than once—in the name of the revolution—tortured innocent people. Yury knew that to be the case. But now the situation was, said Yury—who found it hard to say exactly what he meant—the situation was such that, said Yury—and opened the refrigerator to find a fortifying beer even though it wasn't even twelve noon yet—the situation was such that Marshal Beria had very recently failed with this strategy. A western expert had been kidnapped in Switzerland and taken to Marshal Beria, but it all ended in a dreadful mess. Yury apologized; he didn't want to get into the details, but Allan must believe what Yury had said: What had been learned from the recent failure was that the necessary nuclear advice, according to a decision from above, would be bought in the western market, based on supply and demand, however vulgar that might be. The Soviet atomic weapons program began with a letter from the nuclear physicist Georgy Nikolayevich Flyorov to comrade Stalin in April 1942, in which the former pointed out that there hadn't been a word uttered or written in western, allied media concerning nuclear fission since it had been discovered in 1938.

Comrade Stalin wasn't born yesterday. And just like nuclear physicist Flyorov, he thought that a complete silence of three years around the discovery of fission could only mean that someone had something to hide, such as, for example, that someone was in the process of developing a bomb that would immediately put the Soviet Union—to use a Russian image—in checkmate.

So there was no time to lose, apart from the minor detail that Hitler and Nazi Germany were fully occupied with seizing parts of the Soviet Union—that is everything west of the Volga, which would include Moscow, which was bad enough, but also Stalingrad!

The Battle of Stalingrad was, to put it mildly, a personal matter for Stalin. Although one-and-a-half-million or so people were killed, the Red Army won and started to push Hitler back, in the end all the way to the bunker in Berlin.

It wasn't until the Germans were about to retreat that Stalin felt that he and his nation might have a future, and that's when nuclear fission research really got going.

But, of course, atom bombs were not something you could screw together in a morning, especially when they hadn't even been invented yet. The Soviet atom bomb research had been under way for a couple of years without a breakthrough when one day there was an explosion—in New Mexico. The Americans had won the race, but that wasn't surprising since they had started running so much earlier. After the test in the desert in New Mexico, there were two more explosions that were for real: one in Hiroshima, another in Nagasaki. With that, Truman had twisted Stalin's nose and shown the world who mattered, and you didn't need to know Stalin well to understand that he was not going to put up with that.

—Solve the problem, comrade Stalin said to Marshal Beria. Or to be clearer: Solve the problem!

Marshal Beria realized that his own physicists, chemists, and mathematicians were bogged down, and it wouldn't even help to send half of them to the Gulag prison camps. Besides, the marshal had not received any indication that his agents in the field were getting close to the holy of holies. For the moment it was simply impossible to steal the Americans' blueprints.

The only solution was to bring in knowledge from the outside to complement what they already knew at the research center in the secret city of Sarov, a few hours by car southeast of Moscow. Since only the best was good enough for Marshal Beria, he told the head of the department of international secret agents:

—Pick up Albert Einstein.

—But . . . Albert Einstein . . . said the shocked boss of the international agents.

—Albert Einstein is the sharpest brain in the world. Do you intend to do as I say, or are you nurturing a death wish? asked Marshal Beria.

The boss of the international agents had just met a new woman and nothing on Earth smelled as good as she did, so he certainly wasn't nurturing a death wish. But before he had time to tell this to Marshal Beria, the marshal said:

—Solve the problem. Or to express myself more clearly: Solve the problem!

It was no easy matter to pick up Albert Einstein, and send him in a package to Moscow. First of all, they had to find him. He was born in Germany, but moved to Italy and then on to Switzerland and America, and since then he had traveled back and forth between all sorts of places and for all sorts of reasons.

For the time being he had a house in New Jersey, but according to the agents on the spot, the house seemed to be empty. Besides, if possible Marshal Beria wanted the kidnapping to take place in Europe. Smuggling celebrities out of the USA and across the Atlantic was not without complications.

But where was the man? He rarely or never told people where he was going before a journey and he was notorious for arriving several days late for important meetings.

The boss of the international agents wrote a list of places with some sort of close connection with Einstein, and then he sent an agent to keep an eye on each place. There was his home in New Jersey, and his best friend's house in Geneva. Then there was his publisher in Washington and two other friends, one in Basel, the other in Cleveland, Ohio.

It took some days of patient waiting, but then came the reward—in the form of a man in a gray raincoat, a turned-up collar and hat. The man came on foot and went up to the house where Albert Einstein's best friend, Michele Besso, lived in Switzerland. He rang the doorbell and was heartily and sincerely welcomed by Besso himself, but also by an elderly couple who would need further investigation. The watching agent summoned his colleague who was doing the same job in Basel 150 miles away, and after hours of advanced window watching and comparison with the sets of photos they had with them, the two agents came to the conclusion that it was indeed Albert Einstein who had just come to visit his best friend. The elderly couple was presumably Michele Besso's brother-in-law and his wife, Maja, who was also Albert Einstein's sister. Quite a family party!

Albert stayed there with his friend and his sister and her husband for two well-watched days, before again putting on his overcoat, gloves, and hat and setting off, just as discreetly as he had come.

But he barely made it around the corner before being grabbed and pushed in to the backseat of a car and anesthetized with chloroform. Then he was taken via Austria to Hungary, which had a sufficiently friendly attitude toward the USSR that few questions were asked when the Soviets expressed the wish to land at the military airport in Pécs to refuel, pick up two Soviet citizens and a very sleepy man, and then immediately take off again for an unknown destination.

The next day they started to interrogate Albert Einstein on the premises of the secret police in Moscow, with Marshal Beria in charge. The question was whether Einstein would choose to cooperate, for the sake of his health, or to be obstructive, which wouldn't help anybody.

Regrettably, it turned out to be the latter. Albert Einstein would not admit that he had given a moment's thought to the technique of nuclear fission (even though it was common knowledge that as early as 1939 he had communicated with President Roosevelt about the matter, which in turn had led to the Manhattan Project). In fact Albert Einstein would not even admit that he was Albert Einstein. He maintained with idiotic stubbornness that he was instead Albert Einstein's younger brother, Herbert Einstein. But Albert Einstein didn't have a brother; he only had a sister. So that trick naturally didn't work with Beria and his interrogators, and they were just about to resort to violence when something rather remarkable happened on Seventh Avenue in New York.

There, in Carnegie Hall, Albert Einstein was giving a lecture on the theory of relativity, to an audience of two thousand eight hundred specially invited guests, of which two were spies for the Soviet Union.

Two Albert Einsteins was one too many for Marshal Beria, even if one of them was a long way away on the other side of the Atlantic. It was soon possible to ascertain that the one in Carnegie Hall was the real one, so who the hell was the other one?

Under the threat of being subjected to procedures that nobody willingly undergoes, the false Albert Einstein promised to clarify everything for Marshal Beria.

—You will get a clear picture of everything, Mr. Marshal, as long as you don't interrupt me, the false Albert Einstein promised.

Marshal Beria promised not to interrupt him with anything other than a bullet in the head, and he would wait to do that until it was beyond any doubt that what he had heard was pure lies.

—So please go ahead. Don't let me put you off, said Marshal Beria, and cocked his pistol.

The man who had previously claimed that he was Albert Einstein's unknown brother, Herbert, took a deep breath and started by . . . repeating the claim (at which point a shot was almost fired).

Thereupon followed a story, which, if it was true, was so sad that even Marshal Beria could not bring himself to execute the narrator.

Hermann and Pauline Einstein did indeed have two children: first Albert and then Maja. But Papa Einstein hadn't really been able to keep his hands and other parts of his body away from his beautiful (but dim) secretary at the electrochemical factory he ran in Munich. This had resulted in Herbert, Albert and Maja's secret and not-at-all legitimate brother.

Just as the marshal's agents had already been able to ascertain, Herbert was virtually an exact copy of Albert, although he was thirteen years younger. Herbert had unfortunately inherited all his mother's intelligence. Or lack thereof.

When Herbert was two years old, in 1895, the family moved from Munich to Milan. Herbert followed along, but not his mother. Papa Einstein had of course offered her a suitable solution, but Herbert's mama was not interested. She couldn't contemplate replacing bratwurst with spaghetti, and German with . . . whatever language they spoke in Italy. Besides, that baby had just been a lot of trouble; he screamed all the time for food, and was always making a mess! If somebody wanted to take Herbert somewhere else, that would be fine, but she herself intended staying where she was.

Herbert's mother got a decent sum of money from Papa Einstein. Supposedly she then met a genuine count who persuaded her to invest all her money in his almost-finished machine for the production of a life elixir that cured every existing illness. But then the count had disappeared, and he must have taken the elixir with him because Herbert's impoverished mama died some years later, of tuberculosis.

Herbert thus grew up with his big brother, Albert, and big sister, Maja. But in order to avoid scandal, Papa Einstein referred to Herbert as his nephew. Herbert was never particularly close to his brother, but he loved his sister sincerely even though he had to call her his cousin.

—To sum up, said Herbert Einstein, I was abandoned by my mother, denied by my father—and I'm as intelligent as a sack of potatoes. I haven't done any useful work in all my life, just lived on what I inherited from my father, and I have not had a single wise thought.

Marshal Beria lowered his pistol. The story did have a degree of credibility, and the marshal even admired the self-awareness that the stupid Herbert Einstein had demonstrated.

What should he do now? The marshal got up from the chair in the interrogation room. For purposes of security he had put aside all thought of right and wrong, in the name of the revolution. He already had more than enough problems, he didn't need another one to burden him. The marshal turned to the two guards at the door:

—Get rid of him.

Upon which he left the room.

It would not be pleasant to report on the Herbert Einstein mess-up to comrade Stalin, but Marshal Beria was lucky, because before he had time to find himself out in the cold, there was a breakthrough at Los Alamos.

Over the years, more than one hundred and thirty thousand people had worked on what was called the Manhattan Project, and naturally more than one of them was loyal to the socialist revolution. But nobody had managed to obtain the innermost secret of the atom bomb.

But they had found out something that was almost as useful: a Swede had solved the puzzle, and they knew his name!

It didn't take more than twelve hours to find out that Allan Karlsson was staying at the Grand Hôtel in Stockholm, and that he spent his days just pottering about after the head of the Swedish atomic weapons program had told him that they didn't require his services.

—The question is, who holds the world record in stupidity, Marshal Beria said to himself. The boss of the Swedish atomic weapons program or Herbert Einstein's mom. . . .

This time, Marshal Beria chose a new tactic. Allan Karlsson would be persuaded to contribute his knowledge in exchange for a considerable number of American dollars. And the person who would take care of the persuading was a scientist like Allan Karlsson himself, not an awkward and clumsy agent. The agent in question ended up (to be on the safe side) behind the wheel as the private chauffeur of Yury Borisovich Popov, a sympathetic and competent physicist from the innermost circle of Marshal Beria's atomic weapons group.

And everything had gone according to plan. Yury Borisovich was on his way back to Moscow with Allan Karlsson—and Karlsson seemed positively inclined.

Marshal Beria's Moscow office was inside the walls of the Kremlin, at the wish of comrade Stalin. The marshal himself greeted Allan Karlsson and Yury Borisovich in the lobby.

—You are heartily welcome, Mr. Karlsson, said Marshal Beria and shook his hand.

—Thank you, Mr. Marshal, said Allan.

Marshal Beria wasn't the type to sit and chat about nothing. Life was too short for that (and besides he was socially incompetent). So he said to Allan:

—Have I understood the reports correctly, Mr. Karlsson, in that you are willing to assist the socialist Soviet republic in nuclear matters in exchange for 100,000 dollars?

Allan replied that he hadn't given the money much thought, but that he would like to give Yury Borisovich a hand if there was something he needed help with and there did seem to be. But it would be nice if Mr. Marshal could wait until the next day, because he had traveled an awful lot lately.

Marshal Beria answered that he understood that the journey had been somewhat exhausting for Mr. Karlsson, and told him that they would soon be having dinner with comrade Stalin, after which Mr. Karlsson would be able to rest in the very finest guest suite the Kremlin had to offer.

Comrade Stalin was not stingy when it came to food. There was salmon roe and herring and salted cucumbers and meat salad and grilled vegetables and borsht and pelmeni and blini and lamb cutlets and pierogi with ice cream. There was wine of various colors and of course vodka. And even more vodka.

Around the table sat comrade Stalin himself, Allan Karlsson from Yxhult, nuclear physicist Yury Borisovich Popov, the boss of the Soviet state's security Marshal Lavrenty Pavlovich Beria, and a little, almost invisible young man without a name and without anything to either eat or drink. He was the interpreter, and they pretended he wasn't there.

Stalin was in brilliant spirits right from the beginning. Lavrenty Pavlovich always delivered! Okay, he had put his foot in it with Einstein; that had reached Stalin's ear, but it was history now. And besides, Einstein (the real one) only had his brain; Karlsson had exact and detailed knowledge!

And it didn't hurt that Karlsson seemed to be such a nice guy. He had told Stalin about his background, albeit extremely briefly. His father had fought for socialism in Sweden and then journeyed to Russia for the same purpose. Admirable indeed! His son had for his part fought in the Spanish Civil War and Stalin was not going to be so insensitive as to ask on which side. After that he had traveled to America (he had to flee, Stalin assumed) and by chance had found himself in the service of the Allies . . . and that could be forgiven; Stalin himself had in a manner of speaking done the same thing in the latter part of the war.

Only a few minutes into the main course, Stalin had learned how to sing the Swedish toast *"Helan går, sjung hopp faderallan lallan lej"* whenever it was time to raise their glasses. Allan in turn praised Stalin's singing voice, leading Stalin to tell of how in his youth he had not only sung in a choir but even performed as a soloist at weddings, and then he got up and gave proof of this by jumping around on the floor and waving his arms and legs in every direction to a song that Allan thought sounded almost . . . Indian . . . but nice!

Allan couldn't sing. He couldn't do anything of any cultural value, he realized, but the mood seemed to demand that he attempt something more than *"Helan går . . . ,"* and the only thing he could remember straight off was the poem by Verner von Heidenstam that Allan's village school teacher had forced the children to memorize.

Thus Stalin resumed his seat, while Allan got up and proclaimed the poem in his native Swedish:

As an eight-year-old, Allan hadn't understood what he recited, and now that he declaimed the poem again, with impressive engagement, he realized that thirty-five years later he still hadn't a clue what it was about. The Russian-English (insignificant) interpreter sat in silence on his chair and was even less significant than before.

Allan then announced (after the applause had died down) that what he had just recited was by Verner von Heidenstam. Had he known how comrade Stalin would react to that news, Allan might have refrained from imparting it, or at least adjusted the truth a little.

Comrade Stalin had once upon a time been a poet, indeed a very competent one. The spirit of the times, however, had made him a revolutionary soldier instead. Such a background was poetical enough in itself. But Stalin had also retained his interest in poetry and his knowledge of the leading contemporary poets.

Unfortunately for Allan, Stalin knew all too well who Verner von Heidenstam was. And unlike Allan he knew all about Verner von Heidenstam's love of—Germany. And about the love being mutual. Hitler's right-hand man, Rudolf Hess, had visited Heidenstam's home in the 1930s, and shortly afterward Heidenstam had been awarded an honorary doctorate by the University of Heidelberg.

All of this caused Stalin's mood to undergo an abrupt metamorphosis.

—Is Mr. Karlsson sitting here and insulting the generous host who received him with open arms? asked Stalin.

Allan assured him that such was not the case. If it was Heidenstam who had upset Mr. Stalin, then Allan apologized profusely. Perhaps it might be some consolation that Heidenstam had been dead for some years?

—And *"sjung hopp faderallan lallan lej,"* what did that actually mean? Did you have Stalin repeat a homage to the enemies of the revolution? asked Stalin who always spoke of himself in the third person when he got angry.

Allan answered that he would need some time to think to be able to translate *"sjung hopp faderallan lallan lej"* into English, but that Mr. Stalin could rest assured that it was nothing more than a cheerful ditty.

—A cheerful ditty? said comrade Stalin in a loud voice. Does Mr. Karlsson think that Stalin looks like a cheerful person?

Allan was beginning to tire of Stalin's touchiness. The old geezer was quite red in the face with anger, but about not very much. Stalin went on:

—And what actually did you do in the Spanish Civil War? It would perhaps be best to ask Mr. Heidenstam-lover which side he fought for!

Has he got a sixth sense too, the devil? Allan thought. Oh well, he was already as angry as he could reasonably become, so it was probably just as well to come clean.

—I wasn't really fighting, Mr. Stalin, but at first I helped the republicans, before—for rather random reasons—changing sides and becoming good friends with General Franco.

—General Franco? Stalin shouted, and then stood up so that the chair behind him fell over.

It was evidently possible to get even angrier. On a few occasions in Allan's eventful life, somebody had shouted at him, but he had never ever shouted back, and he had no plans to do so in front of Stalin. That didn't mean that he was unmoved by the situation. On the contrary, he had rapidly come to dislike the little loudmouth on the other side of the table, in his own quiet way.

—And not only that, Mr. Stalin. I have been in China for the purpose of making war against Mao Tse-tung, before I went to Iran and prevented an attempt to assassinate Churchill.

—Churchill? That fat pig! Stalin shouted.

Stalin recovered for a moment before downing a whole glass of vodka. Allan watched enviously. He too would like to have his glass filled, but didn't think it was the right moment for such a request.

Marshal Beria and Yury Borisovich didn't say anything. But their faces bore very different expressions. While Beria stared angrily at Allan, Yury just looked unhappy.

Stalin absorbed the vodka he had just downed and then he lowered his voice to a normal level. He was still angry.

—Has Stalin understood correctly? asked Stalin. You were on

Franco's side, you have fought against comrade Mao, you have . . . saved the life of the pig in London, and you have put the deadliest weapon in the world in the hands of the arch-capitalists in the USA.

—I might have known, Stalin mumbled and in his anger forgot to talk in the third person. And now you are here to sell yourself to Soviet socialism? One hundred thousand dollars, is that the price for your soul? Or has the price gone up during the course of the evening?

Allan no longer wanted to help. Of course, Yury was still a good man and he was the one who actually needed the help. But you couldn't get away from the fact that the results of Yury's work would end up in the hands of comrade Stalin, and he was not exactly Allan's idea of a real comrade. On the contrary, he seemed unstable, and it would probably be best for all concerned if he didn't get the Bomb to play with.

—Not exactly, said Allan. This was never about money. . . .

He didn't get any further before Stalin exploded again.

—Who do you think you are, you damned rat? Do you think that you, a representative of fascism, of horrid American capitalism, of everything on this earth that Stalin despises, that you, you, can come to the Kremlin, to the Kremlin, and bargain with Stalin, and bargain with Stalin?

—Why do you say everything twice? Allan wondered, while Stalin went on:

—The Soviet Union is prepared to go to war again, I'll tell you that! There will be war, there will inevitably be war until American imperialism is wiped out.

—Is that what you think? asked Allan.

—To do battle and to win, we don't need your damned atom bomb! What we need is socialist souls and hearts! He who knows he can never be defeated, can never be defeated!

—Unless of course somebody drops an atom bomb on him, said Allan.

—I shall destroy capitalism! Do you hear! I shall destroy every single capitalist! And I shall start with you, you dog, if you don't help us with the Bomb!

Allan noted that he had managed to be both a rat and a dog in the course of a minute or so. And that Stalin was being rather inconsistent, because now he wanted to use Allan's services after all.

But Allan wasn't going to sit there and listen to this abuse any longer. He had come to Moscow to help them out, not to be shouted at. Stalin would have to manage on his own.

—I've been thinking, said Allan.

—What, said Stalin angrily.

—Why don't you shave off that mustache?

With that the dinner was over, because the interpreter fainted.

P*lans were changed with all haste. Allan was not, after all, housed in* the finest guest suite at the Kremlin, but instead in a windowless cell in the cellar of the nation's secret police. Comrade Stalin had finally decided that the Soviet Union would get an atom bomb either through its own experts working out how to make it, or by good old-fashioned honest espionage. They would not kidnap any more westerners and they would definitely not bargain with capitalists or fascists or both combined.

Yury was deeply unhappy. Not only because he had persuaded the nice Allan to come to the Soviet Union where death now certainly awaited him, but also because comrade Stalin had exhibited such human failings! The Great Leader was intelligent, well educated, a good dancer, and he had a good singing voice. And on top of that he was completely bonkers! Allan had happened to quote the wrong poet and in a few seconds a pleasant dinner had been transformed into a . . . catastrophe.

At the risk of his own life, Yury tried cautiously, so cautiously, to talk to Beria about Allan's impending execution and whether despite everything there was an alternative.

But Yury had misjudged the marshal. He did use violence against women and children, he did torture and execute guilty as well as innocent people, he did that and a lot more besides . . . but however revolting his methods, Marshal Beria did work single-mindedly in the best interests of the Soviet Union.

—Don't worry, my dear Yury Borisovich, Mr. Karlsson won't die. At least not yet.

Marshal Beria explained that he intended to keep Allan Karlsson out of the way as a backup, in case Yury Borisovich and his fellow scientists continued to fail to make a bomb. This explanation had an inbuilt threat, and Marshal Beria was very pleased with that.

While waiting for his trial, Allan sat where he sat, in one of the many cells at the headquarters of the secret police. The only thing that happened besides nothing was that every day Allan was served a loaf of bread, one ounce of sugar, and three warm meals (vegetable soup, vegetable soup, and vegetable soup).

The food had been decidedly better in the Kremlin than it was here in the cell. But Allan thought that although the soup tasted as it did, he could at least enjoy it in peace, without anyone shouting at him for reasons that he couldn't quite follow.

This new diet lasted six days, before the special tribunal of the secret police summoned Allan. The courtroom, just like Allan's cell, was in the enormous secret police headquarters beside Lubyanka Square, but a few floors higher up. Allan was placed on a chair in front of a judge behind a pulpit. To the left of the judge sat the prosecutor, a man with a grim expression, and to the right Allan's defense lawyer, a man with an equally grim expression.

For starters, the prosecutor said something in Russian that Allan didn't understand. Then the defense lawyer said something else in Russian that Allan didn't understand either. After which the judge nodded as if he was thinking, before opening and reading a little crib (to make sure he got it right) and then proclaiming the verdict of the court:

—The special tribunal hereby condemns Allan Emmanuel Karlsson, citizen of the kingdom of Sweden, as an element dangerous to the Soviet socialist society, to a sentence of thirty years in the correction camp in Vladivostok.

The judge informed the convicted man that the sentence could be appealed, and that the appeal could take place within three months of the present day. But Allan Karlsson's defense lawyer informed the court on behalf of Allan Karlsson that they would not be appealing. Allan Karlsson was, on the contrary, grateful for the mild sentence.

*A*llan *was of course never asked whether or not he was grateful, but* the verdict did undoubtedly have some good aspects. First, the accused would live, which was rare when you had been classified as a dangerous element. And second, he would be going to the Gulag camps in Vladivostok, which had the most bearable climate in Siberia. The weather there wasn't much more unpleasant than back home in Södermanland, while farther north and inland in Russia it could get as cold as minus 58, minus 76, and even minus 94 Fahrenheit.

So Allan had been lucky, and now he was pushed into a drafty freight car with about thirty other fortunate dissidents. This particular load had also been allocated no fewer than three blankets per prisoner after the physicist Yury Borisovich Popov had bribed the guards and their immediate boss with a whole wad of rubles. The boss of the guards thought it was weird that such a prominent citizen would care about a simple transport to the Gulag camps, and he even considered reporting this to his superiors, but then he realized that he had actually accepted that money so perhaps it was best not to make a fuss.

It was no easy matter for Allan to find somebody to talk to in the freight wagon, since nearly everybody spoke only Russian. But one man could speak Italian and since Allan of course spoke fluent Spanish, the two of them could understand each other fairly well. Sufficiently well for Allan to understand that the man was deeply unhappy and would have preferred to kill himself, if in his own view he hadn't been such a coward. Allan consoled him as best he could, saying that perhaps things would work themselves out when the train reached Siberia.

The Italian sniffled and pulled himself together. Then he thanked Allan for his support and shook hands. He wasn't, incidentally, Italian but German. Herbert was his name. His family name was irrelevant.

Herbert Einstein had never had any luck in his life. On account of an administrative mishap, he had been condemned—just like Allan—to thirty years in the correction camps instead of the death he so sincerely longed for.

And he wouldn't freeze to death on the Siberian tundra either, the extra blankets would see to that. Besides, January 1948 was the mildest for many a year. But Allan promised that there would be many new possibilities for Herbert. They were on their way to a labor camp after all, so, if nothing else, he could work himself to death. How about that?

Herbert sighed and said that he was probably too lazy for that, but he wasn't really sure because he had never worked in all his life.

And there, Allan could see an opening. In a prison camp you couldn't just hang around, because if you did then the guards would shoot you.

Herbert liked the idea, but it gave him the creeps at the same time. A load of bullets, wouldn't that be dreadfully painful?

A llan Karlsson didn't ask much of life. He just wanted a bed, lots of food, something to do, and now and then a glass of vodka. If these requirements were met, he could stand most things. The camp in Vladivostok offered Allan everything he wished for except the vodka.

At that time, the harbor in Vladivostok consisted of an open and a closed part. Surrounded by a seven-foot-high fence, the Gulag correction camp consisted of forty brown barracks in rows of four. The fence went all the way down to the pier. The ships that were going to be loaded or unloaded by Gulag prisoners berthed inside the fence, the others outside. Almost everything was done by the prisoners, only small fishing boats and their crews had to manage on their own, as did the occasional larger oil tanker.

With few exceptions, the days at the correction camp in Vladivostok all looked the same. Reveille in the barracks at six in the morning, breakfast at a quarter past. The working day lasted twelve hours, from half-past six to half-past six, with a half-hour lunch break at midday. Immediately after the end of the working day, there was supper, and then it was time to be locked up until the next morning.

The diet was substantial: mainly fish admittedly, but rarely in the form of soup. The camp guards were not exactly friendly, but at least they didn't shoot people without cause. Even Herbert Einstein got to stay alive, albeit contrary to his own ambition. He did of course work more slowly than any other prisoner, but since he always stayed very close to the hardworking Allan, nobody noticed.

Allan had nothing against working for two. But he soon introduced a rule: Herbert wasn't allowed to complain about how miserable his life was. Allan had already understood that to be the case, and there was nothing wrong with his memory. To keep on saying the same thing over and over again thus served no purpose.

Herbert obeyed, and then it was okay, just as most things were okay, apart from the lack of vodka. Allan put up with it for exactly five years and three weeks. Then he said:

—Now I want a drink. And I can't get that here. So it's time to move on.

SEVENTEEN

Tuesday, May 10, 2005

The spring sun shone brightly for the ninth day in a row and even though it was cool in the morning, Bosse set the table for breakfast out on the veranda.

Benny and The Beauty led Sonya out of the bus and into the field behind the farmhouse. Allan and Pike Gerdin sat in the hammock sofa and rocked gently. One of them was one hundred years old, and the other felt as if he was one hundred years old. His head throbbed, and his broken ribs made it hard to breathe. His right arm was good for nothing, not to mention the worst of all—the deep wound in his right leg. Benny came by and offered to change the dressing on the leg, but he thought it was perhaps best to start with a couple of strong painkillers. They could then resort to morphine in the evening if necessary.

After which Benny returned to Sonya and left Allan and Pike to themselves. Allan thought that it was high time that the two men had a more serious conversation. He was sorry that—Bolt?— had lost his life out there in the Södermanland forests and that— Bucket?—ended up under Sonya. Both Bolt and Bucket had however been threatening them, to put it mildly, and perhaps that could be a mitigating factor. Didn't Mr. Pike think so?

Pike Gerdin answered that he was sorry to hear that the boys were dead, but that it didn't really surprise him that they had been overpowered by a hundred-year-old geezer, albeit with a little assistance, because they had both been hopelessly daft. The only person who was even more daft was the fourth member of the club, Caracas, but he had just fled the country and was well on his way to somewhere in South America, Pike wasn't really sure where he came from.

Then Pike Gerdin's voice grew sadder. He seemed to feel sorry for himself, because it was Caracas who had been able to talk to the cocaine sellers in Columbia; now Pike had neither interpreter nor henchmen to continue his business. Here he sat, with God knows how many broken bones in his body, and without a clue as to what he should do with his life.

Allan consoled him and said that there was surely some other drug that Mr. Pike could sell. Allan didn't know much about drugs, but couldn't Mr. Pike and Bosse Baddy grow something here on the farm?

Pike answered that Bosse Baddy was his best friend in life, but also that Bosse had his damned moral principles. Otherwise, Pike and Bosse would by now have been the meatball kings of Europe.

Bosse interrupted the general melancholy in the hammock by announcing that breakfast was served. Pike could at last get to taste the juiciest chicken in the world, and with it watermelon that seemed to have been imported directly from the Kingdom of Heaven.

After breakfast, Benny dressed Pike's thigh wound, and then Pike explained that he needed to have a morning nap, if his friends would excuse him?

The following hours at Bellringer Farm developed as follows:
Benny and The Beauty moved things around in the barn so that they could rig up a fitting and more permanent stable for Sonya.

Julius and Bosse went off into Falköping to buy supplies, and while there became aware of the newspaper headlines about the centenarian and his entourage who had evidently run amok across the country.

Allan returned after breakfast to the hammock, with the aim of not exerting himself—preferably in the company of Buster.

And Pike slept.

But when Julius and Bosse came back from their shopping expedition, they immediately summoned everyone to a big meeting in the kitchen. Even Pike Gerdin was forced from his bed.

Julius told them what he and Bosse had read in the newspaper. Anyone who wanted to could read it in peace and quiet after the meeting, but to sum up, there were warrants out for their arrest, all of them except Bosse who wasn't mentioned at all, and Pike who according to the newspapers was dead.

—That last bit isn't entirely true, but I *am* feeling a bit under the weather, said Pike Gerdin.

Julius said that it was, of course, serious to be suspected of murder, even if it might end up being called something else. And then he asked for everyone's views. Should they phone the police, tell them where they were, and let justice run its course?

Before anyone could say what they thought about that, Pike Gerdin let out a roar and said that it would be over his half-dead body that anybody voluntarily phoned and reported themselves to the police.

—If it's going to be like that, then I'll get my revolver again. What did you do with it, by the way?

Allan answered that he had hidden the revolver in a safe place, bearing in mind all the weird medicines Benny had given to Mr. Pike. And didn't Mr. Pike think that it was just as well that it remained hidden a little longer?

Well, okay, Pike could go along with that, if only he and Mr. Karlsson could stop being so formal.

—I am Pike, said Pike, and shook hands with the centenarian.

—And I'm Allan, said Allan. Nice to meet you.

So by threatening to use weapons (but without a weapon) Pike had decided that they wouldn't admit anything to the police and prosecutor. His experience was that Justice was rarely as just as it ought to be. The others agreed. Not least on account of what would happen if Justice this time should turn out to be just.

The result of the short discussion was that the yellow bus was immediately hidden in Bosse's huge warehouse, together with a lot of as yet untreated watermelons. But it was also decided that the only person who could leave the farm without the group's permission was Bosse Baddy—that is, the only one among them who wasn't wanted by the police or presumed dead.

As for the question of what they should do next, what for example should happen to the suitcase with money, the group decided to postpone the decisions until later. Or as Pike Gerdin said:

—I get a headache when I think about it. At the moment I'd pay fifty million for a painkiller.

—Here are two pills, said Benny. And they are free.

It was a hectic day for Chief Inspector Aronsson. Thanks to all the publicity, they were now drowning in tips about where the presumed triple murderer and his companions were holed up. But the only tip-off that Chief Inspector Aronsson had any faith in was the one that came from the deputy chief of police in Jönköping, Gunnar Löwenlind. He reported that on the highway somewhere near Råslätt, he had met a yellow Scania bus with a badly dented front and only one functioning headlight. If it hadn't been for the fact that his grandson had just started throwing up in his babyseat in the back of the car, Löwenlind would have phoned the traffic police and tipped them off.

Chief Inspector Aronsson sat for a second evening in the piano bar at the Hotel Royal Corner in Växjö and once again made the mistake of analyzing the situation while under the influence.

—The northbound highway, the chief inspector reflected. Are you going back into Södermanland? Or are you going to hide in Stockholm?

He decided to check out of the hotel the next day and set off home to his depressing three-room apartment in the center of Eskilstuna. Ronny Hulth from the bus station at least had a cat to hug. Göran Aronsson didn't have anything, he thought, and downed the last whiskey of the evening.

EIGHTEEN

1953

I n the course of five years and three weeks, Allan had naturally
learned to speak Russian very well, but also brushed up on his
Chinese. The harbor was a lively place, and Allan established
contact with returning sailors who could keep him up-to-date on
what was happening out in the world.

Among other things, the Soviet Union had exploded its own
atom bomb one-and-a-half years after Allan's meeting with Stalin,
Beria, and the sympathetic Yury Borisovich. In the West, they suspected espionage, because the Soviet bomb seemed to be built according to exactly the same principle as the Los Alamos bomb. Allan
tried to work out how many clues Yury might have picked up in the
submarine while vodka was being drunk straight from the bottle.

—I believe that you, dear Yury Borisovich, have mastered the
art of drinking and listening at the same time, he said.

Allan also discovered that the United States, France, and Great Britain had combined their zones of occupation and formed a German federal republic. And an angry Stalin had immediately retaliated by forming a Germany of his own, so now the West and East each had one, which seemed practical to Allan.

The Swedish king had gone and died, as Allan had read in a British newspaper that for some obscure reason had found its way to a Chinese sailor, who in turn remembered the Swedish prisoner in Vladivostok and so brought the newspaper with him. The king had admittedly been dead almost a whole year when it came to Allan's attention, but that didn't really matter. A new king had immediately replaced him, so things were fine in the old country.

Otherwise the sailors in the harbor mainly talked about the war in Korea. And that wasn't so surprising. Korea was after all only about 125 miles away.

As Allan understood it, the following had happened:

The Korean Peninsula was kind of left over when the Second World War ended. Stalin and Truman each occupied a bit in brotherly agreement, and decided that the 38th parallel would separate north from south. This was then followed by negotiations lasting forever about how Korea should be able to govern itself, but since Stalin and Truman didn't really have the same political views (not at all, in fact) it all ended up like in Germany. First, the United States established a South Korea, upon which the Soviet Union retaliated with a North Korea. And then the Americans and the Russians left the Koreans to get on with it.

But it hadn't worked out so well. Kim Il Sung in the north and Syngman Rhee in the south, each thought that he was best suited to govern the entire peninsula. And then they had started a war.

But after three years, and perhaps four million dead, absolutely nothing had changed. The north was still the north, and the south was still the south. And the 38th parallel still kept them apart.

When it came to getting that drink—*the main reason to escape* from the Gulag—the most natural way would of course have been to sneak on board one of the many ships that stopped in the harbor in Vladivostok. But at least seven of Allan's friends in the camp hut had thought the same over the years, and all seven had been discovered and executed. Every time it happened, the others in the barrack had mourned. And the biggest mourner was Herbert Einstein, it would seem. Only Allan knew that the reason for Herbert's sadness was that, yet again, he hadn't been executed.

One of the challenges of getting on to a ship was that every prisoner wore black-and-white prison clothes. It was impossible to blend in with the crowd. In addition, there was a narrow passageway to the ship and that was guarded, and well-trained guard dogs sniffed at every load that was lifted onto the ship by crane.

Also, it wasn't exactly easy to find ships where Allan would be readily accepted as a stowaway. A lot of transports went to mainland China, others to Wonsan on the North Korean east coast. There was reason to believe that a Chinese or North Korean captain who found a Gulag prisoner in his hold would either turn back with him or throw him overboard (with the same final result, but with less bureaucracy).

Over land didn't seem much easier. Northward into Siberia where it really was cold was no solution. Nor was going westward into China.

What remained was southward, to South Korea where they would surely look after a Gulag refugee who would be assumed to be an enemy of communism. Too bad that North Korea lay in between.

There would be some stumbling blocks along the way, Allan realized, before he had even had time to work on something vaguely resembling a plan for his overland escape to the south. But there was no point in worrying himself to death because then he'd never get any vodka.

Should he try on his own, or along with someone else? In that case it would have to be Herbert, miserable though he was. In fact, Allan thought he could find some use for Herbert in his preparations. And it would certainly be more fun to be two on the run, than just one.

—Escape? said Herbert Einstein. Over land? To South Korea? Via North Korea?

—More or less, said Allan. At least that's the working plan.

—The chances that we will survive can't be more than microscopic, said Herbert.

—You're probably right about that, said Allan.

—I'm in! said Herbert.

A *fter five years, everybody in the camp knew how little cognitive activity there was in the head of prisoner number 133—Herbert—* and even when there was evidence of *some* activity, it seemed to only cause trouble internally.

This, in turn, had created a certain tolerance in the prison guards when it came to Herbert Einstein. If any other prisoner didn't stand the way he was supposed to in the food line, then at best he would be shouted at, second best he would get a rifle butt in his stomach, and in the worst case it would be good-bye forever.

But after five years Herbert still couldn't find his way around the barracks. They were all just the same brown color, and all the same size; it was confusing. The food was always served between barrack thirteen and fourteen, but prisoner 133 could just as often be found wandering about beside barrack seven. Or nineteen. Or twenty-five.

—Damn it, Einstein, the prison guards would say. The food line is over there. No, not there, there! It has been there the whole damn time!

Allan thought that he and Herbert could make use of this reputation. They could of course escape in their prison clothes, but to stay alive in those same prison clothes for more than a minute or two, that would be harder. Allan and Herbert each needed a soldier's uniform. And the only prisoner who could get anywhere near the soldiers' clothes depot without being shot immediately on discovery was 133 Einstein.

So Allan told his friend what to do. It was a question of "going the wrong way" when it was time for lunch, because it was lunchtime for the staff at the clothes depot too. During that half hour the depot was guarded solely by the soldier at the machine gun in watchtower four. Like all the other guards, he knew about prisoner 133's strange ways, and if he saw Herbert he would probably just shout at him rather than shoot him. And if Allan was wrong about that, it wasn't a huge issue considering Herbert's eternal death wish.

Herbert thought that Allan had worked it out well. But what was it that he was supposed to do, could he tell him one more time?

A*nd of course it went wrong. Herbert got lost and for the first time in ages found himself in the right place for the food line.* Allan was already standing there, and with a sigh he gave Herbert a friendly push in the direction of the clothes depot. But that didn't help; Herbert went the wrong way again and before he knew it he found himself in the laundry room. And what did he find there, if not a whole pile of newly washed and ironed uniforms!

He took two uniforms, hid them inside his coat, and then went out around the barracks again. The soldier in watchtower four saw him, but he didn't even bother shouting. In fact, the guard thought that it looked as if the idiot was actually on the way to his own barracks.

—A miracle, he mumbled to himself and returned to what he

was doing before, which was dreaming that he was somewhere else far away.

Now Allan and Herbert each had a uniform to show that they were proud recruits in the Red Army. Now it was just a matter of the rest of the plan.

Recently Allan had noticed a considerable increase in the number of ships on the way to Wonsan. The Soviet Union was officially not in the war on the North Korean side, but lots and lots of war material had started to arrive by train in Vladivostok, where it was then loaded on to ships that all had the same destination. Not that it was actually advertised where they were going, but Allan had the sense to ask the sailors. Sometimes you could also see what the cargo consisted of—for example, rough terrain vehicles or even tanks—while on other occasions they were just wooden containers.

Allan needed a diversionary tactic like the one in Tehran six years earlier. Following the old Roman maxim of keeping to what you do best, he thought that some fireworks might be just the thing. And that was where the containers to Wonsan came into the picture. Allan couldn't know, but he guessed that several of them contained explosives and if such a container were to catch fire in the dock area and if it started to explode. . . . Well, then Allan and Herbert would have the opportunity to slip around the corner and change into the Soviet uniforms. And then they would have to get hold of a car—which would need to have the keys in the ignition and a full fuel tank, plus no owner in sight. And then the guarded gates would have to open on Allan and Herbert's orders, and once they were out of the harbor and Gulag area, nobody would notice anything strange at all, nobody would miss the stolen car, and nobody would follow them. And all of this before they were even in the vicinity of problems like how they would get into North

Korea and—above all—how they would then move from north to south.

—I might be a bit slow, said Herbert. But it feels as if your plan isn't entirely ready.

—You aren't slow, Allan protested. Well, perhaps a little, but when it comes to this, you are perfectly right. And the more I think about it, the more I think that we should just leave it at that, and you'll see that things will turn out like they do, because that is what usually happens—almost always, in fact.

The escape plan's first (and only) step thus consisted of secretly setting fire to a suitable container. For that purpose they needed 1) a suitable container, and 2) something they could set it on fire with. While waiting for a ship with a suitable container, Allan sent the notoriously stupid Herbert Einstein out on another mission. And Herbert showed that Allan's faith in him was not misplaced by managing both to steal a signal rocket and hide it in his trousers before a Soviet guard discovered him in a place where Herbert had no right to be. But instead of executing or at the very least searching the prisoner, the guard just shouted something about it being not unreasonable to expect that after five years prisoner number 133 should be able to stop getting lost. Herbert said he was sorry, and tiptoed away. For the sake of the charade, he went in the wrong direction.

—The barrack is to the left, Einstein, the guard shouted after him. How stupid can you get?

Allan praised Herbert for a job well done and for acting the part well. Herbert blushed, while dismissing the praise, saying that it wasn't hard to play stupid when you are stupid. Allan said that he didn't know how hard it was, because the idiots Allan had met so far in his life had all tried to do the opposite.

Then, *what seemed to be the right day turned up. It was a cold morn-*
ing, the first of March 1953, when a train arrived with more
wagons than Allan, or at least Herbert, could count. The transport was obviously a military one, and everything was going to be
loaded on to three ships, all destined for North Korea. Eight T-34
tanks couldn't be concealed as part of the load, but otherwise
everything was packed in massive wooden containers without
any labels. But the gaps between the planks were just big enough
to allow a signal rocket to be fired into one of the containers. And
that was exactly what Allan did when he had the chance after half
a day of loading.

Smoke soon began to billow out of the container, but, help-
fully, it took several seconds before the load caught fire, so Allan
could get away and was not immediately suspected of being involved. Soon, the container itself was ablaze, immune to the effects
of the subzero temperature outside.

The plan was for it to explode after the fire reached a hand
grenade or some similar item in the load. That would make the
guards react like headless chickens, and Allan and Herbert would
be able to get back to their barracks for a quick change.

The problem was that nothing ever exploded. There was however an enormous amount of smoke, and it got even worse when
the guards who didn't want to go near the fire themselves ordered
some of the prisoners to pour water onto the burning container.

This, in turn, led three of the prisoners to use the smoke as a
screen while they climbed over the seven-foot-high fence to reach
the open side of the harbor. But the soldier in the watchtower saw
what was happening. He was already sitting behind his machine
gun and now he fired off salvo after salvo of bullets through the
smoke toward the three prisoners. Since he was using tracer ammunition, he hit all three with a large number of bullets and the
men fell to the ground dead. And if they weren't already dead,
then they most certainly were a second later, because it wasn't
only the prisoners who were hit. An undamaged container that

stood to the left of the one on fire also received a hail of bullets. Allan's container held fifteen hundred military blankets. The container next to it held fifteen hundred hand grenades. The tracer bullets contained phosphor and when a first bullet hit a first grenade it exploded, and tenths of a second later it took fourteen hundred and ninety-nine others with it. The explosion was so powerful that the next four containers flew between thirty and eighty yards into the camp.

Container number five held seven hundred land mines and there was soon another explosion just as powerful as the first one, which in turn led to the contents of a further four containers being spread in all directions.

Chaos was what Allan and Herbert had wished for, and chaos was what they got. And yet it had barely begun. The fire reached container after container. One of them was full of diesel and gas. Another was full of ammunition, which took on a life of its own. Two of the watchtowers and eight of the barracks were fully ablaze already before some armor-piercing shells got in on the act. The first shells knocked out watchtower number three; the second went right into the camp's entrance building and, in passing, took the entrance barrier and guard post with it.

Four ships were berthed and ready for loading, and the next salvo of armor-piercing shells set fire to all of them.

Then another container of hand grenades exploded and that started a new chain reaction, which finally reached the very last container at the end of the row. This happened to be a second load of armor-piercing shells, and now these shot off in the other direction, toward the open part of the harbor where a tanker with sixty-five thousand tons of oil was about to berth. A direct hit to the bridge left the tanker drifting, and a further three hits to the side of the tanker's hull started the largest fire of all.

The violently burning tanker now drifted along the edge of the quay toward the center of the town. During this last journey, it set fire to all the houses along its route, a distance of 1.4 miles.

The wind was coming from the southeast that day. So it didn't take more than another twenty-five minutes before—literally—all of Vladivostok was ablaze.

Comrade Stalin was just finishing a pleasant dinner with his hench-men Beria, Malenkov, Bulganin, and Khrushchev in the residence at Krylatskoye, when he received news that, basically, Vladivostok didn't exist any longer, after a fire that had started in a container of blankets had gone amok.

The news made Stalin feel really out of sorts.

Stalin's new favorite, the energetic Nikita Sergeyevich Khrush-chev, asked if he might be permitted to give a piece of good advice on the matter, and Stalin lamely answered that yes, Nikita Ser-geyevich certainly might.

—My dear comrade Stalin, said K., I suggest that what has hap-pened in this case has not happened. I suggest that Vladivostok is immediately sealed off from the rest of the world, and that we then patiently build up the town again and make it the base for our Pacific Fleet, just as comrade Stalin planned earlier. But above all—what has happened has not happened, because the opposite would indicate a weakness that we cannot afford to show. Does comrade Stalin understand what I mean? Does comrade Stalin agree?

Stalin still felt out of sorts. And he was drunk too. But he nod-ded and said that it was Stalin's wish that Nikita Sergeyevich him-self should be responsible for making sure that what had happened, hadn't happened. Having said that, he announced that it was time for him to withdraw for the evening. He wasn't feeling well.

Vladivostok, thought Marshal Beria. Wasn't that where I had that Swedish fascist expert sent to keep him in reserve in case we couldn't build the Bomb by ourselves? I had forgotten all about him. I should have liquidated the devil when Yury Borisovich Popov so brilliantly solved the problem by himself. Anyway, perhaps now he has been incinerated, although he didn't need to take the whole town with him.

At the door to his bedroom Stalin informed his staff that under no circumstances was he to be disturbed. And then he closed the door, sat on the edge of the bed, and undid the buttons of his shirt while he reflected.

Vladivostok . . . the town that Stalin had decided would be the base of the Soviet Pacific Fleet! Vladivostok . . . the town that was to play such an important role in the coming offensive in the Korean War! Vladivostok . . .

Didn't exist any longer!

Stalin just had time to ask himself how the hell a container with blankets could start to burn when it was minus four Fahrenheit. Somebody must be responsible and that bastard would . . .

Upon which Stalin fell headfirst to the floor. There he remained stroke-bound until the following evening, because if comrade Stalin said that he didn't want to be disturbed, then you didn't disturb him.

A llan and Herbert's barrack was one of the first to catch fire, and the friends immediately scrapped their plan of sneaking in and putting on the uniforms.

The fence around the camp had already fallen down, and if there were any watchtowers left standing there was nobody in them to keep guard. So getting out of the camp was not difficult. But what would happen next? They couldn't steal a military truck because they were all on fire. And going into town to find a car was not an option either. For some reason, all of Vladivostok was burning.

Most of the prisoners who had survived the fire and explosions stayed in a group on the road outside the camp, at a safe distance from the grenades and armor-piercing shells and everything else that was flying about in the air. A few adventurous types set off, all of them in a northwesterly direction, because that was the only reasonable direction for a Russian to flee. In the east was water, in the south the Korean War, and directly north was a town that was rapidly burning up. The only option remaining was to walk right into really cold Siberia. But the soldiers had worked that out too, and before the day was over had caught the escapees and sent them to eternity, every one of them.

The only exceptions were Allan and Herbert. They managed to make their way to a hill southwest of Vladivostok. And there they sat down for a short rest and to look at the destruction below.

—That signal rocket burned very bright, said Herbert.

—An atom bomb could hardly have done a better job, said Allan.

—So what are we going to do now? asked Herbert, and in the bitter cold almost longed to be back in the camp, which wasn't there anymore.

—Now we're going to North Korea, my friend, said Allan. And since there aren't any cars around, we'll have to walk. It will keep us warm.

Kirill Afanasievich Meretskov was one of the most skillful and decorated commanders in the Red Army. He was a Hero of the Soviet Union and he had been awarded the Order of Lenin no fewer than seven times.

As commander of the Fourth Army, he had fought the Germans around Leningrad, and after nine hundred terrifying days the siege was broken. No wonder Meretskov was made a marshal of the Soviet Union, in addition to all his other orders, titles, and medals.

When Hitler had been pushed back once and for all, Meretskov went off to the east instead, 6,000 miles by train. He was needed to command the Far East Front, to chase the Japanese out of Manchuria. To nobody's surprise, he succeeded in that too.

Then the world war came to an end, and Meretskov himself was tired. Since there was nobody waiting for him back in Moscow, he remained in the east. He ended up behind a military desk in Vladivostok. A nice desk it was too. Genuine teak.

In the winter of 1953, Meretskov was fifty-six years old, and was still sitting behind his desk. From there, he administered the Soviet nonpresence in the Korean War. Both Marshal Meretskov and comrade Stalin considered it to be strategically important that the Soviet Union did not for now engage in direct combat with American soldiers. Both sides had the Bomb, of course, but the Americans were way ahead. There was a time for everything, and this was not the time to be provocative—which naturally didn't prevent the Soviets from getting involved in Korea: the Korean War could be won, and indeed it ought to be won.

But now that he was a marshal, Meretskov allowed himself to take things a bit easy occasionally. For example, he had a hunting cottage outside Kraskino, a couple of hours south of Vladivostok. He stayed there as often as he could, preferably in the winter— and if possible on his own. Except for his aide, of course; marshals couldn't drive their own cars. What would people think?

Marshal Meretskov and his aide had almost a whole hour's drive remaining to Vladivostok when they saw, from the winding coast road, a pillar of black smoke.

The distance was too great for it to be worth getting the binoculars out of the trunk, so Marshal Meretskov ordered full speed ahead, adding that in the next fifteen minutes the aide should find a place to park with a good view of the bay.

A llan and Herbert had walked some way along the main road when a stylish military green Pobeda approached from the south. The escapees hid behind a snowdrift while the car passed. But then, the car slowed down and stopped about fifty yards away. Out stepped an officer with a chest full of medals, accompanied by his aide. The aide took the officer's binoculars out of the trunk and then the officer and his aide left the car to seek out a place with a better view of the bay on the other side of which Vladivostok had recently stood.

This made it simple for Allan and Herbert to sneak up to the car, seize the officer's pistol and the aide's automatic, and then make the officer and his aide aware of the fact that they were now in a tricky situation. Or, as Allan said:

—Gentlemen, would you kindly take your clothes off?

M arshal Meretskov was furious. You did not treat a marshal of the Soviet Union in that way, not even if you were a camp prisoner. Did the two gentlemen mean that he—Marshal K. A. Meretskov—should enter Vladivostok on foot wearing nothing but underpants? Allan answered that it would be difficult to enter Vladivostok at all, as the town was at that moment burning down, but otherwise that was more or less what he and his friend Herbert meant. The gentlemen would of course be given a couple of sets of inferior black-and-white prisoners' clothes in exchange, and in any case the nearer they got to Vladivostok—or whatever one should call the cloud of smoke and ruins over there—the warmer it would get.

Upon which Allan and Herbert put on the stolen uniforms and left their old prison clothes in a pile on the ground. Allan thought that it would perhaps be safest if he drove the car himself, so Herbert got to be Marshal Meretskov, and Allan his aide. Allan wished the marshal farewell and said that he needn't look so angry, because

Allan was quite sure that it wouldn't help at all. Besides it would soon be spring, and spring in Vladivostok was . . . well, perhaps it wasn't. Anyway, Allan encouraged the marshal to think positively, but added that it was of course entirely up to the marshal himself. If he really wanted to walk along wearing only his underpants and have negative thoughts about life, then he could do so.

—Farewell, Mr. Marshal. And you too, of course, Allan added to the aide.

The marshal didn't reply. He just continued to glare at them, while Allan turned the Pobeda round. And then he and Herbert set off southward.

Next stop North Korea.

The border crossing between the Soviet Union and North Korea was an uncomplicated and quick affair. First, the Soviet border guards stood to attention and saluted, and then the North Koreans did the same. Without a word being exchanged, the barrier was lifted for the Soviet marshal (Herbert) and his aide (Allan). The most devoted of the two North Korean border guards could hardly keep his eyes dry when he thought of the personal commitment he was witnessing. Korea could not have a better friend than the Union of Soviet Socialist Republics. Presumably, the marshal was on his way to Wonsan to make sure that the supplies from Vladivostok arrived safely.

But this particular marshal was not thinking about the well-being of North Korea. It is not even certain he knew in which country he found himself. He was fully occupied with trying to fathom how you opened the car's glove compartment.

What Allan had gathered from the sailors in the harbor in Vladivostok was that the Korean War had come to a standstill, that the two parties were each back on their own side of the 38th parallel. When Herbert heard this news, he suggested that one way to pass from North to South would be to get up speed and jump over the border (as long as it wasn't too wide). There was, of course, a risk that they would get shot when they were jumping, but really that wasn't such a big deal.

But it turned out—still with quite a way left to the border—that a full-scale war was already being waged around them. American planes circled in the air and seemed to be bombing everything they saw. Allan realized that a military-green, Russian staff car would probably be regarded as an excellent target, so he left the main road (without first asking his marshal for permission) and drove inland, on smaller roads with more chance of seeking shelter every time they heard the roar of an airplane above their heads.

Allan continued in a southeasterly direction, while Herbert entertained him with a running commentary while he went through the marshal's wallet, which he had found in an inner pocket of his uniform. It contained a tidy sum in rubles, but also information about what the marshal was called and some correspondence about activities in Vladivostok.

—Maybe he was the one in charge of that train transport, said Herbert.

Allan praised Herbert for that thought, which he found wise, and Herbert blushed.

—By the way, do you think you can memorize Marshal Kirill Afanasievich Meretskov's name? asked Allan. It would be useful.

—I am sure I can't, said Herbert.

When it started to get dark, Allan and Herbert turned into the yard of what looked like a well-to-do farm. The farmer, his wife, and their two children stood to attention in front of the important guests and the fancy car. The aide (Allan) apologized in Russian as well as Chinese for arriving unannounced, but wondered if it was possible to get something to eat. They would of course pay for it, but that would have to be in rubles; they didn't have anything else.

The farmer and his wife hadn't understood a word of what Allan had said. But the eldest son, aged about twelve, had studied Russian at school and he translated for his father. After which, it only took a few seconds before aide Allan and Marshal Herbert were invited in to the family home.

Fourteen hours later, Allan and Herbert were ready to continue on their way. First of all they had had dinner with the farmer, his wife, and the children. They were served a chili-and-garlic-flavored pork dish with rice, and with it—hallelujah!—Korean vodka! Of course, the Korean vodka didn't exactly taste like the Swedish sort, but after five years and three weeks of involuntary sobriety, it was more than okay.

After the dinner, the marshal and his aide were both offered lodging. Marshal Herbert was given the big bedroom while mother and father slept with the children. Aide Allan found himself on the floor of the kitchen.

When morning came, there was a breakfast of steamed vegetables, dried fruit, and tea before the farmer filled the marshal's car with some gas he had in a barrel in the barn.

Finally, the farmer refused to accept the bundle of rubles from the marshal, until the moment the marshal barked out, in German:

—You will take this money now, peasant!

That terrified the farmer to such a degree that he did as Herbert said, without understanding a word of what he had said.

They waved a friendly good-bye and then the journey continued in a southwesterly direction, without any other traffic on the winding road, but with the threatening roar of bombers overhead.

A s the vehicle approached Pyongyang, Allan thought that it might be time to work on a new plan. It was now out of the question to try to reach South Korea.

The plan instead became to try to arrange a meeting with Prime Minister Kim Il Sung. Herbert was after all a Soviet marshal, and that ought to suffice.

Herbert apologized for interfering with the planning, but he wondered what the point was of meeting Kim Il Sung.

Allan answered that he didn't know yet, but that he promised to think about it. One reason he could already give Herbert was that the closer you got to the top dogs, the better the food tended to be—and the vodka.

Allan realized it was only a matter of time before he and Herbert were stopped along the road and checked out properly. Not even a marshal would be allowed just to roll into the capital of a country at war without somebody at least asking a question or two. So Allan spent a couple of hours instructing Herbert as to what he should say—just one sentence in Russian, but a very important one: "I am Marshal Meretskov from the Soviet Union—take me to your leader!"

Pyongyang was protected at this time by an outer and an inner military ring. The outer one, twelve miles from the city, consisted of antiaircraft guns and double checkpoints on roads, while the inner ring was virtually a barricade, a front line for defense against land attack. Allan and Herbert got caught in one of the outer checkpoints first and were met by a very drunk North Korean soldier, with a cocked machine gun across his chest. Marshal Herbert had rehearsed his single sentence endlessly, and now he said:

—I am your leader, take me to . . . the Soviet Union.

By good fortune, the soldier didn't understand Russian, but he did understand Chinese. So the aide (Allan) interpreted for his marshal and then all the words came in the right order.

But the soldier had an almost impossible amount of alcohol in his blood, and was totally incapable of deciding what to do. He did at least invite Allan and Herbert into the checkpoint's sentry box and then he phoned his colleague 200 yards away. After which he sat down on a shabby armchair and pulled out a bottle of rice vodka (the third for the day) from his inside pocket. Then he took a gulp and started to hum to himself, while he looked straight through the Soviet guests with an empty glow in his eyes.

Allan was not satisfied with Herbert's efforts in front of the guard, and he realized that with Herbert as marshal it wouldn't take more than a couple of minutes with Kim Il Sung before both the marshal and his aide would be well and truly arrested. Through the window, Allan could see the other guard approaching.

Now they had to be quick.

—Let's swap clothes, Herbert, Allan said.

—But why? asked Herbert.

—Do it now, said Allan.

And so, in all haste, the marshal became the aide, and the aide became the marshal. The impossibly drunk soldier with the empty stare rolled his eyes and gurgled something in Korean.

A few seconds later, soldier number 2 entered the sentry box and immediately saluted when he saw what a prominent guest he had received. Soldier number 2 spoke Chinese too, upon which Allan (in the guise of the marshal) once again expressed the desire to meet the prime minister, Kim Il Sung. Before soldier number 2 had time to answer, number 1 ceased his gurgling.

—What's he saying? Marshal Allan wondered.

—He says that you just took all your clothes off and then got dressed again, answered soldier 2 truthfully.

—That is quite some vodka! said Allan and shook his head.

Soldier 2 apologized for his colleague's behavior and when number 1 insisted that Allan and Herbert had undressed and then dressed each other, he was given a punch on the nose and ordered to keep his mouth shut once and for all, unless he wanted to be reported for drunkenness.

Soldier 1 decided to keep quiet (and took another gulp) while number 2 made a couple of phone calls before filling in a pass in Korean, signing and stamping it in two places, and handing it over to Marshal Allan. And then he said:

—Mr. Marshal, show this at the next checkpoint. Then you will be guided to the second-in-command of the prime minister's second-in-command.

Allan thanked him, saluted, and returned to the car, pushing Herbert in front of him.

—Since you have just become my aide, you will have to drive from now on, said Allan.

—How exciting, said Herbert. I haven't driven a car since the Swiss police ordered me never to sit behind a wheel again.

—I think it's best if you say no more, said Allan.

—I have a hard time with left and right, said Herbert.

—As already noted, I think it's best if you say no more, said Allan.

The journey continued with Herbert behind the wheel, and it went off much better than Allan had expected. And with the help of the pass there were no problems in getting all the way into the city and right up to the prime minister's palace.

Once there, the second-in-command's second-in-command received them and said that the second-in-command could not receive them until three days later. Meanwhile, the gentlemen would be staying in the guest suite in the palace. And dinner would be served at eight o'clock, if that suited them.

—What did I tell you? said Allan to Herbert.

Kim Il Sung was born in April 1912 to a Christian family on the outskirts of Pyongyang. That family, like all other Korean families, was under Japanese sovereignty. Over the years, the Japanese did more or less what they wanted with people from the colony.

Hundreds of thousands of Korean girls and women were captured and used as sex slaves for needy Japanese imperial troops. Korean men were conscripted into the army to fight for the emperor who had, among other things, forced them to adopt Japanese names and in other respects done his best to eradicate the Korean language and culture.

Kim Il Sung's father was a quiet apothecary, but also sufficiently articulate in his criticism of the Japanese that the family one day found it wise to move northward, to Chinese Mongolia.

But after Japanese troops arrived in 1931 it wasn't all peace and quiet there either. Kim Il Sung's father was dead by then, but his mother encouraged him to join the Chinese guerrillas, with the ambition of forcing the Japanese out of Manchuria—and eventually Korea.

Kim Il Sung made a career in the service of the Chinese, as a communist guerrilla. He gained a reputation for being a man of action, and brave too. He was appointed to the command of an entire division and he fought so fiercely against the Japanese that in the end only he himself and a few more in the division survived. That was in 1941, in the middle of the World War, and Kim Il Sung was forced to flee over the border to the Soviet Union.

But he made a career there too. He was soon a major in the Red Army and fought right up until 1945.

The end of the war meant that Japan had to hand back Korea. Kim Il Sung came back from exile, now as a national hero. All that remained was to build the state; there was no doubt that the people wanted Kim Il Sung as the Great Leader.

But the victors from the war, the Soviet Union and the United States, had divided Korea into spheres of interest. And in the United States, they felt that you couldn't have a documented communist as the head of the whole peninsula. So they flew in a head of state of their own, a Korean exile, and put him in the south. Kim Il Sung was expected to settle for the north, but that is exactly what he didn't do. Instead, he started the Korean War. If he could chase out the Japanese, then he could just as well chase out the Americans and their UN followers.

Kim Il Sung had served in the military in both China and the Soviet Union. And now he was fighting for his own cause. What he had learned during the dramatic journey was, among other things, not to depend upon anybody.

He made only one exception to that rule. And that exception had just been appointed as his second-in-command.

Anybody who wanted to have contact with Prime Minister Kim Il Sung, must first seek a meeting with his son.

Kim Jong Il.

—And you should always let your visitors wait at least seventy-two hours before you receive them. That is how you maintain your authority, my son, Kim Il Sung had instructed him.

—I think I understand, Father, Kim Jong Il lied, after which he sought out a dictionary and looked up the word he hadn't understood.

Three days of waiting didn't bother Allan and Herbert at all, because the food was good and the beds were soft in the prime minister's palace. Besides, it was rare for American bombers to come close to Pyongyang, as there were easier targets to aim for.

Finally, however, the time came. Allan was fetched by the prime minister's second-in-command's second-in-command and was shown along the corridors of the palace to the second-in-command's office. Allan was prepared for the fact that the second-in-command was little more than a boy.

—I am the prime minister's son, Kim Jong Il, said Kim Jong Il. And I am my father's second-in-command.

Kim Jong Il's grip was firm even though his entire hand disappeared inside Allan's hefty fist.

—And I am Marshal Kirill Afanasievich Meretskov, said Allan. I am thankful that the young Mr. Kim agreed to receive me. Would the young Mr. Kim allow me to present my mission?

Kim Jong Il would, so Allan continued with his lying: the marshal had a message for the prime minister directly from comrade Stalin in Moscow. Since there were suspicions that the USA—the capitalist hyenas—had infiltrated the Soviet communication system (the marshal didn't want to go into more detail, and hoped the young Mr. Kim would understand), comrade Stalin had decided that the message should be conveyed in person. And this mission of honor had fallen upon the marshal's shoulders, and those of his aide (whom the marshal had left in their suite to be on the safe side).

Kim Jong Il looked suspiciously at Marshal Allan and seemed to be almost reading from a text when he said that his job was to protect his father whatever the cost. And part of that job was to trust nobody; his father had taught him that, he explained. So Kim Jong Il could not contemplate letting the marshal visit his father, the prime minister, until the marshal's story had been checked with the Soviet Union. Kim Jong Il intended to phone Moscow and ask whether Stalin had in fact sent the marshal.

—It is, of course, not fitting for a simple marshal to sit here and object, but I will nevertheless allow myself to note that one perhaps should not use the telephone to check if it is true that one shouldn't use the telephone.

The young Mr. Kim could see Alan's point. But his father's words echoed inside his head: "Don't trust anybody, my son!" Finally, the boy thought of a solution. He would indeed phone Uncle Stalin, but he would talk in code. Young Mr. Kim had met Uncle Stalin several times and Uncle Stalin used to always call him "the little revolutionary."

—So I shall phone Uncle Stalin, introduce myself as "the little revolutionary," and then ask Uncle Stalin if he has sent anyone to visit Father. Then I don't think we will have said too much, even if the Americans should be listening. What do you think, Marshal?

The marshal thought that he was a devious devil, that boy. How old could he be? Ten? Allan had himself become an adult early. At Kim Jong Il's age he was already working with dynamite for all he was worth at the nitroglycerin factory. Furthermore, Allan thought that things might be moving toward a nasty end, but he couldn't say that. Anyway, things were as they were, and so on.

—I do believe the young Mr. Kim is a very wise boy and is going to go far, said Allan and left the rest to fate.

—Yes, the idea is that I shall inherit Father's job after Father, so the marshal might be right about that. But now, please have a cup of tea while I phone Uncle Stalin.

Young Mr. Kim walked over to the brown desk in one corner of the room, while Allan poured the tea and thought about whether he ought to try to jump out of the window. But he immediately dropped the idea. For starters, he was on the fourth floor of the prime minister's palace, and also, Allan couldn't abandon his comrade. Herbert would have been more than happy to jump (if he had only dared), but of course he wasn't here just now.

Allan's thoughts were suddenly interrupted when young Mr. Kim burst into tears. He put the phone down, and rushed over to Allan, crying:

—Uncle Stalin is dead! Uncle Stalin is dead!

Allan thought that such luck bordered on the absurd, and then he said:

—There, there, young Mr. Kim. Come now and Uncle Marshal will give the young Mr. Kim a hug. There, there . . .

When the young Mr. Kim was more or less consoled, he no longer seemed so precocious. It was as if he couldn't manage to be adult any longer. Sniffling, he reported that Stalin had had a stroke several days earlier and that according to Aunty Stalin (that is what he called her) Uncle had died just before the young Mr. Kim phoned.

While the young Mr. Kim sat on Allan's knee, Allan talked

with feeling about the bright memory of his last meeting with comrade Stalin. They had eaten a banquet meal together, and they had gotten into that really good mood that only arises between true friends. Comrade Stalin had danced and sang before the evening was over. Allan hummed the Georgian folk song that Stalin sang on that occasion, just before something short-circuited inside his head. And the young Mr. Kim recognized the song! Uncle Stalin had sung that song for him too. Thus—if not before—all doubts were swept away. Uncle Marshal was quite clearly who he said he was. The young Mr. Kim would make sure that his father, the prime minister, received him the next day. But now he wanted another hug. . . .

In fact, the prime minister wasn't exactly sitting and governing his half country from an office next door. That would have been far too great a risk. No, if you were going to meet Kim Il Sung you had to embark upon a longer journey, which for reasons of security was undertaken in an SU-122 self-propelled howitzer, because the prime minister's second-in-command would come along too.

The vehicle was not at all comfortable, but that's not really the point of self-propelled howitzers, of course. During the journey, Allan had plenty of time to ponder two not entirely unimportant things. The first was what he would say to Kim Il Sung, and the second was what result he hoped for.

In front of the prime minister's second-in-command (and son), Allan had claimed that he came with an important message from comrade Stalin, and thanks to an amazing stroke of luck it had become easy to deal with this. The false marshal could now say anything at all; Stalin was far too dead to be able to deny it. So Allan decided that the message to Kim Il Sung would be that Stalin was going to give Kim Il Sung two hundred tanks for the communist struggle in Korea. Or three hundred. The higher the figure, the happier the prime minister would be, of course.

The other thing was more awkward. Allan was not particularly interested in traveling back to the Soviet Union after having accomplished his mission with Kim Il Sung. But to get the North Korean leader instead to help Allan and Herbert to South Korea would not be easy. And staying in the vicinity of Kim Il Sung would be more and more unhealthy for every day those tanks didn't turn up.

Could China be an alternative? As long as Allan and Herbert had been wearing black-and-white prison clothes, the answer was no, but they weren't anymore. Korea's gigantic neighbor had possibly been transformed from a threat to a promise, since Allan had become a Soviet marshal. Especially if Allan could trick Kim Il Sung into providing them with a nice letter of introduction.

So, next stop China? And then things would just have to turn out however they did. If no better option turned up en route, they could always traipse over the Himalayas once more.

With that, Allan felt he had reflected enough. First, Kim Il Sung would get three hundred tanks, or even four hundred—there was no need to be stingy. Thereafter, the pretend-marshal would humbly ask the prime minister to help him with transportation and visas for his journey to China, since the marshal had business with Mao Tse-tung too. Allan was pleased with his plan. Toward the evening, the armored convoy with passengers Allan, Herbert, and the young Kim Jong Il rolled into what seemed to be some kind of military camp.

—Do you think we've ended up in South Korea? Herbert asked hopefully.

—If there is anywhere in the world where Kim Il Sung is NOT sitting and keeping his head down, then it is South Korea, said Allan.

—No, of course not. I just thought . . . no, I don't suppose I did really, said Herbert.

Then the ten-wheel tracked armored vehicle jerked to a halt. The three passengers crawled out. They were in a military airfield outside a building that looked like a command center.

The young Mr. Kim held the door open for Allan and Herbert, after which he daintily trotted past the two gentlemen and even held open the next door. With that, the trio had reached the holiest of holies. Inside stood a large writing desk covered with papers. On the wall behind it hung a map of Korea, and on the right were two sofas. Prime Minister Kim Il Sung sat on one sofa, talking to a guest on the other. On the other side of the room, two soldiers armed with machine guns stood to attention.

—Good evening, Mr. Prime Minister, said Allan. I am Marshal Kirill Afanaseivich Meretskov of the Soviet Union.

—You certainly are not, said Kim Il Sung calmly. I know Marshal Meretskov very well.

—Oh, said Allan.

The soldiers immediately stopped standing to attention and instead pointed their weapons at the false marshal and his presumably equally false aide. Kim Il Sung was still calm, but his son broke out into a combination of tears and fury. Perhaps this was the moment when the last fragments of his childhood disappeared. Never trust anybody! And he had sat on the false marshal's lap! Never trust anybody! He would never, ever, trust a single person again.

—You will die! he shouted at Allan amid the tears. And you too! he said to Herbert.

—Yes, you will certainly die, said Kim Il Sung in his still-calm manner. But first we want to find out who has sent you.

This doesn't look good, Allan thought.

This looks good, Herbert thought.

The real Marshal Kirill Afanasievich Meretskov and his aide had had no choice but to walk toward what might remain of Vladivostok.

After several hours, they came to a campsite set up by the Red Army outside the destroyed city. There, the humiliation had been even worse, as the marshal had been suspected of being an escaped prisoner who had regretted his escape. But soon enough, he was recognized and treated in the manner that his position demanded.

Only once in his life had Marshal Meretskov allowed an injustice to pass by, and that was when Stalin's second-in-command, Beria, had had him arrested and tortured for nothing, and would certainly have let him die if Stalin himself had not come to his rescue. Perhaps Meretskov ought to have done battle with Beria after that, but there was a world war to win and Beria was too strong in any case. So he had been obliged to forget it. But Meretskov had said to himself that he would never again allow himself to be humiliated. So now he had to seek out and destroy the two men who had robbed him of his car and his uniform.

Meretskov could not start the hunt immediately because he didn't have his marshal's uniform. And it was not the easiest matter to find a tailor in one of the tent camps, and then they still had problems with something as trivial as needle and thread. All of Vladivostok's sewing workshops—together with the rest of the city—had ceased to exist.

But after three days the marshal's uniform was ready. Of course his medals were missing because the false marshal was flaunting them. Nevertheless, Meretskov would not let that stop him.

Marshal Meretskov managed with some difficulty to arrange a new Pobeda for himself and his aide (most military vehicles had of course been lost in the fire) and set off southward at dawn, five days after the dreadful business started.

At the Korean border he had his suspicions confirmed. A marshal, just like the marshal, and in a Pobeda, just like the marshal's, had crossed the border and continued southward. The border guards didn't know any more than that.

Marshal Meretskov came to the same conclusion that Allan had done five days earlier, namely that it would be suicide to continue toward the front. So he turned off toward Pyongyang, and after a few hours was able to confirm that he had made the right decision. The guards at the outer defense ring told him that a Marshal Meretskov with aide had asked for a meeting with Prime Minister Kim Il Sung and been given an audience with the prime minister's second-in-command. Marshal Meretskov and his aide continued on their way toward Pyongyang.

The real Marshal Meretskov met the second-in-command of the prime minister's second-in-command after lunch the same day. With all the authority that only a Soviet marshal is able to muster, Marshal Meretskov had soon convinced the second-in-command of the second-in-command that both the prime minister and his son were in imminent danger of losing their lives, and that the second-in-command of the second-in-command must now without delay show them the way to the headquarters of the prime minister. Since no time could be lost, they would use the marshal's Pobeda, a vehicle that must be at least four times faster than the self-propelled howitzer in which Kim Jong Il and the criminals were traveling.

—*Well, said Kim Il Sung haughtily but with interest. Who are you, who* has sent you, and what was the purpose of your little deception?

Allan didn't have time to answer before the door opened and the real Marshal Meretskov rushed in, shouting that the two men in the middle of the room were criminal camp prisoners and were planning an assassination.

For a second, there were too many marshals and aides for the two soldiers with machine guns. But as soon as the prime minister satisfied himself that the new marshal was the real one, the soldiers could again focus on the imposters.

—Take it easy, dear Kirill Afanasievich, said Kim Il Sung. The situation is under control.

—You are going to die! said the furious Marshal Meretskov

when he saw how Allan stood there in the marshal's uniform with all his medals on his chest.

—Yes, so they all say, Allan answered. First the young Kim here, then the prime minister, and now you, Mr. Marshal. The only one who hasn't demanded my death is you, said Allan and turned to the prime minister's guest. I don't know who you are, but I'm hoping you have a different opinion on that issue.

—I most certainly do not, the guest smiled back. I am Mao Tse-tung, the leader of the People's Republic of China, and I do not have any particular sympathy with somebody who wishes to harm my comrade Kim Il Sung.

—Mao Tse-tung! said Allan. What an honor. Even if I am soon to be done away with, you mustn't forget to give my regards to your beautiful wife.

—Do you know my wife? said Mao Tse-tung, amazed.

—Yes, unless Mr. Mao has changed wives recently; you've done that from time to time. Jiang Qing and I met in the Sichuan province some years ago. We hiked a bit in the mountains, together with a young boy called Ah Ming.

—Are you Allan Karlsson? said Mao Tse-tung, astonished. My wife's savior?

Herbert Einstein didn't understand very much, but he *did* understand that his friend Allan had nine lives, and that their certain death was on the way to being transformed into something else, again! This must not be allowed to happen! Herbert now acted in shock.

—I'm escaping, I'm escaping, shoot me, shoot me! he shouted and rushed right through the room, opened the wrong door and hurled himself into a cleaning cupboard where he immediately fell over a bucket and mop.

—Your comrade . . . , said Mao Tse-tung. He's not exactly an Einstein, is he?

—Don't say that, said Allan. Don't say that.

There was nothing strange about Mao Tse-tung being in the room, because Kim Il Sung had set up his headquarters in Manchurian China, just outside Shenyang in the Liaoning province, about three hundred miles northwest of Pyongyang. Mao liked to spend time in that area, where he had perhaps his strongest support. And he liked to be with his North Korean friend.

Nevertheless, it took quite a while to sort out everything that must be sorted out, and get all those who wanted Allan's head on a platter to reconsider.

Marshal Meretskov was the first to hold out a forgiving hand. Allan Karlsson had after all suffered from Marshal Beria's madness just like Meretskov himself. (To be on the safe side, Allan excluded the little detail about how he had burned down all of Vladivostok.) And when Allan proposed that he and the marshal should swap uniform jackets so that the marshal got back his medals, the marshal's anger evaporated.

Nor did Kim Il Sung, for his part, feel he had cause for anger.

After all, Allan had never intended to harm the prime minister. Kim Il Sung's only worry was that his son felt so betrayed.

Young Kim still cried and shouted and continued to demand Allan's immediate, and preferably violent, death. In the end, Kim Il Sung just boxed his son's ear and told him to shut up immediately, or else he would get another wallop.

Allan and Marshal Meretskov were asked to sit down on Kim Il Sung's sofa, soon to be joined by a downhearted Herbert, once he had untangled himself from the contents of the cleaning cupboard.

Allan's identity was confirmed definitively when Mao Tse-tung's twenty-year-old cook was called into the room. Allan and Ah Ming hugged each other for a long time until Mao ordered Ah Ming back into the kitchen to make some noodles.

$\mathbf{M}$*ao Tse-tung's gratitude for Allan saving his wife's life knew* no bounds. He was prepared to help Allan and his comrade with whatever they wanted, without limit. That included staying in China, if Allan wished, where Mao Tse-tung would ensure that he, and his comrade too, would live a comfortable life in a position of dignity.

But Allan answered that just now—and Mr. Mao would have to excuse him for this—he had had all he could take of communism, and he longed to be able to relax somewhere where he could drink a glass of something strong without an accompanying political lecture.

Mao could forgive Mr. Karlsson for that, but he said that Karlsson should not have too high hopes for the future because communism was meeting with success everywhere and it would not be long before the entire world was conquered.

Allan asked where the gentlemen thought communism would take the longest to make its entry—preferably a place where the sun shone, where the beaches were white, and where you could fill your glass with something other than Indonesian green banana liquor.

—I think I need a vacation, said Allan. I've never had one.

Mao Tse-tung, Kim Il Sung, and Marshal Meretskov discussed the matter among themselves. Cuba popped up as a possibility, and the gentlemen concluded that you could hardly imagine somewhere more capitalist. Allan thanked them for the tip, but said that the Caribbean was awfully far away; besides he had just realized that he had neither money nor passport, so he must lower his ambitions somewhat.

As for money and passport, Mr. Karlsson would not need to worry. Mao Tse-tung promised to give Allan and his friend false papers so that they could go anywhere they wanted. He would also provide them with a pile of dollars, because he had an excess of them. It was money that President Truman had sent to the

Kuomintang and that the Kuomintang in its haste had abandoned during their flight to Taiwan. But it was true that the Caribbean was on the other side of the globe, so perhaps it wouldn't be a bad idea to think of other options.

While the three arch communists continued their creative discussion about where somebody who was allergic to their ideology ought to go for a holiday, Allan silently thanked Harry Truman for the financial aid.

The Philippines cropped up as a suggestion, but were considered too unstable in political terms. Finally, Mao suggested Bali. Allan had grumbled about Indonesian banana liquor and that had led Mao to think about Indonesia. And it wasn't communist either, even though communism was lurking in the bushes, there as everywhere else, with the possible exception of Cuba. But they would have access to more than banana liquor in Bali, Chairman Mao was sure of that.

—Bali it is, said Allan. Are you coming, Herbert?

Herbert Einstein had slowly accustomed himself to the fact that he was going to live a little bit longer, and he nodded dejectedly. Yes, he would come along, what else could he do?

NINETEEN

Wednesday, May 11–Wednesday, May 25, 2005

The fugitives and the presumed dead managed successfully to keep themselves out of sight at Bellringer Farm. The farm lay two hundred yards from the main road, and from that angle the farmhouse and the barn concealed the farmyard from view. This created a free zone for Sonya. She could have a little walk between the barn and the small wood behind the farm.

Life on the farm was generally quite enjoyable. Benny regularly dressed Pike's wounds and administered a sensible and limited amount of medicine. Buster liked the open views of the Västgöta plain, and Sonya liked it anywhere as long as she didn't go hungry and as long as her benefactor and feeder—The Beauty—was there with a friendly word now and then. Recently, the old guy had joined them too and the elephant thought that made things even better.

For Benny and The Beauty, the sun was always shining whatever the weather, and if they hadn't been on the run from the law, they would probably have gotten married right away. Once you've reached a certain age, it is easier to sense when everything feels exactly right.

At the same time, Benny and Bosse became better brothers to each other. When Benny had managed to make Bosse understand that he was a grown-up even though he drank fruit juice instead of vodka, things went much more smoothly. And Bosse was impressed by everything that Benny knew. Perhaps it hadn't been quite so dumb or such a waste of time to go to school? It was almost as if his little brother had become a big brother, and that actually felt really good, Bosse thought.

Allan didn't make much of a fuss about anything. He sat in his hammock all day long, although the weather had become more like it usually was in Sweden in May. Sometimes Pike sat down near him for a little chat.

During one of these conversations, it transpired that they had a shared image of what nirvana was. Both of them thought that this perfect and absolute harmony was to be found in a beach chair under a parasol in a sunny and warm climate where the staff served chilled drinks of various sorts. Allan told Pike what a delightful time he had had on the island of Bali once upon a time, when he was vacationing with money he had gotten from Mao Tse-tung.

But when it came to what should be in the glasses, Allan and Pike differed. The centenarian wanted vodka cola or possibly vodka grape. On more festive occasions, he preferred vodka straight up. Pike Gerdin, on the other hand, liked more colorful liquids—best of all something orange turning into a golden yellow, a bit like a sunset. And there had to be a little parasol in the middle. Allan wondered what on earth Pike wanted with a parasol in his glass. You couldn't drink it. Pike answered that while Allan had been out and seen the world, and certainly knew a lot more about this and that

THE ONE HUNDRED YEAR OLD MAN

than a simple prison-bird from Stockholm, this was something Allan didn't have a clue about.

And so this friendly bickering on the theme of nirvana went on for a while. One of them about twice as old as the other, and the other about twice as big as the first, but they got along pretty well.

As the days and then weeks passed, journalists found it harder to keep the story alive—the story, that is, about the suspected triple murderer and his henchmen. After only a day or two, TV and the national and local newspapers had stopped reporting, according to the old-fashioned and easily defensible standpoint that if you didn't have anything to say, you said nothing.

The evening papers, the Swedish tabloids, held out longer. If you had nothing to say, you could always interview somebody who didn't realize that he too had nothing to say. The *Express* toyed with the idea of using tarot cards to help them home in on Allan's whereabouts, but dropped it. That was enough about Allan Karlsson. Go and nose out the next piece of shit . . . as one said in the trade. If nothing else was available, you could run an article on the latest miracle diet. That always worked.

So the media was letting the mystery of the centenarian disappear into oblivion—with one exception. In the local paper, there were a number of reports about various items related to Allan Karlsson's disappearance, like, for example, that the ticket office at the bus station had now been fitted with a security door as protection against future attacks. And that Director Alice at the Old Folks' Home had decided that Allan Karlsson had forfeited the right to his room and it would be allocated to someone else, someone who "was more appreciative of the care and warmth of the staff."

In every article, however, there was a short recap of the events that the police believed were a result of Allan Karlsson climbing out of his window at the Old Folks' Home.

The local paper happened to have a dinosaur of a publisher (cum editor in chief), a man with the hopelessly outdated attitude that a citizen is innocent until the opposite is proven. So the paper was careful about which people in the drama they identified by name. Allan Karlsson was indeed Allan Karlsson, but Julius Jonsson was the "67-year-old" and Benny Ljungberg was the "hot-dog-stand proprietor."

This in turn led an angry gentleman to phone Chief Inspector Aronsson at his office. The man said he had a tip about the missing Allan Karlsson, the man suspected of murder.

Chief Inspector Aronsson said that a tip was just what he needed.

Well, the man had read all the articles in the local paper and thought very carefully about what had happened. While he didn't have as much information as the chief inspector, it seemed to him that the police hadn't checked up properly on the foreigner.

—And I am certain that is where you will find the real villain, said the man.

—Foreigner? said Chief Inspector Aronsson.

—Yes, I don't know whether he is called Ibrahim or Muhammed, because the newspapers always call him the "hot-dog-stand proprietor," as if we don't know that he is a Turk or an Arab. No Swede would open a hot dog stand. That would only work if you're a foreigner and don't pay any taxes.

—My, said Aronsson. That was a lot all at once. But you can be a Turk and a Muslim at the same time, or for that matter an Arab and a Muslim, in fact that is quite likely.

—So he's a Turk *and* a Muslim! Even worse! Then check his background thoroughly! And his damned family's. He'll have one hundred relatives here, and they'll all be living on public assistance.

—Not a hundred, said the chief inspector. The only relative he has is actually a brother. . . .

And that was when an idea started to germinate in Chief Inspector Aronsson's brain. A few weeks earlier Aronsson had ordered an inquiry into the families of Allan Karlsson, Julius Jonsson, and Benny Ljungberg. The inquiry had been to see if a female, preferably with red hair, sister or cousin or a child or grandchild, happened to be living in Småland. This was before they had identified Gunilla Björklund. The results had been meager. Just one name had turned up, and at the time it didn't seem the slightest bit relevant, but now? Benny Ljungberg had a brother who lived just outside Falköping. Was that where they were all holed up? The chief inspector's thoughts were interrupted by the anonymous informant.

—And where does the brother have his hot dog stand? How much tax does he pay? This mass immigration has to stop!

Aronsson said that he was grateful for the man's tips even though the hot-dog-stand proprietor in this case was called Ljungberg and was utterly Swedish. Whether or not Ljungberg was Muslim, Aronsson couldn't say. Nor did it interest him.

The man said that he thought he detected something offensive in the chief inspector's answer and that it showed clear signs of socialism.

—There are a lot of people who think like me; we are growing in numbers. You'll see in the elections next year.

Chief Inspector Aronsson told the anonymous man to piss off, and hung up.

A ronsson phoned Prosecutor Ranelid to tell him that early the next day he intended, with the permission of the prosecutor, to go to Västergötland to follow up a new tip in the case of the centenarian and his companions. (Aronsson didn't think he needed to tell the prosecutor that he had known about the existence of Benny Ljungberg's brother for several weeks.) Prosecutor Ranelid wished Aronsson good luck.

It was almost five p.m. and the prosecutor was tidying up for the day while whistling silently to himself. Should he write a book about the case? *The Greatest Victory of Justice*. Would that be the right title? Too pretentious? *The Great Victory of Justice*. Better. And more humble. It fit the writer's character perfectly.

TWENTY

Mao Tse-tung provided Allan and Herbert with false British passports. Their journey took them by airplane from Shenyang, via Shanghai, Hong Kong, and Malaysia. Soon, the former Gulag escapees were sitting under a parasol on a white beach just a few yards from the Indian Ocean.

It would all have been perfect if only the well-meaning waitress didn't constantly get everything wrong. Whatever Allan and Herbert ordered to drink, they got something different—if they got anything at all. Sometimes the waitress lost her way altogether on the beach. The last straw for Allan was when he ordered a vodka and Coca-Cola ("a bit more vodka than cola") and got—Pisang Ambon, a vibrantly green banana liquor.

—Enough is enough, said Allan and was going to complain to the hotel manager and ask for a new waitress.

—Over my dead body! said Herbert. She is absolutely charming!

The waitress was called Ni Wayan Laksmi; she was thirty-two years old and should have been married off long ago. She looked nice, but wasn't from a fine family, didn't have any money, and on top of that it was known that she was about as intelligent as a *kodok*, Balinese for frog. So Ni Wayan Laksmi had been left over when boys chose girls and girls chose boys on the island (insofar as they had a choice).

It hadn't really bothered her very much, because she had always felt rather uncomfortable in male company, in female company, in any company at all, in fact. Up until now! There was something really special about one of the two new white men at the hotel. His name was Herbert and it was as if . . . they had something in common. He must be at least thirty years older than her, but she didn't think that mattered, because she was . . . in love! And her feelings were reciprocated. Herbert had never before met anybody who was anywhere near as slow-witted as he himself was.

When Ni Wayan Laksmi turned fifteen, her father had given her a language book, the idea being that his daughter would use it to learn Dutch, because Indonesia was at that time a Dutch colony. After four years of struggle with the book, a Dutchman came to visit. Ni Wayan Laksmi dared for the first time to try out the Dutch that had been so difficult to learn, and was told that what she was speaking was German. Her father, who wasn't terribly bright himself, had given her the wrong book.

Now, thirteen years later, that unfortunate circumstance had unexpectedly useful results, because Ni Wayan Laksmi and Herbert could speak to each other and declare their love.

Next Herbert asked for half of the pile of dollars that Mao Tse-tung had given to Allan, after which he sought out Ni Wayan Laksmi's father and asked for the hand of his eldest daughter. Her father thought he was being made fun of. Here was a foreigner, a white man with his pockets full of money, who was asking for the hand of by far the most stupid of his daughters. The fact that he even knocked on the door was a sensation. Ni Wayan Laksmi's family belonged to the Sudra caste, the lowest of the four castes on Bali.

—Are you sure this is the right house? asked the father. And is it my eldest daughter you mean?

Herbert Einstein replied that although he usually muddled things up, on this particular occasion he was quite certain he was right.

T*wo weeks later, they were married, after Herbert had converted to . . . some religion the name of which he had forgotten. But* it was quite a fun one, with elephant heads and that sort of thing.

Over this period Herbert had tried to learn the name of his new wife, but in the end he gave up.

—Darling, he said. I can't remember your name. Would you be very sorry if I call you Amanda instead?

—Not at all, dear Herbert. Amanda sounds nice. But why Amanda?

—I don't know, said Herbert. Do you have a better idea?

Ni Wayan Laksmi didn't, so from that moment on she was Amanda Einstein.

Herbert and Amanda bought a house in the village of Sanur, not far from the hotel and beach where Allan spent his days. Amanda stopped waitressing; she thought it was just as well to give her notice—she would be fired someday anyway because she never did anything right. Now they just had to decide what to do for the future.

Just like Herbert, Amanda muddled everything up that could be muddled up. Left became right, up became down, here became there. . . . So she never had any education. The very least it demanded was that you could regularly find your way to school.

But now Amanda and Herbert had an awful lot of dollars and so everything would certainly sort itself out. Amanda was admittedly terribly unintelligent, she explained to her husband, but she wasn't stupid!

And then she told Herbert that in Indonesia everything was for sale, and so anyone who had money could get anything he wanted. Herbert didn't really understand what his wife meant, and Amanda knew what it was like not being able to understand, so instead of explaining it further, she said:

—Dear Herbert, tell me something that you would like for yourself.

—Do you mean . . . like being able to drive a car?

—Yes, exactly! said Amanda.

And then she excused herself, she had some things to do. But she would be back before the evening meal.

Three hours later, she was home again. She had with her a newly issued driver's license in Herbert's name. But that wasn't all. She also had a diploma that showed that Herbert was a certified driving instructor and a receipt showing that she had just bought the local driving school and given it a new name: Einstein's School for Driving.

This was all fantastic, Herbert thought, but . . . it didn't make him a better driver, did it? Well, yes, in a way it did, Amanda explained. Now he had a position. Now he would decide what was good driving and what wasn't. Life worked in such a way that right was not necessarily right, but rather what the person in charge said was right.

Herbert's face lit up: he got it!

E*instein's School for Driving soon became a successful company. Al*most everyone on the island in need of a driver's license wanted to be taught by the nice white man. And Herbert rapidly grew in this role. He gave all the theory lessons himself, and in a friendly yet authoritative manner explained that it was important not to drive too fast because then you might crash. And you shouldn't drive too slowly either, because then you obstructed traffic. The teacher seemed to know what he was talking about.

After six months, the island's two other driving schools closed for lack of customers, and now Herbert had a monopoly. He told Allan about this during one of his weekly visits to the beach.

—I'm proud of you, Herbert, said Allan. That you of all people got involved in driving instruction! And here where they drive on the left. . . .

—Drive on the left? said Herbert. Do they drive on the left in Indonesia?

A*manda had been busy too. First, she had acquired a proper education,* and now she had a degree in economics. It had taken a few weeks and had cost quite a lot, but in the end she had the certificate in her hand. Top grades too, from one of the better universities in Java.

And with a university degree behind her, she had gone for a long walk along the beach at Kuta and thought hard. What could she do here in life that would bring good fortune to her family? Even with her degree in economics it was still rather hard to count. But perhaps she should . . . could she possibly? Yes, I'll damn well do it, Amanda Einstein thought.

—I'll go into politics!

A*manda Einstein founded the Liberal Democratic Freedom Party* (she thought the three words "liberal," "democratic," and "freedom" sounded good together). She immediately had six thousand imaginary members, all of whom thought she should stand for election as governor in the fall. The sitting governor would be standing down for reasons of age, and before Amanda had her idea there was only one likely candidate to take over. Now there were two. One of them was a man of the Pedana caste, the other was a woman of the Sudra caste. The result of the election was preordained, to Amanda's disadvantage. If it wasn't for the fact that she had a pile of dollars.

H*erbert had nothing against his beloved going into politics, but he* knew that Allan disliked politics in general and after his years in the Gulag disliked communism in particular.

—Are we going to become communists? he asked uneasily.

No, Amanda didn't think they would. That word wasn't in the party name. But if Herbert really wanted to become communist, they could probably add it.

—The Liberal Democratic Communist Freedom Party, said Amanda and felt how the name rolled off her tongue. A bit long perhaps, but it could work.

But that wasn't what Herbert meant. Quite the opposite, he thought. The less their party could devote itself to politics, the better.

They discussed how to finance their campaign. According to Amanda, they wouldn't have a lot of dollars left when the campaign was over, because it was expensive to win. What did Herbert think?

Herbert replied that he was certain that Amanda was the one in the family who best understood that matter. There wasn't much competition, admittedly.

—Great, said Amanda. Then we'll use one-third of our capital for my election campaign, one-third for bribes for the heads of the election districts, one-third for muddying the reputation of the main opponent, and then we'll keep one-third to live on if things don't work out. What do you think?

Herbert scratched his nose and didn't think anything at all. But he did tell Allan about Amanda's plans, and Allan sighed at the thought that somebody who couldn't distinguish between banana liquor and vodka now believed she could become governor. But so what, they had started off with a bundle of dollars from Mao Tse-tung, and there was more than enough left of Allan's half. So he promised Herbert and Amanda that he would give them some more after the election. But after that he didn't want to hear of any more projects concerning things that Herbert and Amanda didn't understand.

Herbert thanked him for the offer. Allan was a very kind man; that much was clear.

However, *Allan's help was not needed. The governor's election was a* complete success for Amanda. She won with more than 80 percent of the votes, and her opponent got 22 percent. The opponent thought that the total of more than 100 percent indicated the election wasn't fair, but the court soon dismissed his complaint and threatened him with serious consequences if he continued to defame the governor-elect, Mrs. Einstein. Just before the court announcement, Amanda had happened to meet the court's chairman for a cup of tea.

While *Amanda Einstein slowly but surely took over the island,* and her husband, Herbert, taught people to drive (without sitting behind the wheel himself more than absolutely necessary), Allan sat in his lounge chair beside the sea with a suitable drink in his hand. Since Amanda had given up waitressing, he now (most of the time) got served exactly what he asked for.

Apart from sitting where he sat and drinking what he drank,

Allan thumbed through the international newspapers he had ordered, ate when he got hungry, and had a nap in his room when his head felt too fuzzy.

D*ays became weeks, weeks became months, months became years—* and Allan never tired of being on vacation. And after fifteen years he still had a lot of dollars left. That was partly because there had been a pile of dollars to start with, but also because Amanda and Herbert Einstein had for some time owned the hotel he was staying in, and they immediately made Allan the only nonpaying guest.

Allan was now sixty-three years old and still didn't move around more than necessary, while Amanda went from strength to strength in her political career. She was popular with the masses, as could be seen from the regular opinion polls carried out by the local statistics institute owned and run by one of her sisters. Besides, Bali was ranked by the human rights organizations as the least corrupt region in the country. That, in turn, was because Amanda had bribed the entire investigating committee.

Nevertheless, the campaign against corruption was one of the three things that characterized Amanda's work as governor. She even introduced anticorruption lessons in all of Bali's schools. One headmaster in Denpasar had first protested—in his opinion the whole thing could have the opposite effect. But then Amanda made him chairman of the school board instead, with twice as big a salary, and that took care of him.

The second thing was Amanda's struggle against communism. Before the election she had organized the banning of the local communist party, which was on the way to becoming too big for her own good. This helped her get through the election with a much smaller budget than she would otherwise have needed.

The third thing that contributed to Amanda's success was Herbert and Allan. Through them, she discovered that it was by no means eighty-five degrees Fahrenheit all year round in large parts of the rest of the world. In what they called Europe it was particularly chilly and most of all in the far north where Allan came from. So she stimulated the development of tourism by granting building permission for luxury hotels on land she had just bought herself.

Otherwise, she looked after her nearest and dearest as best she could. Father, mother, sisters, uncles, aunts, and cousins soon all had central and lucrative positions in Balinese society. This led to Amanda being reelected as governor no less than twice. The second time, the number of votes and voters even tallied.

Over the years, Amanda had also given birth to two sons: first Allan Einstein (Herbert had Allan to thank for almost everything), followed by Mao Einstein (in honor of that useful pile of dollars).

But one day everything fell apart. It started when Gunung Agung, the nearly 10,000-foot-high volcano, erupted. The immediate consequence for Allan, forty-five miles away, was that the smoke blocked the sun. For others, it was worse. Thousands of people died, and even more had to flee from the island. Bali's hitherto popular governor didn't make any decisions worth the name. She didn't even realize she had a number of decisions to make.

The volcano gradually calmed down, but the island was still erupting politically and economically—just like the rest of the country. In Jakarta, Suharto took over after Sukarno, and the new leader was certainly not going to be soft on various political deviations like his predecessor. Above all, Suharto had been hunting down communists, presumed communists, suspected communists, possible communists, highly unlikely communists, and the odd innocent person. Soon, somewhere between two hundred and three hundred thousand people had died; the figures were uncertain, because a lot of ethnic Chinese had simply been branded as communists and shipped out of Indonesia, and they had to disembark in China where they were treated as capitalists.

When the smoke had cleared, not a single one of Indonesia's

two hundred million inhabitants still professed communist ideas (to be on the safe side, it had been declared a crime). Mission accomplished for Suharto who now invited the USA and others in the West to share the nation's riches. This in turn got the wheels of the economy turning, people fared better, and best of all Suharto himself soon became almost unbelievably rich. Not bad for a soldier who started his military career smuggling sugar.

A*manda Einstein no longer thought it was fun being governor. As* many as eighty thousand Balinese had lost their lives to the Jakarta government's efforts to make them think correctly.

Amid the mess, Herbert retired and Amanda was considering doing the same even though she wasn't yet fifty. The family owned land and hotels after all, and that pile of dollars that had made the family's prosperity possible had now been transformed into a lot more dollars. It would be just as well to retire, but what should she do instead?

—What about becoming Indonesia's ambassador in Paris? Suharto asked her straight off after first having introduced himself on the phone.

Suharto had noticed Amanda Einstein's work on Bali and her resolute decision to ban the local communists. Besides, he wanted a balance between the sexes when it came to top jobs in the embassies (the balance would be 24:1 if Amanda took the job).

—Paris? Amanda Einstein answered. Where's that?

A*t first, Allan thought that the 1963 volcanic eruption was an act* of providence telling him it was time to move on. But when the sun popped out again from behind the disappearing volcanic smoke, most things returned to what they had been like before (except, for some reason, there seemed to be a civil war in the streets). So Allan remained in his beach chair for a few more years.

And it was thanks to Herbert that he did eventually pack up and move on. One day, Herbert announced that he and Amanda were going to move to Paris, and if Allan wanted to come with them then his friend would arrange a false Indonesian passport instead of the false (and out-of-date) British one that Allan had last used. Besides, the ambassador-to-be would see to it that Allan had a job at the embassy, not so much so that Allan would have to work but because the French could be a bit difficult about whom they let into the country.

Allan accepted the offer. He had had plenty of rest. Besides, Paris sounded like a calm and stable corner of the world, without the riots that had recently raged in Bali, even around Allan's hotel.

They would leave in two weeks. Amanda started her job at the embassy on the first of May.

It was 1968.

TWENTY-ONE

P er-*Gunnar Gerdin was still sleeping when Chief Inspector Göran* Aronsson turned in to Bellringer Farm and to his amaze- ment discovered Allan Emmanuel Karlsson sitting in a hammock on the large wooden veranda.

Benny, The Beauty, and Buster were busy carrying water to Sonya's new stable in the barn. Julius had let his beard grow and had been given the group's permission to go with Bosse to Falköping to buy supplies. Allan had fallen asleep in the ham- mock and didn't wake up until the chief inspector made his pres- ence known.

—Allan Karlsson, I presume? said Chief Inspector Aronsson.

Allan opened his eyes and said that he presumed the same thing. But he, on the other hand, had no idea who was addressing him. Would the stranger be kind enough to shed some light on that?

The chief inspector would. He said that his name was Aronsson and that he was a chief inspector in the police force, that he had been looking for Mr. Karlsson for a while, and that Mr. Karlsson was under arrest on suspicion of having killed people. Mr. Karlsson's friends Mr. Jonsson and Mr. Ljungberg and Mrs. Björklund were, for that matter, also under arrest. Perhaps Mr. Karlsson could tell him where they were?

Allan was in no hurry to answer. He said that he needed to collect his thoughts, he had only just woken up after all, and he hoped the chief inspector understood. You didn't just talk about your friends without having thought things over carefully. Surely the chief inspector agreed?

The chief inspector said that it was not up to him to give advice, but Mr. Karlsson should hurry up and tell him what he knew. But, in fact, the chief inspector was not in a hurry.

Allan found that reassuring and he asked the chief inspector to sit down on the hammock, so that he could get some coffee from the kitchen.

—Would you like sugar in your coffee, Inspector? Milk?

Chief Inspector Aronsson was not one to let arrested delinquents just walk off any old way, not even to an adjacent kitchen. But there was something calming about this particular specimen. Besides, from the hammock the chief inspector would have a good view of the kitchen. So Aronsson thanked Allan for his offer.

—Milk, please. No sugar, he said and made himself comfortable on the hammock.

The newly arrested Allan busied himself in the kitchen. ("A Danish pastry too, perhaps?") while Chief Inspector Aronsson sat on the veranda and watched him. Aronsson found it hard to understand how he could have been so clumsy in his approach. He had, of course, seen a solitary old man on the farmhouse's veranda and thought that it might have been Bo Ljungberg's father, and that he would certainly be able to lead Aronsson to the son and that at the next stage the son would confirm that none of the wanted persons were in the vicinity, and that the entire journey to Västergötland had been for nothing.

But when Aronsson had come sufficiently close to the veranda, it turned out that the old man in the hammock was Allan Karlsson himself. Aronsson had acted in a calm and professional manner, if you could call it "professional" to let a suspected triple murderer go off to the kitchen to brew some coffee, but now he was sitting there and feeling like an amateur. Allan Karlsson, one hundred years old, didn't look dangerous, but what would Aronsson do if the three other suspects also turned up, possibly in the company of Bo Ljungberg, who for that matter ought to be arrested too for harboring a criminal.

—Was it milk but no sugar? Allan called out from the kitchen. At my age, you forget so easily.

Aronsson repeated his request for milk in his coffee, and then pulled out his mobile to phone for reinforcements from his colleagues in Falköping. He would need two cars, to be on the safe side.

But the mobile rang before he could make his own call. It was Prosecutor Ranelid—and he had some sensational news.

TWENTY-TWO

Wednesday, May 25–Thursday, May 26, 2005

The Egyptian sailor who had offered the smelly remains of Bengt "Bolt" Bylund to the fish in the Red Sea had finally reached Djibouti for three days of leave.

In his back pocket he had Bolt's wallet with 800 Swedish crowns. The seaman had no idea what that could be worth, but he had his hopes, and now he was looking for somewhere to change money.

The capital city in Djibouti is, rather unimaginatively, called the same as the country itself, and is a young and lively place. Lively because Djibouti is strategically placed on the Horn of Africa, right next to where the Red Sea joins the ocean and young because the people who live in Djibouti don't live very long. Reaching your fiftieth birthday is something of an exception.

The Egyptian sailor stopped at the city's fish market, perhaps intending to eat something deep-fried before continuing his search for a place to change money. Right next to him stood a sweaty man, one of the locals, restlessly switching his weight from one foot to the other, and with a feverish and roaming look in his eyes. The sailor didn't find it strange that the sweaty man was so sweaty; it was after all at least 95 degrees Fahrenheit in the shade, and besides the sweaty man was wearing two sarongs and two shirts under his pulled-down fez.

The sweaty man was in his midtwenties, and did not have the slightest ambition to become any older. His soul was in revolution. Not because half the population of the country was unemployed, nor because every fifth citizen had HIV or AIDS, nor because of the hopeless shortage of drinking water, nor because of the way the desert was spreading across the nation and swallowing the pathetically small amount of arable land. No, the man was furious because the USA had established a military base in the country.

In that respect, the USA was not alone. The French Foreign Legion was already there. There was a strong link between France and Djibouti. The country used to be called French Somaliland (in French of course) until it was allowed to go into business on its own in the 1970s.

Next to the Foreign Legion's base, the United States had now negotiated the right to establish its own base at a convenient distance from the Gulf and Afghanistan, and indeed with a whole row of Central African tragedies just around the corner.

Good idea, thought the Americans, while nearly all the Djiboutians couldn't care less. They were fully occupied with trying to survive yet another day.

But one of them had evidently had time to reflect upon the American presence. Or perhaps he was simply a bit too religious for his own, worldly good.

Whatever the reason, he was now wandering about in the center of the capital city on the lookout for a group of American soldiers on leave. During his walk he nervously fiddled with the string he was to pull—at the right time—so that the Americans would be blown to hell while he himself would sail off in the opposite direction.

But, as we have already heard, it was hot (as it tends to be in Djibouti). The bomb itself was taped onto his stomach and back and covered by a double layer of garments. The suicide bomber must have been boiling in the sun and in the end the best he could do was to accidentally fiddle a little too much with his string.

In so doing, he transformed himself and the unfortunate people who happened to be standing near him into mincemeat. A further two Djiboutians died from their wounds and ten or so were badly injured.

None of the victims were American. But the man standing closest to the suicide bomber seemed to have been a European. The police found his wallet in sensationally good condition next to the remains of its owner. Besides 800 Swedish crowns in banknotes, the wallet contained a passport and a driver's license.

The following day, the Swedish honorary consul in Djibouti was informed by the city's mayor that all the evidence suggested that Swedish citizen Erik Bengt Bylund had fallen victim to the mad bomb attack in the city's fish market.

Regrettably the city was unable to hand over the remains of the said Bylund because the body was too badly damaged. The pieces had, however, immediately been cremated, under respectful circumstances.

The honorary consul did receive Bylund's wallet, which contained his passport and driver's license (the money had disappeared en route). The mayor expressed his regrets that the city had not been able to protect the Swedish citizen, but he did feel obliged to point out something, if the honorary consul would permit an observation.

Bylund had been in Djibouti without a valid visa. The mayor didn't know how many times he had raised the problem with the Frenchmen and for that matter with President Guelleh. If the French wanted to fly in legionnaires directly to their base, that was their business. But the very same moment a legionnaire left the base to go into the city of Djibouti ("my city" as the mayor put it) as a civilian, he must have valid documentation. The mayor did not for a second doubt that Bylund was a foreign legionnaire. He knew the pattern all too well. The Americans followed the rules, but the French behaved as if they were still in Somaliland.

The honorary consul thanked the mayor for his condolences, and lied and promised on a suitable occasion to discuss the matter of visas with the French representatives.

It was a horrendous experience for Arnis Ikstens, the unfortunate man in charge of the car-crushing machine at the scrapyard in the southern suburbs of Riga, the capital of Latvia. When the last car in the row was squashed completely flat he suddenly noticed a human arm sticking out of the cubic metal package that until recently had been a car.

Arnis immediately phoned the police, and then went home, even though it was the middle of the day. The image of the dead arm would haunt him for a long time to come. He prayed to God that the person was already dead before he squashed the car in his crushing machine.

The chief of police in Riga personally informed the ambassador at the Swedish Embassy that their citizen Henrik Mikael Hultén had been found dead in a Ford Mustang at the car scrapyard in the southern suburbs of Riga.

That is, they had as yet been unable to confirm that it was him, but the contents of the wallet the dead man carried on him would suggest that such was his identity.

A t 11:15 in the morning on the 26th of May, the Swedish Ministry for Foreign Affairs in Stockholm received a fax from the honorary consul in Djibouti, containing information and documentation concerning a deceased Swedish citizen. Eight minutes later, a second fax arrived, on the same theme, but this time dispatched from the embassy in Latvia.

The official on duty in the ministry immediately recognized the names and pictures of the dead men—he had recently read about them in the tabloids. A bit strange, the official reflected, that the men had died so far from Sweden, because that hadn't been the impression given in the newspaper. But that was for the police and prosecutor to sort out. The official scanned the two faxes and then wrote an e-mail containing all the relevant information about the two victims.

Prosecutor Ranelid's life was about to fall apart. The case of the triple-murdering centenarian was to be the professional breakthrough that Ranelid had waited such a long time for, and that he so richly deserved.

But now it transpired that victim number one, who had died in Sörmland, died again three weeks later in Djibouti. And that victim number two, who died in Småland, did the same again in Riga, Latvia.

After ten deep breaths through the open office window, Prosecutor Ranelid's brain started to work again. Must phone Aronsson, Ranelid concluded.

And Aronsson must find victim number three. And there must be some DNA link between the centenarian and number three.

Otherwise Ranelid had made a fool of himself.

W*hen Chief Inspector Aronsson heard Ranelid's voice on the*
phone, he immediately started to tell him how he had just
located Allan Karlsson and that the said Karlsson was now under
arrest (even though he was spending that arrest standing in the
kitchen brewing some coffee for Aronsson).

—As regards the others, I suspect that they are in the vicinity,
but I think it is best that I should first call in reinforcements. . . .

Prosecutor Ranelid interrupted the inspector's report and told
him despairingly that victim number one had been found dead in
Djibouti, and victim number two in Riga, and that the chain of
circumstantial evidence was disintegrating.

—Djibouti? said Chief Inspector Aronsson. Where is that?

—I've no idea, said Prosecutor Ranelid, but as long as it is more
than twelve miles from Åker's foundry village it weakens my case
dramatically. Now, you have to find victim number three!

At that very moment a newly awoken Per-Gunnar Gerdin
stepped out onto the veranda. He nodded politely but somewhat
warily toward Chief Inspector Aronsson who stared at him wide-
eyed.

—I think that number three has just found me, he said.

TWENTY-THREE

1968

The duties involved in Allan's position at the Indonesian Embassy in Paris were not arduous. The new ambassador, Mrs. Amanda Einstein, gave him a room of his own and said that Allan was now free to do whatever he wanted.

—But it would be kind of you if you could help as an interpreter if things should ever get so bad that I need to meet people from other countries.

Allan responded that he couldn't exclude that things would get exactly as bad as that, considering the nature of the assignment. The first foreigner in line would surely be waiting the very next day, if Allan had understood correctly.

Amanda swore when she was reminded that she would have to go to the Élysée Palace for accreditation. The ceremony would last no more than two minutes but that was more than enough for someone who had a tendency to say something stupid, a tendency that Amanda thought she had.

Allan agreed that now and then something unsuitable did come out of her mouth, but that it would be fine with President de Gaulle, as long as she made sure that she only spoke Indonesian during her two minutes, and otherwise just smiled and looked friendly.

—What did you say he was called? asked Amanda.

—Indonesian, speak Indonesian, said Allan. Or even better, Balinese.

Upon which Allan went out for a walk in the French capital. He thought that it wouldn't do any harm to stretch his legs after fifteen years in a beach chair, and also he had just seen himself in a mirror at the embassy, and was reminded that he hadn't had a haircut or a shave since some time after the volcanic eruption in 1963.

It turned out, however, that it was impossible to find an open barbershop. Everything was closed; virtually everybody seemed to have gone on strike and now they were occupying buildings and demonstrating and pushing cars onto their sides and shouting and swearing and throwing things at each other. Riot barriers were being put up along and across the streets where Allan was walking along, keeping his head down.

It was all like the Bali he had just left—just a bit cooler. Allan turned around and went back to the embassy.

There he met a furious ambassador. The Élysée Palace had just called to say that the two-minute-long accreditation ceremony had been replaced by a long lunch and that the ambassador was warmly welcome to bring along her husband and of course her own interpreter, and that President de Gaulle for his part intended to invite the Minister of the Interior Fouchet and—not least—that the American President Lyndon B. Johnson would be there too.

Amanda was in despair. She might have managed two minutes in the company of the president without risking immediate
deportation, but three hours and with yet another president at the
table.

—What's happening and what shall we do, Allan? asked
Amanda.

But the development from a handshake to a long lunch with
double presidents was just as incomprehensible to Allan. And trying to understand things that were incomprehensible was not in
his nature.

—What should we do? I think we should find Herbert and
have a drink. It is already after noon.

An accreditation ceremony with President de Gaulle on the
one side and an ambassador from a distant and unimportant nation
on the other usually lasted at most sixty seconds, but might be
allowed to go on twice as long if the diplomat in question was talk-
ative.

In the case of the Indonesian ambassador it had suddenly become completely different for major political reasons, ones that
Allan Karlsson would never have been able to work out even if
he had cared to try.

As it happened President Lyndon B. Johnson was sitting in the
American Embassy in Paris and longing for a political victory. The
protests the world over against the war in Vietnam were now raging like a hurricane and the person most associated with the war,
President Johnson, was undeniably unpopular everywhere.

Johnson had long since abandoned his plans to run in the November elections, but he wouldn't mind being remembered by
some more attractive epithet than "murderer" and other unpleasant names that were being shouted out all over the place. So first he
had ordered a break in the bombing of Hanoi and had actually organized a peace conference. The fact that there then happened to
be semiwar raging on the streets in the city where the conference
came to be held was something President Johnson found almost

comical. There was something for that de Gaulle to get his teeth into.

President Johnson thought that de Gaulle was a jerk. He seemed to have completely "forgotten" who had rolled up their sleeves and saved his country from the Germans. But the rules of politics were such that a French and an American president can't be in the same capital together without at least having lunch.

So a lunch was booked, and would have to be endured. But luckily the French had evidently messed things up (Johnson was not surprised) and had double-booked their president. So now the new Indonesian ambassador—a woman!—was joining them. President Johnson thought that was just fine; he could talk to her instead of that de Gaulle.

B*ut it wasn't actually a double booking. Instead, President de Gaulle* had personally and at the last moment had the brilliant idea of pretending that was the case. In this way, the lunch would be endurable. He could converse with the Indonesian ambassador—a woman!—instead of that Johnson.

President de Gaulle didn't like Johnson, but it was for historical rather than personal reasons. At the end of the war, the USA had placed France under American military jurisdiction—they had intended to steal his country! How could de Gaulle forgive them that, regardless of whether the sitting president was actually involved? The sitting president, for that matter . . . Johnson . . . He was called Johnson. The Americans simply had no style, thought Charles André Joseph Marie de Gaulle.

A*manda and Herbert soon agreed that it would be best if Herbert* stayed at the embassy during the meeting with the presidents in the Élysée Palace. In this way, they both thought, the risk that something would go totally wrong would be almost exactly halved. Didn't Allan think so too?

Allan was silent for a moment, considering possible answers, before he finally said:

—Herbert, you should stay home.

The luncheon guests were gathered and waiting for their host who in turn was sitting in his office waiting just for the sake of waiting. And he intended to keep on waiting a few minutes more, in the hope that it would put that man Johnson in a very bad mood.

De Gaulle could hear the noise of the demonstrations from far away, as riots raged in his beloved Paris. The Fifth French Republic had started to wobble, suddenly and from nowhere. First, it was some students who were for free sex and against the Vietnam War. As far as that went, this was okay with the president because students will always find something to complain about.

But the demonstrations became bigger and bigger, and more violent too, and then the trade unions raised their voices and threatened to take ten million workers out on strike. Ten million! The whole country would grind to a halt!

What the workers wanted was to work less for a bigger wage. And that de Gaulle resisted. Three wrong out of three, according to the president who had fought and won much worse battles than that. Leading advisors at the Ministry of the Interior told the president to treat tough protests with equal toughness. This was not about anything big—for example, a communist attempt orchestrated by the Soviet Union to try to take over the country. But, of course, over coffee Lyndon Johnson would speculate that this was the case given half a chance. After all, the Americans saw communists hiding in every bush. To be on the safe side, de Gaulle had taken along Interior Minister Fouchet and his especially knowledgeable senior official. These two had been responsible for handling the current chaos in the nation and so they could also be responsible for defending themselves if Johnson started to stick his nose in things.

—Ugh! Damn and blast! (but in French) said President Charles de Gaulle and got up from his chair.

They couldn't delay the lunch any longer.

The French president's security staff had been especially careful when it came to checking the Indonesian ambassador's bearded and long-haired interpreter. But his papers were in order and they had made certain he was not carrying a weapon. Besides, the ambassador—a woman!—vouched for him. Thus, the bearded man was seated at the dining table between a much younger and more smartly dressed American interpreter and, on the other side, a French copy of the same.

The interpreter who was worked hardest was the bearded Indonesian, since Presidents Johnson and de Gaulle directed their questions to Madame Ambassador instead of to each other.

President de Gaulle started by inquiring as to Madame Ambassador's professional background. Amanda Einstein said that really she was rather a blockhead, that she had bribed her way to the position of governor of Bali and then bribed her way to reelection in two subsequent elections, that she had made pots of money for herself and her extended family for many years until the new President Suharto had, quite out of the blue, phoned and offered her the position of ambassador in Paris.

—I didn't even know where Paris was; I thought it was a country, not a city. Have you ever heard anything so crazy, said Amanda Einstein and laughed.

She had said all of this in her mother tongue and the long-haired and bearded interpreter translated it into English, taking the opportunity to change almost everything Amanda Einstein had said into something he felt more appropriate.

When the lunch was coming to a close, the two presidents

were in agreement over one thing, even though they weren't aware of the fact. They both thought that Madame Ambassador Einstein was entertaining, enlightened, interesting, and wise. She might, of course, have shown better judgment when it came to her choice of interpreter, because he looked like the Wild Man of Borneo.

*I*nterior Minister Fouchet's especially knowledgeable senior official, Claude Pennant, was born in 1928 in Strasbourg. His parents were convinced and passionate communists, who had gone to Spain to fight against the fascists when war broke out in 1936. With them they had their eight-year-old son, Claude.

The entire family survived the war and by a complicated path fled to the Soviet Union. In Moscow, they offered their services to further the interests of international communism. And they presented their son, now eleven years old, and announced that he already spoke three languages: German and French from back home in Strasbourg, and now Spanish too. Could that perhaps, in the long term, serve the revolution?

Yes, it could. The young Claude's talent for languages was carefully checked and after that his general intelligence through a number of tests. And then he was put in a language-cum-ideology school and before he was fifteen years old he spoke fluent French, German, Russian, Spanish, English, and Chinese.

When he was eighteen, just after the end of the Second World War, Claude heard his mother and father express doubts as to the course the revolution was taking under Stalin. Claude reported these views to his superiors and before long Michel and Monique Pennant had been both convicted and executed for nonrevolutionary activity. The young Claude thus gained his first award, a gold medal for the best pupil of his year, 1945–46.

After 1946, Claude started to prepare for service abroad. The intention was to place him in the West and let him work his way up in the corridors of power, if necessary as a sleeper agent for dozens of years. Claude was now under the protective hawklike wings of Marshal Beria, and he was carefully kept out of all official engagements where he might possibly end up in a photograph. The only work the young Claude was allowed to do was an occasional bout as interpreter, and then only when the marshal himself was present.

In 1949, at the age of twenty-one, Claude Pennant was sent back to France, but this time to Paris. He was allowed keep his own name, although his life history had been rewritten. He started up the career ladder at the Sorbonne.

Nineteen years later, in May 1968, he had risen to the immediate vicinity of the French president himself. The last two years he had been Interior Minister Fouchet's right hand and as such he now served the international revolution more than ever. His advice to the interior minister—and thus in extension to the president—was to react harshly in the ongoing student and worker uprising. To be on the safe side, he also made sure the French communists sent false signals, implying that they were not behind the demands of the students and workers. The communist revolution in France was at most one month away, and de Gaulle and Fouchet didn't have a clue.

A fter lunch, there was an opportunity for everyone to stretch their legs before coffee was served in the drawing room. Now, the two presidents had no choice but to exchange pleasantries with each other. It was while they were doing this that the long-haired and bearded interpreter came up to them unexpectedly.

—Excuse me for disturbing both the Mr. Presidents, but I have to talk to Mr. President de Gaulle and I don't think it can wait.

President de Gaulle was just about to call a guard, because a French president most certainly did not mix with just anybody in that manner. But the long-haired and bearded man was perfectly polite, so he was allowed to speak.

—Very well, but be quick about it. As you can see I've got more important things to do than chat with an interpreter.

Oh indeed, Allan promised not to go on. The simple fact was that Allan thought the president ought to know that Interior Minister Fouchet's special advisor was a spy.

—Excuse me, but what the hell are you saying? said President de Gaulle loudly, but not so loudly that Fouchet, smoking out on the terrace, and his right hand, also smoking out on the terrace, could hear.

Allan told him how he had had the dubious pleasure of dining with Misters Stalin and Beria almost exactly twenty years earlier, and that the interior minister's right hand was quite definitely on that occasion Stalin's interpreter.

—It was of course twenty years ago, but he looks just the same. I, however, looked different. I didn't have a magpie's nest on my face in those days, with my hair sticking out in all directions. I recognize the spy but the spy doesn't recognize me, because I hardly recognized myself when I looked in the mirror yesterday.

President de Gaulle went bright red in the face, excused himself, and then immediately requested a private conversation with his interior minister ("No, private conversation, I said, without your special advisor! Now!").

President Johnson and the Indonesian interpreter were left behind. Johnson looked very pleased. He decided to shake the interpreter's hand, as a thank-you for him having made the French president lose his mask of superiority.

—A pleasure to meet you, said President Johnson. What was your name?

—I am Allan Karlsson, said Allan. I once knew your predecessor's predecessor's predecessor, President Truman.

—Well, what do you know! said President Johnson. Harry is on his way to ninety but he is alive and well. We are good friends.

—Give him my regards, said Allan, and then made his excuses

so that he could find Amanda (he wanted to tell her what she had said to the presidents at the table).

The lunch with the two presidents came to a rapid end and everyone went home. But Allan and Amanda had only just reached their embassy when President Johnson himself phoned and invited Allan to dinner at the American Embassy at eight o'clock that same evening.

—That would be nice, said Allan. I had anyway intended having a good square meal this evening, because whatever you say about French food, it soon disappears from your plate without your actually having eaten much.

That was an observation President Johnson completely agreed with, and he looked forward very much to the evening's events.

There were at least three good reasons for President Johnson to invite Allan Karlsson to dinner. First, to find out more about the spy and about Karlsson's meeting with Beria and Stalin. Second, Harry Truman had just told him on the phone what Allan Karlsson had done at Los Alamos in 1945. That alone was of course worth a dinner. And third, President Johnson was personally extremely pleased with what happened at the Élysée Palace. At very close range, he had been able to enjoy seeing de Gaulle look aghast and discomfited, and he had Allan Karlsson to thank for that.

—Welcome, Mr. Karlsson, said President Johnson as he greeted Allan with a double handshake. Let me introduce Mr. Ryan Hutton, he is . . . well, he is a bit secret here at the embassy, one could say. Legal advisor, I believe he is called.

Allan shook hands with the secret advisor and then the trio went to the dining table. President Johnson had ordered beer and vodka to be served with the food, because French wine reminded him of Frenchmen and this was meant to be an enjoyable evening.

While they were eating the first course, Allan related some of his life story, up to the dinner in the Kremlin, the one that went wrong. It was there that Interior Minister Fouchet's right hand had fainted instead of translating Allan's final insult to the already furious Stalin.

President Johnson was no longer so amused by the revelation that Claude Pennant turned out to be a Soviet spy in the vicinity of the French president, because he had just been informed by Ryan Hutton that the specialist Monsieur Pennant had in all secrecy also been an informer for the CIA. In fact, Pennant had up to then been the main CIA source of the information that there was not an imminent communist revolution in France although the country was deeply infiltrated by communists. Now the entire analysis would have to be reconsidered.

—That, of course, was unofficial and confidential information, said President Johnson, but I can count on Mr. Karlsson to keep a secret, can't I?

—I wouldn't be too sure about that, Mr. President, said Allan.

And then Allan told of how during that submarine journey in the Baltic he had been drinking with a really extraordinarily nice man, one of the Soviet Union's leading nuclear physicists, Yury Borisovich Popov, and that in the rush of things there had been a bit too much talk about nuclear technology.

—Did you tell Stalin how to build a bomb? asked President Johnson. I thought you ended up in a prison camp precisely because you refused.

—I refused to tell Stalin. He wouldn't have understood anyway. But the day before with that nuclear physicist I may have gone into more detail than I ought to have done. That's what happens when you drink a bit too much vodka, Mr. President. And it wasn't really apparent what a nasty man that Stalin could be, not until the following day.

President Johnson had his palm on his forehead, and pushing his fingers through his hair he thought that the revelation of how you build atomic bombs wasn't something that just happened because alcohol was involved. Allan Karlsson was in fact . . . he was in fact . . . a traitor. Wasn't he? But . . . he was not an American citizen so what did you do then? President Johnson needed time to think.

—And then what happened? he asked, as he had to say something.

Allan thought it best not to leave out too many details now that a president was asking him. So he told him about Vladivostok, about Marshal Meretskov, about Kim Il Sung, about Kim Jong Il, about Stalin's fortunate death, about Mao Tse-tung, about a pile of dollars that Mao had been so kind as to supply him with, about the calm life on Bali and about the not-so-calm life on Bali, and finally about his journey to Paris.

—That's about all, I think, said Allan. But with all this talking I've become really parched.

The president ordered some more beer, but added that a person who spilled atomic secrets in a state of inebriation ought to consider becoming a teetotaler. Then he asked:

—You had a fifteen-year-long vacation, financed by Mao Tse-tung?

—Yes. Sort of. Really it was Chiang Kai-shek's money, and he had gotten it from our mutual friend Harry Truman. Now that you mention it, Mr. President, perhaps I ought to phone Harry and thank him.

President Johnson had enormous problems with the knowledge that the bearded and long-haired man opposite him had given Stalin the Bomb. And had lived a life of leisure paid for by American foreign aid. And on top of it all, you could now faintly hear how demonstrators on the street outside the embassy were shouting: "USA out of Vietnam! USA out of Vietnam!" Johnson sat there in silence, his face a picture of misery.

Meanwhile, Allan emptied his glass while he studied the worried face of the American president.

—Can I be of any help? he asked.

—What did you say? President Johnson said, deep in his own thoughts.

—Can I be of any help? Allan repeated. The president looks dreadful. Perhaps he needs some help?

President Johnson was at the point of asking Allan Karlsson to win the Vietnam War for him, but then he returned to reality and what he saw before him again was the man who gave the Bomb to Stalin.

—Yes, you can do one thing for me, said President Johnson in a tired voice. You can leave.

*A*llan said thank you for the dinner, and went on his way, leaving behind President Johnson and the European CIA director, the oh-so-secret Ryan Hutton.

Lyndon B. Johnson was horrified at the way Allan Karlsson's visit had developed. First such a nice start but then Karlsson sat there and admitted he had given the Bomb not only to the USA but also to Stalin. Stalin! The communist of communists!

—Now, Hutton, said President Johnson. What should we do? Shall we pick up that damned Karlsson again and boil him in oil?

—Yes, said secret agent Hutton. Either that or we could make sure to put him to good use.

*S*ecret agent Hutton was not only secret, he was also well-read on most things of politically strategic interest from the perspective of the CIA. For example, he was very well aware of the existence of the physicist that Allan Karlsson had had such a pleasant drinking session with on the submarine between Sweden and Leningrad. Yury Borisovich Popov had made quite a career from 1949 and on- ward. And his first big break might very well have been thanks to the information that Allan Karlsson had delivered—in fact it was highly likely that such was the case. Now Popov was sixty-three years old and technical director of the entire atomic arsenal of the Soviet Union. As such, he had knowledge that was so valuable to the USA that you couldn't even put a price on it.

If the USA could find out what Popov knew and thereby determine whether the West was in advance of the East when it came to atomic weapons—well, then President Johnson could take the initiative toward mutual disarmament. And the path to such knowledge went via—Allan Karlsson.

—You want to make Karlsson an American agent? said President Johnson while he thought about how some serious disarmament could do a great deal of good for how he would be remembered as a president, regardless of that damned war in Vietnam.

—Yes, exactly, said secret agent Hutton.

—And why would Karlsson go along with that?

—Well . . . because . . . he seems the type. And just a moment ago he sat there and asked the president if there was anything he could do to help.

—Yes, said President Johnson. He actually did.

The president was silent again for a few moments. Then he said:

—I think I need a strong drink.

I nitially, the French government's hard attitude toward the popular dissatisfaction did indeed lead to the country grinding to a halt. Millions of Frenchmen went on strike. The docks in Marseilles closed down, as did international airports, the railway, and all department stores.

The distribution of gas and oil came to a halt and garbage collection stopped. From every side there were workers' demands. For higher wages, of course, and shorter working hours, and better job security, and more influence.

But in addition there were demands for a new system of education. And a new society! The Fifth Republic was threatened.

Hundreds of thousands of Frenchmen demonstrated in the streets, and it wasn't always peaceful either. Cars were set on fire, trees were felled, streets were dug up, barricades were built. . . . There were gendarmes, riot police, tear gas, and shields. . . .

That was when the French president, the prime minister, and his government did a quick about-turn. Interior Minister Fouchet's special advisor no longer had any influence. (He was imprisoned secretly in the premises of the secret police, where he had considerable difficulty in explaining why he had a radio transmitter installed in his bathroom scale.) The workers on general strike were suddenly offered a big increase in the minimum wage, a general increase of wages of ten percent, a three-hour reduction of the work week, increased family allowances, more trade union power, negotiations on comprehensive general wage agreements, and inflation-adjusted wages. A couple of the government's ministers had to resign too, among them Interior Minister Fouchet.

With this array of measures, the government and president neutralized the most revolutionary factions. There was no popular support to take things further than they had already gone. Workers went back to work, occupations stopped, shops opened again, the transport sector began to function. May 1968 had now become June 1968. And the Fifth Republic was still there.

President Charles de Gaulle personally phoned the Indonesian Embassy in Paris and asked for Mr. Allan Karlsson, in order to award him a medal. But at the embassy they said that Allan Karlsson no longer worked there and nobody, including the ambassador herself, could say where he had gone.

TWENTY-FOUR

Thursday, May 26, 2005

*P*rosecutor Ranelid had to try to salvage what could be saved of his career and honor. He arranged a press conference that same afternoon to say that he had just canceled the warrant for the arrest of the three men and the woman in the case of the disappearing centenarian.

Prosecutor Ranelid was good at lots of things, but not at admitting his shortcomings and his mistakes. The prosecutor turned and twisted in his explanation, which consisted of the information that while Allan Karlsson and his friends were not under arrest (they had, incidentally, been found that same afternoon in Västergötland), they were probably guilty anyway, the prosecutor had acted properly, and the only thing that was new was the evidence had changed so dramatically that the arrest warrants for the time being were no longer valid.

The representatives of the media wondered in what way the proof had changed, and Prosecutor Ranelid described in detail the new information from the Ministry of Foreign Affairs with regard to the fate of Bylund and Hultén in Djibouti and Riga respectively. And then Ranelid finished by saying that the law sometimes required that arrest warrants be withdrawn, however offensive that may feel in certain cases.

Prosecutor Ranelid sensed that he had not closed the matter entirely. And that impression was immediately confirmed when the representative of the major national *Dagens Nyheter* peered over his reading glasses and reeled off a monologue containing a host of questions that made the prosecutor especially uneasy.

—Have I understood correctly that despite the new circumstances you still consider Allan Karlsson guilty of murder or manslaughter? Does that mean that you believe that Allan Karlsson, one hundred years old as we know, has forced the thirty-two-year-old Bengt Bylund to follow him to Djibouti on the Horn of Africa and there blown the said Bylund—but not himself—to bits as recently as yesterday afternoon, and then in all haste gone to Västergötland? Can you describe what means of transportation Karlsson is meant to have used, considering that to the best of my knowledge there are no direct flights between Djibouti and the west of Sweden, and considering that Allan Karlsson is said not to have a valid passport?

Prosecutor Ranelid inhaled deeply, and said he had not made himself clear. There was no doubt whatsoever as to the fact that Allan Karlsson, Julius Jonsson, Benny Ljungberg, and Gunilla Björklund were innocent of what they were accused of.

—No doubt whatsoever, as I said, Ranelid repeated, having at the last second managed to convince himself of the matter.

But those damned journalists were not satisfied with that.

—You have previously in some detail described the chronology and geography of the three presumed murders. If the suspects are now suddenly innocent, what does the new course of events look like? wondered the reporter from the local paper.

Enough was enough. The representative of the local paper should not think he could beat up on Prosecutor Ranelid.

—For technical reasons in connection with the investigation, I am unable for the time being to say any more, was Prosecutor Ranelid's closing comment before he got up from his chair.

"Technical reasons in connection with the investigation" had more than once saved a prosecutor in a tight spot, but this time it wouldn't work. For several weeks, the prosecutor had trumpeted out the reasons why the four were guilty, and now the press thought it only right that he devote at least a minute or two to explaining their innocence. Or as the know-all from *Dagens Nyheter* put it:

—How can it be secret "for technical reasons" to tell us what a number of innocent people have been doing?

Prosecutor Ranelid stood there on the edge of a precipice. Almost everything indicated that he would fall over, straightaway or in a day or two. But he had one advantage over the journalists. Ranelid knew where Allan Karlsson and the others were holed up. After all, Västergötland was a large county. This would be his final chance. Prosecutor Ranelid said:

—If for once you could let me have my say! For technical reasons in connection with the investigation I am, for the time being, unable to say any more. But at three tomorrow, I shall arrange a new press conference in these premises and on that occasion I intend to describe exactly what happened, as you have asked me to do.

—Where exactly in Västergötland is Allan Karlsson just now? asked one journalist.

—I am not saying, said Prosecutor Ranelid, and he left.

How could it possibly have ended up like this? Prosecutor Ranelid sat in his room with the door locked and smoked a cigarette for the first time in seven years. He had been going down in Swedish criminal history as the first prosecutor to convict murderers whose victims' bodies had not been found. And then suddenly, the bodies had turned up. And in the wrong places too! And besides, victim number three was still alive, the one who had been the deadest of them all. Just think, what damage number three had done to Ranelid.

—I should kill the devil as a punishment, the prosecutor muttered to himself.

But now it was a matter of saving his honor and his career, and for that reason a murder was not the best solution. The prosecutor went over the catastrophic press conference in his mind. He had in the end been very clear about the fact that Karlsson and his henchmen were innocent. And all of this was because he . . . actually didn't know. What had actually happened? Bolt Bylund *must* have died on that inspection trolley. So how the hell could he die again several weeks later a whole continent away?

Prosecutor Ranelid cursed himself for being so quick to meet the press. He ought to have talked to Allan Karlsson and his henchmen first, investigated everything—and then decided what the media needed to know.

And in his current predicament—in the aftermath of the catastrophic statements about the innocence of Karlsson and his henchmen—if he were to pull them in "to help with inquiries" it would be seen as simply harassing them. Yet Ranelid didn't have many options. He had to find out what had happened . . . and he had to do so before three the following day.

Otherwise, in the eyes of his colleagues he would no longer be a prosecutor but a clown.

Chief Inspector Aronsson was in excellent spirits sitting in the hammock at Bellringer Farm drinking coffee, and with a pastry to dip into it too. The hunt for the disappearing centenarian was over; besides, the sympathetic old man no longer had a warrant out for his arrest. Why the old guy had climbed out of his window almost a month ago, and what had happened since then remained to be discovered, if it needed to be discovered at all.

Nevertheless, there was surely time for a little more small talk first. The man who had been run over and killed and was now risen from the dead, Per-Gunnar "the Boss" Gerdin, turned out to be a perfectly regular sort of guy. He had immediately proposed that they should drop the formal titles, and be on first-name terms, and that he in that case preferred to be called Pike.

—That's fine with me, Pike, said Chief Inspector Aronsson. You can call me Göran.

—Pike and Göran, said Allan. That rolls off the tongue nicely, perhaps you two should go into business together?

Pike said that he wasn't so sure that he had the necessary respect for the internal revenue authorities and their taxes to be able to run a company in partnership with a police chief inspector, but that he nevertheless thanked Allan for the advice.

The mood had thus immediately become jovial. And it didn't get worse when Benny and The Beauty joined them, and shortly after, Julius and Bosse too.

They talked about all manner of things there on the veranda, except how the events of the past month fit together. Allan scored a success when he suddenly led an elephant around the corner and together with Sonya put on a short dance performance. Julius became more and more pleased not to be wanted by the police any longer, and started to cut off the beard that he had felt obliged to cultivate before he had dared show himself in Falköping.

—To think that I have been guilty all my life and now I am suddenly innocent! said Julius. What a delightful sensation!

And Bosse, for his part, thought this was reason enough to

fetch a bottle of genuine Hungarian champagne for his friends
and the chief inspector to toast each other. The chief inspector
lamely protested that he had his car at the farm. A room was re-
served at the central hotel in Falköping, but as a chief inspector he
could hardly drive there if he was a bit tipsy.

But then Benny came to the rescue and said that teetotalers in
general—according to Allan—were a threat to world peace, but
that they were useful to have at hand when you needed a lift somewhere.

—Have a glass of champagne, Inspector, and I shall make sure
that you get safely to your hotel.

The inspector didn't need further persuading. He had long suffered from a chronic lack of social life, and now that he finally
found himself in pleasant company he couldn't sit there and sulk.

—Well now, a little toast for the innocence of all of you, I suppose the police force can go along with that, he said. Or even two
toasts if necessary; there are quite a lot of you. . . .

Thus passed a couple of hours of general merriment before Chief
Inspector Aronsson's mobile rang again. Once more, it was
Prosecutor Ranelid. He told Aronsson that on account of unfortunate circumstances in the presence of the press, he had just
announced that the three men and the woman were innocent,
and he had done so in a manner that hardly allowed for retraction.
Besides, within less than twenty-four hours he must know what
had actually happened between the day when the old geezer
Karlsson climbed out of his window and the present day, because
that was what the press were being summoned to hear at three
tomorrow.

—In other words, you are well up shit creek, said the slightly
drunken chief inspector.

—You must help me, Göran!

—How? By moving corpses geographically? Or by killing

people who have had the poor taste to not be as dead as you would have wished them to be?

Prosecutor Ranelid admitted that he had already considered that last solution, but that it probably wouldn't work. No, he hoped that Göran could cautiously sound out Allan Karlsson and his . . . accomplices about whether Ranelid would be welcome at the farm the following morning for a little—completely informal—chat about this and that in order to bring clarity as to what had recently taken place in the forests of Södermanland and Småland. And for good measure, Prosecutor Ranelid promised that he would apologize to the four innocent citizens on behalf of the Södermanland Police Force.

—The Södermanland Police Force? said Chief Inspector Aronsson.

—Yes . . . Or, no, on my own behalf, said Prosecutor Ranelid.

—Understood. Just take a deep breath, Conny, and I'll ask. I'll call you back in a few minutes.

Chief Inspector Aronsson turned to his companions and announced the happy news that Prosecutor Ranelid had just held a press conference where he had emphasized how innocent Allan Karlsson and his friends were. And then he passed on the prosecutor's request to visit.

The Beauty reacted with an animated lecture saying that no good would come of describing in detail the developments of the last few weeks for the prosecutor. Julius agreed. If you had been declared innocent, then you were innocent, and that was that.

—And I'm not used to that. So it would be too bad if my innocence lasted less than twenty-four hours.

Allan said that he wished his friends would stop worrying about every little thing. The newspapers and TV would certainly not leave the group in peace until they had their story. So wouldn't it be better to tell it to a solitary prosecutor, than to have journalists all over the place for the next few weeks?

—Besides, we've got all evening to come up with a story, said Allan.

Chief Inspector Aronsson would have preferred not to hear the last bit. He got up from his chair to emphasize his presence and stop them from saying any more. It was time to call it a day, he said. If Benny would be so kind as to drive him to his hotel, he would be most grateful. From the car, Aronsson intended to phone Prosecutor Ranelid and tell him that he would be welcome at about 10:00 the following morning, if that was what the group agreed upon. In any case, Aronsson intended to come in a taxi, if only to collect his car. Incidentally, would it be possible to have another half glass of that exquisite Bulgarian champagne before he left? What? It was Hungarian? Well it didn't really matter, to be honest.

Chief Inspector Aronsson was served yet another glass, filled to the brim, which he downed in all haste before rubbing his nose and then getting into the passenger seat of his own car, already driven up to the door by Benny. And then, he declaimed some lines from the Swedish poet Carl Michael Bellman about good friends and Hungarian wine.

Benny, an almost-expert on literature, nodded.

—John 8:7. Don't forget that tomorrow morning, Chief Inspector, Bosse called out in a sudden burst of inspiration. In the Bible, John 8:7.

TWENTY-FIVE

Friday, May 27, 2005

I t takes time to get from Eskilstuna to Falköping. *Prosecutor Conny Ranelid* needed to get up at dawn (and after sleeping badly all night too) to get to Bellringer Farm by ten o'clock. And the meeting couldn't run longer than one hour or his plan would be ruined. The press conference was supposed to start at three.

Conny Ranelid was close to tears as he drove down the highway. *The Great Victory of Justice*—that was what his book would have been called. Hah! If there was any justice at all in this world, then lightning would strike that damned farm and everyone there would burn to death. Then Prosecutor Ranelid could say whatever he wanted to the journalists.

*C*hief Inspector Aronsson slept late. He woke up at nine, with a bit of a bad conscience about the events of the previous day. He had drunk champagne with the potential delinquents, and he had clearly heard Karlsson say that they would make up a story for Prosecutor Ranelid. Was he about to become an accomplice—accomplice to what, in that case?

When the chief inspector had reached his hotel the previous evening, he looked up John 8:7 in the Gideon Bible in his room. This had been followed by a couple of hours of Bible reading in a corner of the hotel bar, in the company of a gin and tonic, followed by another gin and tonic followed by another gin and tonic.

The chapter in question was about the woman who committed adultery and whom the Pharisees had taken before Jesus to place him in a dilemma. If according to Jesus the woman should not be stoned for her crime, then Jesus was rejecting Moses (the Book of Leviticus). If, on the other hand, Jesus was on the same side as Moses, then he would be battling with the Romans who had the monopoly on the death sentence. Would Jesus go against Moses or the Romans? The Pharisees thought that they had the Master cornered. But Jesus was Jesus and after thinking it over he said:

—Let he who is without sin cast the first stone!

Jesus had thus avoided arguing with Moses *and* with the Romans, or for that matter with the Pharisees. The Pharisees went off, one by one (men, in general, are of course not in the slightest bit free of sin). Finally, only Jesus and the woman remained.

—Woman, where are they? Has no one condemned you?

—No one, she answered.

—Then neither do I condemn you, Jesus declared. Go now and sin no more.

*T*he chief inspector still had his policeman's sense of smell intact and he was sure he could smell a rat. But Karlsson and Jonsson and Ljungberg and Björklund and Gerdin were, as of yesterday,

declared innocent by Prosecutor Ranelid, and who was Aronsson
to call them delinquents? Besides, they were actually a rather appealing bunch and—as Jesus so rightly pointed out—who was in a
position to cast the first stone? Aronsson thought back to some
darker moments of his own life, but above all he grew angry over
how Prosecutor Ranelid had wished the thoroughly pleasant Pike
Gerdin dead, just to serve his own purposes.

—No, damn it! You'll have to sort this out yourself, Ranelid,
said Chief Inspector Aronsson and headed for the hotel's breakfast
room.

Cereal, toast, and egg were washed down with coffee and the
two big national dailies, both of which cautiously suggested that
the prosecutor had made something of a fiasco of the case of the
disappearing centenarian who was eventually both accused of murder and declared innocent. The newspapers did, however, have to
admit that they didn't know enough about it. The centenarian himself couldn't be found, and the prosecutor didn't want to tell them
any more until Friday afternoon.

—As noted, Ranelid, you'll have to sort this out yourself, Aronsson murmured.

Then the chief inspector ordered a taxi and arrived at Bellringer Farm at 9:51, just three minutes before the prosecutor.

There was no meteorological risk of what Prosecutor Ranelid so de-
voutly wished for: a lightning strike on Bellringer Farm. But
it was cloudy and chilly. So the inhabitants of the farm planned to
meet in the spacious kitchen.

The previous evening the group had agreed on an alternative
story to present to Prosecutor Ranelid, and to be on the safe side
they had rehearsed the story at breakfast too. Now they were reasonably sure of their roles for the morning's performance, allowing for the fact that the truth is always much simpler to remember
than its opposite. He who tells a big lie can easily find himself in

big trouble, so now the members of the group had to think carefully before they opened their mouths.

—Damn and hell, was how The Beauty summarized the general tension before Chief Inspector Aronsson and Prosecutor Ranelid were led into the kitchen.

The meeting with Prosecutor Conny Ranelid was more fun for some than for others. This is how it went:

—Well, to start with I would like to thank you for letting me come, said Prosecutor Ranelid. And I must apologize on behalf of . . . er . . . on behalf of the prosecutor's office for the fact that several of you had warrants out for your arrest quite without cause. Having said that, I would very much like to know what happened, from the moment you, Mr. Karlsson, climbed out of the window at the Old Folks' Home and right up to the present. Would you like to begin, Mr. Karlsson?

Allan had no objection to that. He thought that this might turn out to be fun.

—I can indeed, Mr. Prosecutor, even though I am old and decrepit, and my memory isn't what it used to be. But I do remember that I climbed out of that window, yes I do. And there were some very sound reasons for that, very sound reasons. You see, Mr. Prosecutor, I was on my way to see my good friend Julius Jonsson here, and you don't show up to visit him without a bottle of vodka and that is exactly what I had been able to obtain after sneaking off to the local state-run alcohol store when nobody was looking. In fact, nowadays you don't even have to go all the way to the state-run alcohol store, you can simply knock on the door of . . . well, I won't tell you his name, Mr. Prosecutor, because that isn't why you are here, but he sells privately imported vodka for less than half the regular price. Anyway, this time Eklund wasn't at home—oh dear, now I've told you his name—and I had no choice but to buy the vodka at the state store. Then I managed to get the bottle into my room and usually at that point I'm home free. But this time I was going to take it out again, and the director was on duty and she has eyes in the back of her head and everywhere else, I can tell you, Mr. Prosecutor. It's not easy to fool Director Alice. So I thought that the window was the best route on this occasion. It was my hundredth birthday that day, and who wants to have his birthday drink confiscated then?

The prosecutor thought that this might drag on. This old Karlsson geezer had already been babbling for quite a while without really saying anything. And in less than an hour, Ranelid had to be on his way back to Eskilstuna.

—Thank you, Mr. Karlsson, for the interesting insights into your difficulties in acquiring a drink on your big day, but I hope you'll forgive me for asking you to be more disciplined in the telling; we don't have much time, as I am sure you understand. What about the suitcase and the meeting with Bolt Bylund at the bus station?

—Well, now, how did that happen? Per-Gunnar phoned Julius who phoned me. According to Julius, Per-Gunnar wanted me to take charge of those Bibles and I didn't want to say no because I. . . .

—Bibles? Prosecutor Ranelid interrupted.

—If you will allow me, Mr. Prosecutor, perhaps I can give a little background information? said Benny.

—By all means, said the prosecutor.

—Well, it's like this. Allan is a good friend of Julius at Byringe, who in turn is a good friend of Per-Gunnar, the man that the prosecutor thought was dead, and Per-Gunnar in turn is a good friend of mine, and I am partly the brother of my brother Bosse, the man who is our host today, partly the fiancé of Gunilla, she is the beautiful lady at the head of the table, and Gunilla busies herself with exegesis and thus has something in common with Bosse who sells Bibles—to Per-Gunnar for example.

The prosecutor sat there with a pen in his hand, but it had all been said so quickly that he hadn't jotted down a single word.

—Exegesis?

—Yes, the interpretation of the Bible, The Beauty explained.

Interpretation of the Bible? thought Chief Inspector Aronsson who sat in silence beside the prosecutor. Was it even possible to interpret the Bible when you swore as much as Aronsson had heard The Beauty swear the previous evening? But he said nothing. This was for the prosecutor to sort out, once and for all.

—Interpretation of the Bible? said Prosecutor Ranelid, but decided in the very same second to move on. Never mind, tell me instead what happened with the suitcase and Bolt Bylund at the bus station.

Now it was Per-Gunnar Gerdin's turn to get in the act.

—Would you, Mr. Prosecutor, allow me to say something?

—Absolutely, answered Prosecutor Ranelid. As long as what somebody says will shed some light on this business, the devil himself can have a say.

—Please mind your language, said The Beauty and rolled her eyes. (The chief inspector was now completely certain that they were making fun of the prosecutor.)

—I don't think "the devil" is a fully adequate description of my humble self since I found Jesus, said Per-Gunnar Gerdin. You, Mr. Prosecutor, will of course have heard that I led an organization called Never Again. The name originally referred to the fact that its members would never find themselves behind bars again even though there might be no lack of legal reasons for such a measure, but as of late the name has acquired another meaning. Never Again shall we be tempted to break the law, not that written by man and absolutely not that written in Heaven!

—Is that why Bolt smashed up a waiting room, beat up an official, and then kidnapped a bus driver and his bus? asked Prosecutor Ranelid.

—Oh dear, now I can definitely feel a certain sarcasm in the air, said Per-Gunnar Gerdin. But just because I myself have seen the light, doesn't mean that my colleagues have done the same.

One of them has indeed gone to South America to do missionary work, but the two others came to an unfortunate end. I had entrusted Bolt with the task of collecting the suitcase with two hundred Bibles on Bosse's route from Uppsala home to Falköping. I was going to use the Bibles to spread joy among the worst villains in the country, if you will excuse my language, Mr. Prosecutor.

Up until now, the owner of Bellringer Farm, Bosse, had kept quiet. But at this juncture he placed a heavy gray suitcase onto the kitchen table and opened it. Inside lay a large number of superslim Bibles bound in genuine black leather, with golden lettering, notations, three marking ribbons, maps in color, and more besides.

—You will not encounter a more magnificent Bible experience than this, Mr. Prosecutor, said Bosse Ljungberg with conviction. Would you allow me to present you with a copy? We must all seek the light, Mr. Prosecutor!

Unlike the others, Bosse actually meant what he said. And the prosecutor must have had an inkling of that, because he began to waiver in his conviction that all this Bible talk was just pretense. He accepted Bosse's Bible and thought that immediate salvation might be his only option.

—Can we once and for all get back to the business at hand? he asked. What happened to that damned suitcase in Malmköping?

—No swearing! lectured The Beauty.

—Perhaps it's my turn again? Allan said. Well, you see, I went to the bus station a little earlier than I had expected, because Julius asked me to. Bolt Bylund had previously phoned Per-Gunnar in Stockholm and had been—if you, Mr. Prosecutor, will again excuse my language—a bit tipsy! And as you will know, Mr. Prosecutor, or perhaps as you may not know because I don't know your drinking habits, but anyhow . . . where was I? Yes, you know, Mr. Prosecutor, how when vodka goes in, common sense goes out, or whatever the saying is. I myself, in a state of inebriation have said more than I should have in a submarine at a depth of seven hundred feet in the middle of the Baltic Sea. . . .

—In the name of God, get to the point! said Prosecutor Ranelid.

—No blasphemy! urged The Beauty.

Prosecutor Ranelid put one hand on his brow while he inhaled deeply a few times. Allan Karlsson went on:

—Well, Bolt Bylund had phoned Per-Gunnar in Stockholm to say that he was resigning from Per-Gunnar's Bible Club, and that instead he intended to join the Foreign Legion but that first of all—and at this point you ought to sit down, Mr. Prosecutor, because what I am going to say is dreadful—he intended to make a bonfire of the Bibles in the main square in Malmköping!

—To be more precise, he is said to have yelled "those damn fucking Bibles," said The Beauty.

—No wonder, then, that I was sent out to find Mr. Bolt and take the suitcase from him before it was too late. We often have little time, and sometimes we have even less time than we can possibly imagine. Like, for example, on the occasion when General Franco in Spain very nearly got blown to bits before my very eyes.

—What has General Franco in Spain got to do with this story? wondered Prosecutor Ranelid.

—Nothing whatsoever, Mr. Prosecutor, other than that I let him serve as an illustrative example. You can never have too much clarity.

—In that case, what if you, Mr. Karlsson, were to bring some clarity to this matter? What happened to the suitcase?

—Well, Mr. Bolt didn't want to give it to me, and my physique didn't really allow me to try to take it by force, not just *my* physique for that matter. In principle I think it's terrible the way people . . .

—Stick to the subject, Mr. Karlsson!

—Yes, my apologies, Mr. Prosecutor. Well, when Mr. Bolt, in the middle of everything, needed to visit the station's public conveniences, then I took my chance. Together with the suitcase, I got on the Strängnäs bus, which took me to Byringe and old Julius here, or Julle as we sometimes say.

—Julle? said the prosecutor, as he felt he had to say something.

—Or Julius, said Julius. Nice to meet you.

The prosecutor sat in silence for a few moments. Now he had actually started making some notes, and he seemed to be drawing connecting lines between the notes.

—But, Mr. Karlsson, you paid for the bus journey with a fifty-crown banknote and wondered how far it would get you. How does that fit in with having a deliberate intention of traveling to Byringe and nowhere else?

—Hah! said Allan. I know perfectly well what it costs to travel to Byringe. I just happened to have a fifty-crown note in my wallet and I simply had a bit of fun with the driver. That's not against the law, is it, Mr. Prosecutor?

Prosecutor Ranelid didn't bother to answer.

—Briefly: What happened next?

—Briefly? Briefly, Julius and I, we had a nice evening together, until Mr. Bolt came and tried to unbolt the door, if you will excuse the pun, Mr. Prosecutor. But since we had a bottle of vodka on the table, and you will perhaps remember from earlier in my tale that that is what I had with me—a bottle of vodka—and, to be honest, not just one bottle but two, one shouldn't tell untruths about less-important details and anyhow who can judge what is more or less important in this tale, that is for you, Mr. Pros . . .

—Go on!

—Yes, my apologies. Well, Mr. Bolt calmed down when he realized there was roast elk and vodka on the menu. During the course of the late evening, he even decided not to burn the Bibles in gratitude for the state of inebriation he had been afforded. Alcohol does indeed have its positive sides, don't you think, Mr. Pros . . .

—Go on!

—In the morning, Mr. Bolt had the worst hangover. I personally haven't been there since 1945, when I did my best to drink Vice President Truman under the table with the help of tequila. Unfortunately, President Roosevelt went and died that same day so we had to break off the party early, and that was probably lucky for me because I can't begin to describe what my head felt like the next day. You could say I only felt slightly better than Roosevelt.

Prosecutor Ranelid blinked rapidly. In the end, his curiosity got the better of him:

—What are you talking about? Were you drinking tequila with Vice President Truman when President Roosevelt died?

—Perhaps we shouldn't get bogged down in details, or what do you think, Mr. Prosecutor?

The prosecutor said nothing.

—Mr. Bolt was, in any case, not in a condition to help us pedal the inspection trolley when it was time to travel to Åker Foundry the following morning.

—He wasn't even wearing shoes, I understand, said the prosecutor. How can you explain that, Karlsson?

—If you, Mr. Prosecutor, had only seen what a hangover Mr. Bolt had that morning. . . . He could just as well have been sitting there in nothing but underpants.

—And your own shoes, Karlsson? They were later found in Julius Jonsson's kitchen.

—Yes, I borrowed some shoes from Julius of course. If you are one hundred years old, you sometimes find yourself going out in slippers, as you'll discover yourself, Mr. Prosecutor, if you wait forty or fifty years.

—I don't think I'll survive that long, said Prosecutor Ranelid. The question is whether I'll survive this conversation. How do you explain that when the inspection trolley was found, a police dog could smell traces of a dead body?

—You tell me, Mr. Prosecutor. Mr. Bolt was of course the last person to leave the trolley, so perhaps he could have told us himself, if he hadn't had the misfortune to die over there in Djibouti. Do you, Mr. Prosecutor, think that I might be the origin of that smell? I'm not dead, that much is for sure, but I am dreadfully old. . . . Can the smell of a dead person sort of come a bit early?

Prosecutor Ranelid was getting impatient. So far they had covered less than one of the twenty-six days. And ninety percent of what came out of the mouth of the old geezer was pure nonsense.

—Go on! said Prosecutor Ranelid.

—Well, we left Mr. Bolt sleeping on the trolley and went for a refreshing walk to the hot dog stand, which of course was run by Per-Gunnar's friend Benny.

—Have you also been in prison? asked the prosecutor.

—No, but I've studied criminology, said Benny quite truthfully, before making up a story about how he had once interviewed inmates in a big prison and had then met Per-Gunnar.

Prosecutor Ranelid seemed to note something down again, after which he monotonously ordered Allan Karlsson to "go on!"

—By all means. Benny was originally going to drive me and Julius to Stockholm so that we could give the suitcase with Bibles to Per-Gunnar. But now Benny said he wanted to make a detour via Småland to see his fiancée, Gunilla. . . .

—Peace be with you, said Gunilla and nodded toward Prosecutor Ranelid.

Allan went on:

—Benny was of course the one who knew Per-Gunnar best and Benny said that Per-Gunnar could wait a few days for the Bibles; he didn't think there was anything with a topical news value in them, and you have to admit he is right about that. But you can't wait in all eternity, because when Jesus actually returns to Earth then all the chapters on his imminent return become obsolete. . . .

—Stick to the subject!

—Of course, Mr. Prosecutor! I shall absolutely stick to the subject, otherwise things can go badly wrong. I probably know that better than anyone. If I hadn't stuck to the subject in front of Mao Tse-tung in Manchuria then I would almost certainly have been shot then and there.

—That would undeniably have saved us a lot of trouble, said Prosecutor Ranelid.

—Anyhow, Benny didn't think that Jesus would have time to return while we were in Småland, and to the best of my knowledge Benny was right about that. . . .

—Karlsson!

—Oh yes. Well, the three of us drove to Småland without first telling Per-Gunnar, and that of course was a mistake.

—Yes, it was, Per-Gunnar Gerdin added at this point. I suppose I could have waited a few days for the Bibles; that wasn't the issue. But, you see, Mr. Prosecutor, I thought that Bolt had come up with something stupid together with Julius, Allan, and Benny. Because Bolt had never liked the idea that Never Again should start spreading the Gospel. And of course I didn't feel any better after reading the papers!

The prosecutor nodded. Perhaps there was something here that resembled logic after all. Then he turned to Benny:

—But when you read about a suspected kidnapping of a centenarian—why didn't you contact the police?

—Well, the thought did occur to me. But when I raised it with Allan and Julius they refused to allow it. Julius said that on principle he never spoke to the police, and Allan said that he was on the run from the Old Folks' Home and absolutely didn't want to be returned to Director Alice just because the newspapers and TV had got this and that wrong.

—You never talk with the police on principle? said Prosecutor Ranelid to Julius Jonsson.

—I have had a little bad luck in my relations with the police over the years. But for pleasant encounters—like with Chief Inspector Aronsson yesterday and with you, Mr. Prosecutor, today—I am happy to make an exception. Would you like some more coffee?

Yes, the prosecutor would indeed. He needed all the energy and strength he could muster to get this meeting into some sort of order and then to be able to present something to the media at three o'clock. Something that was true, or at least credible.

But the prosecutor didn't want to let Benny Ljungberg off the hook.

—And why didn't you phone your friend Per-Gunnar Gerdin? You must have realized that he would read about you in the newspaper.

—I thought that perhaps the police and prosecutor were not yet aware of the fact that Per-Gunnar had met Jesus, and that therefore his phone line was bugged. And you, Mr. Prosecutor, have to admit that I was right.

The prosecutor mumbled something, made a note, and regretted that he had happened to let that detail slip out to the journalists, but done was done. He turned to Per-Gunnar Gerdin.

—Mr. Gerdin, you seem to have been tipped off as to where Allan Karlsson and his friends were situated. Where did that tip come from?

—Regrettably, we'll probably never know. My colleague took that information with him to his grave. Or to the scrapyard to be exact.

—And what was the tip?

—That Allan, Benny, and his girlfriend had been seen in Rottne in Småland. A friend of Bucket called, I think. I was mainly interested in the information as such. I knew that Benny's girlfriend lived in Småland and that she had red hair. So I ordered Bucket to make his way to Rottne and stand outside the supermarket. Because you have to eat. . . .

—And Bucket was happy to oblige, in the name of Jesus?

—Well, not exactly! You've hit it on the head there, Mr. Prosecutor. One can say a lot about Bucket, but . . . religious? No, he was never that. He was, if anything, even more upset than Bolt as to the new direction the club had taken. He talked of going to Russia or the Baltic countries and getting into the narcotics business there. . . . Have you ever heard anything so dreadful? He might have done so, but you'll have to ask him yourself. . . . No, that's not possible. . . .

The prosecutor looked somewhat suspiciously at Per-Gunnar Gerdin.

—We had a tape recording, exactly as Benny Ljungberg just assumed. In it, you refer to Gunilla Björklund as an "old dame" and a little later in the conversation you swear as well. What does the Lord think about that?

—Ah, the Lord is quick to forgive, as you will soon see if you open the book you have just been given.

—"Whoever's sins you forgive, they are forgiven," says Jesus, Bosse chipped in.

—The Gospel according to John? said Chief Inspector Aronsson, who thought he recognized the quote from the hours he spent in the corner of the hotel bar the previous evening.

—Do you read the Bible? Prosecutor Ranelid wondered in amazement.

Chief Inspector Aronsson didn't answer, but smiled piously at Prosecutor Ranelid.

—I chose that tone because I wanted Bucket to recognize the style from the old days; I thought that it might make him follow orders, explained Per-Gunnar Gerdin.

—And did he? wondered the prosecutor.

—Yes and no. I didn't want him to make himself known to Allan, Julius, Benny, and his girlfriend, because I thought that his rather uncouth manner wouldn't really go down well with the group.

—It certainly didn't, The Beauty added.

—How come? wondered Prosecutor Ranelid.

—Well, he came charging up to my farm and was smoking and swearing and wanted alcohol. . . . I can put up with a great deal, but I can't abide folk who have to resort to expletives.

Chief Inspector Aronsson managed to avoid choking on his cake. The Beauty had as recently as the previous evening been sitting on the veranda and swearing almost without a pause for breath. Aronsson felt more and more certain that he never wanted to find out the truth in this mess. Things were all right as they were. The Beauty went on:

—I am pretty sure he was drunk already when he arrived, and, just think, he came in a car too! And then he went around waving his pistol to show off, boasting and saying that he was going to deal drugs in . . . Riga, I think it was. So I roared out, yes, Mr. Prosecutor, I roared out "No weapons on my land!" and made him put his gun down on the veranda. I don't think I've ever met a more bad-tempered and unpleasant man. . . .

—Perhaps it was the Bibles that made him lose his temper, Allan said. Religion can so easily stir up people's feelings. Once, when I was in Tehran . . .

—Tehran? the prosecutor blurted out.

—Yes, it was a few years ago, that's for sure. Things were in order down there in those days, as Churchill said to me when we left there by plane.

—Churchill? said the prosecutor.

—Yes, the prime minister. Or perhaps he wasn't prime minister just then, but earlier. And later, in fact.

—I know bloody well who Churchill was, I just . . . You and Churchill together in Tehran?

—No swearing, Mr. Prosecutor! said The Beauty.

—Well, not together exactly. I was living for a while with a missionary. And he was an expert at getting people to lose their tempers.

And losing his temper was exactly what Prosecutor Ranelid was doing. He had just realized that he was trying to get the facts out of a hundred-year-old geezer who claimed he had met Franco, Truman, Mao Tse-tung, and Churchill. But Ranelid losing his temper didn't bother Allan. He continued:

—Young Mr. Bucket walked around like a human thundercloud the entire time he was at Lake Farm. He only brightened up once, and that was when he finally left. Then he lowered the win-

dow of his car and shouted out: "Latvia, here I come!" We chose to
interpret that as meaning he was on his way to Latvia, but you,
Mr. Prosecutor, are much more experienced in police matters so
perhaps you have a different interpretation?

—Idiot! said the prosecutor.

—Idiot? said Allan. I've never been called that before. Dog and
rat, yes, Stalin let those two epithets slip out when he was at his
angriest, but never idiot.

—Then it's about time, said Prosecutor Ranelid.

Per-Gunnar Gerdin interrupted:

—Now, now, no need to be angry because you can't just lock
up anyone you feel like, Mr. Prosecutor. Do you want to hear the
rest of the story, or not?

Yes, the prosecutor wanted to hear it, so he mumbled an apol-
ogy. Or perhaps "wanted" was not the right word . . . he simply
had to hear it. So he let Per-Gunnar go on:

—So, about Never Again, Bolt went off to Africa to become a
French Legionnaire, Bucket to Latvia to start a drug business, and
Caracas went home to . . . well, he went home. All that is left is little
me, all on my own, with Jesus by my side, of course.

—Right, mumbled the prosecutor. Go on!

—I made my way down to Lake Farm to see Gunilla, Benny's
girlfriend. Bucket had at least phoned and told me the address before he left the country.

—Umm, I have some questions about that, said Prosecutor
Ranelid. The first is to you, Gunilla Björklund. Why did you go off
and buy a bus a few days before you left—and why did you leave?

The previous evening, the friends had decided to keep Sonya
out of it all. Just like Allan, she was on the run, but unlike Allan
she had no citizen's rights. She probably would not be regarded as
Swedish, and in Sweden, just like in most countries, you don't count
for much if you are a foreigner. Sonya would probably be deported
or sentenced to life in a zoo or both.

—It's true that the bus was purchased in my name, said The Beauty, but it was actually Benny and me who bought it together and we bought it for Benny's brother Bosse.

—And he was going to fill it with Bibles? Prosecutor Ranelid burst out. He was no longer capable of minding his manners and temper.

—No, with watermelons, Bosse answered. Do you want to taste the sweetest watermelons in the world, Mr. Prosecutor?

—No, I don't, Prosecutor Ranelid answered. I want to bring some clarity to what remains of the story and then I want to go home and quickly get through a press conference and then I want to take a vacation. That's what I want. And now let's move on. Why the hell . . . umm, why on earth did you leave Lake Farm just when Per-Gunnar Gerdin arrived?

—But they didn't know I was on the way there, said Per-Gunnar Gerdin. Are you finding it hard to follow, Mr. Prosecutor?

—Yes, I am, said Prosecutor Ranelid. Einstein would find it hard to follow if he had to listen to this nonsense talk.

—Now that you mention Einstein . . . , said Allan.

—No, Mr. Karlsson, said Prosecutor Ranelid with a firm voice. I don't want to hear what you and Einstein did together. Instead, I want Mr. Gerdin to explain how the "Russians" come into the picture.

—The Russians? said Per-Gunnar Gerdin.

—Yes, the Russians. Your deceased colleague Bucket talks of "the Russians" in your bugged phone conversation. You complained that Bucket hadn't called your pay-as-you-go phone, and Bucket answered that he thought that only applied when you did business with the Russians.

—That isn't something I want to talk about, said Per-Gunnar Gerdin, mainly because he didn't know what to say.

—But I do, said Prosecutor Ranelid.

There was silence around the table. The papers hadn't mentioned the bit about the Russians in Gerdin's phone conversation, and Gerdin himself hadn't remembered it. But then Benny said:

—*Yesli chelovek kurit, on plocho igraet v futbol.*

They all stared at him.

—"The Russians" refers to me and my brother, Benny explained. Our father—may he rest in peace—and our uncle Frasse—may he also rest in peace—were a bit red. So they made me and my brother learn Russian as children and friends and acquaintances nicknamed us the Russians. That was what I just said, but in Russian of course.

Like so much else this particular morning, what Benny had said had very little to do with the truth. He had simply tried to get Pike Gerdin out of a tight spot. Benny had almost completed a BA in Russian (he never handed in his final essay), but that was some time ago and all Benny could remember in a hurry was:

"If you smoke, you won't be much good at soccer."

But it worked. Allan was the only one there who understood what Benny had said.

It was all too much for Prosecutor Ranelid: First, all these idiotic references to historic figures, and then people speaking Russian. . . .

Can you explain, Mr. Gerdin, how you were first rammed and killed by your friends, and then rose up from the dead and are now sitting here and . . . eating watermelon? And can I taste that melon, after all?

—But of course, said Bosse. The recipe is secret though! Or as the saying goes: "If the food is going to be really tasty then you don't want the food inspector watching you when you make it."

That was not a saying that either Chief Inspector Aronsson or Prosecutor Ranelid had ever heard before. But Aronsson had once and for all decided to keep as quiet as possible, and Ranelid now wished for nothing more than to bring it all to a conclusion . . . whatever that was . . . and leave. So he didn't ask for an explanation. Instead, he noted that the watermelon in question was the tastiest he had ever bit into.

Per-Gunnar Gerdin explained how he had come to Lake Farm just as the bus was driving away, how he had gone to look around before he realized that the bus had probably carried off his friends, and how he had then chased it, overtaken it, and lost control of his car in a skid—and, well, the photos of the wrecked car were not unfamiliar to the prosecutor, he supposed.

—No surprise that he caught up with us, Allan added, after having been quiet for a while. He had more than three hundred horsepower under the hood. Not like the Volvo PV444 that took me to visit Prime Minister Erlander. Forty-four horsepower! That was a lot in those days. And I wonder how many horsepower Gustavsson had when he turned into my yard by mistake. . . .

—Shut it . . . please, Mr. Karlsson, before you finish me off, said Prosecutor Ranelid.

The chairman of Never Again continued his story. He had, of course, lost a little blood in the wrecked car, or actually quite a lot, but he was soon bandaged and he hadn't thought it necessary to go to the hospital for as little as a light wound, a broken arm, a concussion, and a few broken ribs.

—Besides, Benny did study literature, said Allan.

—Literature? repeated Prosecutor Ranelid.

—Did I say literature? I meant medicine.

—I have studied literature too, said Benny. My absolute favorite is probably Camilo José Cela, not least his first novel, from the 1940s, La familia de . . .

—Get back to the story.

The prosecutor, in his appeal, had happened to look at Allan, so Allan said:

—If you'll excuse us, Mr. Prosecutor, we've told you everything. But if you absolutely want to hear us talk some more then I

THE ONE HUNDRED YEAR OLD MAN   335

can probably remember one or two adventures from my time as a CIA agent—or even better from my trip across the Himalayas. And do you want the recipe for making vodka from goats' milk? All you need is a beet and a bit of sunshine. And some goats' milk of course.

Sometimes your mouth seems to go its own way while your brain stands still, and that was probably what happened to Prosecutor Ranelid when—contrary to what he had just decided—he happened to comment on Allan's latest nonsense:

—You crossed the Himalayas? At a hundred?

—No, don't be silly, said Allan. You see, Mr. Prosecutor, I haven't always been a hundred years old. No, that's recent.

—Can we move on. . . .

—We all grow up and get older, Allan continued. You might not think so when you are a child. Take young Mr. Kim Jong Il, for example. That unfortunate child sat crying on my lap, but now he is head of state, with all that entails. . . .

—Never mind, Karlsson.

—I'm sorry. You wanted to hear the story of when I crossed the Himalayas, Mr. Prosecutor. Well, for several months my only company was a camel, and say what you will about camels, they aren't much fun. . . .

—No! exclaimed Prosecutor Ranelid. I don't want to hear that at all. I just . . . I don't know . . .

And then Prosecutor Ranelid was silent for a few moments, before saying in a quiet voice that he didn't have any more questions . . . except possibly that he couldn't understand why the friends had stayed in hiding for several weeks when there was nothing to hide from.

—You were innocent, weren't you?

—But innocence can mean different things depending on whose perspective you adopt, said Benny.

—I was thinking along the same lines, said Allan. President Johnson and de Gaulle for example. Who was guilty and who was innocent when it came to their bad relationship? Mind you, I didn't bring that up when we met, we had other things to talk about, but . . .

—Please, Mr. Karlsson, said Prosecutor Ranelid. I beg you, please be quiet.

—You don't have to go down on your knees, Mr. Prosecutor. I shall be quiet as a mouse from now on, I promise you. During my hundred years, my tongue has slipped only twice. First when I told the West how you build an atom bomb, and then when I did the same for the East.

Prosecutor Ranelid slowly got up, and with a nod quietly thanked them for the melon, for the coffee and the cake, for . . . the conversation . . . and for the fact that the friends at Bellringer Farm had been so cooperative.

After which he got into his car and drove away.

—That went well, said Julius.

—Indeed it did, said Allan. I think I covered most of it.

In his car on the highway, Prosecutor Ranelid's mental paralysis gradually lost its hold. He went over the story he'd been told, adding something here, deleting something there (mainly deleting), and patching and polishing until he felt he had a nicely tidied-up story that would actually work. The only thing that really worried the prosecutor was that the journalists just wouldn't believe that the hundred-year-old Allan Karlsson already carried the scent of death.

Then Prosecutor Ranelid had an idea. That damned police dog . . . Could they blame it all on the dog?

If Ranelid could make it sound as if the dog was crazy, unimagined possibilities appeared for the prosecutor to save his own skin. The story would then be that there never was a corpse on the inspection trolley in the Södermanland forest, and that's why it hadn't been found. But the prosecutor had been fooled into believing the opposite, and that in turn led to a number of logical conclusions and decisions—which had turned out to be completely wrong. But you couldn't blame the prosecutor for that. It was the dog's fault.

This could be brilliant, Prosecutor Ranelid thought. The story of the dog that had lost its touch just needed to be confirmed by another source and then Kicki—was that her name?—had to end her days fast. It wouldn't do for her to prove her skills after the prosecutor had explained what happened.

Prosecutor Ranelid had a hold on Kicki's handler since the time, some years ago, when he had managed quietly to spirit away a case of a police officer suspected of shoplifting at 7-Eleven. A police career shouldn't end because of one muffin that somebody had forgotten to pay for, thought Ranelid. But now it was high time for the dog handler to repay the favor.

—Bye-bye, Kicki, said Prosecutor Ranelid and smiled for the first time in ages.

Shortly afterward, his phone rang. It was the county police chief. The autopsy and identity report from Riga had just landed on his desk.

—The compressed corpse at the scrapyard was Henrik Hultén, said the police chief.

—Nice to hear that, said Prosecutor Ranelid. And a good thing you phoned! Can you connect me to the reception? I need to get hold of Ronny Bäckman, the dog handler. . . .

The friends at Bellringer Farm had waved good-bye to Prosecutor Ranelid and at Allan's suggestion had returned to the kitchen table. There was, he said, a question that needed to be resolved.

Allan started the meeting by asking Chief Inspector Aronsson if he had anything to say about what Prosecutor Ranelid had just been told. Perhaps the chief inspector would prefer to go for a walk while the friends had their meeting?

Aronsson answered that he thought the account had been

clear and sound in every way possible. As far as the chief inspector was concerned, the case was closed, and if they would let him remain seated at the table he would be happy to do so. He himself was not free from sin, said Aronsson, and he was not about to throw the first or even the second stone in this matter.

—But do me the favor of not telling me things that I don't really need to know. I mean, if there should be alternative answers to those you just gave to Ranelid. . . .

Allan promised, and added that his friend Aronsson was welcome to stay.

Friend Aronsson, thought Aronsson. In his work over the years, Aronsson had made many enemies among the country's most unscrupulous villains, but not a single friend. He thought it was about time! And so he said that if Allan and the others would like to include him in their friendship, he would be both proud and happy.

Allan answered that during his long life he had been on comradely footing with both presidents and priests, but not until now with a policeman. And since their friend Aronsson absolutely didn't want to know too much, Allan promised not to say anything about where the group's pile of money had come from. For the sake of friendship, that is.

—Pile of money? asked Chief Inspector Aronsson.

—Yes, you know that suitcase? Before it contained superslim Bibles in genuine leather, it was filled to the brim with five-hundred-crown banknotes. About fifty million crowns.

—What the devil . . . said Chief Inspector Aronsson.

—Swear if you like, said The Beauty.

—Fifty million? asked Chief Inspector Aronsson.

—Minus some expenses in the course of our journey, said Allan. And now the group has to sort out who owns it. And with that I shall ask Pike to speak.

Per-Gunnar Pike Gerdin scratched his ear. Then he said that he would like the friends and the millions to stick together. Perhaps they could go on vacation together, because there was nothing Pike longed for more just now than to be served a parasol drink under a parasol somewhere far, far away. Besides, Pike happened to know that Allan had leanings of a similar nature.

—But without the parasol, said Allan.

Julius said that he agreed with Allan that protection from rain over the vodka was not one of the necessities of life, especially if you were already lying under a parasol and the sun was shining from a clear blue sky. But he also thought that the friends didn't need to argue about that. A shared vacation sounded great!

Chief Inspector Aronsson smiled shyly at the idea, not daring to assume he belonged to the group. Benny noted this, so he put an arm around the chief inspector's shoulder and asked how the representative of the police force preferred to have his holiday drinks served. The chief inspector smiled and was just about to answer when The Beauty put the damper on everything:

—I'm not taking a single step without Sonya and Buster!

And then she was silent for a second before she added:

—Not a snowball's chance in hell!

Since Benny for his part couldn't contemplate taking a step without The Beauty, his enthusiasm rapidly evaporated.

—Besides, I don't suppose half of us even have a valid passport, he sighed.

But Allan calmly thanked Pike for his generosity with regard to how the suitcase money could best be shared. He thought a holiday was a good idea, and preferably as many thousands of miles from Director Alice as possible. If only the other members of the group could agree, they could surely sort out the transportation issues and find a destination where they weren't so fussy about visas for man and beast.

—And how do you intend to take along a five-ton elephant on the plane? said Benny in despair.

—I don't know, said Allan. But as long as we think positively, I'm sure a solution will appear.

—And the valid passports?

—As long as we think positively, as I said.

—I don't think Sonya actually weighs much more than four tons, perhaps four and a half at the most, said The Beauty.

—You see, Benny, said Allan. That's what I mean by thinking positively. The problem immediately became a whole ton less.

—I might have an idea, The Beauty said.

—Me too, said Allan. Can I use your phone?

TWENTY-SIX

1968–1982

Yury Borisovich Popov lived and worked in the city of Sarov in Nizhny Novgorod, about 220 miles southeast of Moscow. Sarov was a secret city, almost more secret than Secret Agent Hutton. It wasn't even allowed to be called Sarov any longer, but had been given the not particularly romantic name Arzamas-16. Besides, the entire city had been rubbed out on all maps. Sarov did and didn't exist at one and the same time, depending on whether you referred to reality or to something else—kind of like Vladivostok for a few years from 1953 on, except the opposite.

Arzamas-16 was fenced in with barbed wire, and not a soul was let in or out without a vigorous security check. If you had an American passport and were stationed at the American Embassy in Moscow, it was not advisable to come anywhere near.

CIA agent Ryan Hutton and his new pupil Allan Karlsson had practiced the spy's ABCs for several weeks before Allan was installed at the embassy in Moscow under the name Allen Carson and with the vague title "administrator."

Embarrassingly for Secret Agent Hutton, he had completely ignored the fact that the target Allan Karlsson was intended to approach was unapproachable, shut in behind barbed wire in a city that was so well protected that it wasn't even allowed to be called what it was called, or to be where it was.

Secret Agent Hutton told Allan he was sorry about the mistake, but added that Mr. Karlsson would surely think up something. Popov must visit Moscow now and then.

—But now you'll have to excuse me, Mr. Karlsson, said Secret Agent Hutton on the phone from the French capital. I have some other business on my desk. Good luck!

Secret Agent Hutton replaced the receiver, sighed deeply, and returned to the mess of the aftermath of the military coup in Greece the previous year—supported by the CIA. Like so much else in recent times, it had not exactly turned out as intended.

Allan, for his part, had no better idea than to take a refreshing walk to the city library in Moscow every day and sit there for hours reading the daily papers and magazines. He was hoping that he would come across an article about Popov making a public appearance outside the barbed wire that fenced in Arzamas-16.

The months went by and no such news items cropped up. But Allan could read about how the presidential candidate Robert Kennedy met with the same fate as his brother and how Czechoslovakia had asked the Soviet Union for help getting its socialism in order.

Furthermore, Allan noted one day that Lyndon B. Johnson had been succeeded by a man called Richard M. Nixon. But since he was still getting his expenses from the embassy in an envelope every month, Allan thought that he had better keep on looking for

Popov. If anything changed, then Secret Agent Hutton would no doubt get in touch.

1 968 turned into 1969 and spring was approaching when Allan in his everlasting thumbing through newspapers at the library came across something interesting. The Vienna Opera was going to give a guest performance at the Bolshoi Theatre in Moscow, with Franco Corelli as tenor and the international Swedish star Birgit Nilsson in the role of Turandot.

Allan scratched his (now again) beardless chin and remembered the first and only entire evening that he and Yury had spent together. Late in the night, Yury had started to sing an aria. "Nessun Dorma" is what he had sung—nobody is allowed to sleep! Not long afterward, he had for reasons connected with alcohol fallen asleep anyway, but that was another matter.

To Allan's way of thinking, a person who at one time could manage a more or less good rendering of Puccini and Turandot at a depth of seven hundred feet, would hardly miss a guest performance from Vienna with the same opera at the Bolshoi Theatre in Moscow, would he? Especially if the man in question lived only a few hours away and had received so many medals that he would have no problem getting a seat.

Or perhaps he might. And, in that case, Allan would have to continue his daily walks to and from the library. That was the worst that could happen, and that wasn't so bad.

For the time being, Allan worked on the assumption that Yury might turn up outside the opera, and then all he had to do was to be standing there and remind him of their last drinking bout. And that would be that.

Or it wouldn't.

Not at all, in fact.

On the evening of March 22, 1969, Allan placed himself strategically on the left of the main entrance to the Bolshoi Theatre. The idea had been that from such a position he would be able to recognize Yury when he passed by on his way into the auditorium. There turned out to be a problem, however: all the visitors looked almost identical. They were men in black suits under a black coat and women in long dresses that showed under a black or brown fur coat. They all came in pairs and rapidly went from the cold outside into the warmth of the theater, past Allan where he stood on the magnificent stairway's top step. And it was dark too, so how on earth would Allan be able to identify a face he had seen for two days twenty-one years ago? Unless he had the incredible luck that Yury recognize him instead.

No, Allan didn't have any such luck. It was of course far from certain that Yury Borisovich was now inside the theater, but, if he was, he had passed a few yards from his old friend without noticing. So what could Allan do? He thought aloud:

—If you have just gone into the theater, dear Yury Borisovich, then you will pretty certainly be coming out again in a few hours through the same door. But then you are going to look just the same as when you went in. So I am not going to be able to find you. That means you will have to find me.

So be it. Allan went back to his little office at the embassy, made his preparations, and returned well before Prince Calàf had made Princess Turandot's heart melt.

More than anything, secret agent Hutton had impressed upon Allan the word "discretion." A successful agent never made any noise. He should melt into the setting where he was active to such a degree that he was almost invisible.

—Do you understood, Mr. Karlsson?

—Absolutely, Mr. Hutton, Allan had answered.

B irgit Nilsson and Franco Corelli were called back to the stage twenty times by the applauding audience; the performance was a huge success. So it took an extra-long time before people who all looked alike started to stream down the steps again. What everyone then noticed was the man standing in the middle of the bottom step, with both arms in the air holding a homemade poster on which could be read:

I AM
ALLAN
EMMANUEL

Allan Karlsson had of course understood Secret Agent Hutton's sermons; he simply paid no attention to them. In Hutton's Paris it was spring, but in Moscow it was both cold and dark. Allan was freezing, and now he wanted results. At first he had intended to write Yury's name on the poster, but eventually decided that if he was going to be indiscreet then it should be on his own behalf.

L arissa Aleksandrevna Popova, Yury Borisovich Popov's wife, lovingly held on to her husband's arm and thanked him for the fifth time for the fantastic experience they had just shared. Birgit Nilsson was pure Maria Callas! And the seats!

The fourth row, right in the middle. Larissa was happier than she had been for a long time. And besides, this evening she and her husband would be staying at a hotel, and she wouldn't have to go back to that horrid city behind the barbed wire for almost twenty-four hours. They would have a romantic dinner for two . . . just her and Yury . . . and then perhaps. . . .

—Excuse me, darling, said Yury and stopped on the top step just outside the theater doors.

—What is it, my dear? Larissa asked anxiously.

—It's probably nothing. . . . But do you see that man down there with the poster? I have to go and have a look. . . . It can't be . . . but the man is dead!

—Who's dead, darling?

—Come on! said Yury and negotiated his way down the steps with his wife.

Three yards from Allan, Yury stopped and tried to make his brain understand what his eyes had registered. Allan saw his crazily staring friend from long ago, lowered his poster, and said:

—Was she good, Birgit?

Yury still didn't say anything, but his wife whispered— Is this the dead man? Allan said that he wasn't dead, and if the Popov couple wanted to make sure he didn't freeze to death it would be best if they could immediately lead him to a restaurant where he could get some vodka and perhaps a bite to eat.

—It really is you. . . . Yury finally managed to exclaim. But . . . You speak Russian . . . ?

—Yes, I went on a five-year course in your country's language shortly after we last met, said Allan. The school was called Gulag. What about that vodka?

Yury Borisovich was a very moral man, and during the last twenty-one years he had felt very guilty for having involuntarily lured the Swedish atom-bomb expert to Moscow for subsequent transport to Vladivostok, where the Swede presumably—if not earlier—would have died in that fire that all reasonably well-informed Soviet citizens knew about. He had suffered for twenty-one years, because he had instantly liked the Swede and his—so it seemed—unstoppable ability to look on the bright side.

Now Yury Borisovich was standing outside the Bolshoi Theatre in Moscow, where it was just about zero Fahrenheit, after a warming opera performance and . . . no, he couldn't believe it. Allan Emmanuel Karlsson had survived. He lived. And he was standing in front of Yury this very moment. In the middle of Moscow. Speaking Russian!

Yury Borisovich had been married to Larissa Aleksandrevna for forty years and they were very happy together. They hadn't been blessed with children, but their mutual trust knew no bounds. They shared everything for better or worse and Yury had more than once expressed to his wife the sorrow he felt over the fate of Allan Emmanuel Karlsson. And now, while Yury still tried to make sense of events, Larissa Aleksandrevna took command.

—If I understand correctly, this is your friend from the old days, the man you indirectly sent to his death. Dear Yury, would it not be a good idea if in accordance with his wishes we take him quickly to a restaurant and provide him with some vodka before he dies for real?

Yury didn't answer, but he nodded and let his wife drag him over to the waiting limousine in which he was seated beside his until recently dead comrade while his wife gave instructions to the driver.

—The Puskhin Restaurant, please.

They needed two good drinks for Allan to thaw out and two more for Yury to come to his senses again. In between, Allan and Larissa got to know each other.

When Yury was finally able to replace shock with joy ("Now we're going to celebrate!"), Allan thought it was time to get down to business. If you had something to say, better just to say it right away.

—What do you think about becoming a spy? asked Allan. I myself am one, and it is actually rather exciting.

Yury choked on his fifth drink.

—Spy? asked Larissa while her husband coughed.

—Yes, or "agent." I don't really know what the difference is, actually.

—So interesting! Tell us more, please, Allan Emmanuel.

—No, don't, Allan, Yury coughed. We don't want to know any more!

—Don't be silly, dear Yury, said Larissa. Let your friend tell us about his job; you haven't seen each other for so many years. Go on, Allan Emmanuel.

A*llan went on and Larissa listened with interest while Yury hid his face in his hands.* Allan told them about the dinner with President Johnson and Secret Agent Hutton from the CIA and the meeting with Hutton the following day during which Hutton suggested that Allan should travel to Moscow and find out how things were with the Soviet missiles.

The alternative that Allan saw before him was to stay on in Paris where he would certainly have his hands full with preventing the ambassador and her husband from creating diplomatic crises just by opening their mouths. Since Amanda and Herbert were two, and Allan couldn't possibly be in more than one place at a time, he agreed to Secret Agent Hutton's proposal. It sounded less stressful. Besides, it would be nice to meet Yury after all these years.

Yury still had his hands over his face, but he was peeping at Allan between his fingers. Had Yury heard Herbert Einstein's name mentioned? Yury remembered him and it would certainly be good news if Herbert too had survived the kidnapping and the prison camp that Beria had sent him to.

Oh, yes, Allan confirmed. And then he told the story briefly, the story of the twenty years together with Herbert; about how his friend first wanted nothing more than to die, but when he finally did do so, dropping dead at the age of seventy-six last December in Paris, he had completely changed his mind about that. He left behind him a successful wife—now widow—who was a diplomat in Paris, and two teenaged children. The last reports from the French capital said that the family had coped well with Herbert's death, and that Mrs. Einstein had become something of a favorite in important circles. Her French was admittedly dreadful, but that was part of her charm; now and then she said stupid things that she couldn't possibly mean.

—But we seem to have gotten off our subject, said Allan. You forgot to answer my question. What about becoming a spy. Isn't it time for a change?

—But Allan Emmanuel, my good friend. This simply can't be happening! I am more honored for my services to the mother country than any other nonmilitary person in the modern history of the Soviet Union. It is absolutely out of the question that I should become a spy! said Yury and raised his glass to his mouth.

—Don't say that, dear Yury, said Larissa, and let her husband knock back drink number six, as he had knocked back number five.

—Isn't it better to drink your vodka instead of spraying it all over? Allan asked kindly.

Larissa Popova expanded upon her reasoning, while her husband again put his hands in front of his face. She and Yury would both be sixty-five soon, and what did they actually have to thank the Soviet Union for? Yes, her husband had received lots and lots of decorations and awards, and that in turn led to fine tickets at the opera. But otherwise?

Larissa didn't wait for her husband's answer, but went on to say that they were both shut up inside Arzamas-16, a city the very name of which would make anybody depressed. And behind barbed wire too. Yes, Larissa knew that they were free to come and go as they wished, but now Yury mustn't interrupt her because she was far from finished.

For whose sake had Yury slaved day after day? First it was for Stalin, and he was completely mad. Then it was Khrushchev's turn, and the only sign that man showed of any human warmth was that he had Marshal Beria executed. And now it was Brezhnev—who smelled bad!

—Larissa! exclaimed Yury Borisovich in horror.

—Now don't you sit there and Larissa me, dear Jilij. That Brezhnev smells—those are your own words.

She went on to say that Allan Emmanuel had come at a most opportune moment, because she had recently become more and more depressed at the thought of dying inside that barbed wire fence in the city that officially didn't exist. Could Larissa and Yury even count on real gravestones? Or would you need coded language on them too, for security reasons?

—Here lies comrade X and his dear wife Y, said Larissa.

Yury didn't answer. His dear wife might have something of a point there. And now Larissa delivered the knockout blow:

—So why not spy for a few years together with your friend here, and then we'll be helped to flee to New York and once there we can go to the Metropolitan every evening. We'll get a life, dear Yury, just before we die.

While Yury looked as if he was giving in, Allan went on to explain in more detail how this had come about. He had by a rather roundabout route met a Mr. Hutton in Paris, and this Hutton was a man who seemed to be close to ex-President Johnson and also to have a high position within the CIA.

When Hutton heard that Allan knew Yury Borisovich from long ago, and that Yury possibly owed Allan a favor, then Hutton had worked out a plan.

Allan hadn't listened very carefully to the global political aspects of the plan, because when people started talking politics then he stopped listening. It sort of happened by itself.

The Soviet nuclear physicist had come to his senses, and now he nodded in recognition. Politics wasn't Yury's favorite subject, not in any way. He was of course a socialist heart and soul, but if anybody asked him to elaborate, he'd run into problems.

Allan attempted to summarize what Secret Agent Hutton had said. It had something to do with the fact that the Soviet Union would either attack the USA with nuclear weapons, or it wouldn't.

Yury agreed that such was the situation. Either-or and not much space between the alternatives.

Furthermore, the CIA man Hutton, as far as Allan could remember, had expressed concern as to the consequences a Soviet attack would have for the USA.

Because even if the Soviet nuclear weapon arsenal was only big enough to wipe out America once, Hutton thought that was bad enough.

Yury Borisovich nodded a third time, and said that without a doubt it would be pretty bad for the American people if the USA was wiped out.

But how Hutton tied all the ends together, that Allan couldn't really say. For some reason, he wanted to know what the Soviet arsenal consisted of. When he had found out, he could recommend that President Johnson start negotiations with the Soviet Union over atomic disarmament. Although now, of course, Johnson wasn't the president any longer, so . . . no, Allan didn't know. Politics was often not only unnecessary, but sometimes also unnecessarily complicated.

Yury was the technical boss of the entire Soviet nuclear weapons program, and he knew everything about the program's strategy, geography, and force. But during his twenty-three years in the service of the Soviet nuclear program, he hadn't thought—and hadn't needed to think—a single political thought. That suited Yury and his health exceptionally well. He had over the course of the years survived three different leaders as well as Marshal Beria. To live so long and stay in a high position was not the fate of many powerful men in the Soviet Union.

Yury knew what sacrifices Larissa had had to make. And now, when they really deserved a pension and a dacha by the Black Sea, the extent of her self-sacrifice was greater than ever. But she had never complained. Never ever. So now Yury listened all the more closely when she said:

—Beloved, dear Yury. Let us, together with Allan Emmanuel, contribute a little to peace in this world, and let us then move to

New York. You can give the medals back and Brezhnev can stuff them up his backside.

Yury gave up and said "yes" to the whole deal (except for the bit about Brezhnev's backside) and soon afterward, Yury and Allan agreed that President Nixon probably didn't need to hear the entire truth, but rather something that would make him happy. Because a happy Nixon would please Brezhnev, and if they were both happy then there surely couldn't be a war, could there?

Allan had just recruited a spy by holding up a poster in a public place, in the country with the world's most effective secret police apparatus. Both a military GRU captain and a civilian KGB director were also at the Bolshoi Theatre the evening in question, together with their wives. Both of them, like everybody else, had seen the man with the poster on the bottom step. And both of them had been in the business far too long to sound the alarm to some colleague on duty. Anybody who was doing anything of a counter-revolutionary nature did not do so in such a public way.

Nobody could be that stupid.

In addition, there were at least a handful of professional KGB and GRU informers at the restaurant where the actual recruiting was successfully carried out that evening. At table number nine, a man spluttered vodka over the food, hid his face in his hands, waved his arms about, rolled his eyes, and was told off by his wife—in other words, a completely normal scene in any Russian restaurant. Not worth noting.

So it came about that a politically blind American agent was allowed to cook up a global peace strategy together with a politically blind Soviet nuclear weapons boss—without either the KGB or the GRU putting in their veto. When the European CIA boss in Paris, Ryan Hutton, received notice that the recruitment was completed, he said to himself that Karlsson had to be more professional than he seemed.

The Bolshoi Theatre renewed its repertoire three or four times a year. In addition, there would be at least one annual guest performance like the one from the Vienna Opera.

Thus there were a handful of occasions every year when Allan and Yury Borisovich could meet discreetly in Yury and Larissa's hotel suite to cook up some suitable nuclear weapons information to be sent to the CIA. They mixed fantasy with reality in such a way that from an American perspective the information was both credible and encouraging.

One consequence of Allan's intelligence reports was that President Nixon's staff at the beginning of the 1970s started to work on Moscow to bring about a summit meeting with mutual disarmament on the agenda. Nixon felt safe knowing that the USA was the stronger of the two.

Chairman Brezhnev, for his part, was not actually against the idea of a disarmament treaty, because his intelligence reports told him that the Soviet Union was the stronger of the two. What complicated the picture was that a cleaning lady at the CIA section for intelligence reports had sold some remarkable information to the GRU. She had gotten hold of documents sent from the CIA office in Paris, which indicated that the CIA had a spy placed at the center of the Soviet nuclear weapons program. The problem was that the information he sent was not correct. If Nixon wanted to disarm on the basis of false information that a Soviet mythomaniac sent to the CIA in Paris, then of course Brezhnev had nothing against it. But the whole thing was so complicated that it required time to think. And the mythomaniac had to be found.

Brezhnev's first measure was to call in his technical nuclear weapons boss, the unswervingly loyal Yury Borisovich Popov, and ask for an analysis of where the disinformation to the Americans could have originated. Because even if what the CIA had obtained severely underestimated the Soviet nuclear weapons capacity, the way the documents were formulated showed a worryingly good insight into the topic. Which was why expert assistance was needed from Popov.

Popov read what he and his friend Allan had cooked up, and shrugged his shoulders. Those documents, Popov said, could have been written by any student at all after a bit of research in a library. It was nothing for comrade Brezhnev to worry about, if comrade Brezhnev would allow a simple physicist to have an opinion on the matter?

Yes, that was exactly why Brezhnev had asked Yury Borisovich to come. He thanked his technical nuclear weapons boss heartily for his help, and sent his regards to Larissa Aleksandrevna, Yury Borisovich's charming wife.

W*hile the KGB set up discreet surveillance on literature related to* nuclear weapons at two hundred libraries in the Soviet Union, Brezhnev continued to wonder how he should respond to Nixon's unofficial proposals, right up until the day—the horror of it!—when Nixon was invited to China to meet that fatty, Mao Tse-tung! Brezhnev and Mao had recently told each other to go to hell once and for all, and now there was suddenly a risk that China and the USA might form an unholy alliance against the Soviet Union. And that must not be allowed to happen.

So, the following day, Richard M. Nixon, President of the United States of America, received an official invitation to visit the Soviet Union. This was followed by hard work offstage and when one thing had finally led to another, Brezhnev and Nixon had not only shaken hands but also signed two separate disarmament treaties: one concerning antiballistic missiles (the ABM Treaty) and the other concerning strategic weapons. As the signing took place in Moscow, Nixon seized the opportunity to shake hands with the agent at the American Embassy who had so brilliantly supplied him with information about the Soviet nuclear weapons capacity.

—You're welcome, Mr. President, said Allan. But aren't you going to invite me to dinner too? They usually do.

—Who does? asked the astounded president.

—Well, said Allan. The people who were satisfied with my
help . . . Franco and Truman and Stalin . . . and Chairman Mao . . .
although he didn't give me anything but noodles . . . but it was very
late in the evening of course . . . and the Swedish prime minister
only gave me coffee, when I come to think of it. Mind you, that wasn't
so bad either, considering there was rationing in those days. . . .

Luckily President Nixon had been briefed as to the agent's
past, so he could calmly say that there was regrettably not time for
dinner with Mr. Karlsson. But then he added that an American
president could not readily be less obliging than a Swedish prime
minister, so a cup of coffee was definitely called for, and cognac to
go with it. Now this very minute, if that suited?

Allan thanked him for the invitation, and asked if a double cognac
might be in order if he refrained from the coffee. Nixon answered
that the American national budget could probably support both.

*The two gentlemen had a pleasant hour together, or at least, as pleas-
ant as it could be for Allan to listen to President Nixon talk
politics. The American president asked about how the political
game worked in Indonesia. Without naming Amanda by name, Allan described in detail how careers in politics came about there.
President Nixon listened carefully and seemed to be giving the subject his serious attention.

—Interesting, he said. Interesting.

*Allan and Yury were pleased with each other and with the develop-
ments. It seemed that the GRU and KGB had calmed down
when it came to searching for the spy, and Allan and Yury found
that comforting. Or as Allan put it:

—It is better not to have two murder organizations on your heels.

Then he added that the two friends ought not spend too much time on the KGB, GRU, and all the other abbreviations, which they in any case couldn't do anything about. Instead, it was high time to cook up the next intelligence report for Secret Agent Hutton and his president. Considerable rust damage to the middle-range missile store in Kamchatka, could they elaborate on that?

Yury praised Allan for his delightful imagination. It made it so easy to put the intelligence reports together. And that meant more time for food, drink, and good company.

Richard M. Nixon had every reason to be satisfied with most things. Right up until the time when he didn't have any reason at all.

The American people loved their president and reelected him in 1972, in a landslide. Nixon won in forty-nine states; George McGovern managed to win just one.

But then everything got more difficult. And even more difficult. And in the end, Nixon had to do what no other American president had done before.

He had to resign.

Allan read about the so-called Watergate scandal in all the available papers at the city library in Moscow. In summary, Nixon had evidently cheated on his taxes, received illegal campaign donations, ordered secret bombings, persecuted enemies, and made use of break-ins and telephone bugging. Allan thought that the president must have been impressed by that conversation over a double cognac in Paris. And then he said to the newspaper picture of Nixon:

—You should have gone in for a career in Indonesia instead. You would have gone far there.

THE ONE HUNDRED YEAR OLD MAN   357

The years went by. Nixon was replaced by Gerald Ford who was re-placed by Jimmy Carter. And all the while Brezhnev stayed where he was. Just like Allan, Yury, and Larissa. The three of them continued to meet five or six times a year, and they had just as good a time on every occasion. The meetings always resulted in a suit-ably imaginative report about the current status of the Soviet arse-nal of nuclear weapons. Over the years, Allan and Yury had chosen to tone down the Soviet capacity more and more, because they noticed how much more satisfied this made the Americans (regard-less of who the president was, it seemed) and how much more pleasant the atmosphere then seemed to be between the leaders of the two countries.

But what joyous thing lasts forever?

One day, just before the SALT II treaty was signed, Brezhnev thought that Afghanistan needed his help. So he sent his elite troops into the country, and they happened to kill the sitting president, so that Brezhnev had no choice but to appoint his own.

This of course irritated President Carter (to put it mildly). The ink on the SALT treaty had barely dried. So Carter arranged a boy-cott of the Olympic Games in Moscow as well as increasing the se-cret CIA support to the Mujahedin, fundamentalist guerrilla forces in Afghanistan.

Carter didn't have time to do much more than that, because very soon Ronald Reagan took over and he had a much shorter temper when it came to communists in general and the old relic Brezhnev in particular.

—He does seem to be dreadfully angry, that Reagan, Allan said to Yury at the first agent-spy meeting they had after the new president had been sworn in.

—Yes, Yury answered. And now we can't dismantle any more of the Soviet arsenal of nuclear weapons because then there would be nothing left.

—In that case, I suggest we do the opposite, said Allan. That is bound to soften up Reagan a bit, just wait and see.

So the next spy report to the USA, via Secret Agent Hutton, bore witness to a sensational Soviet initiative in their missile defenses. Allan's imagination had gone right out into space. From up there, Allan thought up the idea that Soviet rockets would be able to pick off everything that the USA intended to attack with down on Earth.

With that, the politically blind American agent Allan and his politically blind Russian nuclear weapons boss Yury had laid the foundations for the collapse of the Soviet Union. Because Ronald Reagan blew his top when he read the intelligence report that Allan sent, and he immediately embarked upon his Strategic Defense Initiative, also known as Star Wars. The description of the project, with its satellites with laser guns, was almost a copy of what Allan and Yury had cooked up some months earlier, in a hotel room in Moscow, under the influence of what they thought was a suitable amount of vodka. The American budget for defense against nuclear weapons reached astronomical sums. The Soviet Union tried to match this, but couldn't afford it. Instead the country started to crack at the seams.

Whether it was from the shock over the secret American military plans (Reagan wouldn't even tell the American people about it until March 23, 1983), or for some other reason, one can't say, but on November 10, 1982, Brezhnev died of a heart attack. The following evening, Allan, Yury, and Larissa happened to have one of their intelligence meetings.

—Isn't it time to stop all this nonsense? Larissa asked.

—Yes, let's stop this nonsense, said Yury.

Allan nodded, and agreed that everything must come to an end, especially nonsense perhaps.

And he added that the following morning he was going to phone Secret Agent Hutton. Thirteen-and-a-half years of service to the CIA was enough; that most of it had been make-believe was neither here nor there. All three agreed that it was best to keep that part secret from Secret Agent Hutton and his so-irascible president.

Now the CIA would have to see to it that Yury and Larissa were airlifted to New York; they had already promised that, while Allan himself was wondering what things were like in good old Sweden.

The CIA and Secret Agent Hutton kept their promise. Yury and Larissa were transported to the USA, via Czechoslovakia and Austria. They were given an apartment on West 64th Street in Manhattan, and an annual stipend that wildly exceeded their needs. And it wasn't particularly expensive for the CIA either, because in January 1984 Yury died in his sleep and three months later his Larissa followed him, dying of sorrow. They were both seventy-nine years old and they had their happiest year together in 1983, which was when the Metropolitan Opera celebrated its one hundredth anniversary, with an endless array of unforgettable experiences for the couple.

Allan, for his part, packed his bags and informed the administrative section of the American Embassy in Moscow that he was about to leave for good. That was when the section discovered that Allen Carson for unclear reasons had only been paid his additional foreign allowance during the thirteen years and five months he had been in service.

—Didn't you ever notice that you didn't get a salary? asked the official.

—No, said Allan. I don't eat much and vodka is cheap here. I thought it was more than enough.

—For thirteen years?

—Yes, how time flies.

The official gave Allan a strange look and then promised to make sure that the money would be paid via check as soon as Mr. Carson, or whatever he was really called, reported to the American Embassy in Stockholm.

TWENTY-SEVEN

Friday May 27–Thursday June 16, 2005

Amanda Einstein was still alive. She was now eighty-four years old and lived in a suite at the luxury hotel in Bali that was owned and run by her elder son, Allan.

Allan Einstein was fifty-one years old and had quite a brain, just like his one-year-younger brother, Mao. But while Allan had become a business specialist (for real) and eventually hotel director (he had been given the hotel in question by his mother on his fortieth birthday), his little brother Mao went in for engineering. At first things hadn't gone too well with his career, because Mao was exceedingly fussy about details. He had been given a job in Indonesia's leading oil company with the task of ensuring the quality of the production system. Mao's mistake was that he did. Suddenly, all the midlevel management in the company found that they were no longer able to siphon off various sums under the table when they had to order repairs, because there was no longer any need to order any repairs. The efficiency of the oil company increased by 35 percent and Mao became the most unpopular person in the organization. When the general bullying from his colleagues turned into more direct threats, Mao Einstein thought it wise to withdraw and instead got a job in the United Arab Emirates. He soon increased efficiency there too, while the company in Indonesia to everyone's relief soon returned to its old level.

Amanda was endlessly proud of her two sons. But she couldn't understand how they could both be so clever. Herbert had once told her that there were some good genes in his family, but she couldn't really remember what he was referring to.

Be that as it may, when Amanda received the telephone call from Allan she was overjoyed and she wished him and all his friends a warm welcome to Bali. She would immediately discuss the matter with Allan Junior; he would have to kick out some other guests if the hotel happened to be full. And she would phone Mao in Abu Dhabi and order him to come home for a holiday. And, of course, they served drinks at the hotel, with and without a parasol. And yes, Amanda promised not to get involved in the actual serving of the drinks.

Allan said that they would all turn up soon. And then he ended with some encouraging words about how he thought that there wasn't a single person in the world who had gone so far with such a limited intelligence as Amanda had done. And Amanda thought that was so beautifully said, that tears came to her eyes.

—Hurry up and get here, Allan dear. Hurry up!

P*rosecutor Ranelid opened the afternoon's press conference with the* sad revelation about police dog Kicki. She had indicated the presence of a corpse on that inspection trolley at Åker Foundry, and that in turn had led to a number of assumptions on the part of the prosecutor—which of course were correct when based on the dog's indications, but nevertheless wrong, so very wrong.

It had now come to light that just before this assignment the dog in question had lost her mind and was on that account not to be trusted. There was, to put it simply, never any corpse in that place.

It had just come to the prosecutor's notice that the police dog had been put down, and the prosecutor thought that was a wise decision by its handler. (Kicki, under an assumed name, was on her way instead to the dog handler's brother in the north of Sweden, but the prosecutor never got to know that.)

Furthermore, Prosecutor Ranelid regretted that the Eskilstuna Police had neglected to inform him as to the new, and most honorable, evangelical direction of the Never Again organization. Had he been in possession of that knowledge, the prosecutor would most certainly have given other instructions to further the efforts of the investigation. On behalf of the police, Prosecutor Ranelid would like to apologize for the conclusions that he had drawn. They were based partly on a crazy canine, partly on the information supplied—and wrongly so—by the police.

As for the discovery of the corpse of Henrik Bucket Hultén in Riga, it was likely that a new murder investigation would be instigated. The case of the similarly deceased Bengt Bolt Bylund was, however, now closed. There were strong indications that the said Bylund had joined the French Foreign Legion. Since all legionnaires join up under a pseudonym, it was not possible to confirm definitively, but it was nevertheless highly likely that the said Bylund was a victim of the suicide bombing that had taken place in the center of Djibouti a couple of days earlier.

The prosecutor presented a detailed account of the various protagonists' relationships, and in that context showed the assembled media representatives the copy of the superthin Bible that he had received earlier that day from Bosse Ljungberg. At the end of the press conference, the journalists wanted to know the whereabouts of Allan Karlsson and his entourage so as to obtain their version of events, but Prosecutor Ranelid had no information to give them on that score (he had absolutely nothing to gain from allowing the senile geriatric to spout on about Churchill and God knows what else with representatives of the press). So the focus of the journalists was now switched to Bucket Hultén. He had presumably been murdered, and the previously presumed murderers were no longer suspected. So who had killed Hultén?

Ranelid had hoped that the matter would be conveniently forgotten, but now he had to emphasize that the investigation would be started immediately after the conclusion of the press conference and he said that he would return to that subject on a later occasion.

To Prosecutor Ranelid's amazement, the journalists accepted that, and all the rest of what he had said. Prosecutor Ranelid, and his career, had survived the day.

A*manda Einstein had asked Allan and his friends to hurry up and travel to Bali, which was what the friends wanted too.* At any moment, a far-too-skillful journalist might find his way to Bellringer Farm, and it would be safest for all concerned if the place was abandoned. Allan had done his bit by contacting Amanda. The rest was up to The Beauty.

Not far from Bellringer Farm lay the Såtenäs military airfield and there was a Hercules plane that could swallow an elephant or even two with ease. The plane in question had on one occasion roared over Bellringer Farm and almost scared the elephant to death, and that was what had given The Beauty the idea.

The Beauty spoke to a colonel at Såtenäs, but he was far more stubborn than he needed to be. He wanted to see every manner of certificate and permission before he could even think of intercontinental transport assistance for a number of people and animals. For example, the military was absolutely forbidden from competing with commercial airlines, and they would need a certificate from the Department of Agriculture that such was not the case. A transport would further require four stopovers, and at each airport a vet would have to be present to check the status of the animal. And as regards the elephant, there was no question of anything less than twelve hours' rest between flights.

Damn and blast the Swedish bureaucracy, said The Beauty and instead phoned Lufthansa in Munich.

They were only slightly more cooperative. They could of course pick up an elephant and a number of accompanying travelers, and that could be done at Landvetter Airport near Gothenburg, and they could of course transport them all to Indonesia. All that was required was a certificate of ownership of the elephant, and that a registered veterinarian accompanied them in the aircraft. And of course necessary documents would need to be provided for admittance to the Republic of Indonesia, for people as well as animals. When those conditions were fulfilled, the airline's administration could plan the transport within the next three months.

—Damn and blast the German bureaucracy, said The Beauty and instead phoned Indonesia.

It took a while, because in Indonesia there are fifty-one different airlines and not all of them have English-speaking staff. But The Beauty didn't give up, and finally she succeeded. In Palembang, on Sumatra, there was a transport company that for a reasonable fee would be happy to make a round-trip to Sweden. They had a Boeing 747 suitable for that purpose, a machine that had recently been purchased from the Azerbaijani army. (Luckily this was before all Indonesian airlines were blacklisted by the European Union and forbidden from landing in Europe.) The company promised to arrange all the papers for the landing in Sweden, while it was the customer's responsibility to arrange landing permission for Bali. A vet? Why?

All that remained was the matter of payment. The price went up by 20 percent before The Beauty with a maximal use of her rich vocabulary got the company to agree to be paid in cash in Swedish crowns on arrival in Sweden.

As the Indonesian Boeing took off on its flight to Sweden, the friends held a council. Benny and Julius were entrusted with the falsification of some papers that they could wave in front of what they assumed would be fussy officials at Landvetter Airport, and Allan promised to arrange the Balinese landing permission.

They had a few problems at the airport outside Gothenburg, but Benny not only had his false veterinary certificate, but also the ability to reel off some professional-sounding veterinary phrases. This, together with the certificate of ownership and the certificate of health for the elephant, and a whole bundle of credible documentation written by Allan in Indonesian, meant that they could all board as planned. Since the friends amid the general falsification had also said that the next stop was Copenhagen, nobody asked for their passports.

The traveling party included the hundred-year-old Allan Karlsson; petty thief Julius Jonsson (now declared innocent); eternal student Benny Ljungberg; his fiancée, the beautiful Gunilla Björklund; both of her pets, elephant Sonya and Alsatian dog Buster; Benny Ljungberg's brother, the newly religious food wholesaler Bosse; the previously so-lonely Chief Inspector Aronsson from Eskilstuna; the former gangster boss Per-Gunnar Gerdin; and his mother, eighty-year-old Rose-Marie, she who at one time had written an unfortunate letter to her son while he was incarcerated at the Hall Prison.

The flight took eleven hours, without lots of unnecessary stops en route, and the group was in good condition when the Indonesian captain informed his passengers that they were now approaching Bali's international airport and that it was time for Allan Karlsson to pull out that landing permission. Allan asked the captain to let him know when the air traffic controller at Bali got in touch. Allan would take care of the rest.

—Here they are, said the worried captain. What do I tell them? They could shoot us down any minute!

—Don't worry, said Allan and took over. Hello? Is that Bali Airport? he said in English, and received the answer that they should immediately identify themselves unless they wanted to face the Indonesian Air Force.

—My name is Dollars, said Allan. One Hundred Thousand Dollars.

The air traffic controller was completely silent. The Indonesian captain and his copilot looked at Allan in admiration.

—At this very moment the controller and his closest colleagues are counting how many are getting a share, Allan explained.

—I know, said the captain.

Another few seconds passed before the flight leader contacted them again.

—Hello? Are you there, Mr. Dollars?

—Yes, I am, said Allan.

—Excuse me, what is your first name, Mr. Dollars?

—One Hundred Thousand, said Allan. I am Mr. One Hundred Thousand Dollars, and I want permission to land at your airport.

—Excuse me, Mr. Dollars. The sound is very poor. Could you please be so kind as to say your first name once more?

Allan explained to the captain that the controller had now started to negotiate.

—I know, said the captain.

—My first name is Two Hundred Thousand, said Allan. Do we have your permission to land?

—One moment, Mr. Dollars, said the flight leader, and checked with his colleagues. He then said:

—You are most welcome to Bali, Mr. Dollars. It will be a pleasure to have you here.

Allan thanked the flight leader.

—This must not be your first visit, said the captain, and smiled.

—Indonesia is the country where everything is possible, said Allan.

When the high-ranking officials at Bali International Airport realized that several of Mr. Dollars's fellow travelers didn't have passports, and that one of them weighed in at nearly five tons and had four legs instead of two, it cost a further fifty thousand dollars to arrange the customs documents and suitable transport for Sonya. But an hour after landing, the entire group was in place at family Einstein's hotel, including Sonya, who had been transported there with Benny and The Beauty in one of the airport's catering trucks (that afternoon's flight to Singapore, incidentally, unfortunately lacked lunch trays).

Amanda, Allan, and Mao Einstein received their guests, and after a bout of hugging and kissing, they were shown to their rooms. Sonya and Buster could meanwhile stretch their legs in the hotel's enormous fenced-in garden. Amanda had already expressed her regret at the lack of elephant friends for Sonya on Bali, but she would immediately arrange that a potential boyfriend be delivered from Sumatra. When it came to girlfriends for Buster, he would probably find them himself; there were lots of pretty girl-dogs roaming around the island.

And Amanda promised that toward the evening there would be one hell of a Balinese party for them all, and she urged them to have a nap first.

All except three abided by that recommendation. Pike and Pike's mama couldn't wait any longer for that parasol drink and the same applied to Allan, minus the parasol.

All three made their way to the lounge chairs beside the water, made themselves comfortable, and waited for the delivery of what they had just ordered from the bar.

The waitress was eighty-four years old and had taken over from the barman.

—Here's a red parasol drink for you, Mr. Gerdin. And a green parasol drink for you, Mrs. Mama Gerdin. And . . . but wait a moment . . . You didn't order milk, did you, Allan?

—I thought you had promised not to get involved with serving the drinks, dear Amanda, said Allan.

—I lied, dear Allan. I lied.

D*arkness descended upon the paradise and the friends gathered for a* three-course meal, invited by their hosts Amanda, Allan, and Mao Einstein. For starters they were served *sate lilit*, for the main course *bebek betutu*, and for dessert a *jaja batun bedil*. They drank *tual wayah*, palm-tree beer, except for Benny who drank water.

The very first evening on Indonesian soil was almost as long as it was pleasant. The food came to an end and it was rounded off with Pisang Ambon for everyone except Allan who had a vodka and Benny who had a cup of tea.

Bosse felt that this day and evening of excess needed a bit of spiritual balance so he stood up and quoted Jesus from the Gospel according to Matthew ("Happy are they . . . their spiritual needs"). Bosse believed they would all benefit from listening to God and learning from God. And then he put his palms together and thanked the Lord for an extremely unusual and unusually good day.

—Everything will work out just fine, said Allan in the silence created by Bosse's words.

B*osse had thanked the Lord and perhaps the Lord thanked them in* return, because their good fortune lasted and grew. Benny asked The Beauty if she would marry him, to which she replied: Yes, damn it! Now straightaway! The ceremony took place the following evening and lasted three days. Rose-Marie Gerdin, eighty years old, taught the members of the local pensioners' club how to play the Treasure Island Game (but no better than her so that she

herself could win every time); Pike lay on the beach under a parasol day in and day out, drinking parasol drinks in all the colors of
the rainbow; Bosse and Julius bought a fishing boat that they
rarely left; and Chief Inspector Aronsson became a popular member of the Balinese upper classes: he was a white man after all, and
a detective chief inspector too, and if that wasn't enough, he had
come from the least-corrupt country in the world. You couldn't get
more exotic than that.

Every day, Allan and Amanda went on suitably long walks
along the glowing white beach outside the hotel. They always had
lots to talk about, and they felt better and better in each other's
company. They didn't go very fast, because she was eighty-four
years old and he was now in his hundred-and-first year.

After a while they started to hold each other's hand, for balance.
Then they decided to dine, just the two of them, on Amanda's terrace in the evenings, as it got too much with all the others. And in
the end, Allan moved in with Amanda for good. In that way, Allan's
room could be rented to a tourist instead, and that was good for the
hotel's balance sheet.

During one of the following day's walks, Amanda raised the
question of whether they should just do the same as Benny and
The Beauty, that is, get married, when they were living together
anyway. Allan said that Amanda was a young girl in comparison
with him, but that he could bring himself to ignore that circumstance. And nowadays he mixed his own drinks so there was no
problem there either. So, in short, Allan couldn't see any decisive
objection to what Amanda had just proposed.

—Then it's a plan? said Amanda.

—Yes, it's a plan, said Allan.

And they held each other's hand extra hard. For balance.

*The investigation into Henrik Bucket Hultén's death was short and
without result. The police looked into his past and interrogated Bucket's former companions in Småland (not far from Gu-*

nilla Björklund's Lake Farm, in fact), but they hadn't heard or seen anything.

The colleagues in Riga sought out the drunkard who had taken the Mustang to the scrapyard, but they couldn't get a sensible word out of him until one of the police colleagues thought of priming him with a bottle of wine. Then the drunkard suddenly started to tell them—that he had no idea who it was who had asked him to take the car to the scrapyard. Somebody just turned up at the park bench one day with a whole bagful of wine bottles.

—I wasn't sober, admittedly, said the drunkard. But I never get so drunk that I'd say no to four bottles of wine.

Only one journalist got in touch a few days later to find out how the investigation about Bucket Hultén's death was going, but Prosecutor Ranelid wasn't there to take the call. He had gone on holiday, booking a cheap last-minute charter flight to Las Palmas. What he really wanted to do was to get away from everything, and he had heard that Bali was nice, but that flight was fully booked.

The Canary Islands would have to do. And there he sat now in a lounge chair under a parasol, with a parasol drink in his hand, wondering where Aronsson had gone off to. He had apparently given his notice, taken all the vacation days due to him, and just disappeared.

TWENTY-EIGHT

1982–2005

The salary from the American Embassy had come in handy when Allan returned to Sweden. He found a little red cottage just a few miles from where he had grown up, which he paid for in cash. Making the purchase he had to argue with the Swedish authorities about whether he existed. In the end, they gave in and started to pay him a pension—much to Allan's surprise.

—Why? asked Allan.

—You're a pensioner, said the authorities.

—Am I? said Allan.

And he was, of course, and by a good margin too. The following spring he would be seventy-eight, and Allan realized that he had gotten old, against all odds and without having thought about it. But he was going to get much older. . . .

The years passed, at a leisurely rate and without Allan influencing world developments in any way at all. He didn't even influence things in the town of Flen, into which he occasionally ventured to buy some groceries (from the grandson of wholesale merchant Gustavsson who now ran the local supermarket and to his good fortune hadn't a clue that Allan was who he was). The public library in Flen didn't, however, get any new visits, because Allan had realized that you could subscribe to the newspapers you wanted to read and they landed neatly in the mailbox outside his cottage. Very practical!

When the hermit in the cottage outside Yxhult turned eighty-three he thought all that biking back and forth to Flen was getting hard, so instead he bought a car. For a moment he thought about combining this with the acquisition of a driving license, but as soon as the driving instructor had mentioned "sight test" and "provisional license," Allan decided to do without. When the instructor went on to list the "books," the "theory lessons," the "driving lessons," and the "final double test," Allan had long since stopped listening.

In 1989, the Soviet Union had started to fall to bits, which didn't surprise the old man in Yxhult with his own vodka distillery in the cellar. The new youth at the helm, Gorbachev, had started his era in power with a campaign against the massive vodka drinking in his nation. That wasn't something that would get the masses on your side, was it?

That same year, in fact on Allan's birthday, a kitten suddenly appeared on the porch steps, and signaled that it was hungry. Allan invited it into his kitchen and served it milk and sausage. The cat liked that so much that it moved in.

It was a tiger-striped farmyard cat, a male, who was given the name Molotov, not after the minister but after the cocktail. Molotov didn't say very much, but he was extremely intelligent and fantastic at listening. If Allan had something to say, he only had to call the cat; he always came skipping along, unless he was occupied with catching mice (Molotov knew what was important). The cat jumped up into Allan's lap, made himself comfortable, and made a sign with his ears to show that Allan could now say what he had to say. If Allan simultaneously scratched Molotov on the back of his head, and on his neck, there was no limit to how long the chat could last.

And when Allan got some hens, it was enough to tell Molotov one single time that he shouldn't go running after them, for the cat to nod and understand. The fact that he ignored what Allan said and ran after the hens till he didn't find it fun anymore, that was another matter. What could you expect? He was a cat after all.

Allan thought that nobody was craftier than Molotov, not even the fox that was always sneaking around the henhouse looking for gaps in the netting. The fox also had designs on the cat, but Molotov was much too quick for that.

Mⁿore years were added to those that Allan had already collected. And every month the pension money arrived from the authorities without Allan doing anything in return. With that money, Allan bought cheese, sausage, and potatoes and now and then a sack of sugar. In addition, he paid for the subscription to the local paper, and he paid the electricity bill whenever it appeared.

But there was still money left over every month, and what good was that? Allan once attempted to send the excess back to the authorities in an envelope, but after a while an official came to Allan's cottage and informed him that you couldn't do that. So Allan got his money back, and had to promise to stop arguing with the authorities.

Allan and Molotov had a good life together. Every day, weather allowing, they went for a little bike ride along the gravel roads in the area. Allan pedaled, while Molotov sat in the basket and enjoyed the wind and the speed.

The little family lived a pleasant and regular life. And this went on until one day it turned out that not only Allan but also Molotov had gotten older. Suddenly, the fox caught up with the cat, and that was just as surprising for the fox and the cat as it was sad for Allan.

Allan was more sad than he possibly ever had been earlier in his life, and the sorrow soon turned to anger. The old explosives expert stood there on his veranda with tears in his eyes and called out into the winter night:

—If it's war you want, it's war you'll get, you damned fox!

For the first and only time in his life, Allan was angry. And it wasn't dispelled with vodka, a drive (without a driver's license) in his car, or an extralong bike ride. Revenge was a poor thing to live for, Allan knew. Nevertheless, just now that was precisely what he had on the agenda.

Allan set an explosive charge beside the henhouse intended to go off when the fox got hungry next time and stretched its nose a little too far into the hens' domain. But in his anger, Allan forgot that right next to the henhouse was where he stored all his dynamite.

Thus it was that at dusk on the third day after Molotov's ascent to heaven, an explosion was heard in that part of Södermanland, the like of which hadn't been heard since the late 1920s.

The fox was blown into little bits, just like Allan's hens, his henhouse, and woodshed. But the explosion took the barn and cottage too. Allan was sitting in his armchair when it happened, and he flew up in the air in the armchair and landed in a snowdrift outside his potato cellar. He sat there looking around him with an astonished expression on his face, before finally saying:

—That was the end of the fox.

By now, Allan was ninety-nine years old and he felt so knocked about that he stayed where he was. But it wasn't hard for the ambulance, police, and fire brigade to find their way to him, because the flames reached high into the sky. And when they had made sure that the geriatric in the armchair in the snowdrift beside his own potato cellar was uninjured, it was time for the social services to be called in.

In less than an hour, social worker Henrik Söder was by his side. Allan was still sitting in his armchair, but the ambulance men had wrapped a couple of hospital blankets around him, which wasn't really necessary because the fire from the house that had almost burnt to the ground still gave off quite a lot of heat.

—Mr. Karlsson, I understand that you have blown up your house? said social worker Söder.

—Yes, said Allan. It's a bad habit of mine.

—Let me guess that you, Mr. Karlsson, are no longer in possession of an abode? the social worker continued.

—There is some truth in that, said Allan. Do you have any suggestions, Mr. Social Worker?

The social worker couldn't think of anything on the spot, so Allan—at the expense of the social services—was carted off to the hotel in the center of Flen, where the following evening Allan, in a festive atmosphere, celebrated New Year's with, among others, social worker Söder and his wife.

Allan hadn't been in such fancy surroundings since the time just after the war when he had stayed at the luxurious Grand Hôtel in Stockholm. In fact, it was high time he paid the bill there, because in the rush to leave it never got paid.

A t the beginning of January 2005, social worker Söder had located a possible place of residence for the nice old man who had happened to become suddenly homeless a week earlier.

So Allan found himself at Malmköping's Old Folks' Home, where room 1 had just become available. He was welcomed by the director, Alice, who smiled a friendly smile, but who also sucked the joy out of Allan's life in laying out for him all the rules of the home. Director Alice said that smoking was forbidden, drinking was forbidden, and TV was forbidden after eleven in the evening. Breakfast was served at 6:45 on weekdays and an hour later on weekends. Lunch was at 11:15, coffee at 15:15, and supper at 18:15. If you were out and didn't keep track of the time and came home too late, you risked having to go without.

After which, Director Alice went through the rules concerning showers and brushing your teeth, visits from outside, and visits to other resident senior citizens; what time various medicines were handed out; and between which times you could not disturb Director Alice or one of her colleagues unless it was urgent, which it rarely was, according to Director Alice, who added that in general there was too much grumbling among the residents.

—Can you take a shit when you want to? Allan asked.

Which is how Allan and Director Alice came to be at odds less than fifteen minutes after they had met.

Allan wasn't pleased with himself over the matter of the war against the fox back home (even though he won). Losing his temper was not in his nature. Besides, now he had used language that the director at the home might well have deserved, but which nevertheless was not Allan's style. Add to that the mile-long list of rules and regulations that Allan now had to abide by. . . .

Allan missed his cat. And he was ninety-nine years and eight months old. It was as if he had lost control of his own spirit, and Director Alice had had a lot to do with that.

Enough was enough.

Allan was done with life, because life seemed to be done with him, and he was and always had been a man who didn't like to push himself forward.

So he decided that he would check into room 1, have his 18:15 supper and then—newly showered, in clean sheets and new pajamas—he would go to bed, die in his sleep, be carried out, buried in the ground, and forgotten.

A *llan felt an almost electric sense of pleasure spreading through his* body when, at eight o'clock in the evening, for the first and last time he slipped into the sheets of his bed at the Old Folks' Home. In less than four months, his age would reach three figures. Allan Emmanuel Karlsson closed his eyes and felt perfectly convinced that he would now pass away forever. It had been exciting, the entire journey, but nothing lasts forever, except possibly general stupidity.

Then Allan didn't think anything more. Tiredness overcame him. Everything went dark.

Until it got light again—a white glow. Imagine that, death was just like being asleep. Would he have time to think before it was all over? And would he have time to think that he had thought it? But wait, how much do you have to think before you have finished thinking?

—It is a quarter to seven, Allan, time for breakfast. If you don't eat it up, we shall take your porridge away and then you won't have anything until lunch, said Director Alice.

Besides everything else, Allan noted that he had grown naive in his old age. You can't simply go and die to order. And there was now a considerable risk that the following day too he would be woken by that dreadful woman and be served the almost equally dreadful porridge.

Oh well. There were still a few months to go to one hundred, so surely he would manage to kick the bucket before that. "Alcohol kills!" was how Director Alice had justified the "no alcohol" rule in residents' rooms. That sounded promising, thought Allan. He'd have to sneak out to the state alcohol shop.

D*ays passed and turned into weeks. Winter became spring and* Allan longed for death almost as much as his friend Herbert had done fifty years earlier. Herbert didn't have his wish fulfilled until he had changed his mind. That wasn't a good omen.

And what was even worse: the staff at the Old Folks' Home had started to prepare for Allan's coming birthday. Like a caged animal he would have to put up with being looked at, sung to, and fed with a birthday cake. That was most definitely not something he had asked for.

And now he had just a single night in which to die.

TWENTY-NINE

Monday, May 2, 2005

You might think he could have made up his mind earlier and been man enough to inform his surroundings of his decision. But Allan Karlsson had never been given to pondering things too long.

So the idea had barely taken hold in the old man's head before he opened the window of his room on the ground floor of the Old Folks' Home in the town of Malmköping, and stepped out into the flower border.

This maneuver required a bit of effort since Allan was one hundred years old, on this very day in fact. There was less than an hour to go before his birthday party would begin in the lounge of the Old Folks' Home. The mayor would be there. And the local paper. And all the other old people. And the entire staff, led by bad-tempered Director Alice.

It was only the Birthday Boy himself who didn't intend to turn up.

EPILOGUE

A llan and Amanda were very happy together. And they seemed made for each other. One was allergic to all talk of ideology and religion, while the other didn't know what ideology meant and couldn't for the life of her remember the name of the God she was supposed to pray to. Besides, it transpired one evening when the mutual closeness was especially intense, that Professor Lundborg must have been a bit careless with the surgical knife that August day in 1925, because Allan—to his own surprise—was capable of doing what he hitherto had seen only in movies.

On her eighty-fifth birthday, Amanda's husband gave her a laptop with an Internet connection. Allan had heard that this Internet thing was something that young people enjoyed.

It took Amanda some time to learn how to log in, but she didn't give up and within a few weeks she had created her own blog. She wrote all day long, about things high and low, old and new. For example, she wrote about her dear husband's journeys and adventures the world over. Her intended public was her lady friends in Balinese society. Who else would find their way to it?

One day, Allan was sitting as usual on the veranda enjoying his breakfast when a gentleman in a suit turned up. The man introduced himself as a representative of the Indonesian government and said that he had read some amazing things in a blog on the Internet. Now, on behalf of the president, he wished to make use of Mr. Karlsson's special knowledge, if what he had read turned out to be true.

—And what do you want me to help you with if I may ask? said Allan. There are only two things I can do better than most people. One of them is to make vodka from goats' milk, and the other is to put together an atom bomb.

—That's exactly what we're interested in, said the man.

—The goats' milk?

—No, said the man. Not the goats' milk.

Allan asked the representative of the Indonesian government to sit down. And then he explained that he had given the Bomb to Stalin and that had been a mistake because Stalin was as crazy as they come. So first of all Allan wanted to know about the mental state of the Indonesian president. The government representative replied that President Yudhoyono was a very wise and responsible person.

—I am glad to hear it, said Allan. In that case I'd be happy to help out.

And that's what he did.

ACKNOWLEDGMENTS

An extra thank-you
to Micke, Liza, Rixon, Maud, and Uncle Hans.

—Jonas